She had three men, three lives, three loves. . . .

MARK DAMIAN: He discovered her in a dirt-poor Texas town, and transformed a naive, barefoot teenager into a Hollywood idol who lost her innocence on the path to fame.

BENJAMIN LORD: He rescued her when greed and betrayal threatened her very existence and showered her with the good things of life, wrapping her in the security of his love.

DREW MALLORY: He awakened her to a sensuality she had never known, directing her on the Broadway stage, and challenging her to once again risk her heart.

TORY HOUSTON

THE LEGEND OF LACY BLACK

LEISURE BOOKS  NEW YORK CITY

A LEISURE BOOK®

June 2002

Published by

Dorchester Publishing Co., Inc.
276 Fifth Avenue
New York, NY 10001

ISBN 0-8439-5021-8

Printed in the United States of America.

This one's for you, Hal, my beloved son, and you know why.
—Pamela Monck

To you, Pamela.
It was so much fun creating Lacy Black with you.
I admire your talent and dedication, and I love
you as my daughter and my writing partner.
—Constance O'Banyon

THE LEGEND OF LACY BLACK

Prologue

A mountainous area in California
January 2002

It was a slow news week; otherwise the discovery of the skeletal remains of two people inside the rusted-out cockpit of a 1940s vintage aircraft would have gone virtually unnoticed.

A group of hikers had happened upon the gruesome sight in a desolate area of the Sierra Nevadas and had immediately notified the authorities. When the FAA determined that the wreckage was from the private plane that had carried the legendary movie star Lacy Black to her death almost sixty years earlier, it caused a media frenzy. Reporters from all over the globe converged on the scene, each hoping to be the one to unearth the truth behind the screen goddess's tragic disappearance.

A retired airport mechanic had his fifteen minutes of fame as the last person to speak to Lacy Black before she boarded the ill-fated flight. He recalled that she had seemed upset that night and had demanded that her pilot take off in a dangerous thunderstorm. The mechanic sadly reminisced about how Lacy Black had been so well loved that even a world at war had paused to mourn her passing, and how her husband, producer Mark Damian, had never recovered from her untimely death.

As the days passed, shocking evidence emerged from the wreckage—evidence that proved Lacy Black had not died in the crash after all. Using dental records and the latest forensic technology, experts had positively identified the pilot's remains, but whoever his mysterious female passenger was, she was definitely not Lacy Black!

The CBS camera focused on Dan Rather, who was reporting from the crash site.

"What is it that makes a legend? What magic makes some people become objects of worship and fanatic devotion, even after death? What is that rare ingredient in their personalities that makes them bigger than life? I can count only a handful of people in this century who have affected the world as deeply as Lacy Black—John F. Kennedy, Marilyn Monroe, Princess Diana, and, most recently, John Kennedy, Jr. There seems to be an irony to all this—an unwritten law—that if you are one of the worshiped, you must die young. We were deprived all too soon of the brilliance of these unique individuals who dwelled among us mortals so briefly."

The camera swept over the rusted, twisted metal that was strewn across the crash site, focusing in on the technicians who were still sifting through the debris.

Dan Rather continued. "It is said that Lacy Black was every man's fantasy, and every woman's ideal. Doubtless she would have been a sensation in any decade. Because of the interest this discovery has generated, we are told that Lacy's old films have been resurrected, and video stores throughout the country are raking in the profits. Those who remember her movies from Hollywood's heyday are now joined by a new generation of fans who have just discovered her."

The newscast cut to the anchorwoman in New York. "Dan, we are showing pictures of Lacy here in the studio. It's easy to see why she was once given an award for being the most beautiful woman in the world. She has often been compared to Jean Harlow, and though Lacy had the same platinum hair as Harlow, and we lost them both too soon, there the resemblance between the two sex goddesses of the thirties ends. They were both beautiful, to be sure, but Lacy had something beyond mere beauty—a vulnerability and a sadness that reach out to us even after all this time."

Dan Rather glanced down at his notes. "What everyone seems to overlook is that even if Lacy was not the woman who died in this plane, she ceased to exist the night it went down. There are questions here that may never be answered. Since Lacy didn't die in this crash, then who did? And," he concluded dramatically, "more intriguing still—what really happened to Lacy Black?"

Part One
Mark

Chapter One

Snyder, Texas
1937

"Step on a crack, break your mother's back!" Seventeen-year-old Lucinda Blackburn chanted the nonsensical children's rhyme, then deliberately ground her foot on a jagged crack in the uneven sidewalk, as if the gesture could actually inflict pain on the mother who had abandoned her.

Suddenly feeling self-conscious, Lucinda looked about, hoping that no one had observed her childish antics. She needn't have worried, though, because she seemed to be the only person foolish enough to be out on the street at midday. Most people had gone indoors to escape the grueling west Texas heat.

As Lucinda neared the town square, she glanced longingly at the tall, sturdy elms that surrounded the dome-shaped courthouse, wishing she could linger beneath the shade of one of those trees. But she dared not—she was late already, and her daddy would be furious if his lunch wasn't on the table at twelve sharp.

She wiped sweat from her face with the sleeve of her thin cotton dress, then glanced down at her finger, gently touching the golden band in the shape of two hands clasping. It was the only thing she possessed that had belonged to her mother, and she was careful not to wear it when her father was around; it would only send him into one of his tirades.

There was a constant battle raging inside Lucinda: sometimes she hated her mother for leaving her, and other times she wished her mother would return for her and take her away from this small, dusty town where nothing ever happened.

Reluctantly, Lucinda turned her footsteps in the direction of home, thinking of all the chores she had to do before dinner. No matter what she did or didn't do, she could never please her daddy. In his eyes, her older half sister, Ruth, had all the virtues, while she had all the faults. Why couldn't he see that Ruth was manipulative and sly, and cared only about herself?

As Lucinda neared home, she saw her daddy watching her with his usual intimidating stance—hands on hips, eyes gleaming with condemnation. Quickly putting her mother's ring in her pocket and out of sight, she approached him with trepidation.

Sam Blackburn was a man of medium height, with rawboned features, a ruddy complexion, and wide, muscular shoulders. He had been handsome at one time, but hard work and bitterness had aged him beyond his years.

He was the only mechanic in Snyder, and he constantly reminded his daughters that it was his toil and sweat that put food in their bellies when much of the country was going hungry. They lived in a small apartment he'd built above the garage, and on hot days like this one, the smell of oil and gas permeated every room.

Lucinda saw the coldness in her father's eyes and the tightening of his jaw. Nervously, she dropped her gaze to stare at his work-worn hands. Grease was embedded under the chipped nails, and she couldn't remember a time when his nails had been clean.

"Well, miss," he said harshly, "while you've been frittering your morning away, doing heaven only knows what, your sister's been hard at work, doing her chores and yours as well. Most likely you've been out trying to tempt every boy in town, just like your ma used to do."

Lucinda swallowed past the lump in her throat. "No, Daddy, I wasn't . . . I didn't—"

Sam grabbed her arm and yanked her forward. "Don't lie to me, girl, or I'll know it. The Bible warns us against the seed of the adulterer and the whore—that's what you are."

"I'm *not* like her, Daddy," Lucinda protested.

They were both distracted when a roadster with steam hissing from under the hood pulled up to the garage. Sam and Lucinda stared in astonishment at the sleek black automobile.

A well-dressed man emerged from it and walked to the front of the car, where he paused as if uncertain how to unlatch the hood. He was tall and blond, with bronze skin. His hair was swept across his high forehead, giving a rakish air to his boyishly handsome face.

Sam regained his composure and assumed a businesslike manner. "Mighty fancy automobile you got there," he drawled. "Never expected to see a Cord in these parts."

The stranger looked annoyed. "I hope you aren't going to tell me you don't know how to repair it."

Sam was plainly upset as he reached forward and unlatched the hood, raising it over his head. "I 'spect I know more about it than you do. Bet you've never even seen the motor."

The newcomer's eyes flashed in anger. "Why should I? I'm not a mechanic. I hire people to take care of things like that for me."

Sam's eyes narrowed at the man's arrogance. "Good thing you stopped when you did, mister. I'd say you've got a hole in your radiator, maybe even a busted block. Either way, you got troubles."

"What do you mean?" the stranger demanded. His voice was clipped and deep, his eyes piercing and suspicious.

"I mean there ain't nobody around here got an automobile like this, so I don't stock the parts. If you want it fixed, I'll have to send all the way to Dallas for what I'll need."

The man looked at Sam impatiently. "Are you the only mechanic in town?"

"Yep. Name's Sam Blackburn, and you might say I'm the only mechanic within a hundred miles. If you've a mind to, you could take your chances on the road, but you wouldn't get far."

"Just how long would it take you to get the parts?"

Sam bent his head and looked at the radiator, which was still hissing steam. "Well . . . if you are of a mind to pay someone to drive to Dallas, he could be back day after tomorrow, if he didn't dawdle. If not, you'd have to rely on the bus, and that'd take a week, maybe more."

The man gave an exasperated glance at the heavens and crammed his hands into his pockets. "What in the hell do you expect me to do?"

"I don't expect you to do anything," Sam snapped, his nostrils flaring with anger. "And I don't hold with profanity. I'll tell you this right now—keep a decent tongue in your head if you expect me to work on your car."

Lucinda saw something dangerous spark in the stranger's eyes. It was obvious that he was unaccustomed to being spoken to with such scorn. On closer inspection, she thought the man looked familiar, but she couldn't think why. Her eyes followed him as he opened the passenger's side of the car and an elegant young woman joined him.

Even with the dust from the drive smudging her cheeks, she was beautiful. Her platinum hair was clipped short and framed her face. She was willow-thin and petite, and she wore the most wonderful dress that Lucinda had ever seen—bright purple, and so shiny it had to be silk.

With a gasp, Lucinda recognized the woman—it was Dolores Divine, the famous Hollywood movie star! She'd seen her picture in the fan magazines that Ruth kept hidden beneath her mattress, and on occasion she had gone with friends to the Aztec

Theater to see a Dolores Divine film. Lucinda looked closer at the man as realization dawned on her. It was Mark Damian, owner of Pinnacle Pictures! She could hardly believe they were there, at her daddy's garage!

Dolores spoke in a voice that carried to Lucinda and her father. "How in God's name do you expect me to wait around for days while you have your new toy put in working order?" She looked about her contemptuously. "I can tell you right now, Mark Damian, I have no intention of staying in this backwater town for one minute longer than it takes me to catch a train out."

Mark spoke appeasingly. "It won't be so bad, baby. And besides, it'll give us more time to be alone."

"I never should have listened to you, Mark. The biggest publicity scheme in the history of pictures, my ass!" She tried to mimic him: " 'Let's promote your latest picture in Texas, because westerns do so well there.' " She stomped her foot petulantly. "Of course westerns do well here, Mr. Genius Producer," she ranted. "These people haven't got anything else to entertain them!"

Dolores then pushed past Mark, fanning herself with a beaded handbag. "I doubt there's even a hotel in this town. I warn you, I'll not stay in another dump like we did last night." She glanced down at her hands and held one up for his inspection. "Just see how dry my skin is, and I'll never get the tangles out of my hair! Suppose someone were to photograph me in this condition? I'm ready to escape this hellhole of a state and get back to Los Angeles, where civilized people live."

Mark Damian turned to the mechanic. "Have you a hotel in town, Mr. . . . uh . . . Black . . . whatever?"

"Blackburn," Sam stated, his eyes narrowing. "And, yes, there's the Manhattan Hotel on the south side of the square." His eyes ran disapprovingly over the platinum blonde, noting her tight dress and the heavy makeup she wore. His lips curled in distaste. "Ain't much of a hotel, and I expect it wouldn't meet your needs, being as it ain't fancy."

"What time is the next train heading west?" Dolores demanded, glancing with revulsion at the mechanic's greasy hands. This person wasn't even worth the charm she normally exerted when she found herself in the company of a man.

"There's not a westbound train till six tomorrow morning," Sam replied, focusing his attention under the hood of the Cord.

"Impossible!" Dolores stated angrily. "I won't have it, I tell you."

Sam shrugged. "There's a westbound bus, but it don't come through until tomorrow afternoon."

The movie star glared at him. "Is there a place where I can at least get out of this heat until you *gentlemen* decide what to do? I damn sure don't intend to stand around in this filthy old garage while you make up your minds."

Lucinda could see her daddy's lips tighten in a disapproving line. He was a hard, unyielding man who despised everything the actress represented, and it was obvious, to Lucinda at least, that he was fighting to conceal his disgust.

"If you want to, you can wait in my place," Sam said grudgingly. "Mind you don't go filling my daughters' heads with any of your fancy notions." He nodded in Lucinda's direction. "You can go with Lucinda now, as long as you remember that I'll not have cussing under my roof."

For the first time, Mark and Dolores turned their attention to Lucinda, and embarrassment stained her cheeks. If only she'd worn shoes, she thought woefully. What must they think of her, barefoot and in her shabby dress?

The actress dismissed Lucinda as unimportant, but Mark Damian scrutinized her closely. He couldn't help noticing how her faded print dress clung to her sweet young body. Wisps of sable-colored hair were plastered to her forehead, and her jade-green eyes were noticeable even from where he stood. When he gave her a half smile, she returned it tentatively.

Seething inwardly, Dolores watched Mark's reaction to the mechanic's young daughter. It was always the same with him when he saw a pretty female. But he wouldn't get to this one, she thought maliciously—the girl's father would see to that.

"Good afternoon, Miss Blackburn," Mark said, suddenly his most charming, his eyes running with appreciation over her shapely young body.

Lucinda was so shy she could only nod.

"I'm Mark Damian, and this is Dolores Divine. I'm sure you've seen her latest picture, *Pioneer Spirit*. It's playing in the movie theaters now."

Sam snorted contemptuously. "My girls don't go to the movies—I don't hold with 'em. These young'uns are exposed to enough sinful temptations without that flesh-peddling, ungodly pastime." He would like nothing better than to order the strangers out of his garage, but these were hard times, and he couldn't afford to turn away business. "Now, young man, do you want me to fix your car or not?"

Having no other option, Mark nodded, then turned to Dolores. "You go on up with Miss Blackburn. I'll come get you soon and we'll go to the hotel."

With a sigh of martyrdom, Dolores followed Lucinda through the garage and up the splintered stairs that led to the living quarters.

Lucinda was so in awe of her famous guest that she didn't speak until they reached the top step. "You'll find it's cooler inside, Miss Divine," she said, opening the door and allowing the actress to enter. "Since we have windows on both the north and south sides, we catch a good crossbreeze."

Seeing Dolores Divine's lip curl in disgust when she looked about the room, Lucinda was made painfully aware of the shabbiness of the furnishings. Before now, she hadn't noticed that the blue linoleum with the pink roses was cracked and worn. She had looked past her daddy's frayed green chair with the dark stain on the back where his head always rested.

"Charming," Dolores offered mockingly. "Simply charming."

Lucinda resented the actress's rudeness. The room might not be fancy, but it was spotlessly clean.

Unaware that she had offended the young girl, Dolores spoke

directly to her for the first time. "How can you live in a place like this? I'd rather be dead!"

Lucinda moved across the room to tie back the frayed lace curtains, allowing the slight breeze to help cool her anger. "This is all I know, Miss Divine. It's my home."

"Lord, I never dreamed anyone could exist in such a place. This must be hell."

"Miss Divine," Lucinda answered carefully, attempting to hide her growing dislike of the actress, "you can rest in my bedroom and I'll get you a drink of water. I can put ice in it if you'd like."

Dolores tossed her handbag on the sagging divan and pushed her damp platinum hair away from her face. "Right now I'd sell my soul to the devil for a very large, very dry martini."

Lucinda looked puzzled. "I can run to the drugstore and get you a Coca-Cola or a Grapette."

"My God!" Dolores exclaimed, looking at the young girl in horror. "You don't even know what a martini is, do you? I've come to the ends of the earth!"

Chapter Two

Lucinda spent most of the afternoon catering to Dolores Divine, who was demanding, hard to please, and ungrateful. Finally, Lucinda excused herself and sought the sanctuary of the kitchen, where she began to prepare the evening meal.

Glancing at the wall clock, she wondered where her sister was. Ruth hadn't been home all afternoon, and despite what their daddy thought, she hadn't done any of the chores before she left.

Lucinda was annoyed as she crumbled several slices of bread in a bowl and gathered the rest of the ingredients to make bread pudding. It appeared that they would be having company for supper, so she took down the large baking dish.

The heat from the oven made the kitchen unbearable, so Lucinda dampened a washcloth and wiped her face and the back of her neck. While she worked, she speculated on the glamorous lives Mark Damian and Dolores Divine must lead. Ruth had once told her that Mark Damian had a twenty-room mansion in the hills of Hollywood and gave parties that were attended by such stars as Joan Crawford, Marlene Dietrich, and Clark Gable.

Before today, if anyone had told her that Dolores Divine would be staying under her roof, Lucinda would have been thrilled. But now that she had spent the afternoon with the temperamental movie star, she was not so impressed.

With a resigned sigh, she noticed the puddle of water on the floor near the icebox. Grabbing up a rag, she sank to her knees to sop it up, irritated because she'd neglected to empty the tray—just another aggravation to add to a day filled with aggravations.

She frowned when she saw that the window screen was unlatched, and realized that Ruth had taken her usual exit, slipping through the window and dropping to the ground. With a shake of her head, Lucinda wondered what their father would do if he found out that Ruth was sneaking out to meet her boyfriends.

Dolores fanned herself with a religious magazine she'd found on the scarred coffee table. Her anger had been building all afternoon. How dared Mark dump her in this nasty little apartment and then neglect her! Some honeymoon this was turning out to be. With a toss of her platinum hair, she wondered what had possessed her to marry Mark. It had seemed the right thing at the time—a full moon hanging over Dallas, Mark with his boyish charm, making love to her and swearing it would be like that forever. Well, forever to Mark lasted only until the next attractive female came along—in this case, the Blackburn girl.

Hearing a train whistle in the distance, Dolores glanced at her handbag on the divan, glad that she'd had the foresight to tuck fifty dollars into the zipper compartment. Tomorrow she would be on that train for Los Angeles, and to hell with Mark Damian!

Hearing heavy footsteps on the stairs, Dolores turned to watch Mark enter the room. She stiffened when he took her in his arms, and glared at him when he gave her that boyish smile that had once sent her heart pounding. After today, she vowed, his smooth-talking approach would no longer work on her.

"Baby," he cajoled, trying to appease her, "I really missed you this afternoon."

Despite her anger, she felt herself melting against him. "I missed you, too," she admitted. "But we can make up for it tonight."

Mark shook his head regretfully. "I'm afraid that won't be possible." Then he gave her an apologetic smile. "The car repairs are going to cost more than I anticipated, but I know you'll be understanding."

Dolores moved out of his arms. "Just what is that supposed to mean?"

"It took most of my cash to pay for the parts and repairs. Until I can get someone to wire money, we're broke."

Dolores stared at him, her anger ablaze again. "I promise you, Mark, if you don't get me out of here at once, we're through . . . finished . . . washed up!"

He pulled her stiff, unyielding body against his. "Come on, baby, don't be that way." His hand ran up her arm, and he fondled her breasts through the thin material of her dress. "I'll make this up to you." He nipped at her ear. "You know I will."

Dolores twisted out of his arms, but Mark captured her in an embrace and pressed his lips to her neck. "You know how good it is between us."

"It won't work, Mark," she said flatly. "If what we have is so good, why haven't you announced that we are married?"

"Now, baby, you know we agreed that we wouldn't tell anyone until we can do it right. I want a party with the press and everyone who's anyone in Hollywood before I drop that little bombshell."

She tapped her foot in irritation. "Meanwhile, we are stuck in this hick town."

He touched her cheek and smiled. "It won't be so bad. The car will be repaired in a few days and we'll be on our way again. Just think about the party we'll throw to tell the world we're married."

She eyed him suspiciously. "Just where do we stay while your car's being repaired?"

He made a wide sweep with his hand. "Why, we'll stay here. Mr. Blackburn has reluctantly offered us his hospitality, such as it is." He laughed with real amusement. "That old hypocrite thinks you're a decadent influence on his two daughters, but since he demanded full payment before he'd work on my car, he said it was only 'Christian' to provide us with a place to eat and sleep—but in separate beds, of course."

Dolores pushed him away. "I'll be on that train tomorrow morning when it pulls out. Dolores Divine doesn't sleep in a hovel!"

There was a sharp edge to Mark's voice. "I don't see that we have a choice."

Her face became distorted with rage. "How dare you treat me this way—you forget who I am!"

"You're wrong," Mark said coldly. "When I found you, you were no more than a barefoot farm girl by the name of Glenda Huddelton. Don't tell me you've started believing the publicity the studio puts out. Dolores Divine is my creation, and you'd better remember that."

Dolores didn't like being reminded of her humble beginnings, and she wanted to strike out at him, to hurt him. "Who in the hell are you to drag up the past? You were an actor down on your luck before you found a wealthy sucker who made you his partner. It was mighty convenient of Ted Morris to die and leave Pinnacle Pictures to you. Without me, your studio would have gone under long ago."

Mark laughed sardonically. "I hate to disillusion you, baby, but anyone could do what you do, and do it better."

She shook her head. "We both know that isn't true, Mark. I might have been nobody when you found me, but I'm somebody now."

Ruth Blackburn had entered the apartment so silently, Mark and Dolores were unaware that they had an audience.

"Excuse me," Ruth interrupted. "Just who *are* you?"

Mark and Dolores swung around to stare at the newcomer, wondering how much of their conversation she had overheard.

Lucinda broke an awkward silence when she came into the room, carrying a worn tablecloth and mismatched napkins to place on the rickety dining room table.

"Ruth," Lucinda said as easily as if she had been introducing any ordinary strangers, "this is Mark Damian and Dolores Divine. Their car broke down and Daddy's fixing it."

Ruth's mouth dropped open and she was speechless as she looked from Mark to Dolores. She murmured something unintelligible under her breath and hurriedly left the room.

Lucinda became aware that Mark Damian was watching her every move, and it made her uncomfortable. Under his watchful gaze, she spread the tablecloth, taking particular care to press the wrinkles out with her hand. She looked up and met his eyes. "Supper will be at six, Mr. Damian," she told him, then hurried back to the kitchen.

"I wonder what culinary delights our little country mouse is going to surprise us with," Dolores said sharply. She wasn't a fool; she knew what Mark had in mind, and even though she had decided to leave him, it made her furious.

Lucinda was thinking about Mark Damian and how gracious his manners were compared to Miss Divine's. He was nice, she mused, dipping pork chops in flour, then placing them in hot grease. Mark Damian was polished and sophisticated, and like no man she'd ever met before.

The kitchen door was shoved open and Ruth entered, wearing her new yellow Sunday dress, a look of amazement etched on her face. "I can't believe it! Dolores Divine and Mark Damian in our living room! Won't everyone envy me when I tell them?"

Lucinda speared one of the pork chops with a fork and turned it over. "As you come to know Miss Divine, you'll be less and less impressed with her. She fits Daddy's description of 'all that glitters is not gold.' From seeing her movies, I thought she'd be a nice person, but she's not." Mischievously, Lucinda smiled at her sister. "Maybe she's a better actress than the critics give her credit for."

Ruth picked up a carrot that had been arranged on the relish tray and chewed on the end. "That may be true, but Mark Damian is even handsomer in person than in the movie magazines. He's a perfect dream." She sighed. "And to think he's been here all afternoon."

"That reminds me," Lucinda said. "Where were you today? I could have used your help."

Ruth shrugged her shoulders. "I met Bobby Franklin and we went to a movie," she admitted, knowing that Lucinda would never tell their father.

"Well, now that you're here, why don't you see to our company? I'd much rather cook the whole meal than spend five more minutes with that woman."

"They've gone out walking down by Deep Creek. Do you suppose they'll mind that the creek's dry?"

Lucinda glanced up at the kitchen clock. "I don't know, or care. But I do hope they're back in ten minutes, because it's almost six, and Daddy'll expect to eat on time, whether we have company or not."

Ruth assessed her young half sister with a critical eye. They were about the same height, and their hair was the same rich brown color, but there the resemblance ended. She was big-boned, while Lucinda was delicately built. She wore her straight hair long, while Lucinda's was cropped short so that ringlets covered her head. Though Ruth knew she was pretty, she was aware that Lucinda was the beauty in the family, and she'd always resented her for it.

The front screen door slammed and Lucinda removed the pork chops from the pan and placed them in a platter. "That'll be Daddy; I need to hurry."

Ruth's eyes took on a cunning gleam. "You worked hard all afternoon. Go on in and greet Daddy, while I bring everything to the table."

Lucinda was grateful. "I *would* like to run a brush through my hair before we sit down to eat."

"Go along, and I'll finish up here," Ruth offered. "That's the least I can do, since you did my chores."

Lucinda quickly removed her apron and dashed out the kitchen door. If she hurried, she'd have time to change her dress while her father washed for supper.

Ruth tied the flour-splattered apron about her waist before carrying the platter of pork chops into the dining area. "Hello, Daddy," she said sweetly. "We're having your favorite for supper tonight."

Sam nodded. "You're a good girl, Ruth." His eyes hardened when he looked at his younger daughter's bedroom door. "That's more than I can say for your sister."

Ruth said nothing, but tried to look dutiful, all the while smiling smugly to herself. She felt no guilt for taking the credit for Lucinda's labor. As her father was fond of reminding them, "The Lord helps those who help themselves."

Meanwhile, Lucinda was hurriedly changing into a dress that Ruth had outgrown. She tugged it into place, thinking it was almost too small, but it was all that she had, and it would have to do. As a final touch, she tied a pink ribbon in her hair.

When Lucinda entered the living room, she was glad to see that their guests had returned from their walk and her father appeared to be talking amiably with Mark Damian. She wasn't surprised that Dolores Divine had a bored expression on her face as she flipped through the pages of a seed catalog.

Mark was aware of Lucinda's presence, and almost reluctantly his eyes strayed to her. He didn't notice that her dress was a hand-me-down. But he did notice how snugly it fit across her breasts and how it came only to her knees, showing a very shapely pair of legs.

Lucinda approached her father. "Supper's ready."

Sam glared at her. "No thanks to you. Once again your sister's been left with all the work, while you did nothing."

Lucinda opened her mouth to protest, but knew it would do

no good—it never did. She resented the fact that Ruth twisted every situation to her own advantage.

Choking back her indignation, Lucinda glanced up and caught Mark Damian's eyes. She knew that he understood what she was feeling—he'd seen Ruth arrive home only thirty minutes ago. She raised her head proudly, not wanting a stranger to witness her humiliation or to pity her.

Sam Blackburn moved his stout frame across the room and seated himself at the head of the table, looking impatiently at everyone else.

"Please, sit here," Lucinda said to Dolores and Mark, indicating the two chairs opposite her and Ruth.

After they complied, Sam cleared his throat and said grace in a booming voice that made Mark wonder if he thought God was hard of hearing.

Mark glanced across the table at Lucinda. She was fresh, innocent, and lovely—a rose among thorns, or, more aptly, a pearl among swine. Her eyes were closed in prayer, and the shadow of her long lashes rested against her pale cheeks. Her lips were full and pink, and dimples danced intriguingly as she whispered the prayer.

Mark found himself fantasizing about being the man who brought awareness to her. His attention was so focused on Lucinda that he didn't realize the prayer had ended until she raised her head and blushed under his close scrutiny.

There was a long silence while the food was passed around and plates were filled.

"Surely you don't expect me to eat that!" Dolores exclaimed as she was handed a bowl of green beans in sauce with a thin sheen of grease floating on top.

Sam's eyes flashed with anger. "Whether you eat or not makes no difference to me, ma'am, but if what we have isn't good enough for you, you can leave others to eat in peace."

Dolores tapped Mark on the shoulder. "I can't believe you're going to let him speak to me that way."

Mark was inclined to let Dolores take care of herself, but

whatever their differences, they did have a public image to maintain. "Miss Divine is not at her best today," he said apologetically. "As she is Pinnacle Pictures' biggest star, I'm afraid we spoil her—and rightly so." The statement sounded false, even to his ears.

Sam waved his fork in the air. "No one is pampered in this house. If either of you don't like it, you can leave—now."

Dolores pushed back her chair and stormed across the floor, making her departure as dramatic as she could before entering Lucinda's bedroom and slamming the door.

She flung herself on the narrow bed, half hoping that Mark would come after her, but he didn't—not this time.

Instead, it was Lucinda who tried to go to Dolores. She didn't care much for the movie star, but the actress was a guest in their home.

Sam gruffly ordered Lucinda to sit back down and finish her meal, and she obeyed.

Mark unfolded his napkin and placed it across his lap. "Everything looks delicious to me," he said cheerfully.

Ruth went to the kitchen and returned with a plate of corn bread. She served her father first, then moved to Mark's side. When she offered him the plate, her body pressed against his and her eyes gleamed invitingly as she smiled down at him.

Mark was amazed that the bold little baggage was offering herself to him right in front of her father. Normally he wouldn't have minded, but his real interest was in Lucinda, who had lowered her head, apparently embarrassed by her sister's outrageous behavior.

There was a tenseness in the air, and Sam Blackburn looked around suspiciously. Something wasn't right, but he couldn't quite see what the trouble was. "Pass the gravy," he bellowed, glaring around the table at no one in particular.

Mark was startled when he felt Ruth's bare foot travel up his leg. His gaze met hers across the table, and she smiled at him boldly. *Just what I need with all my other problems,* he thought, *a car that's costing me almost every cent I have, a temperamental star who also happens to be my wife, and a promiscuous teenager trying to get me in trouble with her sanctimonious father.*

Mark decided that it was best all around to avoid both Blackburn girls, so he attempted to engage their father in conversation. "I certainly appreciate your hospitality, Mr. Blackburn, and I feel I must apologize for any inconvenience we've caused you."

If possible, the tension in the room heightened. Lucinda and Ruth exchanged glances before they turned anxious eyes on their father. They knew what Mark Damian did not—no one was allowed to speak at the evening meal. Nothing was more certain to incur their father's wrath. His rule was that absolute silence would be observed at the supper table, for that was the time Sam had set aside for his family to reflect on their actions of the day and to prepare for the hour of Bible reading and prayer that began when the table was cleared and the dishes were washed.

Lucinda placed a finger to her lips, trying to warn Mark, but he didn't see her.

"On my walk this afternoon, I looked around, and I think Snyder might be an ideal location for a western," Mark continued obliviously. "The cactus, the tumbleweeds, the mesquite trees, the—"

Sam Blackburn's bushy eyebrows met in a frown above his nose. "Is there a point you're trying to make, young man?" he barked. "If there is, make it, so me and my daughters can get on with our meal. If you're through eating, you can be excused from the table, and you and that woman are welcome to join us for Bible reading and evening prayers in an hour."

Undaunted, Mark wiped his mouth on the napkin and stood up, sliding his chair back. "I don't want to upset your usual routine, Mr. Blackburn. My evening is going to be spent trying to pacify Dolores. Her feathers have been ruffled, and she needs to have them stroked. You know how it is when you're dealing with a temperamental female."

Sam's expression hardened as his eyes followed Mark across the room. A painted actress and a slick-talking Hollywood man staying under his roof. He never thought he'd live to see this day.

Chapter Three

Mark entered the bedroom to find Dolores pacing the floor furiously.

"So you were finally able to drag yourself away from that little twit with the mooning eyes. Well, you're too late, Mark. Nothing you can say will make up for the way you've treated me today. We're finished!"

"Now, baby," he coaxed, moving toward her. "You're just tired; you don't mean that. You're my wife—we're a team. Together we'll turn on all the lights in Hollywood."

She shook her head and looked at him in disgust, the last remnants of her infatuation for him stripped away. "You just don't understand, Mark. I want a divorce."

His voice became cold, unloving, that of a stranger. "No, it's you who doesn't understand, Dolores. You seem to forget that I own you!"

Dolores's voice trembled, but she met Mark's eyes squarely. "And you seem to forget that we never formalized our working relationship. You outsmarted yourself this time. You wouldn't sign a contract with me because you wanted to be able to drop me if my pictures weren't successful. Well, that little safeguard works both ways; I can walk away, and there's nothing you can do to stop me."

He looked at her distastefully. "Go to hell, Dolores. I made you my wife, and that's the greatest compliment I've ever given any woman."

She sat on the edge of the bed, her eyes downcast. "I'll be a big star someday and you'll be sorry you weren't nicer to me."

Mark crossed the room with angry strides. Roughly, he jerked her chin up and forced her to meet his eyes. "Have you looked in the mirror lately? No amount of makeup can cover the lines of hard living, baby. You may get one or two good parts, but before you know it, you'll be just a character actress, then a walk-on, then gradually you'll fade away until no one will even remember your name."

He hadn't raised his voice, but there was something in his eyes that made Dolores tremble. Fear gripped her, and she moved to the middle of the bed, just out of his reach.

For a long moment they stared at each other, until at last Mark smiled mockingly and gave her a stiff salute. "So long, baby." He opened the door and left, closing it softly behind him.

Dolores lay back on the bed, clutching a pillow in front of her. She hadn't really meant to push him so far, but now there was no turning back. Mark was an unforgiving man—no one got a second chance with him.

One of the first things she'd do when she got home would be to cross the border into Mexico and get a quick divorce. Then she'd be free of Mark once and for all. She didn't need him—she didn't need anyone. She was Dolores Divine!

Just after dawn, while everyone was asleep, Dolores slipped out of the apartment and caught the westbound train. She wondered what Mark would do when he found her missing. She wondered if he'd even care.

* * *

After Mark had explained to the Blackburns that Dolores had felt compelled to return home, no further mention was made of her absence. Lucinda observed that Mr. Damian seemed more at ease now. She came to the conclusion that the fan magazines had been mistaken about any romance between them. Somehow the realization that Mark didn't love the temperamental actress pleased Lucinda, although she could not have said why.

Lucinda tossed and turned, unable to sleep. For the past week, she'd been sharing a room with her sister so Mark could have her bedroom. Ruth had slipped out just after their daddy had gone to bed, and had been gone all night.

When Ruth finally tiptoed into the bedroom, Lucinda groaned and rolled out of bed, glancing at the clock. It was a quarter to six, and time to start her daddy's breakfast.

Lucinda removed her nightgown and neatly folded it and laid it on a chair. She slipped into a brown skirt and white blouse, ran a comb through her hair, and quietly went to the kitchen, leaving Ruth asleep.

She placed the coffeepot on a burner and reached for the ancient cutting board, carving off several thick slices of bacon and slapping them into an iron skillet. While the bacon sizzled and the aroma of coffee filled the tiny kitchen, she sliced the last of the homemade bread and placed it on a platter. Knowing she would need a fresh loaf for lunch, she reached for the flour and mixing bowl, humming to herself.

"Hello, Miss Blackburn," a friendly voice said some time later. "Don't you know what time it is? How can you be so cheerful this early in the morning?"

Lucinda glanced up at Mark. Although he was immaculately dressed, his blond hair was tousled, giving him a boyish look. He jauntily leaned against the doorjamb, watching her knead the dough.

"My God, I didn't know anyone made their own bread anymore."

"Good morning, Mr. Damian," she answered shyly. "There's

coffee on the stove and a cup on the shelf behind you, if you would like to help yourself. I've got bacon frying and I'll make you some eggs as soon as I put the bread to rise."

When he made no effort to move, Lucinda looked at him nervously. "I would get the coffee for you, but I'm rather a mess." As proof she held up her hands, which were covered with dough.

He didn't answer, but instead slowly sauntered toward her, very aware of the effect he was having on the young, inexperienced girl. He knew he courted folly in pursuing this little beauty, but she was so ripe and ready for a man, he couldn't seem to help himself.

"Tell me, baby, have you ever thought about being in the movies?" he asked, reaching over her head for a chipped coffee cup. "You're mighty easy on the eyes, you know." He'd used those same words countless times before with great success. He hadn't meant them in the past—he didn't mean them now. She was no more than a pleasant diversion to pass the long hours since Dolores had run out on him.

Lucinda looked at him thoughtfully. "To be honest, I don't think I'd like it."

He'd expected her to react with enthusiasm—to be starstruck, as most girls were when he fed them his line. Lucinda was different; he'd sensed it from the beginning.

Leaning closer, he brushed flour from her cheek, then allowed his finger to trail to her throat, where her pulse beat furiously. "You'd be a natural on the big screen, baby," he said, making each word a caress. "The audience would just eat you up." He tilted her face to examine it in the light. "Yes, you do have something. But you're so young—you need to be older . . . and more experienced," he said regretfully.

At that moment, the door swung open and Sam entered, quickly assessing the situation. He saw Mark's hand drop away from his daughter's face, and he was enraged.

When Lucinda saw the look in her daddy's eyes, she backed

away from Mark so quickly that she stumbled against the icebox.

"I might have known something like this would happen," Sam roared, his eyes moving from his daughter's flushed face to the seemingly innocent look on Mark Damian's. "I'll not allow fornication in my own home."

"Daddy, I never . . . We weren't—"

"Just like your mother," he raged. "I always knew you wouldn't amount to nothing, and you've proved me right."

Lucinda ran from the room, her hands over her ears.

Mark's eyes hardened. "Mr. Blackburn, I can assure you—"

"Enough!" the outraged Sam ordered. "Your flowery speeches may fool my daughter, but not me. I know what I saw." He threw an automobile key on the table. "Your car's ready, and I'll thank you to be leaving." Sam turned to take the burning pan of bacon off the stove. "That girl never does anything right," he said in disgust. "Such carelessness and waste is a sin."

Ruth suddenly appeared at her daddy's side, trying to look as cheerful as she could, considering she had a hangover from the bootleg whiskey she'd consumed the night before. She'd been awakened by the sound of her daddy's shouting, and had hurriedly dressed and made her way to the kitchen to see what had happened.

"Here, Daddy, you sit down and let me get your breakfast," she offered solicitously.

"You're a good girl, Ruth. I don't know what I'd do without you."

Disgusted by Ruth and her father, Mark hurried to the bedroom, where he started cramming his belongings into a suitcase. He couldn't get away from this house fast enough. He paused for a moment, pitying Lucinda. Poor little fool—her father and sister treated her like hell. But that was none of his affair. He had problems of his own.

Sam had just sat down at the table when someone knocked on the front door. With muttered fury, he lumbered to the door to admit Ed Burton and his son. Ed looked angry, while the gawky teenager looked scared and kept staring down at his feet.

"I'm sorry to be bothering you this early, Sam, but I need to talk to you."

"What's the trouble, Ed?"

The man was twisting his worn cowboy hat in his hands. "This ain't easy to say, Sam, but I want you to keep your daughter away from my boy."

"What do you mean?" Sam roared indignantly.

Ruth hurried into the room when she heard her daddy shout, and when she saw who their early morning visitors were, she turned pale and began to tremble.

Nobody noticed Mark, who stood in the bedroom door observing them with a cynical twist to his lips.

"You'd better explain yourself," Sam said in a dangerous tone.

Ed looked at Ruth, then glanced away. "Your girl and Ed Junior, here, snuck off last night to the old abandoned Johnson barn, where they met up with some of the boys from town and got all liquored up. I don't know what all took place, but I thought you ought to know that there was four boys there, and your daughter was the only girl. I wouldn't want a girl of mine there, and I don't want my boy there again, so I'm asking you to keep your daughter away from him."

Sam stared at his neighbor, shame filling his very soul. "I'll see to it, Ed," he choked out. "It's best you leave now."

The room was filled with silence after the Burtons departed. Sam stood for a long time, clenching and unclenching his hands.

Ruth was almost paralyzed with fear. "Daddy," she said in a squeaky voice. "I . . . I—"

"I know, Ruth," he said grimly, "and I'm sorry for your sake, but I knew this day would come. Lucinda's just no good, and never has been." He reached for a thick leather strap that hung beside the front door.

"Lucinda!" Ruth exclaimed in relief. She certainly wasn't going to confess that she'd been the one with the boys last night, not if her crimes were being laid at her sister's feet.

Sam flung open the bedroom door and slammed it behind him.

Mark flinched when he heard the sound of the strap striking again and again. When he heard Lucinda cry out, he turned on Ruth. "You cunning bitch," he said snarling. "We both know it was you that man was talking about and not Lucinda. Why didn't you tell the truth?"

Ruth looked at him without shame. "Why didn't you?"

"He wouldn't have believed me," Mark said as he pushed past her. "I don't know why I should get involved, but that old man will probably kill your sister if someone doesn't stop him."

Mark shoved the bedroom door open and caught Sam's wrist just as he was about to deliver another blow. Lucinda was huddled in a corner, trying to protect her face.

"Stop it, you fool!" Mark commanded. "Can't you see she's had enough?"

Sam shoved Mark away so forcefully that he was slammed against the wall. The old man stood staring down at his younger daughter, his breathing labored from his exertions. He dropped the strap and then turned to Mark.

"My business isn't yours. You got your car; now get out!" Sam said in a snarl as he stalked out of the room.

Lucinda hung her head, too ashamed to meet Mark's eyes. "Daddy's right," she whispered. "Please go away."

Mark was inclined to do just that. The money he'd been waiting for had arrived the day before. What happened here was none of his business. If he were to return in ten years he'd probably find Lucinda Blackburn work-worn and fat, with five or six kids clinging to her, and married to a man of her father's intelligence.

Pity, he thought. She was such a lovely creature.

Chapter Four

Lucinda was in the kitchen applying a damp cloth to her face when her daddy found her. She cringed when he stood over her, his arm raised menacingly.

"Well, girl, you've shamed me for the last time. I want you out of this house today."

She shook her head in disbelief as fear of the unknown made her tremble and hysteria rose up inside her, grabbing and twisting her insides until she wanted to scream. She must not give in to the terror that threatened to consume her. Taking a big gulp of air, Lucinda met his eyes squarely.

"I haven't done anything wrong," she protested.

"Trickery is the tool liars use when they're trapped—and you're finally found out, girl, so save your lies." Sam's face was red from the anger he was trying to suppress. "Just see that you're gone before I come home for supper. And I don't ever want to lay eyes on you again—is that clear?"

Lucinda was stunned. He couldn't mean to throw her out of the house. "Daddy, I have no place to go. What will happen to me?" she pleaded, wanting to cry out at the hardness she saw in his eyes.

"Go to the devil for all I care," Sam answered, poking his hands in his pockets so he could resist the urge to strike her again. "I always knew you'd end up just like your mother," he said cuttingly.

Lucinda glanced past her daddy and saw Ruth standing there, thinly veiled triumph on her face. "Don't you have something to say to Daddy?" Lucinda asked, hoping Ruth would admit the truth.

Ruth looked undecided for only a moment and then shook her head. "Not a thing. And," she added pointedly, "you'd better not say anything either. Daddy wants you gone, and so do I."

Sam nodded grimly in agreement.

In that moment Lucinda felt the pain of betrayal. She raised her head and looked from her father to her sister. There was nothing for her here. There never really had been; she'd just never realized it before.

Her back stiff with pride, she walked across the living room without pausing. The screen door slamming shut behind her brought a feeling of finality. Nothing would ever induce her to return to this house again. Her daddy and Ruth deserved each other.

Mark was stowing his suitcase in the trunk of his car when Lucinda approached him. He paused to look at her. "Are you all right?"

"My daddy threw me out, Mr. Damian. Please take me with you," she said in desperation. "I have nowhere to go."

Mark slid behind the wheel, impatient to leave. "I can't take you with me, Lucinda. Even if I wanted to, your father would come after me with a shotgun."

"No, he wouldn't, Mr. Damian. He doesn't care what happens to me." Tears pooled in her eyes and ran down her cheeks. "I won't be a burden to you, I promise. Just take me away from Snyder; that's all I ask."

Mark stared at Lucinda while he calculated what her request

would mean for him. "If I take you, I want it understood that I make no promises," he warned. "You should know that about me, Lucinda—I am selfish to the core and will always do what's in my own best interest."

She quickly ran around the car and climbed into the passenger's seat before he could change his mind. No matter what he said, he was the kindest man she'd ever known. "Thank you," she said, her eyes shining with gratitude. "I really won't cause you any trouble."

"You may not thank me before this trip's over, baby. I never do anything for nothing."

In her innocence, she misunderstood him. "I'll always be grateful to you, Mr. Damian, for letting me come with you when I had no place else to go."

She was naive as hell, Mark thought, feeling confused because her vulnerability made him want to protect her. If she but knew it, the person she needed the most protection from was him. He slammed his foot on the accelerator with such force that the tires squealed, leaving black marks on Sam Blackburn's driveway.

If Lucinda could have seen the envious expression on her sister's face when Ruth peered out the window and watched them pull away, she might have derived some small satisfaction from it.

"If it's any consolation to you, your father will soon realize his mistake," Mark said. "Without you around to take the blame, Ruth will soon show her true nature."

Lucinda stared at him in surprise. "You don't believe I did what my daddy accused me of?"

"Of course not," he said scornfully. "I have eyes."

She leaned back against the red leather seat and stared at the dashboard where M. D. had been initialed in gold. "Was it so obvious, what Ruth was doing?"

Mark sneered. "It would be to any man who knows women. My job is to know when someone's real and when they're not. Your sister couldn't fool anyone with half a brain."

"She always fools Daddy," Lucinda said sadly.

Mark gave her a telling glance. "Let me explain something to you, Lucinda Blackburn," he said reflectively. "I'd be willing to bet that Ruth is wishing she had confessed her sins so she could be on her way to Hollywood with me—though I can say with all honesty that I wouldn't have taken *her*."

Lucinda's eyes widened. "Do you mean it? Are you going to take me all the way to Hollywood?"

"Sure, baby. Why not? In for a penny, in for a pound."

Her slender hand moved to his arm. "I haven't thanked you for coming to my rescue."

Mark frowned when he saw the bruises that had formed on Lucinda's face and forearms. "Did he hurt you?"

She avoided his eyes. "No, not so much. Mostly I feel ashamed that Daddy would think so badly of me."

Mark didn't reply, but his lips thinned.

After a while, Lucinda relaxed and watched the mesquite trees whiz by as the finely tuned engine hummed down the narrow road.

"You know, Mr. Damian," she said at last, "this is the first time I've been outside Scurry County, unless you count the time I went with Daddy and Ruth to Lubbock."

"Oh, well," Mark said facetiously. "If you've seen Lubbock, Texas, you've seen the world."

She smiled at him and he smiled back; then they both started laughing.

It was after midnight, and Mark had misjudged the distance between towns. Unable to find a place to stop for the night, he pulled off the road to sleep for a while.

The Cord was a two-seater, so there was little room for Mark and Lucinda to stretch out in comfort. She curled up by the door and was soon asleep, while Mark restlessly watched the full moon play across her face. She slept the sleep of the innocent, and he envied her for that. Had he ever been as trusting as Lucinda? He didn't think so.

Mark muttered an oath when he bumped his knee on the steering wheel, but at last he, too, slept. Just before daylight, he awoke and they resumed their journey.

It was late afternoon when Mark pulled into a run-down tourist court on the outskirts of Tucson, Arizona. After eating at a diner that served greasy hamburgers, he took Lucinda to the small room they would be sharing. While he bathed and shaved in the men's bathroom, Lucinda bathed in the women's.

She had only the skirt and blouse she'd been wearing when they left Snyder, so she washed them in the public sink and returned to the room, where she hung them on the window ledge to dry.

Wearing only the burgundy robe that Mark had loaned her, she stood before him, anxiously knotting the sash that held the robe together.

"My clothes will be terribly wrinkled in the morning because I don't have an iron."

Mark was lounging on the bed, thinking how tempting she looked with her damp hair curling around her freshly scrubbed face. She had no idea how she excited him. "Come here, Lucinda," he said softly, patting the mattress beside him.

She perched on the edge of the bed, as far away from Mark as she could get, not sure just why. She gave him a tentative smile and blurted out the first thought that came to her mind: "I never had a shower before. They're really quite nice."

The sagging bed creaked as Mark leaned forward and gently placed his finger on her lips to silence her. She stared at him, her eyes wide and questioning.

Slowly his finger moved over her mouth, tracing the outline of her full lips. Lucinda closed her eyes and felt herself move toward him. She'd been hurt so deeply and wanted to be in the shelter of his comforting arms.

At first, that was all it was—Mark holding her and she curling up next to him, feeling safe.

"Lucinda, Lucinda, you don't even know the effect you have on men, do you? I saw how all the men in the diner stared at you tonight, and I knew what they were thinking."

She laughed. "I noticed that too. I'm sure they were wondering what a man like you was doing with a ragtag girl like me."

"Innocent," he said softly against her ear. "If you're wise, you'll run from me before you get hurt."

Impulsively, Lucinda leaned forward, pressing her smooth cheek to his rough one. "We haven't known each other very long, Mr. Damian, but I trust you more than anyone I know."

His hand froze at the belt of her robe. "Damn," he said, shoving her away. "Trust is not a word anyone has ever used in connection with me, baby." He stood up and went to the window, where he pushed the cheap curtain aside and stared out at the flashing neon sign. "You can have the bed," he said gruffly. "And stop calling me Mr. Damian. My name's Mark—use it!"

Lucinda slipped off the bed and went to him. "Can't we both sleep on the bed, Mark? I'll try not to disturb you."

He swung around to her, his eyes sweeping her face. "If I get on that bed with you, I can't answer for what might happen. You do know that, don't you, Lucinda?"

She was quiet for a moment. "I told you, I trust you."

"Well, don't," he said in irritation. "I'm not made of stone, and I damn sure don't wear the halo you've placed on my head."

Taking his hand, she led him toward the bed. "You sleep here, and I'll curl up in the chair."

He let out an exasperated breath. "Have it your way, Lucinda."

He groaned when she pressed her body against his and raised her face to him.

"I would do anything for you, Mark. I owe you so much."

His eyes were on her lips. "Don't say that unless you mean it."

Lucinda felt a warmth spread throughout her body. No one in her whole life had touched her in quite the same way he did. In a move that took them both by surprise, she brushed her lips against his. "I love you," she said, her eyes shining softly.

Mark could no longer deny the desire that had raged through

him since their first meeting. "Don't love me, baby," he whispered. His hands expertly moved across her back, and he pressed her against him so tightly that he could feel each breath she took.

Every move he made, every word he spoke, was meant to stir her budding desire. "I'll never ask for—nor do I want—your love. What I want, you must give freely—do you understand, Lucinda?"

She nodded, and her nervousness melted away, lost in the passion she saw in his eyes. She didn't really understand what he wanted, but it didn't matter because she belonged to him. When Mark pushed aside the robe and placed his hand against her bare breast, she trembled with a powerful longing that rocked her whole body.

Mark lowered her against the bed and slipped the robe off her shoulders, his eyes running appreciatively over the most perfect body he'd ever seen.

Lucinda knew she should feel embarrassed, but something miraculous was happening to her with each stroke of his hand, each kiss, each murmured word. Although Mark had warned her not to, she loved him so much it hurt.

With calculated manipulation, Mark stroked, caressed, and kissed her until she clung to him with newly awakened desire.

Lucinda didn't realize that Mark had undressed until he gripped her hips and slid her along his naked body. She was mindless with a building excitement, an ache deep inside that left her breathless. She turned her head to follow his lips, wanting his kiss.

Mark knew without being told that she was a virgin, and he held his body taut, trying to restrain his need so he wouldn't hurt her needlessly. When Lucinda threw back her head, offering her body, he lost control. He hurt her—he knew that when he heard her whimper—but he could not stop.

Lucinda bit her lip and slipped her arms around his waist, opening herself to him. This was the man she loved, and she had no guilt in surrendering her body to him. It was all she had to give him.

Lucinda was too filled with emotion to speak. Tonight she'd left all childhood fantasies behind and had become a woman—Mark's woman. There was something warm and gratifying about that. For the first time in her life, she belonged to someone.

Mark felt strangely tender toward Lucinda. Inexperienced as she was, she had still satisfied him more fully than any woman ever had. He pushed her tumbled hair out of her face and looked into her luminous eyes. "You will never do this with anyone but me," he said forcefully.

"No, I won't," she promised.

"You're mine," he said, wondering why he felt so possessive of her.

"As long as you want me," Lucinda said simply.

He gathered her close, cradling her head against his arm. "You make me feel . . . different," he admitted. "If I had known you before, you might have been my saving grace, but it's too late for that now."

She pressed a kiss on his cheek. "Why, Mark?"

He closed his eyes. "I didn't get where I am without losing pieces of my soul along the way. There is very little left of me, Lucinda. Pray you never find out how little."

He was tormented, and the realization made her incredibly sad. "I'll help you find your soul again, Mark."

He opened his eyes and stared at her. "Be careful that I don't take your soul instead," he warned. Then he took a deep breath and closed his eyes, soon falling asleep.

Lucinda watched him for a long time. He was a very complex man. Even though she knew little of life, she sensed that Mark needed her. She pressed her body against him, her hand resting on his. Lucinda had given herself to Mark, heart and soul.

Although it was still early morning when they drove into Phoenix, the heat was already oppressive. Mark parked the car, and he and Lucinda went into a dry-goods store, where she bought a change of clothing and a few other items she needed.

The plain green dress she chose was serviceable rather than pretty, but it was all she could afford, and she wouldn't take Mark's money.

When they left the store, they were approached by a haggard man in shabby overalls.

"Damn migrants think they can find the promised land out west, when all they really find is more misery," Mark muttered.

Lucinda glanced with pity at the man, who removed his battered hat and raised hopeful eyes to Mark.

"Mister, I've had me a bit of hard luck, and my family's hungry. I'll wash your car, work for you in any way you want, if you'll just give me fourteen cents for a loaf of bread to feed 'em."

"Out of my way," Mark said, shoving him aside. The man lost his balance and fell backward, landing in the dirt.

A grim-faced woman, apparently his wife, rushed to him.

Horrified, Lucinda bent to help the man, but his wife pushed her hand away. At that moment, Lucinda turned to look at the dilapidated truck that was parked next to Mark's car. It was piled high with mattresses and furniture, but her attention was focused on the sickly-looking children who peered back at her, their sunken faces and large eyes betraying their hunger.

"Mark, you have to help them," she pleaded, tugging at his sleeve. But he was unmoved by her plea and shook his head, his lips pressed together tightly in anger.

"Mark, look at the children," she urged. "They're so hungry."

The migrant shook his head and spoke proudly. "Thank you all the same, ma'am, but I don't reckon we need your help, after all."

Frantically, Lucinda looked about her, knowing she must do something. She still had two dollars of her own money, but she sensed that the man would not humble himself by taking it from her. Unmindful of Mark's displeasure, she walked determinedly back to the store. Once inside, she looked about frantically for anything that the children could eat.

Grabbing up a handful of chocolate bars, Lucinda paid for them and hurried to the truck. She handed each child a candy bar, and watched with sadness as five pairs of eager hands tore at the wrappers and the children crammed the candy into their mouths, ravenously devouring it.

They were so young, so helpless; it tore at Lucinda's heart to see their sunken eyes and swollen bellies. She quickly pressed what remained of her money into the hand of the oldest child and whispered hurriedly in his ear, "Give this to your mama once we are gone."

Wordlessly, the child closed his grimy fist on the money as if he feared she might take it back.

Lucinda knew that the children's haggard faces would be burned in her memory forever. She hurried away, fearing she would cry in front of them. What kind of a world was it when children were forced to endure such hardship?

Mark was leaning against the car, watching Lucinda's actions with a stony face. When she got into the car, he slid in beside her. "You made a spectacle of yourself, Lucinda. Don't ever embarrass me again."

Her green eyes blazed as if on fire, and Mark stared at her, mesmerized. He'd never seen her angry, and she'd never looked more beautiful than she did at that moment.

"I don't care if you were embarrassed, Mark. I'll never stand by and watch children starve—not if I can help it."

Mark surprised her when he reached into his pocket, withdrew several bills, and tossed them on the ground in the direction of the ragged man.

"I hope you're satisfied, Lucinda," he said as he started the engine. "But don't think you've done them any favors. If they don't die here, they'll die on the road. There isn't enough food in all of California to feed the stream of worthless trash that chokes the roads these days."

Lucinda watched the man stand erect and proud, but the woman, her face incredibly sad, scooped up the money that would feed her starving children. Lucinda didn't understand the callous way Mark had humiliated those people, but perhaps she shouldn't judge him too harshly. After all, he had given them the money they so desperately needed.

Chapter Five

Mark switched on the car radio, but picked up only static. He turned it off in annoyance, his grip tightening on the steering wheel. "I'll be damn glad to get back to Hollywood, where everything works."

Lucinda sat quietly, leaning her head against the back of the seat and pondering the fate of the migrants. She wished there were more she could have done for the children. With a sigh, she turned her head to stare out the window, hoping to get their forlorn little faces out of her mind.

Becoming bored, Mark looked sideways at her. "One of the features I like about this car is how easy it is to control," he said in a deep, meaningful voice.

She looked at his strong, tanned hands as they slid up and down the wheel almost caressingly.

Mark's voice was hypnotic as he continued: "This car is my most prized possession. See how easily she responds to me?"

His words made Lucinda shiver, and she ached to have him touch her with such gentleness.

Mark took one hand off the wheel and reached under the

hem of her skirt to lay it on her knee. She flinched, and he paused. "I want you to be another of my prized possessions, Lucinda, and I also want you to respond to me when I want you."

She had never had anyone to belong to, and his words struck a chord in her heart. "I feel like I am your possession already, Mark."

He began stroking her knee gently with light, circular motions. When she didn't protest, Mark allowed his hand to continue its journey up her thigh.

Delicious sensations rippled through Lucinda wherever he touched, but she was frightened as well.

Seeing her reluctance, he removed his hand and smiled. "You'll learn, baby. You'll see."

"Is what I did with you wrong, Mark?"

He laughed and tousled her hair. "Did it feel wrong?"

"No," she said without hesitation.

"Then there's your answer." He pulled her to him, pressing her head against his shoulder. "I should be bored with you—but I'm not. Don't ask me why."

Mark was shocked to realize that he'd just spoken the truth. Lucinda might not have the polish and sophistication of the women he was accustomed to, but there was something intriguing about her that he'd never found in another woman, although he could not have said what it was.

"Do you really want to put me in a movie?" Lucinda asked, still unimpressed by the prospect.

"Sure, baby, sure," he replied automatically.

"I don't think you'd better—I can't act." She snuggled next to him. "I just like being with you."

Mark was startled by her admission. Was it possible that Lucinda liked him for himself, and cared nothing about what he could do for her? In that case, she really was a rarity. He suddenly assessed her with a director's eye, speculating on her potential. Even though she was young, there was a radiance about her that would be enhanced by makeup and the right clothes.

If only he could capture her seductive innocence on the screen, he'd show Dolores he didn't need her. Mark hadn't allowed himself to dwell on how he'd resolve his predicament with Dolores once he returned to Hollywood. He didn't have the money to woo an already established name, so he'd have to create a new star. Lucinda would do just as well as anyone. She was available, unencumbered, and would work cheap because she wouldn't expect anything. She was infatuated with him, so he could use that devotion to control her.

"The one thing I know is how to build an image," he said, excitement creeping into his voice. "I'll make you into the hottest star Hollywood has ever known. Move over Harlow, because Lucinda Blackburn is coming to town."

"I can't be a star," she stated emphatically. "I'm too young, Mark, and I don't have talent."

"Just put yourself in my hands, baby, and I'll make Lucinda Blackburn a name the world will never forget." He was quiet for a long time; then he spoke slowly. "No . . . Lucinda Blackburn just won't do. Lucinda Black—no . . . that's not right either. Let me see . . . Lucy . . . Lacy?" Excitement brightened his eyes. "I've got it!"

"What, Mark?"

"Lacy Black!"

It was dusk when Mark maneuvered his car down Sunset Boulevard. Lucinda was so excited about being in Hollywood that she craned her neck, looking at all the billboards and flashing neon lights. Suddenly she sat back in her seat and looked at Mark.

"So this is Hollywood?"

He could see her disappointment. "Most people expect it to be washed in silvery light and spun of dreams, with a movie star standing on every corner. Well, this is the reality, baby. Look carefully; the people standing on every corner are bums, beggars, degenerates, and prostitutes."

There was a catch in Lucinda's throat. "In Ruth's movie magazines, everything looked so . . . glamorous."

"Don't worry, baby; when the spotlights come on for a premiere and the stars parade around in their furs and jewels, you'll see the Hollywood you imagined. I wonder if you'll like it?"

"I'm sure I will," she said, puzzled by his cynicism. "Will I see your studio tonight?"

Mark shook his head. "I'll give you the nickel tour in a week or so. Right now I'm going to take you to a hotel because I have something to do and I can't take you with me."

She nodded, frightened at the thought of being separated from him. She was quiet as he pulled onto a side street and stopped in front of a small, two-story building with *vacancy* flashing in red neon lights.

"Wait here while I get a key," Mark said, sliding out of the car and slamming the door.

It was a balmy night, and the tall palm trees seemed to dance in a gentle breeze. Lucinda breathed in air that was perfumed by exotic flowers, not noticing that the hotel was in need of paint and the streets were littered with trash. It was certainly finer than anything in Snyder, but so strange to her, all the same.

When Mark beckoned her, Lucinda grasped the paper bag that contained her belongings and got out of the car, trying not to panic. Mark wouldn't leave her here for long—he would come back for her soon; he just had to.

Mark pressed his foot on the accelerator and the Cord sped along the winding road up Mulholland Drive. Pulling through the open gate of his estate, he turned off the ignition and stared at the sprawling, Spanish-style house, wondering if he'd find Dolores inside.

He slammed the car door and hurried up the brick walk. Inserting his key into the lock, he opened the door and switched on the light.

He was filled with rage as his footsteps echoed in the empty room. Dolores had been here, all right, and she'd taken everything—even the rugs, damn her greedy little heart.

He searched each room, finding the same emptiness, until he came to his bedroom. There, taped to the mirror, was an envelope. He ripped it open, his hands shaking with rage. It was, of course, from Dolores.

Mark,
By the time you read this, we'll no longer be married. I got a divorce in Mexico and am free of you and Pinnacle Pictures. As you see, I took the furniture as payment for the shortest, most miserable marriage on record. I left the bed, knowing you could hardly do your casting without it. And, of course, I leave you the house, since its mortgage is tied in with the studio. I wish you all the misery you caused me and even more.
The former (thank God)
Mrs. Mark Damian

Mark crumpled the note in his fist. One day she'd pay! He'd see to that. Dolores had been a fool to cross him.

He moved to the living room and pushed a button. A bar swung out of the wall. Grabbing a bottle of scotch, he walked outside to the pool and sat down in a lounge chair. Unbuttoning his shirt, he raised the bottle to his lips, hoping to drink himself into forgetfulness.

He gave little thought to the forlorn young girl he'd left alone in a strange city, without a friend in the world. His heart was filled with hatred as he planned his revenge on Dolores.

Lucinda emptied her pocket and counted what remained of the five dollars that Mark had left her: one dollar and forty-five cents wouldn't last long. She walked to the window and stared at the ocean, which was visible from her small room. She had spent many hours in solitary walks on the beach, collecting seashells and thinking about Mark.

He'd promised he would return, but she hadn't heard from

him in over a week. If he didn't come tomorrow, she'd have to find a job and a cheaper place to live.

Lucinda glanced up at the stars that twinkled in the ebony sky, feeling unbearably lonely. Even if Mark never returned, she wouldn't go back to Snyder. She had severed all ties with the past; her life was here now.

She curled up on the rickety iron bed and, with a melancholy song playing on the radio, finally fell asleep.

The room was in darkness when Lucinda awoke, feeling someone's weight pressing against her. She would have screamed, but a hand was clamped over her mouth.

"Don't be frightened. It's me," Mark muttered, pressing his mouth over hers.

Joyfully, Lucinda wound her arms around his neck, and she wondered if it was liquor she tasted on his lips.

She made no protest when Mark pushed her skirt up and immediately thrust deep inside her. She sensed the turbulence in him and gave herself to him completely.

Mark made love to her with an urgency bordering on desperation. Only Lucinda could cast out his demons. After his body trembled with a shuddering release, he rolled over and lay back on the bed.

Lucinda reached for his hand in the darkness. "I was afraid you'd forgotten me, Mark."

"Not hardly, baby. The thought of your sweet body kept haunting me, and I had to have you again."

"I . . . was afraid."

He pushed her tousled hair out of her face. "Didn't I tell you I'd be back?" he asked with a little more gentleness.

She pressed her lips against his neck. "Yes, Mark."

Slowly he removed her clothing and ran his hand down her naked body. "There's something special about you, Lucinda. I can't get you out of my mind. All I want to do is make love to you."

She closed her eyes, happy that she pleased him.

"Tomorrow, baby," Mark whispered, "your new life begins. I'm taking you to the studio, and I'm going to make you a star!"

The security guard swung wide the wrought-iron gate at the entrance of Pinnacle Pictures. "Welcome back, Mr. Damian," he said with a friendly salute.

Mark motioned for the ruddy-faced guard to approach. "Any problems while I was gone, Joe?"

"No, sir, Mr. Damian. I followed your instructions and didn't allow Miss Divine on the lot. She was sure sore. I'm glad you're back so you can deal with her."

Mark's jaw muscle twitched. "You did good, Joe. Miss Divine is still to be kept off the lot—is that understood?"

"Yes, sir," the man said with confidence. "She won't get past me, Mr. Damian."

Driving on, Mark refused to let his problems with Dolores ruin the day. He was in high spirits because he knew that his fortunes were about to change, and all because of the unsuspecting girl who sat beside him.

Lucinda had paid no attention to the exchange between Mark and the guard. Her attention was focused on the movie lot, which seemed like a fantasyland, with people strolling about in costumes from different eras. She laughed when she saw a man resembling Abe Lincoln offering a hot dog to a portly Henry VIII.

They drove past a set that looked like an authentic western town and another that depicted an English village complete with castle and moat.

Mark explained that Pinnacle Pictures had been built on seven acres of what had once been an orange grove.

"It's wonderful!" Lucinda exclaimed as she watched two knights jousting on horseback while cameras followed them and a man in a director's chair shouted instructions.

"They look real, don't they?" Mark said proudly. "But most of the sets are fake fronts and can be changed to look like Anytown, U.S.A."

He stopped the car before the executive office building, smiling as he opened the car door for Lucinda. "You haven't seen anything yet, baby."

Mark ushered her to his office. The walls and carpet were red, and the furniture and accents black. Lucinda thought the room was without harmony, almost garish—but then, what did she know?

While Mark sorted through the stack of mail on his desk, Lucinda sat quietly studying the massive red-and-black paintings that hung on the walls. She didn't know much about art, but she could see no substance in the intertwining circles and cubes that filled the canvases.

After a while, Mark put his work aside and led Lucinda to a small studio, where he introduced her to George Levine, the photographer who would be doing her publicity stills.

A hairdresser was sent for, and after throwing his hands up in horror, he deftly smoothed Lucinda's natural curls until they formed loose waves. A woman from wardrobe appeared with an armload of clothing, and Mark selected a green dress with a wide white collar. Lucinda was hustled behind a screen, where she was helped into the skintight dress.

Then she was seated under the hot lights, taking direction from George Levine.

"Let me see you pout, Miss Black. Yes, that's good. Now look upward as if you were thinking of something very pleasant."

Lucinda thought of Mark, and her face took on a delicate glow. The photographer hissed through his teeth. "Wonderful, wonderful, hold that look." Levine studied her critically. "Something's not right. That white collar makes you look like a nun." He reached for a black fringed shawl that was draped over a chair. "Here. Let's try this."

After he placed the shawl about Lucinda's shoulders, he shot her from several different angles in various poses, nodding in approval each time the flashbulb exploded.

* * *

Lucinda had been posing for what seemed like hours. Her neck was stiff and she was hungry. "Will this go on much longer?" she asked Mark, who was seated nearby, silently observing.

"Just a few more shots, Lucinda. If you're going to be in the movies, you'll put up with a lot worse than this, believe me."

She was relieved when the photographer indicated that he had everything he needed.

"I'll develop these, Mr. Damian, and get them back to you this afternoon. I believe I saw something in the lens that's going to please you."

Mark came up behind Lucinda, his strong fingers massaging her aching shoulders. "You did good, baby—you're a real trouper."

She beamed up at him, basking in his praise. "What do we do now, Mark?"

"Now we eat."

He took her arm and led her down the hallway to his office, where he seated her on the couch before he moved to his desk and pressed the intercom, buzzing his secretary. "Helen, have lunch for two sent in. I'll have a steak, rare, a baked potato, and a salad. Miss Black will have a hamburger, well done, chips and a milk shake. And see if you can find a slice of chocolate cake."

Lucinda protested. "I could never eat all that, Mark."

He seemed to change right before her eyes. His smile disappeared, and his eyes sparked dangerously. She flinched when he reached out and gripped her face in his hand.

"You'll eat what I say and do what I say. You're too skinny, and I need to put weight on you, or you won't be any good to me at all."

"Yes, but—"

"There are no buts, Lucinda. Either you do as I say, or I'll get someone who will."

She lowered her head and whispered the question that had been nagging at her. "Will Miss Divine come back, Mark?"

His eyes hardened even more. "Dolores will never come back.

I don't even want her name to pass your lips—do I make myself clear?"

Lucinda had not seen this side of Mark since the incident with the migrants in Phoenix. When he was like this, she hardly recognized him. At last, she nodded. "Yes, Mark, I understand—I think."

"And you'll do whatever I say without question?"

"Yes, Mark. I'll do whatever you say."

He pushed her back against the leather cushions of the couch, his hands fumbling with the buttons of her dress.

She was horrified. "Mark, surely you aren't—"

His mouth smothered her protest. "All the while Levine was posing you, I could only think of what I wanted to do to you," he whispered thickly. "I could see he was hot for you too, but he can't have you—I don't share with anyone, baby."

Lucinda's eyes went to the door, as if she feared someone would appear.

Mark laughed when he saw her concern, his hand roughly massaging her breasts. "No one would dare come through that door, baby. They know what we're doing."

His hot mouth was draining her of any protest. He had the power to make her surrender as his hands moved across her hips and positioned her beneath him. Tears lingered just behind Lucinda's eyelids, and she willed them not to fall. He was humiliating her, but she wouldn't let him see her cry.

There was no gentleness in Mark's lovemaking, but Lucinda bore it in silence. She had the feeling he was trying to teach her a lesson, although she didn't know what the lesson was.

After he had taken his pleasure, Mark showed her to his private washroom, his mood lighter, as if nothing had happened. "Make yourself presentable, Lucinda. We have work to do."

George Levine thumbtacked Lucinda's pictures to a bulletin board and illuminated them with a spotlight. "Look at this, boss," he said excitedly. "Do you see what I see? Notice how she was transformed when I draped her in black."

"Damn!" Mark exclaimed as he looked at a pose where Lucinda was staring right into the camera. Her eyes were wide and innocent, while the natural pout to her lips gave her the look of a seductress. "She's got that something that comes along only once in a lifetime, George."

The photographer nodded in agreement. "In all my years of photographing women, I've never seen one to rival her, and I've done them all. The camera picks up her inner self and gives her an aura. She'll be big, boss—real big. With her looks, it won't even matter if she can't act."

"I knew she'd be good!" Mark said with pride, as if he had invented Lucinda himself. "And to think I almost left her in Texas."

Mark rushed to the intercom and buzzed Helen. "Have the makeup department ready in twenty minutes and have wardrobe standing by. I want the heads of production and publicity to meet me here at four this afternoon, and tell them to be prepared to stay late. And locate Miss Black and tell her I want to see her at once."

George Levine still stared at the glossies. "You'd better tie her up with a contract, boss. If L. B. Mayer gets wind of her, he'll steal her from you."

"Let him try," Mark replied smugly. "She's loyal to me, and I intend to keep her that way."

There was a soft knock on the door, and Mark rushed forward to admit Lucinda. He smiled at her and raised her hand to his lips. "Come in; I want you to meet someone very important."

She looked around, puzzled. There was no one in the room but Mark and Mr. Levine, both of whom she already knew.

Mark slid his arm around her shoulders and led her forward until she stood before her own photographs.

"I'd like to introduce you to Lacy Black, the new queen of Pinnacle Pictures!"

Her eyes widened as she stared at the stranger that was herself. She was beautiful, she thought in shock. The artfully applied makeup made her appear older than her age and definitely more worldly.

"Is that really me?" she asked, her eyes seeking Mark's.

"No one else, baby. You are going to have a life that most women only dream of."

"I don't know if—"

He placed a finger over her lips, silencing her. "Let me decide what's best for you. Now, about your new background—you're to forget your family, and we'll give you a new one—understood?"

She nodded.

"You have that Texas accent, so we'll have to keep you in the South. I think we can pass you off as a native Virginian. Yes, the daughter of a poor but proud doctor, now deceased."

"That orphan shit works well, boss," George Levine said. "You'd think the public would get wise to it, but they don't. Lacy Black is all alone in this wide, cruel world."

Mark grinned down at her. "We'll wring the public's heart right out of them. Every woman in America will want to look like you, and every man will wish you belonged to him."

Lucinda looked dazed. "Lacy Black," she said, testing her new identity. Her eyes went to Mark. "I feel like a part of me just died."

Chapter Six

"No, that's not what I want," Mark said impatiently, taking the scissors out of the hairdresser's hand and turning Lacy's head toward him. "Angle it a little more, and take some off the length. And you don't have the color right. I want it lighter—it has to be platinum."

"But Mark," Lacy protested. "I like my own color. I don't want to look like Jean Harlow."

"I've learned never to tamper with success," Mark responded, brushing her objections aside. "It worked well for her; it'll work even better for us." He handed the scissors back to the hairdresser. "Lighten her hair and shave her eyebrows. I want them penciled in a lighter shade. And add a beauty mark—there, at the side of her mouth. I'll be back to pick her up later this afternoon."

Lacy, as Lucinda was now known, spent a miserable day being fussed over by one studio department after another. She was so exhausted by the end of the day that she groaned when she was sent to wardrobe.

Meg Chandler, the wardrobe mistress, was a full-figured

woman in her forties, her hair prematurely white. Although it was her job to design glamorous costumes for others, her own wardrobe was plain and tailored.

Mark watched while Meg looked Lacy up and down.

Dressed in only a black slip, Lacy felt like a piece of meat being inspected.

"She's got long, shapely legs, Mr. Damian, and she'll need no padding. I'd say she's built as perfectly as a woman can be—I see no flaws except youth, and she'll outgrow that."

Lacy felt uncomfortable being talked about as if she weren't there. When she would have spoken up, Mark made an observation.

"I like the effect of the black against her white skin." He walked around her, taking in every detail. His eyes lit up with sudden inspiration. "Chandler, I want you to make her a complete wardrobe and spare no expense. My only stipulation is that everything be black. Lacy Black wears only black."

Meg Chandler smiled radiantly. "I think you have something there, Mr. Damian. Dressing her in black should add to the mystique you're trying to create and set her apart from other actresses."

Mark drew Lacy into his arms. "Damn right it'll set her apart from the others. Call a furrier and have coats made up for her in mink and fox, all in black. Hats, shoes, lingerie, all in black—you get the idea."

Lacy felt her life spinning out of control, and she couldn't stop it. Lacy Black was Mark's creation and had no real substance. She was a fraud from the tip of her lightened hair to the past that had been invented for the benefit of fans.

"Come, my little starlet," Mark said, draping his coat about her shoulders. "We'll be in my office, Meg. After you've finished something, bring it there at once."

The dressmaker nodded, feeling pity for the young girl, who was bound to be consumed by Mark Damian. She'd seen him do this to other women, but never with the same intensity, and never with one so young. Meg gave a resigned sigh and moved to the workroom, where several women were bent over sewing machines. She had been around this business long enough to recognize that special something in Lacy Black that made a star. Whether stardom would bring her happiness was another matter.

Mark borrowed heavily to pay for Lacy's wardrobe and to rent her an apartment in a respectable Bel Air neighborhood. He explained to Lacy that no scandal must touch her, or her career would be over before it started. He insisted that they keep up appearances, so each evening he entered her apartment through the back door and slipped out before dawn.

Lacy worked long hours at the studio every day. She was taught how to walk and how to sit. She was grilled on her new persona and every detail of her newly acquired background until she knew it better than her real identity.

Mark allowed bits and pieces of information about a new and exciting star at Pinnacle Pictures to leak to the press, but he refused to give the gossip columnists a personal interview, hoping to sharpen their curiosity.

At last the night arrived when Mark was ready to present Lacy to the public. He'd chosen the premiere of Dolores's last film with Pinnacle Pictures because every major newspaper and movie magazine would be represented.

Lacy's makeup had been carefully applied, and she now had a distinctive beauty mark just to the left of her mouth. She wore a long black satin gown that clung to every curve of her body and flared out just below her knees. Her penciled eyebrows were thinly arched, and her lipstick matched the red polish on her manicured nails.

She nervously turned away from the mirror, wondering if she would fool anyone into thinking she was an actress.

Mark smiled as he carelessly draped a full-length black mink about her shoulders. "Are you ready to meet your public, Miss Black?"

She turned troubled eyes to him. "I'm frightened."

"Don't be. I'll be beside you the whole time. Everyone will be stunned by my creation," he bragged. "Just remember everything I've told you."

He offered her his arm and escorted her outside, where he helped her into a sleek, chauffeur-driven limousine. As they approached the motorcade of cars that was lined up before Grauman's Chinese Theater, Lacy kept going over in her mind how she must act and what she must say.

Suddenly their limousine came to a stop, and spotlights hit with such a blinding force that Lacy had to shield her eyes. She had no time to think because the car door was whisked open and she was met by the sound of a cheering crowd. Lacy glanced at a sea of faces that were no more than a blur, and her heart began thundering so loud that she feared everyone could hear it.

Mark led her down the long red carpet to where a man stood at a microphone. Lacy was dismayed to see that Dolores Divine was just ahead of them.

Dolores stared at Lacy in startled recognition, but when she looked at Mark, it was with pure poison. Aware that the cameras were focused on her, she turned toward them and flashed a brilliant smile.

"And now, ladies and gentlemen," the announcer boomed, "the head of Pinnacle Pictures, Mark Damian. Mr. Damian, tell us something about the picture we'll be seeing tonight."

Mark's cold glance raked Dolores for the briefest moment before he answered. "*Lift the Banner* speaks for itself. It's Dolores Divine in her usual form."

The crowd, unaware of the tension between Mark and Dolores, pressed against the restraining ropes for a better glimpse of the celebrities.

"Mr. Damian," the radio announcer said, smiling at Lacy, "maybe you could tell us about this beauty with you."

Mark preened as flashbulbs erupted. He was aware that Dolores had turned away and walked into the theater. This was his moment of triumph, because the crowd had turned its attention to Lacy. In a town where boredom was rampant, her newness made her intriguing, and it hadn't hurt that he'd sent out press releases announcing that his new star would be accompanying him to the premiere.

"While I was touring our great country," Mark began, "I discovered this talented young woman, Lacy Black, who is destined to have all Hollywood at her feet."

Lacy smiled tentatively while flashbulbs exploded all around her.

"Am I right in assuming that we will soon see Miss Black on the screen?" the announcer asked, his eyes assessing Lacy with appreciation.

"Indeed you shall. She is the newest and brightest star in Pinnacle Pictures' heaven," Mark said ceremoniously.

Lacy struggled to keep her smile in place while her trembling hand tightened on Mark's arm. A few weeks ago she had been one of the masses sitting by the radio, eagerly listening to every word from Hollywood. Now she was in the spotlight and she felt like an intruder, a fraud.

Mark waved to the crowd and steered Lacy away from the microphone, cutting the interview short. He smiled down at her and whispered so only she could hear, "Never give too much—always leave them asking for more. Tomorrow everyone will want to know about you."

Lacy's heart didn't stop pounding until they were in the darkened theater, away from curious, probing eyes.

Soon the movie lit up the screen and Dolores's face illuminated the darkness. Dolores had been cast as a French patriot who, at the cost of her own life, saved her village from the Germans during the Great War. Even to Lacy's untrained ear, the dialogue was stilted, and Dolores delivered her lines as if she were reading from a script. Toward the finish, it was apparent that the audience was becoming restless, and not one tear was shed when Dolores met her tragic end.

"A damned fiasco," Mark muttered, his grip tightening painfully on Lacy's hand. His sentiment was soon substantiated by the comments that were overheard when they left the theater.

On the ride home, Mark seemed to retreat into silence. And when he did speak, his tone was harsh. "More than Dolores's character died tonight; her career is dead."

"I feel sorry for her," Lacy said softly.

"Well, don't. Next month I'll release that western we filmed in Texas and it'll be a flop too." He ground his teeth. "She's finished in this town." His voice deepened with satisfaction. "She'll never get another decent part."

Lacy was puzzled by his mood. He seemed more pleased that Dolores had failed than upset that he'd lost money on the film.

"Have you no pity for her, Mark? She must have been humiliated tonight."

He glanced down at Lacy as if thinking how to answer her. At last he gave her a humorless smile. "She doesn't deserve your pity, and she wouldn't waste any on you if the situation were reversed."

Lacy didn't like Dolores, but she didn't wish her ill, and it bothered her that Mark was so unfeeling toward a woman he'd once loved. They passed beneath a streetlight and she shivered at the dark hatred she saw etched on Mark's handsome face. She was learning that he could be ruthless to anyone who crossed him.

When the car stopped at Lacy's apartment and the driver opened the door, Mark merely nodded at her.

"Aren't you coming in?" she asked, when he made no move to get out of the limousine.

He shook his head and looked right past her. "Not tonight, baby."

She watched the car pull away, not understanding his moodiness. One moment he would be laughing and happy; then, without warning, he'd turn brooding and silent.

The smoke-filled room was in shadow except for the green felt table that was awash with light from the naked lightbulb swinging above it. Mark sat at the table with five other men, clutching what he hoped was the winning hand—a pair of jacks and a pair of deuces.

Four of the players had folded, and Mark's eyes were riveted on Joe Hollister, a tall, lanky man who owned several movie theaters on the West Coast. Joe covered Mark's bet and raised it by a hundred dollars. Mark raised another hundred.

Joe Hollister stared at the beads of sweat that had formed on Mark's upper lip. He laughed aloud. "I call."

Mark turned his hand over. "Two pair!" he said triumphantly.

Hollister chomped his teeth on his Cuban cigar and grinned. "Read 'em and weep. Three ladies."

Mark shoved the table, and money and cards went flying. "You cleaned me out," he said peevishly.

Hollister nodded for his companions to pick up the money, while he turned to Mark. "You've got a real problem, Damian. You like to play cards, but you don't like to lose."

Mark glared at him. "I always lose when I play with you. I wonder why?"

Hollister rose to an imposing six feet. "I hope you aren't implying that I cheat. I wouldn't like that."

Mark stepped back two quick paces and met Hollister's hostile glance. "Maybe not cheat, but you're sure as hell lucky."

Hollister took a step closer to Mark. "We all took a vote before you came tonight, and it was unanimous—we don't want you in our game anymore, Damian. You're a sore loser, and we just don't like snivelers."

Mark bit back his anger. "There are other poker games; this isn't the only one in town."

"Want some advice?" Hollister asked, sitting down at the table and masterfully opening a new deck and shuffling the cards.

"I pay minions for advice; I don't need any from you," Mark said sourly, moving to the door.

"Well, I'm going to give you some anyway," Hollister replied, blowing a smoke ring and watching it disappear before he spoke again. "You bet rashly, Damian. I've seen men like you, where gambling's a sickness. If you don't stop, you'll end up with nothing."

"Go to hell," Mark muttered, walking out the door and slamming it behind him.

The sun was just coming up as Mark made his way to his car. He didn't have a problem with gambling. He could stop anytime he wanted to.

Lacy had not seen Mark in over a week—not since the premiere of Dolores's picture. She was just bursting with happiness and couldn't wait to share her good news with him. She pressed her forehead against the windowpane and stared at the street, as if wishing for Mark would make him appear. He would be thrilled when she told him that she was going to have his baby; she was sure of it. He'd probably insist that she give up her acting career. Lacy placed her hand against her stomach, in awe of the new life that nestled there. Now she could be Mark's wife and make a home for him. She would have a family of her own, just as she'd always dreamed.

Another two days passed and still she had heard nothing from Mark. When he finally did come, his arrival caught her unaware.

Lacy was in the kitchen, washing dishes, when Mark appeared behind her. She was startled when his arms went around her waist and he turned her toward him.

"I need you tonight, baby. I feel like hell."

She wanted to ask him where he'd been, but she had already discovered that Mark did not like to be questioned. All that mattered was that he was with her now. Later, when the moment was right, she'd tell him about the baby.

It was after dinner when Lacy entered the bedroom, her filmy black negligée trailing behind her as she walked. Mark was standing by the open French windows, popping the cork on a bottle of champagne. He looked so handsome in his burgundy robe that she longed to run into his arms and pour out her love for him, but that would come later.

Mark handed Lacy a glass and raised his in a toast. "Tomorrow's the big day, baby. We start casting *Mata Hari*."

"Oh, Mark," Lacy said under her breath, setting her champagne glass aside untasted, "I never thought I could be this happy."

"Just wait, baby; it's only the beginning." His eyes roamed over the exquisite body that was enticingly revealed rather than concealed by the sheerness of her negligée. "I've missed you," he told her softly.

Lacy went into his arms, snuggling her head against his chest. "You haven't asked me why I'm happy, Mark."

"I know why. It's always this way at the beginning of a new picture." He lifted her chin. "And this will be your first. No matter how many pictures you make, none of them will ever compare with the first time you step before a camera."

"That's not it, Mark." She felt shy and lowered her lashes. "There's a small clinic a few blocks from here, and I went there on Monday."

He studied her face with concern. "Were you sick?"

"No, not sick exactly."

"You look thin. Have you been eating enough?"

She smiled. "Yes. In fact I eat too much."

He tensed. "Then what's wrong?"

She could hardly contain her joy. "Nothing's wrong—we're going to have a baby!"

The smile froze on his face. "What did you say?"

"A baby, Mark. Our very own baby."

He paled, and his lips compressed. "Oh, no, you're not, Lacy. I'm not going to have some brat spoil all the plans I've made."

She was devastated by his reaction. Her mouth trembled as she tried not to give in to tears. "I thought you'd be as happy as I am." Her eyes followed him as he paced back and forth across the room.

"You said you went to a clinic. Well, doctors can make mistakes, Lacy. I'm sure that's what happened."

"There's no mistake," she said in bewilderment. "I haven't been feeling well—"

"You never said anything to me."

"I didn't want to worry you. I'm three months pregnant."

His face reddened with rage. "Why didn't you do something to prevent this? It's all your fault."

Her eyes held a wounded expression. "I thought when two people love each other the way we do . . ." Her voice choked. "I wouldn't have known how to prevent it; no one ever told me."

He was so angry, he longed for the relief it would give him to feel his hands around Lacy's creamy throat, squeezing the life from her. Not even Dolores in her hatred had ruined his ambitions as Lacy was threatening to do out of love.

"How could you do this to me?" he asked, his face distorted with the rage he was feeling.

Lacy backed away from him, her eyes wide with alarm. This was a Mark she'd never seen, and he frightened her. "I . . . never . . ."

He loomed over her, his face twisted with fury. "I could kill you for this." He struck her a stunning blow, and she stumbled backward, falling against the wall and sliding to the floor.

Without a backward glance, Mark stalked out of the room, shouting profanities. She heard the door slam and knew he'd gone. How could she have misjudged his reaction to the baby? she wondered, trying to rise, but falling back to her knees.

After several attempts, Lacy managed to stand up and inch along the wall until she reached her bedroom. She climbed into bed and cried herself to sleep. Throughout the night she awoke repeatedly, listening for Mark, hoping he would return when he'd had time to think.

Late the next afternoon, Lacy heard a key in the lock. With a feeling of dread, she watched Mark enter. For a long moment they stared at each other, until at last he held his arms out to her.

"Can you forgive a fool?" he asked, giving her that boyish smile that always melted her heart.

She raced to him, and he gathered her in his arms.

"Oh, Mark, I love you so. I've been so miserable without you."

His manner was solicitous as he led her to the couch and seated her there. "I've ordered dinner to be brought in—would you like that?"

She glowed under his tender care. "Yes, very much."

"While we wait for our food," he said, moving to the bar and placing two bottles of wine on the smooth surface, "let's celebrate." Mark poured a glass of wine and handed it to her. "Forgive my behavior last night. I was caught unaware, that's all. If you're happy about the baby, then so am I. We'll get married right away; how would you like that?"

"Oh, Mark," Lacy cried, smothering his face with kisses. "You're the most wonderful man in the world!"

He laughed and pulled her onto his lap. "I'm glad you think so, baby."

Lacy ate very little at dinner, but Mark kept filling her wineglass and urging her to drink. She didn't like the wine—it was bitter-tasting—but to please him, she drank it anyway. After a while she began to feel dizzy and stood up unsteadily.

"Forgive me, Mark . . . too much wine, I'm afraid."

He was kind and considerate as he helped her to bed, plumping her pillow and pulling the blanket over her. "Just rest, Lacy. Everything will be all right when you wake up."

Her eyes were heavy, and she soon gave in to the darkness that consumed her.

The night passed in a haze of nightmarish agony for Lacy. She had visions of a strange man bending over her and inflicting terrible pain. The man would often pause in his work to take a drink from a whiskey bottle. She moaned in her sleep, feeling as if her insides were being ripped out. There was blood—oh, so much blood—on his hands, on the bed, everywhere. She tried to push him away, and eventually he did disappear, but the nightmare continued and she could not fight her way out of it.

Chapter Seven

When Lacy awoke the next morning, her head ached and her mouth felt dry, as though she'd swallowed cotton. She tried to sit up, and pain ripped through her body.

"Careful now," Mark said, as he knelt down beside her and gripped her hand in his.

"What happened?" she asked in confusion.

He looked worried. "I'm so sorry, Lacy, but you lost the baby." There were tears in his eyes. "I know how much it meant to you. I wanted it too."

Deep, wrenching sobs shook her body, and she laid her hand against her stomach. "I thought I was having a nightmare. I remember a man here. It seemed he was trying to tear the baby from my body."

"There was a doctor here because I called him when you started hemorrhaging—don't you remember? He couldn't tell me what had caused your miscarriage, but he suggested you wait at least a year before trying to become pregnant again."

"My poor baby." Lacy moaned, her eyes blinded with tears of loss and grief.

"I know how you feel. It was my baby, too. The doctor said you should stay in bed for a few days, and I'll stay with you and be your nurse. We don't want anyone asking too many questions, now, do we?"

"Mark," she said, looking deeply into his eyes, "was the doctor . . . did he drink?"

"Of course not, Lacy," he said indignantly. "The doctor's a specialist, and good at what he does."

She believed him, even though her dream had seemed so real. However, after she had recovered and was cleaning her bedroom, an empty whiskey bottle rolled out from under her bed. She decided not to confront Mark with the evidence because she was afraid of the truth.

Being young and strong, Lacy healed quickly, at least physically, if not emotionally. She knew deep within her heart that she would never completely recover from losing her baby.

Mark said they'd still get married, but not until her first film was completed. Lacy looked forward to being Mark's wife, and he seemed as impatient for their wedding as she was.

The night before the shooting of *Mata Hari* began, Lacy was too nervous to sleep. She was up by five the next morning and drove herself to the studio in the new Ford convertible Mark had given her.

Lacy read over her lines one last time while she was in the makeup chair. She was surprised at how easily she had memorized her part, and she hoped that Mark would be proud of her accomplishment.

The director, Sidney Greenway, had been brought to Pinnacle Pictures by Mark's former partner, and was still contractually obligated to direct one more picture.

When Sidney first saw Lacy, he looked at Mark with disgust. "Another of your tarts you promised to propel to stardom?"

Mark knew Sidney hated him, and it didn't bother him overmuch; he didn't like Sidney either. But he was one of the best directors in Hollywood, and Mark wanted him to direct Lacy's first picture.

"Work with Lacy today, Sidney," Mark said in a cajoling voice, "and if you don't agree that she has talent, I'll pay you off and you can leave Pinnacle Pictures with no hard feelings."

Sidney's eyes hardened and he said in a snarl, "It won't take me a day to break this one and send her crying out the studio gates."

The crew gathered, watching silently as the new star came forward shyly. Lacy was unaware of the sneers and smirks behind her back, or the remarks that she would turn out to be no more than another beautiful body who couldn't act.

Mark himself was plagued with doubts, so he planned to use the camera to capture Lacy's sensuality and not rely on her acting ability. It had worked with Dolores, at least for a while, so why not with Lacy?

A disgruntled Sidney motioned for the cameras to roll. "Let's go, Miss Black," he said as if he were speaking to someone witless. He waved his hands like a maestro conducting an orchestra and called loudly, "Action!"

For a terrified moment, Lacy stared at the director, who was tall, with black hair and a pencil-thin mustache that gave him the sinister appearance of a villain right out of the movies. From his expression, she could tell he didn't like her, and she wondered why.

"I said, 'Action,' Miss Black," Sidney said in a booming voice. "That means you can start acting now!"

Lacy swallowed her fear and moved forward. She thought of Mark and all he'd done for her—she couldn't let him down. Glancing up at the illuminating lights, she was instantly transformed.

Sidney was startled by the sudden metamorphosis—Lacy Black actually became the beautiful courtesan who had spied for the Germans in the Great War. The wind machine was blowing her hair and molding the filmy black costume to her body. She moved gracefully through the exotic dance that had been choreographed for her. Her hips swung sensuously and her dainty hands wove artfully above her head.

The cast and crew were stunned. Something extraordinary was happening before their very eyes, and everyone was caught up in the magic.

Sidney sat forward, his eyes wide with interest. The girl had something he hadn't seen in all his years of directing. It was the kind of magnetism that only the camera could define. The other actors and actresses on the set seemed to pivot around Lacy as she played off them, giving them substance and making everyone believe she really was Mata Hari.

Weeks passed, and the picture reached its final scene, in which the luckless Mata Hari was caught by the French and executed for spying. Several of the crew members actually cried as Lacy spoke her lines. When the shots from the firing squad rang out, tearing into Mata Hari's body, Lacy crumpled to the ground. The cameras didn't cease rolling until she drew her last labored breath and her beautiful face was stilled by death.

For a long moment no one spoke, and then suddenly applause broke out among the cast and crew as they paid tribute to Lacy's performance. Lacy had no way of knowing that it was something that rarely happened on the set of a movie. She blinked her eyes as she was yanked back to reality. It took her a moment to shake off the heaviness in her heart, for she had taken the pain of the tragic Dutch spy as her own.

She was still lying on the ground when Mark ran forward and pulled her to her feet.

"You were magnificent, baby—magnificent!" His eyes went to the director. "Don't you agree, Sidney?"

Sidney merely clamped his teeth on his cigar. "Wait until we see today's rushes," he said sourly, reluctant to agree with Mark on anything.

With astonishment, Lacy accepted the congratulations of her fellow actors. She had not wanted to be an actress, but now it was as if she was compelled to act—to become the character she was playing. She was so involved in the role, she'd almost felt the bullets riddle her body in the final scene.

Later, as Mark and Sidney viewed the day's rushes, they

watched Lacy explode on the screen, overshadowing the other characters.

Neither spoke until the last frame ended; then Mark looked at Sidney, whose expression was unreadable. "When Lacy's in a scene, I don't see anyone else—what about you?" he asked. "Her performance is extraordinary for someone who has never been in a film before."

Sidney stubbed out his cigar and thought before he answered. "I think Hollywood," he said at last, choosing his words carefully, "has never seen her like before, and probably never will again. She's got talent in every move of her body—every fiber of her being. Even when she's silent, you can read what she's thinking because the camera captures her inner self." His eyes shifted to Mark. "She'll make it big even if you've cheapened her by bleaching her hair and dressing her like a tramp. If you don't have her under contract, you'd better sign her before this picture hits the screen."

Mark raised a glass of brandy to his lips and took a sip, the color of his face heightened by amazement; he couldn't remember a time when Sidney had praised any actress, and certainly not in such glowing terms. "I'm not worried. She won't leave me."

Sidney merely stared at Lacy's face as he replayed a closeup, her expression soft and tears in her eyes. "Then she's a fool."

Mark chose to ignore Sidney's barbed remark because he needed the director. "With my help, she'll become another Harlow."

"You're such a shortsighted bastard, Damian. The world doesn't need another Harlow. I'd advise you to take Lacy's hair back to the original color, whatever the hell it was, and give her parts worthy of her talent."

Mark glared at Sidney. "Mr. Hotshot Director, I know all about developing a star, so you just stick to directing and leave the rest to me. I'll cast her as the dumb blonde with a big heart who always snares the rich playboy in the end. I want the public lusting after her and begging for more, so I'll make Lacy's costumes as skimpy as we can get by with."

"Since Mr. Hays is the watchdog of movie morality, it wouldn't be in your best interests to draw his attention," Sidney warned, with a sick feeling in his stomach. Mark would use this girl in every cheap way possible, overlooking her real qualities.

"Ah, but think of the publicity," Mark said audaciously.

"You are nothing but a little man with big ideas, Damian."

Mark seemed unaffected by Sidney's assessment of his character. "You think so? Well, let's talk business. Now that this picture's finished, you're at the end of your contract, Sidney. But I tell you what I'm willing to do. I'll give you a new contract—what do you say?"

Sidney didn't hesitate. "I'll stay, Damian, on the condition that no one directs Miss Black but me."

Mark stuck out his hand, satisfaction etching his boyish features. "So much for my little ideas." He shrugged. "We have a bargain!"

Sidney ignored Mark's hand. "A handshake won't do, Mark. Put it in writing; otherwise, I walk."

Mark beat down his anger. He'd like nothing better than to throw this pompous ass out, but Sidney was the best. "If you want a contract, you'll get one," he said in a snarl, stalking out of the viewing room.

Sidney reached over and killed the projector, and Lacy's image disappeared from the screen. All he wanted from Miss Black was a good performance; in that respect, he was little different from Mark Damian.

Mark, wanting to test an audience's reaction to *Mata Hari*, decided to run a sneak preview at a local theater. He and Lacy attended without fanfare, entering the theater after the movie had started.

Lacy felt sick inside as she watched herself on the screen. She had no talent, and she hated the sight of her face and the sound of her voice. In humiliation, she sank lower in her seat, covering her eyes with her hands. When the movie ended, she avoided looking at Mark, fearing his reaction.

The houselights came on, but the audience didn't move or attempt to leave. Men and women alike were crying in reaction to the poignant death scene.

Mark gripped Lacy's arm and quickly led her out of the theater. "I knew you had something special, baby—you killed them!"

Lacy was stunned. Hysterical laughter was trapped in her throat as Mark rushed her to the limousine that waited at the curb. Once she was seated in the car, she clasped her trembling hands together.

"I was so afraid, Mark."

He lit a cigarette and leaned back to observe her face. "You came off better than even I imagined, Lacy—you're a star! They'll beg for more and more of you, and we'll give it to them."

She lowered her eyes, feeling strangely deflated. Tonight Lucinda Blackburn had disappeared forever, and Lacy Black had taken her place.

Mark stubbed out his cigarette and took her into his arms. "I want to make love to you all night, baby. We'll pretend you're Mata Hari and I'm a poor, unsuspecting fool who's caught in your lair."

Lacy pressed her head against his shoulder, knowing that after tonight, her life would never be the same.

Mata Hari was an instant smash. Overnight the name Lacy Black was on everyone's lips. Reporters flocked to Lacy's door, and the fan letters she received were so numerous that three secretaries were hired just to answer them.

Mark walked with a new swagger. MGM, Fox, and Warner Brothers had contacted him, wanting to buy Lacy's contract. He'd turned them down with great satisfaction, even refusing Jack Warner when he asked to have Lacy on loan to star in a film they were doing with Errol Flynn called *Robin Hood*.

He'd show the folks in this town who they were dealing with

now that he had something everyone wanted, and she belonged exclusively to him.

Mark hosted a party for the press, where waiters in uniform served French champagne and Russian caviar. When everyone was assembled, he escorted Lacy into the room. She wore a black satin gown, high-necked in the front and plunging to her waist in back; daring, yet innocent, Mark had called it.

Lacy felt ill at ease as flashbulbs popped and strangers asked the most intimate questions of her. What color was her bedroom? Did she sleep in the nude, as was reported? Was it true that she wore only black?

Mark drew her into the circle of his arms. "I called you all here today to make an important announcement. Lacy is about to wear a color other than black."

The reporters watched as Mark withdrew an oblong box from his breast pocket and handed it to Lacy.

She opened it with a gasp. With trembling fingers, she held up the shimmering emerald-and-diamond necklace for all to see.

Mark took it from her and clasped it around her neck. "This necklace, ladies and gentlemen, is the famous Raja Star; nothing is too good for my little star."

Once again the flashbulbs exploded and reporters were in a frenzy to have their questions answered.

"I heard it carries a curse," someone called out.

"I'm hoping it'll be lucky for me," Mark answered.

"But it must have cost millions," another reporter observed.

"It did," Mark lied, smiling down at the startled look on Lacy's face. "But you see, my friends, I have an ulterior motive." He was the center of attention, and plainly enjoying himself. "This is my early wedding gift to Lacy, and I wanted to share this moment with you."

Lacy smiled up at Mark with all the love she felt for him shining in her eyes.

He gave her a chaste kiss on the forehead, then turned her around to face the reporters.

Questions were hurled at them. "When will the ceremony take place—will the press be invited?"

Mark, ever the showman, merely smiled. "Lacy has asked for, and I have granted her, a private wedding, but I promise you'll get all the details later." He gripped Lacy by the arm and steered her to the door. "I'm sure you'll understand that we want to be alone. Eat, drink, and be merry. Thank you all for coming."

Mark closed the door on the reporters and took Lacy in his arms, his mouth covering hers in a long, deep kiss.

"Happy, baby?"

Her eyes were sparkling.

"Yes, Mark, very happy." She nuzzled her face against his rough jacket. "I can't wait to be your wife."

He moved away from her and gave her a smile that sent her heart soaring. "Let me have the Raja Star so I can lock it up, then go along and make yourself look like a bride while I talk to Helen. Tonight we drive to San Francisco to be married."

"But Mark, I don't have anything but black dresses."

He was thoughtful for a moment. "So wear black."

Lacy had never heard of a bride wearing black, but she was too happy to care. She had everything she could ever want. Did anyone have the right to be so happy?

The ceremony, which took place in the dimly lit living room of a justice of the peace, was over so quickly that Lacy was stunned. Mark pushed a large diamond ring on her finger and rushed her to the waiting car.

Snuggled in the seat beside him, she linked her arm through his and laid her head against his shoulder. "Mrs. Mark Damian," she said, testing her new name.

He glanced down at her. "There are those who will probably call me Mr. Black," he said in a hard tone. "Let them say what they will; you belong to me now."

He maneuvered the Cord beneath a streetlight, and she saw his jaw tighten. "Just remember to keep me happy."

"I will, Mark," she said with sincerity.

"You will for a while, Lacy, and then you'll be like all the rest."

She was hurt that he would compare her with other women. "No, I won't, Mark, because I love you."

They pulled beneath the awning of the elegant Mark Hopkins Hotel and left the car with the valet. Mark quickly guided Lacy through the lobby and across the marble floor to the elevator. When they stopped at the twelfth floor, he startled the elevator operator by scooping Lacy into his arms and carrying her into the hallway.

He turned to the man, smiling. "It's our honeymoon."

"I see, sir."

"Have you seen *Mata Hari* yet?" Mark asked.

"Mata who, sir?"

Mark turned away, laughing as the elevator door closed smoothly behind them. "Poor fool, he'll never know that Lacy Black was in his elevator tonight."

She gently touched his face. "Forget about him, Mark. This is our wedding night."

Mark's eyes softened in a way she'd never seen before, and there was a hint of sadness reflected there.

"You're going to break my heart one day, Lacy—I know you will."

Chapter Eight

Mark maneuvered his Cord up the twisting curves of Mulholland Drive while Lacy sat beside him, her head on his shoulder.

He planted a kiss on the top of her head and she snuggled closer to him.

"I hope you'll like the house, Lacy. I hired a decorator to completely redo the place so it would be the perfect backdrop for you. I threw out all the old furniture—everything's new."

"Everything?" Lacy asked, unable to comprehend that he had gone to such extravagance just for her.

He smiled as if enjoying a private joke. "Yes. All but my bed—our bed." Then he pointed out the window. "Just around the next curve, you can see your new home."

Lacy sat forward in anticipation as they drove past a wrought-iron gate and down a long driveway lined with tall palms. She stared at the sprawling Spanish-style house, thinking how far removed it was from the shabby little apartment over her father's garage.

When the car stopped, she thrust open the door and rushed up the wide steps that led to the ornately carved front door.

Mark inserted a key and pushed the door open, allowing Lacy to precede him. He was caught up in her infectious excitement as he followed her into the living room.

When they stood before the huge floor-to-ceiling window with its magnificent, sweeping view of the hills, he gripped her shoulder and turned her toward him, pressing his lips on hers.

"Seeing this through your eyes makes it seem like the home it's never been. Until now this has been only a house where I entertained. I've never really spent much time here. But that will change now that you're with me."

Lacy sensed a sorrow in him that he hadn't revealed before. But the one thing she'd learned was that Mark would not talk about his past. "I'll make it a home for you," she said softly, pressing her cheek against his. "I'll spend my life making you happy."

Neither of them heard the housekeeper, Consuela, come up behind them. She cleared her voice to make her presence known. "Welcome home, Señor Damian."

"Lacy," he said smiling, "Consuela keeps the house running smoothly. Consuela, this is my wife, Miss Black."

"I am so happy to meet you, señora," Consuela said. "If you need anything, you have only to ask."

Lacy smiled. "Thank you, Consuela."

Mark looked at his watch. "Consuela will show you the rest of the house while I call the studio. We'll have lunch together by the pool in about an hour."

The housekeeper eyed Mr. Damian's wife warily. She hoped this one wouldn't be like the other women he'd brought to the house—spoiled and demanding, making life difficult for her. "If you will come with me, señora," she said, "we'll start with the downstairs."

As Lacy followed Consuela across the white marble floor from the living room to the formal dining room, the sound of their footsteps echoed loudly. There was no denying that the house was lovely enough to grace the pages of a decorating magazine, but it felt more like a museum than a place where people actually lived, so she could understand why Mark had never felt at home in it.

She also understood what he'd meant about it being the perfect backdrop for Lacy Black. It was a world of white—white walls, white floors, white furniture, gleaming crystal chandeliers—everything cold, impersonal, and sterile. The contrast to her black wardrobe would be dramatic. Every room was perfect, almost too perfect.

After the official release of *Mata Hari*, Lacy's fame grew to stellar proportions, just as Mark had predicted. Lacy Black hit the moviegoing public like an explosion that rocked Hollywood to its core. She was sought after by an insatiable press and admired by a multitude of fans.

Lacy was always exhausted, and she and Mark never had any time alone, but she didn't complain when Mark rushed her through two more pictures that were short on plot, but long on portraying Lacy Black as a sultry seductress.

Mark should have been happy. It fed his ego to be married to the most coveted woman in Hollywood. Lacy had brought him everything he'd ever wanted—respectability, success, and wealth—but still it wasn't enough. He'd started seeing other women, and he'd also resumed his old gambling habits. Twice a week he played poker, and he spent most weekends at the racetrack—not that he was lucky at either one, but now he could afford to lose.

After an unusually tiring day of shooting, Lacy collapsed on the overstuffed couch in her dressing room. When the phone rang, she groaned and lifted it to her ear. "Hello."

"Miss Black?"

"Yes," she answered wearily.

"This is Ada Miller, from Hands of Hope. I've been wanting to talk to you for months. It took quite a bit of detective work on my part to learn that you are our mysterious benefactress."

Lacy held her breath. "I'm afraid I don't know what you are talking about."

"Why, Miss Black, I'm talking about the large donations you make to our organization every month to help the children of migrant workers."

Lacy gripped the phone, remembering the desperate family she and Mark had encountered in Phoenix. The children's faces had haunted her until she'd discovered a way to help others like them through this organization. She'd kept her donations a secret, though, because she didn't want Mark to find out.

"You are mistaken, Mrs. Miller," she said at last. "I know nothing about your charity."

"Miss Black, the manager of the bank unwittingly let it slip that you are our benefactress. It wasn't his fault—you see, he thought I knew all about you."

Lacy sighed in defeat. "Have you told anyone else?"

"Well . . . no. I wouldn't do that without your permission. That's another reason I'm calling. I'd like to use your name as a sponsor to gain the support of other Hollywood stars."

"You can't do that, Mrs. Miller. I won't allow anyone to exploit those children."

There was a long pause. "Naturally not. But surely if your fans were to learn of your generosity, it would only help your career. And think of the publicity—"

"I'm not doing this for the publicity, Mrs. Miller. If I were, do you think I'd have gone to such pains to set up a private account for the monthly checks?"

"No. I suppose not."

"This must remain between the two of us," Lacy reiterated. "If it gets out, I'll deny it. And then I'll find another way to help the children. Is this understood?"

"Yes, I do understand," Ada Miller replied with growing respect for the actress. "Please forgive my intrusion; I won't bother you again, Miss Black."

"Wait—don't hang up. I said I won't endorse your project,

but I would be willing to donate additional money on one condition."

Lacy heard the relief in the woman's voice. "I'll agree to anything if it'll help the children."

"What I'm about to suggest will be just between the two of us."

"You can trust me."

"I know that. I want to start a school for the children. I want it to be a place where they can get free clothing, food, and books, as well as an education."

"This has been my wish all along." There were tears in Ada's voice. "You don't know how I've prayed for this."

"So have I," Lacy said softly.

"If only we could call it the Lacy Black School."

"No! It will be known as the Phoenix School. The children, like the fabled bird, will rise out of their misery and have an education and at least one hot meal a day."

"It will be expensive."

"I'll leave all the details to you."

"Oh, Miss Black, you are an angel."

"No, I just love children like you do, Ada—may I call you Ada?"

"Oh, yes, please do." Again there was a pause. "How will I get in touch with you?"

"Through our mutual friend at the bank. He'll be instructed to give you the money you need."

Then Lacy hung up the phone.

When she left her dressing room and walked through the darkened studio, she found herself wishing she had someone with whom to share her excitement about the new school. She should have been able to confide in Mark, but he was the last person she would ever tell.

"It's hell, isn't it?"

She glanced up in surprise to find that Sidney Greenway was waiting for her.

"I don't know what you mean."

He motioned for her to sit down in a chair, and he pulled up a stool beside her. "I mean stardom. Is it all you thought it would be?"

Although his manner was often brusque, Lacy liked the director. "I never wanted to be an actress, Sidney. That was Mark's doing."

He clamped his teeth on his unlit cigar. "What do you do with yourself on the evenings when Mark is . . . working late?"

She smiled wearily. "I study my lines for the next day." Lacy leaned forward, suddenly needing Sidney's opinion. "I know that I have been successful, but am I a good actress?"

"You don't like the roles you're cast in, do you?"

"No, not much. But you didn't answer my question. Don't be afraid to hurt my feelings."

Sidney studied the delicate face whose expression he'd directed in different roles. He probably knew her better than she knew herself, and he liked her. "You have the potential to become one of the greatest actresses that ever lived. I think you know the difference between being a movie star and being an actress."

She was stunned by his praise. "Yes, I know the difference. A movie star is cardboard, and an actress lives and breathes—I'm cardboard."

He stood up. "No, you're not, but there are those who would have you so." He moved away from her and then stopped and turned back. "Don't let him destroy you, Lacy. There are people who care about you, you know. Anytime you feel the need to talk, I'm a good listener."

She stared after his retreating figure, wondering what he meant. Did he know that she and Mark were seldom together anymore? Did he sense, as she did, that Mark had his dark side? Feeling disloyal to her husband, Lacy left the soundstage and moved out into the gathering darkness. Climbing into the waiting limousine, she dreaded the thought of spending another night alone in that big, empty house.

* * *

Mark had been planning the lavish party for weeks. Invitations had gone out to everyone of importance in Hollywood. The other studio heads had ignored him in the past and ridiculed his movies, and Mark knew that if just one of them attended tonight, he would be vindicated.

It was late afternoon when an exhausted Lacy stumbled into her dressing room. She'd arrived at the studio at five o'clock that morning, and had been working under hot lights almost nonstop since then.

She stood before the full-length mirror, careful not to wrinkle her costume until someone from wardrobe arrived to help her undress. She stared at Mark's interpretation of Lacy Black as the Egyptian queen Nefertiti. The sheer black gown was adorned with beads and revealed rather than concealed her long, shapely legs when she moved. Her black headdress was shaped like a falcon and cleverly covered her platinum hair. Her eyes were boldly outlined, and glitter had been generously applied to the upper eyelids.

"This is the big day," Mark announced, coming up behind her and massaging her shoulders. "I want you to look particularly beautiful tonight. I've had a special dress made just for this occasion."

Lacy gave herself up to the soothing ministrations of Mark's hands. "If only the party wasn't tonight." She sighed. "All I want is a hot bath and to crawl into bed."

Mark's grip on her shoulders tightened painfully, and Lacy cried out.

"You'll come to my party, and you'll act like you're enjoying yourself," he said, intensifying his grip. "Tonight is too important to me for you to ruin it with silly little tantrums."

Lacy was shocked by Mark's sudden cruelty. "You're hurting me," she said angrily. "Surely you don't want to damage the merchandise," she added defiantly, in her first show of rebellion since that day in Phoenix.

Their eyes warred in the reflection of the mirror, and finally Mark capitulated, dropping his hands. "Quite right. We can't have bruises—can we?" He smiled without humor. "I'll meet you at the house later. I want you to make a grand entrance tonight, but don't be too late."

When Mark left, Lacy dropped into a chair and buried her face in her hands, wondering what had gone wrong between them. During those first glorious weeks of marriage she'd felt so cherished; now she felt more like a commodity, something to parade before the press, to show off to the world in the same way Mark had exhibited the Raja Star.

After the makeup artist had removed Lacy's makeup and the wardrobe assistant had helped her out of her costume, she quickly dressed in a simple skirt and blouse and rushed to the waiting limousine. When she climbed into the backseat, she noticed that the sky was overcast and threatening rain. As the car pulled through the gates of the studio, rain was pelting against the windows. Lacy found herself wishing for a flood so that all Mark's guests would have to stay home tonight and she could get some rest.

"Forty days and forty nights," she said wistfully.

The chauffeur met her eyes in the mirror. "Did you say something, Miss Black?"

She looked out the window, where already the rain had stopped and the sky was clearing. "I was just thinking about a flood, Benson."

"Oh, you needn't worry about that, Miss Black," he said with assurance. "It almost never floods here. I can't even think when we last had a good rain."

"Pity," she murmured to herself.

Benson drove around to the side of the house so Lacy could take the back entrance unobserved. When she entered her bedroom, she found Meg Chandler had already arrived from the studio to help her dress.

"I've run you a hot bath, Lacy. You'd better hurry, though. Mark's already been here twice looking for you."

Lacy and the wardrobe mistress exchanged glances. Over the

months, they had become friends, and they both knew that Mark had to be appeased.

Lacy glanced at the black satin creation lying across the bed. "My new gown?" she asked, her lips pressed together in distaste.

"Yep. Nothing new, though—thin black chiffon over a nude-colored underskirt. A plunging neckline, perhaps a little more tight-fitting than usual, but typically Lacy Black. You won't be able to wear any undergarments with this one. Every seam would show."

Lacy rolled her eyes. "It's a wonder that Mark hasn't thought of painting a dress on me." They both laughed, knowing he'd do just that if he thought he could get away with it.

Lacy actually nodded off to sleep in the tub, and was awakened when Meg knocked on the door.

"Time to dress. The guests have already started to arrive."

With a groan, Lacy stepped out of the tub and wrapped herself in an oversize towel. Somehow she would get through this evening—she had to.

She was powdered and perfumed, her hair arranged in a soft style and her lips painted bloodred to match her long fingernails. Lacy inhaled deeply while Meg tugged the skin-tight gown across her hips. "If I breathe, I'll burst a seam," she complained.

"That's nothing, honey," Meg said, grabbing up a needle. "Just wait until I sew you into it." She saw Lacy grimace as she began stitching up a seam at the back that had been left open so Lacy could get into the dress. "I know, I know. It was Mark's idea. I told him you wouldn't like it."

Mark chose that moment to enter. "Beautiful," he said approvingly. "You'll knock them dead, baby."

Meg bit the thread off and stood back. "Not hardly—she can't even move in this gown, Mark. I told you it was too tight."

Lacy added her protests to Meg's. "I can't even sit in it!"

He turned Lacy around and examined her from front to back. "So don't sit. Circulate, work the crowd." Elation danced in his eyes. "Everyone who is anyone is here tonight, and they're here to see you, baby. Go out and give them what they came for. I'll go on ahead to prepare for your entrance. When I introduce you, you come down the stairs."

He left Lacy's bedroom and moved to the landing, where he stood for a moment, looking down at the distinguished guests milling about, savoring his triumph. They were all there: Sam Goldwyn, Jack Warner, even Louis B. Mayer, himself! And the reporters would capture his victory for all the world to see.

His eyes moved to the tables that were laden with hors d'oeuvres and delicacies catered by Romanoff's. Champagne flowed like water in the smoke-filled room. It was hard to be heard above the din of voices. Mark moved about the crowd, strutting proudly. He knew that Lacy was the real reason the Hollywood elite had come, but what did it matter? She was his, and if they wanted to see her, they had to include him.

He tapped a spoon against his champagne glass. When the room fell silent, he spoke distinctly: "Ladies and gentlemen, I give you my wife, Lacy Black!"

Lacy carefully descended the stairs, while faces of strangers swarmed before her. When she reached the bottom step, flash-bulbs burst all around her, momentarily blinding her.

Mercifully, Mark's hand closed around hers, and he led her forward. Everyone seemed to press in on her, and her grip tightened on Mark's hand. Gossip columnists from all the fan magazines vied for space at her side, their notepads ready to jot down anything she said to use for tomorrow's headlines.

For what seemed like hours, she was fawned over, adored, and paid homage. She had long since lost sight of Mark. When at last there was a break in the conversation, she excused herself and fled to the terrace for a breath of fresh air.

Standing beneath the moonlight, she felt removed from her surroundings. Tonight she had realized the price of fame, and she wondered if it was worth it. Inside she was the same little girl from Snyder, Texas, no matter how much Mark tried to make her believe she was the glamorous Lacy Black.

"Well, you wowed them; how does it feel?"

Lacy turned at the familiar voice of Sidney Greenway. "It feels like sliding down a razor's edge—one slip either way and it's all over, and who would mourn?"

Sidney stepped out of the shadows and leaned against the stucco pillar next to her, smoke from his cigar curling about his head. "A bit dramatic, don't you think? But you're right. There isn't a person in that room who wouldn't push you off the edge if they thought they could gain by it."

She met his eyes. "But not you, Sidney?"

"No, never me. If you were wise, you'd leave this town while you still have the chance, and never look back."

"Sometimes . . . I wish I could. But you see, Sidney, I have nowhere to go."

He drained his glass and turned toward the door. "I'm going home. Why don't you chuck this party and go to bed? They've sucked enough blood out of you for one night."

"I can't. Mark wouldn't like it."

Sidney took her hand, holding it gently in his. "He'll suck more blood out of you than all the others put together." Then he dropped her hand and turned to the door. " 'Night, Lacy."

She watched him disappear into the house, thinking that her only friend was gone.

Suddenly she heard voices coming from the direction of the stone steps that led to the garden. Not wanting to talk to anyone, she pulled back into the shadows, hoping the newcomers wouldn't see her as they passed.

She heard a woman's high-pitched giggle, followed by a man's deep laugh—the man was Mark, she was almost certain. Then they were so close that she could have reached out and touched him.

Lacy actually thought she could feel her heart break as she watched the scene that unfolded before her.

"You never noticed me before, Joan. What changed your mind tonight?" Mark asked, holding the woman in his arms.

Joan Montana was one of the biggest stars at Metro. She rubbed her body against his. "I wanted to find out what it is about you that keeps little Lacy happy."

"And did you?"

Joan raised her face to his, her hands moving to intimate places on his body. "I never make a judgment on first contact." She laughed, pressing her lips to the corner of Mark's mouth. "Do you want me again?" she purred.

"You know I do," Mark said as he ravaged her mouth with his kisses.

Lacy closed her eyes, pressing her body against the wide pillar, clamping her hands over her mouth to keep from crying out in agony. Eventually, she heard their footsteps fade away, and only then did she cry.

"Why, Mark, why?" She moaned, raising her face to the pale moon as something inside her died. When there were no more tears left, she went down the steps and around to the kitchen entrance, knowing she couldn't face anyone else tonight. She made her way up the back stairs to her bedroom and ripped the gown from her body, tearing it to shreds.

She'd been manipulated by men all her life—first her father, and then Mark. She had grown up tonight, and it had been a painful experience, but one that would make her strong. Never again would she give Mark, or any man, the power to hurt her.

Climbing into bed, she switched off the lamp, not caring that the party downstairs was growing wilder. Emotionally drained and heartsick, she soon fell asleep.

She didn't know what time it was when Mark entered the room and switched on the light. She raised herself on an elbow, glaring at him. "Turn that light off, Mark."

He dropped down on the bed and gripped her by the shoulders. "Just what in the hell do you think you're doing? You're supposed to be downstairs entertaining my guests."

"You entertain them. I'm tired," Lacy said, pushing his hands away. "I want to sleep . . . alone." At that moment, the sight of him sickened her. She toyed with the notion of telling him that she'd seen him with Joan Montana, but decided against it. She just didn't care. That realization brought her peace—and something else: courage.

Mark could sense a change in Lacy, but he didn't know what it meant. "Sure, baby," he said uncertainly. "Whatever you say. You get some rest. Everything will be back to normal after a good night's sleep." He bent to kiss her, but she turned away.

After a long moment of silence, he went downstairs.

Long after the last guest had departed, Mark sat in the dark, his thoughts troubled. What should have been the greatest triumph in his life had turned sour. Something had happened tonight that had made Lacy turn against him, and he didn't know what it was. Someone must have told her about Joan or one of the others, but who?

Why was he worrying? he wondered. He knew how to handle Lacy. First thing tomorrow, he'd confess his sins and allow her to forgive him. Still, doubts nagged at his mind. She'd tried to assert her independence several times today, and he felt his control of her was slipping.

Chapter Nine

Mark was up just after sunrise, although he hadn't slept well at all. Since Lacy had to be at the studio early, he knew he'd find her already having breakfast on the terrace, and he had to see her before she left.

Lacy watched Mark's approach from behind the shield of her dark sunglasses. She usually wore them whenever she was outside in the bright California sun, but today there was an added reason—her eyes were swollen and red from hours of crying, and she didn't want Mark to know how he had hurt her. Now she was able to observe him without his seeing the loathing in her eyes. She had replayed the scene between him and Joan Montana over and over in her mind until she could stand it no longer.

Mark said a cheerful good morning to Consuela, and leaned down to kiss Lacy, but she pulled away from him. He shrugged and sat down at the table opposite her, just oozing charm.

"You look beautiful today, baby," he said as he unfolded his napkin and ceremoniously placed it on his lap.

"I'm not your baby, Mark," Lacy told him angrily.

Mark let out his breath slowly. Yes, he'd been right. Somehow she had found out about him being with another woman—but which one? "Sure, you're my baby," he said appeasingly. "You're mine to take care of, and I love you, Lacy."

With a vengeance, she stabbed her spoon into the grapefruit she was eating. She wanted to hurt him as he had hurt her, but she didn't know how. "You look like hell, Mark," she said in disgust. "Hungover?"

This was the opening he needed. "I did have too much to drink last night," he admitted sheepishly. He reached for her hand and she drew hers away. "Please, baby, don't turn away from me—not when I need you. You see, I have a vague memory of something happening between me and Joan Montana last night." He saw her stiffen and knew he was divulging the right indiscretion. "I'm not saying it happened—I'm saying it could have. I'm telling you this because I never want there to be any secrets between us."

"I don't want to discuss it, Mark," Lacy said, trying to keep the tears at bay.

"Baby . . . Lacy, don't you know a heartfelt confession when you hear one?"

Mark was never better than when he was humbling himself. "What makes you think I care what happened between you and that . . . woman?" Lacy asked, wanting to believe him, but knowing what she had witnessed.

He grabbed her hand and raised it to his lips, and this time she didn't pull away. "Because we love each other. You aren't going to allow one little mistake to come between us, are you? We have too much going for us."

There had been a time when she would have gullibly swallowed anything he told her. But not after last night.

Her voice was cold when she said, "If you will excuse me, I'm due in wardrobe."

When she stood, he pulled her onto his lap. "I need you, Lacy," he said, nuzzling her neck. "Don't leave me," he pleaded.

"Remember what we are to each other. Don't throw that away just because I was a fool."

She stiffened. "I don't know, Mark. I have to think about it. Right now I have to get to the studio—you know how Sidney feels about punctuality."

Mark held her to him. "All right. But I'll make this up to you, Lacy—you'll see. Just give me a chance."

"You have to give me time, Mark."

He released her and drew in a deep breath. "I'll do anything that will make you happy. You aren't going to leave me, are you?"

For the first time since she'd known him, she saw uncertainty in his eyes, and knew it was genuine. It softened her heart just a bit. "No. I won't leave you."

With relief, he watched her walk away. She hadn't capitulated, but she hadn't turned away from him either. Lacy was changing, and if he was going to hold on to her, he'd have to change too.

Strangely, Lacy and Mark never again discussed the night of his party or his infidelity with Joan Montana. As time passed, their marriage entered a different phase. Mark was more considerate to her and far less demanding. But she wasn't the same trusting little girl she'd once been, and he was no longer her whole world. She was kind to him and tried to act as if nothing had changed, but she couldn't help feeling guilty—she didn't love him as she had before.

Lacy threw herself into her work, determined to become the best actress she could be. She took direction from Sidney, knowing he would take the trite films Mark found for her, and turn them into box office successes.

It was a bright Sunday morning, and Lacy and Mark were eating a leisurely breakfast on the terrace. The view overlooked the new Olympic-size swimming pool, and the tennis courts were just visible through a tall oleander hedge.

Lacy was reading the script that she had decided to do to please Mark, while he scanned the headlines of the newspaper.

"Those damned bureaucrats in Washington are going to drag us into war before the year is out," Mark said in disgust.

Lacy pushed her sunglasses to the top of her head and laid her script aside. "Sidney thinks the United States should join the war. He says Germany won't stop until it steamrolls over Europe. Surely we can't just look the other way if that happens?"

"Sidney thinks he's an expert on everything," Mark snapped. "He's a Roosevelt man and mimics the president's scare tactics. The way I see it, if we go to war, we'll all be living on Roosevelt's new welfare program."

"Someone has to put a stop to that monster, Hitler. You don't really think he'll be satisfied with just Europe, do you?"

"Sidney's words again," Mark said with naked jealousy in his eyes. "Don't you have a thought in your head that wasn't put there and directed by Sidney?"

At that moment, Consuela interrupted them. "Excuse, señora, a Ruth Blackburn is at the door. She says she is your sister."

Lacy looked at Mark in horror. There had always been the possibility that her past would intrude on her new life. What Ruth and her daddy had done to her was unforgivable, and she'd hoped that she would never have to see either of them again.

Sending her a warning look, Mark neatly folded the newspaper and laid it on the table. "I guess you'd better show her in, Consuela," he said, his mind racing ahead on how to deal with the unwelcome intruder.

"Perhaps Ruth's sorry for what she did and wants to make amends, Mark," Lacy said hopefully. "Maybe she's brought an apology from Daddy."

"Yeah, and maybe I can sprout wings and fly," Mark said scornfully.

Lacy stood up when Ruth approached. For a long moment the two sisters stared at each other, surveying the changes in each other since they'd last been together.

Ruth saw an elegant, polished beauty with little resemblance to her younger sister. For a moment she felt nervous as she looked with uncertainty into cold green eyes, seeing no welcome there. When Ruth's gaze fell on Lacy's hand, and she caught sight of the biggest diamond ring she'd ever seen, she could hardly choke back her resentment. Lacy was everything that Ruth had always wanted to be. If she'd been the one kicked out by their father, as she should have been, it would be her sitting where Lacy was now. Mark Damian would have been her husband, and *she* would be a famous movie star.

Lacy felt a sudden rush of pity for Ruth, who looked terrible. She'd put on several extra pounds. Her dress was rumpled, and her hair was coarse and limp, as if it hadn't been washed in days. Why had Ruth lost pride in her appearance, when it had always been her primary concern?

"How have you been, Ruth?" Lacy asked, not knowing what else to say to her sister. Mark wasn't any help—he'd picked up the newspaper and pretended to be reading, totally ignoring Ruth.

"Forget about me," Ruth answered with thinly veiled spite. "It seems you've done pretty well for yourself, Lucinda. I congratulate you."

Mark crumpled the newspaper and his eyes narrowed. "What do you want, Ruth?" he asked venomously.

Ruth turned her attention to her sister's husband, who was even more handsome than she'd remembered. "Why, Mark, no kiss of greeting for your sister-in-law?"

He looked at her in distaste. "I asked you what you want," he repeated.

Ruth shrugged. "Imagine my surprise when I read an article about the famous Lacy Black in *Look* magazine, and my sister's face jumped right off the cover at me. I thought Lucinda might be missing her family, since the article said she didn't have any."

Mark's lips tightened. "The Lucinda you knew no longer exists. And Lacy Black has no immediate family other than her husband, is that clear?" he asked harshly.

Ruth turned her speculative gaze back to Lacy. "So just where does that leave me?"

At that moment, a balding, middle-aged man came out on the terrace, staggering a little as he walked. "Hey, Ruthie," he said, "I got tired of waiting. What's taking so long? I've got to get on the road again and make more calls, or we won't eat next month."

"This is Howard," Ruth said casually, not even bothering to introduce Lacy and Mark to him. "He's the southwest regional sales representative for the Acme Wholesale Coat Hanger and Dry Cleaning Supply Company of Muncie, Indiana. He was *my* ride out of Snyder," she said in a self-deprecating tone of voice.

"Come on, Ruthie, you've had your fun," Howard said, slapping her bottom familiarly, "but we've got to be going. And even if you lost the bet, I'll still buy you that rabbit stole you have your heart set on."

The man turned his attention to Mark and Lacy. "Sorry to disturb you folks," he said apologetically, obviously feeling out of place in the grand surroundings. "Ruthie here bet me she'd prove that Lacy Black was her little sister. I brought her here 'cause I like to humor the little woman, but we'll just be going along now. Sorry we bothered you." He bowed awkwardly in Lacy's direction, then attempted to pull Ruth to his side.

"Let go, you fool," Ruth muttered, jerking her arm away from him. "I'm not leaving with you."

The bleary-eyed salesman looked at Ruth in confusion. "You mean she really is your sister?"

Ruth's eyes met and held Lacy's gaze. "No, it appears Lacy Black has no family—but I think she'll take care of me all the same. Isn't that right, Lacy?"

The hint of threatened exposure was not lost on Mark. Ruth could destroy everything he'd worked so hard to build if she told the press about Lacy's background.

Lacy was unaware of Ruth's threat. She only knew that this was her sister, and she couldn't turn her away, not when she looked so pathetic. "Mark, can she stay for a short visit?"

"Suit yourself," he said, standing up and throwing his napkin on the table. "I have an appointment and won't be home before dinner. Make sure you're ready for the party tonight. Wear the new black lace gown that arrived yesterday, and use a little more makeup. You've been looking pale lately." Without a word to Ruth or Howard, he pushed past them.

There was an awkward silence after his departure. At last Ruth spoke. "Well, Howard, I guess this is good-bye."

Howard looked about him in confusion. He had the feeling that he'd been used, but he wasn't quite sure how. "Ruthie, are you sure . . . ?"

"Good-bye, Howard."

Twisting his hat in his hands, he left the terrace, all the while stealing glances over his shoulder at Ruth.

Ruth pulled out a chair and seated herself next to Lacy. "I might as well make myself at home. Do you think that maid of yours could find me some strong coffee and fried eggs? I'm starved."

Lacy rang for Consuela, and while they waited for her to appear, she searched Ruth's face. "How is Daddy?"

Ruth shrugged indifferently. "Daddy is always the same. That old fool doesn't even know that his daughter is the famous Lacy Black. I don't think anyone back home knows but me, and I didn't find out until just recently."

"Why did you leave Snyder?"

"I was ordered out, just as you were. After you left, Daddy found out it was me who was with Eddie and the other boys that night." She laughed in amusement. "He sure felt bad for what he'd done to you. Course, he'll get over it. I think he hopes you'll come home so he can do penance."

"I'll never go back."

"Why should you?" Ruth reached for a flaky biscuit and attacked it with gusto. "You know, Lucinda, I could get used to living this way. Who'd ever believe that the Blackburn sisters would be living in a mansion in Hollywood with servants waiting on them?"

Lacy's eyes were troubled. "Ruth, Mark was serious about not telling anyone of my past. He has carefully built my image, and he won't allow you to tear it down. You must never tell anyone that we're sisters, or Mark will make you leave."

"So I'm not good enough for the high-and-mighty Lacy Black to acknowledge as family." Ruth tossed her head defiantly. "We both know you're not any better than I am. Put on airs and call yourself whatever name you want to, but your daddy was still a mechanic and your mama a whore."

Lacy lowered her eyes to hide the pain that Ruth's words caused. She'd often heard them from her daddy, and they still had the power to hurt her. Slowly Lacy raised her head and met Ruth's gaze. "Don't ever say that to me again, Ruth. This is my home, and I don't owe you anything. If you stay, it's only because I allow it."

Ruth shrugged. "We both know you won't toss me out, and you won't let your husband, either. I'll keep your secrets, *Lacy*, but don't *you* ever forget who I am."

"I could never forget you, Ruth. You remind me of Daddy. Having you here is like having him looking over my shoulder again, condemning my very being."

Ruth looked puzzled. "I'm not religious the way Daddy is."

"Yes, but you are both cut from the same cloth. You think the world revolves around you and no one else."

Ruth eyed her sister with a hard glare. "Well, it doesn't, does it, Lucinda, or Lacy, or whatever you want to be called? The way I see it, the world revolves around *you*."

Lacy drew in a deep breath. "Looks can be deceiving," she whispered.

Ruth's eyes gleamed. She knew her little sister well enough to realize that she wasn't happy. There was something wrong, and she intended to find out what it was. Maybe Mark wasn't as much in love with Lacy as he pretended to be.

Lacy was seated at the vanity table, applying her makeup, when she heard Mark enter. She met his gaze in the reflection of the mirror, and before she could duck her head, he grabbed her chin, pulling her face into the light.

"You've been crying," he accused.

Lacy pulled away from him. "It's nothing, Mark. Ruth and I just had a little . . . misunderstanding."

His mouth tightened and his eyes narrowed. "I won't allow that scheming little bitch to upset you. If she starts trouble, out she goes, family or not." He handed Lacy her compact. "See if you can do a better job covering up your swollen eyes." He smiled at her and gave her a wink. "Just remember that you're Cinderella, and she's the stepsister."

Lacy felt a rush of gratitude because Mark was protective of her—he'd never allow Ruth to hurt her as their father had. In that moment, her heart softened toward Mark, and she startled him when she stood and embraced him.

"Thank you for understanding," she said softly.

He stared at her for a long moment. This was the first time in months that she'd come into his arms willingly. Maybe Ruth's coming wasn't such a bad thing after all—not if Lacy looked to him for comfort. He pulled her closer and rested his chin on the top of her head. He'd allow Ruth to stay, but only so long as it suited his purpose.

"You finish making yourself beautiful, Lacy. Just come to my study when you're ready to leave."

Ruth found Mark sitting at his desk, but he didn't look up when she entered.

"My, my, but you are a busy little man, always working," she said, bending forward so her cleavage showed.

Mark glanced up in irritation. "What do you want, Ruth?"

"Just thought we should get to know one another. I think you'd like me if you gave me a chance."

Mark's eyes narrowed when he noticed that Ruth was wearing Lacy's new sequined evening gown. She looked like a bad caricature of Lacy—hard where Lacy was soft, cold where Lacy was warm. Ruth's body was overdeveloped, so the gown clung unflatteringly to her hips and exposed the top half of her breasts.

"What are you doing in that dress?" he demanded.

Ruth flashed him a slow, suggestive smile. All men were the same when it came right down to basic needs—and she knew a lot of tricks to make a man want her.

"Don't you like it?" she purred, strutting around him, swaying her hips.

"Not on you," he said brutally. "I paid five hundred dollars for that dress, and it belongs to Lacy. Take it off, *right now.*"

Ruth shrugged and gave him a slight grin. "Whatever you say, Mark." And she proceeded to slip the straps off one of her shoulders, revealing a soft breast.

Lacy was about to enter the room, but when she saw the scene before her, she stopped, backing into the shadows, overcome with emotion. She knew what Ruth was like, but she hadn't expected her sister to go after Mark. She knew what Mark was like, too. *Please, God, don't let Mark betray me with my own sister,* she prayed silently.

Unknown to Lacy, Mark had seen her before she retreated from the room. Acting for Lacy's benefit, he grabbed Ruth's wrists and turned her toward him.

"You're hurting me," Ruth said in a husky voice, rubbing her body against his. "Do you like it rough, Mark? I can oblige you, if that's your need."

"Don't try any of your ineffective charms on me, Ruth," Mark replied, flinging her from him. "I love my wife, and I don't even like you. Go take Lacy's dress off." His tone was cruel and stinging. "You'd better understand that I don't want you here at all. You're a guest in Lacy's home, and you remain only as long as you remember that everything here, including me, belongs to Lacy."

Ruth was at a loss for words for the first time in her life, and she could only stare at Mark.

"Do you understand your position in this house?" Mark asked harshly.

She turned on him, her eyes bitter and full of resentment. "I understand that Lacy has everything and is everything—and I have nothing and am nothing."

Mark gave her a smile that didn't reach his eyes. "Then we understand each other very well."

Ruth stormed out of the room and passed Lacy without seeing her.

When Lacy entered the room a moment later, Mark acted as if nothing had happened. He congratulated himself on a brilliant performance, although it wasn't hard to show his distaste for Ruth—she just wasn't his type.

"You look stunning, baby," he said smoothly. "But have you been crying again?"

She pressed her cheek against Mark's shirtfront, finally convinced that he really loved her.

"Come, Lacy," Mark said gently. "We're already late for the party."

When they reached the front door, Ruth was leaning against the wall, smoking a cigarette, a sneer on her face as she surveyed her sister from head to toe. Lacy was stunning in a black lace gown, the fabulous Raja Star circling her neck. Ruth looked with envy at the rich sable coat that was carelessly draped around Lacy's otherwise bare shoulders.

"Enjoy your party," Ruth said peevishly. "Don't you worry about me; I'll just go to bed early."

Remembering the scene in Mark's study, Lacy felt the need to put some distance between her and Ruth. "We're late," she said hurriedly.

"Did you know that Mark belittled and humiliated me this afternoon?" Ruth asked, expecting Lacy to come to her defense.

Lacy gripped Mark's arm, while he remained silent.

"I won't apologize for my husband, Ruth," she said angrily. "If you don't like it here, I'll see that you have the money to find a place of your own somewhere far away."

Ruth had no intention of leaving this cozy little setup. But she would have to handle things differently. If she wasn't nicer to her sister, she'd find herself on the streets, with only men like Howard to take care of her. She moved forward and put her arms around Lacy, who pulled away. "Don't you worry about me. I'm just out of sorts because I'm tired. Now go and have a good time. Maybe tomorrow we can go shopping." She smiled at Mark. "That is, if your husband doesn't object. He didn't seem to like what I was wearing earlier."

In that moment, the tension between Mark and Ruth was so oppressive that Lacy experienced a feeling of uneasiness, almost like a premonition of tragedy. Between them, they could destroy her completely.

Chapter Ten

September 1939

Mark's studio prospered with the release of each new Lacy Black film. Fans around the world worshiped her, and the magazines and newspapers couldn't print enough stories to satisfy the public's curiosity about her life.

Sidney had been summoned to Mark's office to discuss Lacy's next movie. Enraged, he slammed the script down on the desk and glared at Mark. "It's the same trite plot. Why don't you find something worthy of Lacy's talent? She's capable of much more demanding roles."

Mark looked unruffled. "We've had this conversation before and my answer's still the same. We stick with what works. Her 'trite' pictures, as you call them, pay your salary, Sidney."

"She won't like this one," Sidney said, his hand on the doorknob. "She's getting tired of playing the same old part, and you know it."

Mark laced his hands together and rested them on the top of

his desk, looking composed. "You talk to her, Sidney, and convince her to do it—she listens to you."

"I'll talk to her," the director said, moving through the open door. "But if she doesn't want to do it, I'm on her side."

When the door closed, the smile left Mark's face and his gaze hardened. In a rage, he swept his hand across the desk, sending the script scattering to the floor. It was intolerable that Lacy valued the director's advice over his. But he was forced to endure Sidney's influence—at least for now.

Lacy was listening to the radio, her eyes wide with anxiety as the London correspondent's voice crackled and faded in and out.

"Britain and France have declared war on Germany! The word from the White House is that the United States will remain neutral. However, young American men who want to get into the war are flocking to Canada to enlist. . . ."

Mark came up behind Lacy and switched off the radio. "This war may turn out to be advantageous for us after all. I hadn't counted on the American public's craving for war news. I've had my writers working overtime on a new script for you."

She met his eyes. "Lacy Black goes to war?"

He pulled her to her feet and chuckled. "More like, Lacy Black keeps the fighting men happy."

Mark was plainly excited about something. "We'll discuss your next picture later, baby. Right now, I have a surprise that I think you'll really like," he said, leading her down the hallway to his study.

Lacy watched with interest as he reached for a crowbar and pried the top off a huge wooden crate that had been placed in the middle of the room.

"Look what I bought at the art auction this morning," he boasted, lifting a huge painting and turning it toward Lacy for her inspection.

She looked at the portrait of a man, thinking that it seemed vaguely familiar. "Who is it?"

"This is a self-portrait by Rembrandt. I got it for a mere fifteen thousand dollars. Look how well the dark colors will match the decor of my office. That was what drew me to it in the first place."

Lacy's hand trembled as she reached forward reverently to touch the painting. "It's magnificent, Mark! I know you are proud of it."

He nodded. "Damn right. I never thought I'd own a Rembrandt. I've got a crew coming to the studio tomorrow to install special locks on the doors to protect it. Can't take a chance on its being stolen."

"That's a good idea," Lacy agreed. She moved to the door and paused to smile at him. "Thanks for showing it to me, Mark. Now I need to dress for Mayer's party, if you're sure you still want to go."

"Yes, hurry, baby. I want to get there early so I can see Mayer's face when I tell him about the auction he missed today."

It was the fifth night in a row that Lacy and Mark had attended a party, and she looked around her with boredom. Every night it was the same people doing the same things—drinking too much, talking too loudly, and many of them sneaking off for sordid little rendezvous.

To Lacy, this was the superficial side of Hollywood that the rest of the world never heard about. The public thought of movie stars as American royalty, but many of them were without substance, shallow, and self-centered. They were beautiful people, all right, but they weren't necessarily intelligent, and many of them weren't kind or even pleasant to be around.

Only two years ago, she would have been thrilled for a chance to meet these people, who were more real on the screen than they were in person. Now she knew how impossible it was to have a serious conversation with people who thought only about their appearance or the money they'd earned on their last picture.

Walking down the hallway, away from the noisy crowd, she

found a small alcove where she hoped to escape the pall of cigarette smoke that hung over the huge living room. She could still observe the party, but didn't have to be a part of it. Her back ached, her feet hurt, and she was just plain tired.

Thinking she was alone, she sat on the overstuffed couch, leaned her head back, and closed her eyes.

"Excuse me," a masculine voice said from behind her.

She turned her head to find a man executing a drunken, but nonetheless gallant bow. He was a famous swashbuckling film star that the world had once adored. Now he couldn't even get a bit part in a movie.

"Beautiful lady," he said, slurring his words. "At last I find you. I have been in love with you since first I saw you. I need you to bring meaning into my life. I have a feeling that we are kindred souls, and I will wander forever in darkness if you are unkind to me."

Recognizing the lines from one of his movies, Lacy laughed. "Foolish gallant," she said, "if my husband, Mark Damian, discovers your infatuation, you'll be forced to have your teeth recapped on Monday."

His bleary eyes widened, and he staggered backward and placed his hand to his lips. "Shh, pretty vision, if we don't tell him, he'll never know."

With a smile of amusement, she watched as the man meandered back into the living room, where he approached a young starlet. Bowing before her, he repeated. "Beautiful lady, at last I find you. I have loved you since first I saw you . . ."

"Well, look who's here," a shrill voice called out. "If it isn't little Miss Grapette from small-town Texas."

The odor of perfume and liquor that emanated from the woman made Lacy feel sick. "Hello, Miss Divine."

"You think you're really something now, don't you, kid?" the older actress said so loudly that her voice drifted across the room.

"I don't know what you mean."

"Big star at the box office . . . wife to a big-shot Hollywood producer." She jabbed her finger at Lacy's shoulder to emphasize her words. "Living in a big mansion in Beverly Hills. Well, let me tell you, enjoy it while you can, because it won't last."

"Miss Divine, you've had too much to drink. Why don't you let me call your driver to take you home?"

"I decide what I drink, and when I go home. Nobody asked for your opinion."

Lacy was relieved when she saw Mark appear behind Dolores. His face was white, and he was tight-lipped and angry as he stepped between them.

"Don't let anything Dolores says upset you, Lacy," Mark warned her. "She's just envious of your success."

Dolores let out a loud burst of laughter that ended in a screech. "Don't you believe that, kid." Now she was jabbing at Mark. "I was about to tell your little *wife* that I once had everything she has, including you and your Beverly Hills mansion, but thank God *I* wised up and left."

"Why don't you get smart and leave now?" Mark suggested. "Face it, Dolores, you're a loser. Things didn't go as well for you as you expected, did they? While I, on the other hand, did just what I told you I would do. Lacy Black is a hundred times more successful than you ever thought about being. The best favor you ever did me was to walk out on me in Texas."

"Mark, please," Lacy pleaded. "Is this necessary?" She didn't care for Dolores, but it was cruel to taunt her so mercilessly.

To her surprise, Dolores burst out laughing. "Well, Mark, it's nice to see you haven't changed. But I'm not going away yet. I'd like to talk to you in private, and I think you'll be interested in what I have to say. In fact, I'll bet on it."

There was something reckless, but at the same time triumphant, in Dolores's demeanor, and Mark decided he'd better see what she had to say. Already her actions were drawing attention, and people were beginning to move toward the alcove to satisfy their curiosity.

Without a word to Lacy, Mark grabbed Dolores by the arm and pulled her through the crowd, not releasing his hold on her until they reached their host's private study, where he closed the door behind them.

"Well," he said impatiently. "What do you have to say that you think will be so interesting to me, Dolores?"

Her only reply was to curl her arm around his neck and press herself to him.

He shoved her away. "No, thanks, I'm not desperate. And if that's all you wanted, I'll leave now."

Mark expected his rejection to be met with anger and insults, but instead Dolores merely laughed.

"You're a bitch, Dolores," he said, looking at her suspiciously. "I don't have time to waste on your games." He turned to the door and was about to leave when her words stopped him cold.

"Yes, hurry back to your little star," Dolores called out, "and make sure you treat her well. She's a very valuable piece of property . . . to both of us."

Mark turned and glared at her. "What do you mean?"

"I mean, *husband* dear, that I am very interested in Lacy Black's success. In fact, I have what you might call a vested interest. You see, I couldn't afford the very best legal advice when I went to Mexico for our divorce. Can you imagine my horror when I learned just last week that it was never finalized? You and I are still married, and you and Lacy Black aren't," she taunted. "And in case you don't know, under the laws of the state of California, I own a half interest in all property you have acquired since our marriage, and that includes Lacy Black's contract!"

Mark's face drained of color. "You're lying, and you know it."

Dolores smiled maliciously. "It's easy enough to check, Mark. I believe you'll find that I'm still your legal, if not loving, wife."

"If you tell your lies to anyone else, it'll be the last thing you ever say," he warned.

Her voice became hard. "Don't threaten me, Mark. I've outsmarted you this time, and there's nothing you can do about it."

Dolores noted with satisfaction the nervous tic that was

twitching on his face. She'd spent many angry and sleepless nights since she'd discovered that Mark had taken the Blackburn girl and made her a success, giving her everything that Dolores felt she should have had.

Strangely enough, she did not resent Lacy. In fact, she felt sorry for the kid, because her life was controlled by a ruthless manipulator. Mark was the one she wanted to punish. He'd ruined her life, and he would pay—he'd pay very well.

"What do you want?" Mark asked, knowing that Dolores wasn't stupid enough to fabricate a story that would be so easy to verify.

"I don't want so much, Mark. Not really. I only want one little thing. The problem is, which one? You see, I could either expose you as a bigamist and brand Lacy Black as your mistress, which would ruin you both in Hollywood forever—or I could keep quiet and enjoy my share of Lacy Black's no doubt substantial earnings for the rest of my life."

"You have no claim on Lacy."

The look Dolores gave him was wide-eyed and innocent. "Oh, but I do, Mark. Surely you didn't make the same stupid mistake with her that you did with me. I'm willing to bet that you had her sign such an ironclad contract that the only way she can get out of it is by death."

His angry silence told her that she was right.

Dolores let out an exaggerated sigh. "My dilemma is which to choose. Should I go for financial security, or tear your rotten heart out?"

Mark paled. "This isn't the time or place to be having this conversation," he said nervously. "If someone overhears us, that choice will be taken out of your hands."

She trailed her finger across his cheek. "We wouldn't want that, now, would we? I'll call you to set up a meeting so we can decide what to do. And if you don't show, my next call will be to the newspapers."

Hatred coiled inside Mark like a venomous snake, and he shoved her hand away. "I'll see you in hell, Dolores!" He moved away from her, his footsteps taking him to the door, and the sound of her triumphant laughter followed him out of the room.

Mark found Lacy where he'd left her. With anger still smoldering in his eyes, he grabbed her wrist and pulled her toward the front door, ignoring her protests.

Once they were inside the Cord, she placed her hand on his arm, but he shook it off. "Is something the matter, Mark? What did Dolores do to make you so angry?"

He turned cold eyes on her. "Just shut up, Lacy. I'm not in the mood for conversation with any woman at the moment."

She sat, hurt and silent, as he sped away and drove up the hills so fast that the wheels screeched on the curves. It didn't help his mood any when he was pulled over by a policeman and issued a ticket for speeding.

When they finally reached home, Mark went to his study and slammed the door, leaving Lacy without an explanation.

What could have happened between him and Dolores to make him so angry? Lacy wondered. There had been something almost sinister about his actions tonight—something that frightened her.

She switched off the light and climbed into bed, unable to sleep for a long time. She had just dozed off when she felt the mattress sag.

Mark pulled her against him roughly. "You're mine," he muttered, grinding whisky-wet lips against hers. "And no one will take you away from me—not ever!"

Mark paced back and forth, gnawing on his lip as he tried to decide what he was going to do about Dolores. Two days had passed since she'd made her blackmail demands, and he'd heard nothing from her. He'd tried to find her by contacting her old friends, but without success. He knew her petty little mind—she would make him suffer before she made her final demands.

She'd given him two choices, and either one meant financial ruin. Rage swelled inside him and his eyes burned with hatred. If only Dolores would meet with a timely accident.

He'd thought their divorce was final when he'd married Lacy, but that wouldn't matter to the Hollywood gossips and the fans—and it sure as hell wouldn't matter to the law. Not only would he be ruined—he might even go to jail!

Mark paused at the window that gave him a sweeping view of the studio lot. Signs of prosperity were everywhere. The fact that Sidney Greenway had remained as Pinnacle Pictures' head director had brought them respectability. Mark was aware of the joke that was circulating among his competitors. They called Pinnacle Pictures "the house that Black built." So it was; he didn't deny that. And no one, especially not Dolores, was going to get any part of what belonged to him.

The phone rang, and Mark stared at it for a long moment. Helen's voice came over the intercom. "Miss Divine wishes to speak to you. Shall I tell her you're not in, Mr. Damian?"

"I'll take it, Helen." He lifted the receiver. "Yes?"

"It's time we meet," Dolores said without preamble.

"When?"

Her voice was clipped and cold. "Tomorrow at noon at that little inn we used to frequent during our more . . . intimate days." There was a click, and she was gone.

Mark slammed down the phone and continued his pacing. She would probably expect him to pay her something tomorrow. He'd never convince her that most of Lacy's money had gone back into Pinnacle Pictures, that the rest had been used to discharge his staggering gambling debts.

Somehow he had to find a way to silence Dolores. He visualized her death in every painful way imaginable, then smiled malevolently. He knew what he must do—the bitch was just asking for it.

Mark felt a sudden rush of pleasure. He hadn't gotten where he was without learning how to deal with people who got in his way.

He heard a tentative knock at the door.

"Mark, are you all right?" Lacy asked in concern.

He threw open the door and pulled her into his arms, startling her with his exuberance. "I've never felt better in my life, baby."

"I've been worried about you the last few days. Please tell me what's been bothering you."

Mark shrugged and gave her one of his lopsided, boyish grins. "Just working out a few technical difficulties with my next project. And I just figured out what I need to do, so don't worry." He nuzzled her neck. "Everything's going to be fine, baby—just fine."

She laughed in delight as he scooped her up in his arms and carried her to his leather couch. She lost one of her shoes as he tossed her down and landed beside her.

"What about Helen?" she halfheartedly protested.

"You know that she never intrudes when we're alone. And no one else will get past her either."

Late that afternoon Mark and Lacy entered their home arm in arm. They were both laughing as they passed Ruth's closed bedroom door, but she heard them and was filled with jealousy. Every day she resented her sister more and more.

Two days later, Lacy and Ruth were seated at the breakfast table, Lacy reading her script for the day and Ruth the morning paper. Ruth gave a startled gasp, and Lacy looked up questioningly.

"Dolores Divine is dead! She was killed in an automobile accident at that bad curve here on Mulholland Drive. She went over the cliff!" Ruth exclaimed.

Lacy was horrified. "I can't believe it! I was talking with her just a few nights ago."

Mark entered the room with a smile for them both and gave Lacy a kiss. Ruth's presence didn't seem to bother him this morning as it usually did.

"Why's everyone so gloomy?" he asked cheerfully.

"Oh, Mark, it's terrible," Lacy said. "Dolores is dead."

Mark frowned, and his eyes narrowed. "What does the newspaper say?"

Ruth handed him the front section of the paper. "It says that her car burst into flames." She shuddered. "What a horrible way to go."

Mark quickly scanned the newspaper's account, aware that Lacy was watching him closely. He felt the tension drain from his body when he read that Dolores's death had been ruled accidental. He smiled slightly and folded the newspaper, handing it back to Ruth. "It would be hypocritical on my part to pretend grief. Dolores was bound to meet a tragic end—she just had that kind of personality."

Then he bent down and kissed Lacy briefly. "If you don't mind, I'll skip breakfast this morning. The work's piled up at the studio, and I'm sure we'll be bombarded by reporters and grieving fans, since Pinnacle Pictures made all of Dolores's better films. You stay here and study your lines. I want to start shooting the new picture in the morning." Shaking his head, he sauntered to the door. "She should have been more careful."

Ruth's expression was sardonic. "He doesn't seem to be too heartbroken. But he's probably acting for your benefit. You saw how close they were in Snyder—do you suppose he still loves her?"

Lacy gathered up her script and rose from the table. "Sometimes, Ruth, you're just unbearable."

Lacy went up to her room and flung herself across the wide bed, finding no comfort in the coolness of the satin bedspread beneath her. She remembered the day that Dolores and Mark had come into her life. It seemed so long ago, but it had been little more than two years.

Dolores had once lived in this same house, probably even slept in this bed. And yet today Mark had dismissed her death as coldly as he would a stranger's.

Lacy couldn't help comparing her life to Dolores's. Would Mark grieve if something happened to her? She felt a shiver run down her spine and quickly pushed her disloyal thoughts aside. She was letting her imagination run wild. Mark loved her; she was his wife.

Tears flowed freely down Lacy's cheeks and stained the delicate satin coverlet. Of all those who had known Dolores Divine, Lacy, who hadn't even liked her, was the only one who mourned her passing.

Lacy found it extremely distasteful when Mark announced that he would release all Dolores's films. When she protested, he said it was good business—and what Dolores would have wanted him to do.

With promotional fanfare, Mark hired five Rolls-Royces to head Dolores's funeral procession. The automobiles were crowded with studio bosses and crew members who had worked with her. Lacy and Mark rode alone in the lead car. The ceremony was held at the grave site, with uniformed policemen keeping the curious crowd behind a roped-off area. Even with this precaution, the crowd disrupted the funeral by chanting: "Lacy! Lacy! Lacy!"

She stood beside Mark while he delivered the eulogy. His voice was emotionless as he wove the story of a woman who had risen from obscurity to grace the screen until her name was immortalized for all time. Lacy thought he sounded more like a publicist than a mourner.

As the crowd began to disperse, Lacy took a single long-stemmed red rose and placed it on the bronze casket, feeling a strong kinship with the dead woman, though she didn't know why.

Chapter Eleven

Mark considered it his ultimate triumph when Lacy was given the title Most Beautiful Woman in the World by the Board of Artistic Acknowledgment.

Deep inside, although she hadn't dared admit it to Mark, Lacy was embarrassed by the whole situation. However, she was excited about going to New York City, where she would be presented with a special award in a nationally broadcast ceremony.

Mark's busy schedule wouldn't allow him to accompany her, so he arranged for her to travel by train with Bonny Tate, one of the publicists from the studio.

The day of her departure, Mark escorted Lacy aboard the Silver Streak early, to the private compartment Helen had reserved. Before he left, he gave Lacy a lingering kiss, then smiled down at her. "I never thought I'd be married to the most beautiful woman in the world."

"If I'm beautiful, it's because you have made the image, Mark," Lacy said uncomfortably. If she didn't like to hear the title from Mark's lips, how would she accept it from strangers?

He winked at her. "I had a lot to work with."

Lacy checked her watch. "We'll be pulling out soon."

"I'll miss you, baby. I've instructed Bonny to smooth the way for you, so you shouldn't have any trouble."

Lacy looked up at him. "I wish you were coming with me. I'm nervous about meeting so many new people."

"Just be your charming self and they'll love you. If you need me, you can reach me at the studio. I'll probably sleep there too. You know I can't stand being near your sister."

Lacy smiled sympathetically. "I know. Ruth wanted to come with me, but I told her no. The thought of listening to her complain all the way across the country was more than I could endure."

Mark dipped his head and brushed her lips. "I have to leave now, baby. Call me when you reach New York."

At that moment, Bonny entered with the porter and the luggage, so Lacy wished Mark a hasty good-bye. She looked out the window and watched him disappear into the crowd.

It was past midnight and Bonny had gone to her own compartment. Lacy was having trouble falling asleep because of the constant motion of the train, and the small space seemed to be closing in on her. She had to get out of her compartment, if only for a short while.

She slid out of bed and quietly dressed, thinking she wouldn't have to worry about anyone recognizing her so late at night. Still, she took the precaution of wearing her dark glasses and cramming her platinum hair beneath the brim of a floppy hat.

She made her way down the dimly lit corridor to the drawing room car, which was deserted, except for three men playing cards.

Lacy sat down near a window and picked up a magazine, mindful that her own face leaped off the front cover. There was a restlessness within her that she neither understood nor welcomed.

Bored, she tossed the magazine aside and stared into the darkness for a long time. Occasionally the train would pass a small town and lights would pierce the darkness for a few moments.

"Excuse me, is this seat taken?"

Lacy glanced around at the carful of empty seats and wondered why the man chose to bother her. "None of them are," she said, turning her head to stare back into the darkness.

She was aware that the stranger sat down across from her anyway. After a long moment of silence, she glanced sideways and saw that he had picked up the magazine she had tossed aside. Not wanting to be recognized, she pulled the brim of her hat lower over her forehead and turned back to the window to stare at the man's reflection. His face was more arresting than handsome. His profile was rugged, his jaw stubborn. Since he had dark hair, she guessed his eyes would also be dark, but she couldn't tell because he was looking down at the magazine.

Glancing back at him, she saw that while he was dressed casually, his taste was impeccable, and his clothes were obviously expensive. She leaned her head back and closed her eyes, hoping he would leave.

"Do you always wear sunglasses at night?" he asked.

Lacy stared at him through her tinted lenses. "Do you always strike up conversations with women you don't know?" she responded with asperity.

A smile transformed his rugged features, and he turned the magazine cover toward her. "But you see, I do know you, Miss Black—at least by reputation."

She had started to rise when he spoke again. "No, don't go. Bart Henley asked me to introduce myself to you when he found out that we'd be traveling on the same train."

Lacy had never met Bart Henley, who was the president of the Board of Artistic Acknowledgment.

"Oh, you know Mr. Henley?"

He extended his hand. "We went to school together and now live in the same apartment building in New York. My name's Andrew Mallory."

Lacy recognized his name at once. "The Broadway producer?"

"I plead guilty, but I'm surprised you know who I am."

She took his outstretched hand. "Of course I've heard about you. Hasn't everyone?"

"Have you seen any of my plays?"

Lacy removed her dark glasses and stared into piercing, probing brown eyes. "No, but I hope to while I'm in New York."

"I'll see that you have tickets." He laughed softly. "I've seen every one of your pictures. *Mata Hari* I saw twice."

She found herself blushing like a schoolgirl. "I'm flattered that you've taken notice of me, Mr. Mallory." She became aware that he still held her hand, and she quickly drew hers away.

His eyes flickered just the merest bit. "It's not often that one has the opportunity to talk to the most beautiful woman in the world."

She glanced at him, looking for sarcasm, but found none. "I can assure you the title is an empty one, and I view it as such."

In a move that surprised her, he reached for her right hand, turning it over to inspect the ring she wore.

"What's the story behind this little ring? For a woman who possesses the Raja Star, it seems unpretentious, to say the least."

"It was my mother's, and it means more to me than all my other jewels put together," she answered, wondering why she felt the need to explain to him.

He arched an inquiring eyebrow. "More than your wedding ring?" he asked, indicating the large blue-white diamond that sparkled even in the dimly lit coach.

Lacy jerked her hand free and stared at him in disbelief. Andrew Mallory might be dubbed "the genius of Broadway," but he was rude, and she didn't like him in the least. "Mr. Mallory," she said coolly, "perhaps you think something must be expensive to be valued—I do not."

He leaned back and stared long and hard at the flawless perfection of her face. "Beauty, brains, and sentimentality—remarkable." Now his voice did have a biting tone. "Somehow I hadn't expected you to possess such qualities."

Her anger took her by surprise, and she quickly retaliated.

"That's odd—I expected a wunderkind like you would possess both genius *and* manners. It looks like we were both mistaken."

He was clearly amused. "Touché. If I appear less than dazzled by your luster, Miss Black, it's merely because I have to spend most of my days attempting to placate temperamental actresses. I find your breed, for the most part, shallow and self-centered. Perhaps when I come to know you better, I'll find out that you're different."

Lacy stood up abruptly, shoving her dark glasses back in place. "Don't trouble yourself about me, Mr. Mallory. I will wish you a good night and a good journey. And should we chance to meet again, don't feel that you have to acknowledge me."

As she walked away, she could feel his eyes on her, and she found it very unsettling.

Drew Mallory prided himself on being a good judge of character, but he'd certainly misjudged Lacy Black. He'd been truthful about seeing all her pictures—in fact, he was almost obsessed with her, although he hadn't admitted it to himself until now.

He glanced down at the magazine cover, and Lacy's green eyes seemed to look right into his soul. He'd been rude to her tonight and he hadn't meant to be. Had he been testing her, or maybe himself?

He stared out into the darkness, overcome with a sudden feeling of emptiness. They would meet again—of that he was certain.

New York City was every bit as exciting as Lacy had hoped it would be. In Hollywood it had become impossible for her to walk down the street like a normal person because she was immediately recognized and mobbed. But now, with her floppy hat and dark glasses in place, she found anonymity and enjoyed the freedom it afforded her.

She and Bonny blended in with the other tourists. They rode an open-air bus through Central Park and took a boat trip to view the Statue of Liberty. Lacy was awed by Manhattan's sky-climbing buildings and the soaring bridges that connected the city to the boroughs.

True to his word, Andrew Mallory sent tickets to the Plaza Hotel, where Lacy was staying. That night, she and Bonny were going to the Mary Lord Theatre to attend his latest play, *Upon a Moon-dark Night*. It was the Broadway season's most acclaimed drama, and Lacy wanted to see it, even though she disliked the arrogant director.

Lacy was enthralled from the moment the curtain rose on the first act until it came down on the last. She was on her feet applauding louder than anyone. Andrew Mallory was indeed a genius!

That night, Lacy discovered a new love, a new world—the theater. The actors and actresses on the stage had brought a freshness to their performances that could never be captured on the screen. She realized that she would never feel complete until she'd smelled the aroma of greasepaint and performed before a live audience.

As she and Bonny left the theater, Lacy became aware that she was being surrounded by a loud throng of people who had recognized her. As she tried to duck away the crowd became like a wild thing. The frenzied fans screamed her name and tore at her clothing; rough hands reached out to her, inflicting pain.

"It's Lacy Black!"

"Get a lock of her hair!"

"Take a bead from her jacket—grab her!"

Lacy was swept away by the crowd. She twisted and turned, trying to escape, but the unruly press of humanity pushed her against the wall, and she was afraid that she would be crushed. Until that moment, she hadn't known that there was a sinister side to being adored by the public.

The circle closed in around her, and she couldn't breathe or move. She shut her eyes, sobbing in terror.

"Leave me alone! Please go away!"

* * *

Drew Mallory frantically elbowed his way through the crowd to get to Lacy. Something sharp hit him above the eye, but he ignored the pain, forcefully shoving people out of his way until at last he reached her. When he was close enough to touch her, he stepped between Lacy's trembling body and her overzealous fans.

Thinking that he was one of her tormenters, she struggled against him until he stilled her movements by lifting her in his arms.

"Lacy, don't fight me. It's Drew Mallory, and I'll get you out of here."

Relief washed over her, and she buried her face against his shoulder as he commanded the crowd to move aside. Strangely, a path opened, and he carried her away from harm.

When they reached the front of the theater, a badly shaken Bonny greeted them, her hat missing and the sleeve of her blue evening gown torn.

"I tried to hold on to you, Miss Black, but they shoved me down and I couldn't get to you. Are you hurt?" she asked in concern.

Drew set Lacy on her feet, and she leaned heavily on him for support. Suddenly she felt the ground tilt, and she would have fallen had he not caught her in his arms.

Lacy opened her eyes and blinked in bewilderment. This was definitely not her hotel room. Slowly elevating herself to a sitting position on the green tweed sofa, she observed her surroundings.

It was a small room, and every available space was cluttered with papers. Shelves were overflowing with books, and those volumes that wouldn't fit in the shelves were piled on the floor. A painting of an English hunting scene hung on the wall above the fireplace, and numerous theatrical awards were crowded on the mantel.

"So you're awake." Drew's face was creased with concern as he emerged from the dimly lit kitchenette carrying a damp cloth, which he applied to her head. He handed her a glass of amber liquid. "Here, drink this and you'll feel better."

Hoping it would help her stop shaking, Lacy took a large sip of the liquor. She coughed and her eyes watered, but warmth spread through her body as she pushed the glass away.

"Better?"

She nodded.

"Good."

At last, when she could speak, her eyes ran the length of the room. "Where's Bonny?"

"I'm not sure. When you fainted, the crowd surged around us again, and I had to get you out of there fast. My apartment was nearby, so I brought you here."

Lacy saw that Drew was bleeding above his eye. "You're hurt."

He touched his brow and looked at the blood on his hand. "I'll go take care of this. Don't you move until I get back."

Lacy closed her eyes, still feeling shaky. She didn't think she could move if she wanted to.

Drew soon reappeared with a bandage taped above his eye.

"Was the wound deep?" Lacy asked him.

He smiled down at her. "Let's just say that I'll always have a reminder of this night."

"Perhaps you need stitches. Do you think it'll leave a scar?"

His eyes danced mockingly. "It doesn't matter about me—I'm not receiving a beauty award."

She made an attempt to stand, but she was shaking so much that she sat down again. "I must call the hotel; Bonny will be frantic."

Drew moved to an end table and picked up the phone. Clicking it twice, he spoke into the receiver. "Nancy, connect me with the Plaza Hotel." He placed his hand over the mouthpiece. "What's Bonny's room number?"

"Nine-twenty."

"Have them ring nine-twenty, Nancy." There was a short pause before he spoke again. "Hello, is this Bonny? No need to worry; Miss Black's unharmed. She's still a little shaky, though.

I'll bring her to the hotel as soon as she feels better. No, it won't be necessary for you to come here. Yes, I'm sure Mr. Damian will know you did your duty. Good-bye, Bonny."

He hung up and looked sideways at Lacy. "Is she your watch-dog to see that you don't stray from the fold?"

Lacy took exception to his tone. She'd been so grateful to him for rescuing her, she'd forgotten how much she disliked him. She stood on wobbly legs. "I'll be leaving now. Thank you for your kindness. I don't know what would have happened if you hadn't come along when you did."

"I didn't just happen along. I was told that you were in the audience and I went out front looking for you." He took her arm and gently pushed her back onto the sofa. "You aren't ready to leave yet. You're still pale, and you can't even walk unas-sisted."

She leaned her head back, too weak to protest. "I've never fainted in my life, but those people frightened me."

He sat down beside her, studying her closely, his features unreadable. In spite of her slinky dresses and sexy appearance, she was an innocent, and younger than she looked on the screen. He could smell the alluring aroma of her perfume, and he could remember the feel of her trembling body against his. "The price of fame," he said harshly. "If you want it, you must to be willing to pay the price."

"Fame shouldn't include being trampled and pawed." Lacy tugged at the torn sleeve of her black beaded evening gown, which had been ripped in several places. "Look at this," she said. "It's ruined, and there isn't an inch of my body that doesn't ache." She fought back tears. "I . . . was so frightened until you came along."

She seemed so vulnerable that Drew had to fight the urge to take her in his arms and comfort her. Instead, he lit a cigarette and handed it to her, but she shook her head.

"I've seen you smoke in your pictures," he commented.

"I don't smoke unless the script calls for it. Sometimes Sidney has to do several takes, because when I inhale, I usually choke."

"I see that you are a dedicated actress to the end—do whatever it takes to make a picture."

She had the feeling he was mocking her. "Isn't that what you expect out of your actresses?"

"Of course, but I sure as hell don't know what to expect from you," he said as he pulled her to him. "Maybe a taste of paradise," he murmured, lowering his head and gently touching his lips to hers.

Drew's hold on Lacy was not confining, and yet she couldn't move. She had never known that a kiss could be so soft and yet so exciting. When his hands tangled in her hair and he brought her closer to him, she remembered Mark, and struggled to get out of Drew's arms.

"No!" she said through trembling lips. "I can't do this to my husband."

Drew released her abruptly and rose to put some distance between them.

"I must leave now," Lacy said, avoiding his eyes because she didn't understand what had just happened between them. He had excited her in a way that Mark never had, and she felt disloyal. "Mark . . . my husband will be phoning tonight, and he'll be upset if I'm not there to take his call."

Drew shoved his hands in his pockets, angry with himself, but lashing out at her because she was the reason for his frustration. "So among your other virtues, I can add that you're a faithful little wife—the tally grows."

"Yes, as a matter of fact, I am faithful to my husband. Did you imagine that I'd be so grateful to you for rescuing me that I'd fall into bed with you?"

Drew gave her a whimsical smile. "I could only hope."

Lacy's anger gave her the strength to stand up and move to the door. "Good-bye, Mr. Mallory."

He imagined her walking out of his life forever, and he was beside her in an instant, turning her to face him. "I wouldn't blame you if you left, but I'm asking you not to until I explain some things. Could we start all over and pretend that we've just met, and that we admire each other's work?"

"I do admire your work, Mr. Mallory." She looked at him through sooty lashes. "I can admire the work and not like the man."

"Although the man has been saying and doing all the wrong things, he admires the lady more than any woman who ever breathed," Drew said as though the admission had been torn from him. "Had you known me better, you would have seen through me from the very beginning."

Green eyes met dark eyes, and Lacy shook her head in disbelief. "Must you taunt me?"

He reached out to touch her face softly and she saw that his hand trembled. "I have been merely taunting myself, Lacy. If you only knew," he continued, slowly pulling her resisting body closer to his, "how much courage it took for me to approach you that night on the train. Or that while you were watching my play tonight, I was pacing the lobby, hoping for a chance to speak to you again." He took in a deep breath before he continued. "When I thought the crowd had trampled you, I was like a man possessed until I got to you and saw that you were safe."

She looked into his eyes and knew that he was speaking the truth. "How can this be, Drew? We don't even know each other."

He raised her chin and she was lost in his lustrous brown eyes.

"It's as if I've known you all my life, and have only been waiting to find you. I knew the night on the train that you would be my one and only love."

She shook her head as feelings she had been trying to suppress spilled out. "I . . . can't love you."

He laid his rough cheek against her smooth one. "But you do, Lacy. I couldn't love you this much if it weren't returned."

She hid her face against his shirtfront as the most powerful emotions she'd ever felt shook her slender body. The attraction between them was overwhelming, but how could it have happened so fast?

Slowly she raised her face and looked at him. "Drew, I'm so confused. Please don't say any more."

He nodded. "Could I ask just one thing of you?"

Her eyes swam with tears. "If I can grant it, I will."

He dipped his dark head. "Kiss me willingly. Give me that to remember you by."

She didn't feel herself moving forward, but she did. His lips touched hers softly, reverently, and it was as if the earth opened up and swallowed her. There was no today; there was no tomorrow; there was only this moment when true love was discovered, treasured, and then denied.

Suddenly Drew lifted his head and ran his hand nervously though his hair. "I dare not do that again," he said, turning away and closing his eyes.

When he turned back a moment later, he appeared perfectly composed. "Come, I'll see you to your hotel now."

He hurriedly guided Lacy out the door and into the elevator, as if he couldn't get rid of her fast enough. They were silent as he led her across the lobby and out to the street, where he instructed the doorman to hail a cab.

Drew helped her inside and climbed in beside her, sitting near her, but not touching her. "To the Plaza," he said in an emotionless voice that made Lacy wonder if she'd only imagined what had happened between them.

The driver stared at Lacy for a long moment. "Aren't you Lacy Black?" he asked with a thick Brooklyn accent.

"No, she's not," Drew said in pretended irritation. "Everyone thinks she resembles that actress, but I can't see it. It's getting so I can't take her anywhere without being mobbed."

The driver pulled down his visor and stared at the picture that was attached. It was Lacy dressed as Mata Hari. "Too bad. Lacy's my dream girl. What I wouldn't give to spend a few moments alone with her."

Drew glanced down at Lacy with a look that was like a caress. "Believe me, mister, a few moments wouldn't be enough."

Chapter Twelve

When she returned to her suite at the Plaza, Lacy had to contend with an overwrought Bonny, who was sure Mark would blame her for what had happened at the theater.

After calming Bonny down and sending her off to bed, Lacy soaked in a hot bath, too exhausted to think. She was still wide-awake when she slid into bed and turned off the bedside lamp.

Staring into the darkness, she was deeply troubled. Why had she allowed Drew to kiss her tonight? And why did she feel this emptiness inside, as if she'd lost something very precious? She tried not to remember how it felt to be in Drew's arms and to have his lips on hers.

"No!" she cried, burying her face in her pillow. "I can't love you, Drew; it would be against everything I believe. I won't be like my mother."

Lacy was startled out of her misery when she heard the shrill ring of the telephone. She lifted the receiver, her heart pounding with some uncontrollable excitement. She expected it to be Drew, and her voice was breathless. "Hello?"

"Oh, baby," Mark said from across the miles, "the way you

sound, I wish I was with you now. Are you in bed?"

She sat up, suppressing her disappointment and feeling guilty for wanting the caller to be Drew. "Yes, Mark, I am."

She could hear him breathing into the phone. "Can you feel me there with you?"

"I'm tired, Mark. I was mobbed by a crowd at the theater tonight."

"Yeah, baby, I know. I heard about it on Walter Winchell's broadcast. It couldn't have been better staged if I'd planned it myself. It's been picked up by every newscast from coast to coast."

Lacy's grip tightened on the phone. "The crowd tried to trample me."

"That's what's so great, baby. You're the hottest news item right now. Your new picture comes out in three weeks. We'll try to ride this for all it's worth. We couldn't buy publicity like this."

A lone tear rolled down Lacy's cheek. "Yes, you're right, Mark. We can't buy publicity like that."

In that moment, Lacy wondered if Mark loved her at all or just the image he'd created.

"I hear music and someone laughing. Are you having a party?" she asked.

"Uh, yes. I'm having a few department heads over as a way of thanking them for pulling together on my last project." There was a pause. "I may as well tell you now. If I don't, Ruth will. I didn't want her hanging around the house, so I sent her to a hotel for the weekend. You know how I feel about her."

"Yes, I know. I'm tired now, Mark. I'm going to sleep."

"Sure, baby, sure. You have to look fresh for the awards tomorrow night."

Lacy heard the click on the other end of the wire and it went dead—as dead as she felt inside. Not once had Mark asked how she felt or if she'd been injured. She didn't really understand his kind of love.

So much had happened in the space of one day, it was hours

before Lacy finally fell asleep. She tried not to think about Drew Mallory, who kept pushing his way into her mind, and she refused to think of Mark. It was too painful.

When Mark hung up the phone after talking to Lacy, he turned, smiling at the pretty redhead who leaned against the door, a glass of champagne balanced in her hand. "I should leave now, Mr. Damian," she said, looking wide-eyed and innocent. "Everyone else has gone."

Mark moved slowly toward her. "Has anyone ever told you, baby, that you have the kind of face that would light up the screen?"

"Do you really think so, Mr. Damian?" she asked breathlessly.

He moved toward her and held out his hand. "Yes, I do." He pulled her against his body. "I want you in my bed, baby."

She smiled up at him coyly, running her fingers up the buttons of his shirtfront. "I've heard you called a womanizer, Mr. Damian. Could it be true?"

"Would it make any difference?"

"No." She snuggled up against him. "But what about your wife? I can't believe that anyone married to Lacy Black would be interested in me."

Mark gripped her chin painfully and forced her face up until she looked into his eyes. "My wife has nothing to do with you and me. Do you want my help or don't you?"

She looked uncertain, then nervously nodded. "I do. I want to learn everything you can teach me."

Mark took her hand and led her to the stairs toward the bedroom. "You'll get your first lesson tonight."

Lacy awoke when the telephone rang. Lifting the receiver, she said sleepily, "Hello?"

"Sorry to disturb you so early," Drew said, "but I was worried about you."

She heard genuine concern in his voice.

"I'm fine," she replied, snuggling beneath the bedcovers and savoring the sound of his deep voice.

"I also had another reason for calling. I wanted to tell you that I'm sorry about last night."

She sat up slowly, a deep ache forming inside. So he was having regrets about what had happened between them, while she couldn't stop thinking about him. "No apology is necessary, Mr. Mallory," she said coolly.

"Lacy," he said carefully, "don't misunderstand me. I meant every word I said to you, and I'm not sorry I kissed you. What I'm apologizing for is taking advantage of you when you were at your most vulnerable."

"We'll pretend that last night didn't happen," she said with difficulty.

There was a long pause. "I don't think either of us will be able to forget, Lacy."

"Good-bye, Drew," she said softly.

"No, not good-bye. I'll see you tonight at the awards ceremony."

She closed her eyes, trying to think of something clever to say. Then she realized that there could be no pretense between them. "Until then."

With great effort, she hung up the phone, breaking the connection to something very precious in her life—a love that she had no right to, a love that could never be.

The ballroom of the Plaza was filled with New York's elite. The governor, a senator, and even a prince from an Arabic country was present. But none of them received the attention that Lacy Black did when she was escorted to the head table by the mayor of New York City.

She was dazzling in a tight-fitting red dress that sparkled with thousands of hand-sewn sequins.The red dress had been Mark's idea. Always keep them guessing, he had told her.

Drew, who was already seated at the head table, watched

Lacy's progress. To the others she might appear calm and poised, but he knew she was frightened and shy. For the briefest moment, her eyes met his, and he nodded ever so slightly.

The before-dinner speeches seemed to go on forever, with each politician trying to outdo his predecessor. At last, dinner was over and it was time to present the awards. There was an award given to an American poet, a South American violinist, and an English author. Finally, it was time to present the award that the audience had been waiting for—The Most Beautiful Woman in the World.

Lacy tightly clasped her hands together beneath the table to still their trembling. She'd dreaded this moment and prayed that she would get through it without a serious blunder.

Her eyes widened in amazement when Drew was introduced as her presenter.

He looked handsome in his black tuxedo, and Lacy was sure there wasn't a woman in the audience who wasn't aware of his maleness and sensuality.

Drew smiled after the flowery introduction he received from Bart Henley.

"Troy had its Helen, Napoléon had his Josephine, and we have Lacy Black," he began and then smiled. "That, ladies and gentlemen, was the beginning of the speech that was given to me to deliver tonight. But after I met the real Lacy Black, I knew that she wouldn't like the comparisons, and she doesn't care for flattery. So I stayed up half the night writing my own speech, and then threw it in the trash this morning. Let me say simply that Miss Black is as beautiful of heart as she is of face. Like the rest of the world, I fell under her spell, and like the rest of the world, she took my heart. It is my very great honor to present to you at this time the most beautiful woman in the world, Lacy Black."

Everyone in the audience stood, applauding vigorously.

There were tears in Lacy's eyes as she rose and walked to Drew. He winked at her and then formally kissed her on both cheeks before handing her a crystal statue and a framed certificate.

Drew took his seat and Lacy looked out on a sea of faces. She was frightened at first, but suddenly warmth spread over her and she could almost feel Drew sending her courage. Ignoring the speech that Mark had insisted she memorize, she simply said what was in her heart.

"I've never thought of myself as beautiful, but I have to say that coming here to New York City to accept this award has been the happiest time of my life. I wouldn't have missed it for the world. Thank you."

Lacy received a standing ovation as she made her way back to her seat. If she had looked at Drew at that moment, she would have seen a bittersweet smile on his face. It had been the happiest few days of his life as well—and the saddest.

Back in Hollywood, Mark angrily switched off the radio. What did Lacy think she was doing? That wasn't the speech he'd prepared. She was supposed to thank him and mention his name three different times, but she hadn't even mentioned him once.

By the time she returned to Hollywood, Lacy acknowledged to herself that she no longer loved Mark. She was riddled with guilt because of her feelings for Drew, and it took her several days before she gathered the courage to tell Mark about Drew and how he'd been the one to save her from the mob.

Mark scoffed. "I've never met him, but I once attended a party that was given in his honor. He was an arrogant bastard, although I hear the women like him well enough. He's never had to work for anything in his life. He was born into old money and educated at one of those fancy private schools. He wrote his first hit play at age twenty. They call him a genius and a boy wonder, but I don't see it."

"He saved my life, remember?"

"So he got to play Sir Galahad to your damsel in distress. Don't think I'm jealous of him, baby. I could tell even over the radio that he was in love with you. He probably wanted you real bad, maybe even has fantasies about you, but you belong to me."

Lacy never again mentioned Drew to anyone, but he wasn't ever far from her thoughts. Memories of him often lulled her to sleep. She supposed the experts would probably say that people couldn't fall in love so quickly—but the experts would be wrong. She did love him.

There would always be something missing from her life, something she could never have—fulfillment with Drew.

Chapter Thirteen

Two more Lacy Black war pictures were rushed into production, and when they opened, the tickets were sold out for weeks in advance.

At the mansion on Mulholland Drive, Lacy and Mark slipped into an uneasy alliance. They spent less and less time together, and it suited them both. Lacy devoted herself to her work, leaving the house before dawn and not returning until long after dark. She didn't know how Mark occupied his time outside the studio, and she really didn't care. After almost three years of marriage, she still had no insight into Mark's inner thoughts; in fact, she didn't know him at all.

Ruth stepped out onto the veranda with a cup of coffee in her hand. She had cleverly ingratiated herself into the household, becoming indispensable, and there was no longer any mention of her leaving. She planned the menus, hired and fired the help, and arranged the glamorous parties that Mark was so fond of hosting. Of course, she resented the fact that she was never invited to those parties.

Leaning against the banister, she watched Lacy on the tennis court with the pro whom Mark had hired to give her lessons. The man was tan, blond, and good-looking, and obviously enamored of his pupil. Ruth ground her teeth together—of course perfect little Lacy didn't even seem to notice he was a man.

She watched Lacy serve the ball with a powerful backhand. The ball hit in bounds, but the instructor was unable to return it, giving Lacy the game point. Everything Lacy did came easily to her, whether it was playing tennis, acting, or learning to drive. Ruth was filled with envy because she couldn't have what she coveted most—she wanted to be Lacy Black!

Lacy came up the walk with a healthy glow on her face. She was in such good physical condition that she was hardly out of breath. "You should try tennis, Ruth," she said enthusiastically. "It's great exercise."

"Not me. I'm not going to make an ass out of myself chasing after that little ball."

Lacy tossed her racket on a lounge chair and moved into the house. "I'm going for a swim to cool down. If Mark calls, let me know."

"I'm not your secretary," Ruth snapped.

Lacy sighed, trying not to lose her patience. "Ruth, why do you insist on being difficult? I'd do the same for you."

"I don't get any calls."

"Never mind. Consuela will do it."

Ruth watched her sister disappear upstairs just as the phone rang. She quickly lifted the receiver. "Hello?"

"Ruth, let me speak to Lacy."

"Sorry, Mark. She's at the pool and doesn't want to be bothered."

She could hear the impatience in his voice. "Tell her that I'll be home within an hour, and I need to see her. I have to go back to the office tonight, and can only stay long enough to explain this new scene to her."

"Sure, Mark, I'll tell her." Ruth smirked. *Go back to the office indeed,* she thought, hanging up the phone. Everyone knew that

Mark was seeing other women—that is, everyone except Lacy. Or if she did know, she chose to ignore it. Wouldn't Lacy be a laughingstock if her fans ever learned that the world's most famous sex symbol couldn't even keep her own husband satisfied?

Ruth's breath came out in a soft pant as she envisioned luring Mark into her bed. She knew a lot of ways to satisfy him and keep him coming back for more.

At that moment Lacy reappeared, wearing a bathing suit. "Was the phone for me?" she asked as she pushed her platinum curls into a bathing cap.

"No. Wrong number."

The cab stopped before the sprawling Spanish-style house, and a man got out, climbed up the steps, and rang the doorbell.

"Señor, are you expected?" Consuela asked as she stared up at the tall stranger.

"Not exactly, but I'm a friend of Miss Black's. If you would just tell her I'm here, I know she'll see me."

"And your name, señor?"

"Who is it, Consuela?" Another woman appeared behind the housekeeper—a woman who bore a faint resemblance to Lacy.

"I'm a friend of your daughter's from New York. Perhaps Lacy's told you about me. My name's Andrew Mallory."

Ruth let out her breath in a hiss. "I'm nobody's mother, Mr. Mallory. And if you want to see her, you'll need an appointment."

Drew looked uncomfortable. "I'm sorry if I offended you. Please tell Lacy I'm here. I'm leaving the country, and I must see her before I go."

Ruth was angry. How dare this man mistake her for Lacy's mother! She would have sent him away immediately but for something she saw in his eyes. There was a softness when he spoke of Lacy, and a desperation when he thought he wouldn't get to see her.

Ruth's eyes narrowed calculatingly. Andrew Mallory was in

love with Lacy! It looked like her sister wasn't the innocent she pretended to be. Maybe more had happened between them in New York than Lacy was telling.

Ruth opened the door wider. Mark was expected home at any moment. It might prove interesting if he saw Lacy and this man together.

"Come in, Mr. Mallory. I'll show you the way. You'll find Lacy at the pool."

Lacy arched into a swan dive and swam underwater to the shallow end of the pool. She climbed up the steps and removed her swimming cap, tossing it onto a glass tabletop. The sun was bright, so she put on her sunglasses. She reached for a glass of lemonade and was about to raise it to her lips when a shadow fell across her face.

She glanced up, her heart stopping as Drew smiled down at her.

"Can you spare a thirsty man a glass of that lemonade?"

She tried to reply, but seeing him again so unexpectedly robbed her of speech.

She handed him her glass, able to speak at last. "You're a long way from home, Drew. What are you doing in California?"

Drew's hand closed around hers and lingered there for a moment before he took the glass from her. "I came to see you."

Lacy was glad she was wearing her sunglasses, because he couldn't see that her eyes had filled with tears. She hadn't known until that moment just how much she'd needed to see him again. Her eyes lingered on the scar over his eyebrow—the scar he'd gotten the night he'd rescued her.

"It's good to see you." She tried to make her voice sound casual, but she felt a tear roll from beneath her sunglasses, betraying her true feelings.

Love was being acknowledged without the touch they longed for, without the kiss they ached for, merely with two hearts beating as one.

"Why, Drew?"

"I could tell you that I haven't been able to get you out of my thoughts—day or night. Or that I've never felt about a woman the way I feel about you."

Lacy brushed the tear away. "No, please don't. I don't want to hear this."

"Lacy, I'm going away, and I needed to see you this last time. Will you remove those damned glasses so I can see your eyes?"

She reached up and removed the sunglasses, and he stared into misty green eyes that reflected the same tragic love he felt.

"I knew I couldn't be wrong. You feel it too."

"No, Drew, no."

At that moment, Lacy glanced up the path and saw Mark walking toward them. She could tell by his jerky motions that he was angry.

Drew turned to follow her gaze, then turned back to her. "I don't have much time, so I'll just say that I love you and I want you to leave him."

He watched her eyes glow with happiness, then fill with pain.

"I can't, Drew," she whispered. "You know that."

By now Mark was within hearing distance, and Lacy turned to him. "Mark, this is Andrew Mallory. You remember I told you about him."

The two men shook hands, eyeing each other with hostility all the while. "Of course, Mallory. What brings you to our sunny shores? Finally decided to give Hollywood a try? I might be able to use a man of your talents at Pinnacle Pictures."

Drew's eyes moved to Lacy. "Thank you, but I'm leaving in the morning."

Mark possessively slipped his arm around Lacy. "What is it about Broadway directors that makes them shun our humble art form?"

Drew refused to be baited by Mark, who was deliberately being offensive. For Lacy's sake, he wouldn't retaliate, but he couldn't help saying, "Actually, I'd love the chance to direct Lacy on Broadway."

"My wife works only for me," Mark said. In a calculated

show of ownership, he bent to give her a kiss, but Lacy turned her head, and his lips only brushed her cheek.

Drew realized that his presence was only causing Lacy pain. He placed his glass on the table. "I must be going, but before I do, I'd like to invite the two of you to dinner tonight."

Mark shook his head. "Sorry, I have to get back to the studio, and Lacy won't go without me. Perhaps some other time."

"I'm returning to New York in the morning. After I settle my affairs, I'll be going to Canada, where I'll be training with the RAF. After that, I'll be reporting to a base somewhere in England."

Lacy gasped. "You're not British. Why would you get involved in their war?"

Drew's eyes went to Lacy, as if Mark's presence didn't matter. "My mother was English, and I spent much of my childhood in London. My grandmother still lives there."

Mark looked at Drew as if he'd lost his mind. "You're an artist, not a flyer."

"At the risk of sounding maudlin, I believe we should each, in our own way, fight against Nazism. If we stop Hitler in Europe, we won't have to fight him here."

"Ah, a misguided hero," Mark said dismissively. "I'm a coward myself."

Lacy wanted to beg Drew not to go. She couldn't bear to think of him being in danger, but she had no right to ask him to stay. "You feel you must do this?"

Drew gave her a half smile. "Call me a fool—everyone else has."

She shook her head. "No. You are a hero to me."

Mark's hand gripped Lacy's wrist so tightly that pain shot through her arm. "Sorry if I seem inhospitable, Mallory, but I really must talk to my wife. You will let us hear from you, won't you?"

Drew's eyes locked with Lacy's. "You can bet on it."

Lacy pushed Mark's hand away and offered her hand to Drew.

"You must take the greatest care of yourself. Don't let anything . . . happen to you."

Drew felt her press something into his hand, and he realized that she had given him her mother's ring, her most prized possession. He understood the significance of the gesture.

"Good-bye, Mr. Mallory," she said softly, her eyes incredibly sad.

"Good-bye, Miss Black." His words sounded impersonal, but the love he felt for her was there for all to see.

Drew turned away abruptly, without speaking to Mark. He wished he'd never come, because it was tearing out his heart to leave her.

When he stepped into the waiting cab, he slipped her ring on his little finger. He would wear it as long as he lived. It gave him some comfort to know that he had something she treasured.

Mark stared at Lacy suspiciously. "Just what went on between the two of you in New York? And for that matter, what was going on right here under my nose?"

She retrieved her bathing cap and placed it on her head. "I was just saying farewell to a good friend."

Mark grabbed her by the chin and forced her to look at him. "I know what I saw, and it wasn't just friendship that passed between the two of you."

Lacy pushed his hand away and walked quickly around the pool, where she climbed up to the high diving board. If Mark wanted to talk to her, he'd have to go in the pool to do it. She dove under the water, where she could camouflage her tears and hide her broken heart.

When at last she surfaced at the side of the pool, Mark was waiting for her with a heavy bath towel. When she climbed out, he wrapped it around her. "I'm sorry, baby. I guess I'm just jealous of anyone you admire."

"You don't have to worry about Andrew Mallory, Mark. He knows I'm your wife."

Mark slid his arm around her, leading her toward the house. Perhaps he'd been too neglectful of her lately and needed to spend more time with her.

"I tell you what, baby. I'll stay home tonight and we can dine together—would you like that?"

"If that's what you want, Mark." All she could think of was Drew, and she was having trouble controlling the need to cry.

Ruth, who had witnessed the incident from the veranda, had been too far away to sense the tension. She saw Mark put his arm around Lacy as they walked toward the house. Apparently her little plan hadn't worked.

Chapter Fourteen

Lacy and Mark were having dinner alone, and though Mark was his most charming, she contributed very little to the conversation. Drew's departure had left her feeling devastated. Pleading a headache, she went to bed early to curl up with the new script that Mark wanted her to read. As she scanned the first page, her stomach twisted into a sick knot. Halfway through the script, she threw it across the room in disgust.

She slid out of bed and, not bothering to put on her robe, marched out of her bedroom and into Mark's study, ready for a confrontation.

He was talking on the phone and looked up at her questioningly.

"No!" she said hotly. "Emphatically, no!"

He covered the mouthpiece and said, "I beg your pardon. What do you mean, 'no'?"

"I won't do this movie, Mark. It's vulgar and I won't do it!"

His eyes narrowed dangerously. "Hold on a minute, Helen," he said, speaking to his secretary. Then his gaze bore into Lacy. "Damn it, can't this wait? You can see I'm on the phone."

Lacy planted her body in front of him and shook her head. "No, it can't wait. I want to talk to you now! This script is nothing more than flesh peddling. I've never read anything in such bad taste. I refuse to play a fallen woman who is intimate with every man in the French foreign legion!"

The sight of her half-clad body, and the passion ignited by her anger, stirred Mark's desire. He dragged his eyes away from the sight of her breasts straining against the thin material of her nightgown. He couldn't think about how desirable she was just now because he had to remain in control so he could bend her to his will. "You'll do as you're told, just like any bit player who is under contract to my studio."

"Don't talk to me about a contract, Mark. I'd rather give up acting altogether than do a picture like this one."

Without saying good-bye to Helen, he slammed down the telephone and grabbed Lacy, slinging her onto the sofa. Before she could scramble away, he was on top of her. "You'll do what I say—everything I say."

His hand moved up her leg and she pushed it aside, violently struggling to get away from him, but he held her there while his hands moved over her breasts.

"No, I won't, not this time. Nothing you say or do will make me change my mind."

Unknown to Lacy and Mark, Ruth had quietly slipped downstairs and observed them from the darkness of the hallway, her eyes gleaming at the sight of Mark's unleashed passion. She licked her lips, pretending it was her mouth that was crushed against his and not Lacy's. She moaned with desire when she watched him expose Lacy's breasts. Ruth's hand went to her own breasts and she fantasized that Mark was touching her.

Lacy's voice cut through Ruth's illusion and also halted Mark.

"Get off me; leave me alone!" Lacy demanded. She couldn't stand the feel of Mark's hands on her body. "I don't want you to touch me."

Lacy had never refused him before. At first he was stunned by her denial, and then he became enraged. He jerked her head forward, pressing his thumbs painfully against her temples, his face distorted. "Don't ever think you can defy me, Lacy. I tell you what to do and when to do it. You are nothing without me."

There had been times when Lacy had been afraid of Mark, but never more than now. She shoved him aside and managed to get away from him. With fear driving her, she hurried toward the door, leaning against it for support.

"I won't do that picture, Mark. Don't ever ask me to again." Without giving him time to reply, she rushed from the room, not seeing Ruth, who had stepped back into the shadows.

Lacy reached her bedroom and closed the door, fearful that Mark might come after her. She had never defied him so openly, but no matter what he did to her, she wasn't going to back down this time. She swallowed the knot of fear that had stuck in her throat, prepared to face his anger—but he didn't come.

When several moments passed and she realized he hadn't followed her, she retrieved the scattered script, ripped it up, and threw it in the trash can in her dressing room.

Strangely enough, Lacy felt calm as she climbed into bed, switched off the light, and closed her eyes. She had taken a stand against Mark tonight and it felt wonderful. Knowing and loving a man like Drew had given her the courage she'd needed to take her first step toward escaping Mark's iron-tight grip on her life. The more she loved Drew, the less she could tolerate Mark's selfish demands, and the more she hated the thought of him making love to her.

"Drew, oh, Drew," she whispered. "I pray that God will keep you safe, wherever you are."

Mark would have gone after Lacy, but Ruth sauntered into the room, her flowered robe unbelted, her body clearly visible through the transparent nightgown she wore.

"What you need, Mark, is a woman who knows how to treat you. Lacy knows nothing about satisfying a man."

Anger still smoldered in his eyes. "I have no doubt that you do."

Catlike, she moved toward him. "I know things that would keep you in bed for a week," she purred.

His eyes dipped to her breasts, which were so large they bounced with each step she took. Suddenly, he wanted to touch them, to bury his face in them and feel their softness. He managed to keep control, but just barely. "You're disgusting, Ruth."

Wetting her red lips, she pressed against him. "Don't act pure, Mark. I know about your women. Even though my sister is blind to your affairs, I know they are numerous."

He gave her a prolonged look, but his words held a distinct threat. "Have you told Lacy?"

"Of course not." Ruth slid her hand up his arm. "Why should I? She's getting what she deserves."

"You're a bitch, Ruth."

She rubbed against him and smiled when she felt his arousal swell against her thigh. "Have you ever been in bed with a bitch in heat?"

Hot passion thundered through Mark's body, and he grabbed Ruth, yanking her forward and grinding his mouth against hers. She rubbed her body along his, wanting to tear her nightgown off and feel him inside her.

A bolt of electricity went through Mark's body as Ruth jammed her tongue into his mouth, plunging back and forth while her hand went down to unzip his pants, her fingers sliding across his naked flesh.

When she heard a hiss issue from deep inside him, she turned, closed the door, and shot the lock.

Mark watched, fascinated, while she dropped her robe and then her gown.

Ruth was stockier than Lacy, and didn't have her delicate features, but she had something that set Mark on fire. She swung her hips as she walked toward him, her voluptuous breasts bouncing their invitation.

Mark had always despised Ruth, but right now he wanted

her more than he loathed her. He grabbed her and their bodies fused together as he gave her a passionate kiss. They dropped to the floor, frantically making love. Afterward, when he was sure he could give no more, she stroked him into hardness and again the ritual was repeated.

Daringly, Ruth took his hand and led him up the stairs, past Lacy's closed door, to his bedroom. Once inside, she turned on the shower and pulled an eager Mark in with her. While water cascaded down on them, Ruth dropped to her knees, lathering him with soap, starting at his toes and working upward.

Mark groaned as her soap-slicked hands worked him up and down. When he could stand it no longer, he picked her up and she latched her legs around his waist. Pounding her against the walls of the shower, he yelled out in total satisfaction, unmindful of Lacy in the next room.

"Damn, you're good," he said under his breath against her ear. "I can't seem to get enough of you."

Slyly Ruth stepped out of the shower and tossed him a towel. "There will be other nights and other surprises."

He wrapped the towel about his waist and stared at her. There was no remorse in either of them, just an unspoken understanding that they would do this again, often. Mark was excited at the thought that Ruth would be available to him anytime he wanted her.

"Of course, you won't tell Lacy about this," he said, trying to appear nonchalant. He didn't want to do anything to upset Lacy at the moment.

Ruth tossed her damp hair. "No. Lacy will never know."

"You'll come to me whenever I want you?"

She could hardly keep the satisfaction from showing on her face. "I'll be here for you anytime you want me. I always have been."

Mark was still pressing Lacy to do his film about the foreign legion, and she still refused. A battle of wills had developed, and there was now cold silence between them.

Lacy lay stretched out on the wooden lounge chair in a semi-reclining position, her eyes closed against the glare of the sun. Mark insisted that she sunbathe for at least an hour every day to maintain the tanned perfection of her skin.

Ruth brought Lacy a tall, frosty glass of juice, while she smiled at Mark over Lacy's head.

"This isn't fresh-squeezed, Ruth," Lacy observed in irritation as she saw the wink Mark gave Ruth.

"No, it isn't. Consuela has not gotten around to squeezing orange juice yet, so I just poured some from a can."

Lacy shoved the glass away. "Tell Consuela I'll wait for fresh juice."

Ruth shoved the glass back at her sister, something she would never have done before Mark became her lover. "Tell Consuela yourself. I'm sick of waiting on you like I'm one of the servants."

Lacy was no longer intimidated by her sister, and her anger flared. "No, you aren't a servant, Ruth; the servants earn the money I give them—you don't."

Ruth caught Mark's eye and grinned. "Oh, I earn my keep. Don't you think so, Mark?"

His mouth tightened, and he sent Ruth a warning glance. "You are being hard on your sister, Lacy. You should try to be more understanding."

All her life, Lacy had been manipulated by others: first by her father and Ruth, and then by Mark. Loving Drew made her realize that there were people in the world who loved unselfishly. She had grown more confident and refused to be pushed around anymore. She was going to make changes in her life, starting now.

"Ruth, I've allowed you to stay this long because I felt sorry for you and you had nowhere else to go. Now I want you to find a home of your own."

Ruth was stunned, and a little frightened that Lacy might be serious. Hatred swelled inside her, and venom poured from her lips. "I'm not leaving just because you say so. I met Mark the same time you did, and I have just as much right to be here as you do. You're no longer the kind-spirited girl you used to be. You're only a facade. I don't know why you think you're so special; you're no more an actress than I am," Ruth ranted. "It's just like Mark says. All you have to do is wiggle your ass and no one notices that you can't act."

Mark's voice was harsh. "Ruth, you go too far."

Lacy held out her hand to silence Mark. She stood slowly, her face suddenly tragically sad, while tears swam in her green eyes. "How can you say that to me, Ruth? You, who took care of me after Mama ran off. Since Daddy disowned me, you're the only family I have left. We're sisters, and that should mean something."

By now tears were streaming down Lacy's face, and Ruth looked puzzled, her face softening slightly. "Lacy, I never knew you felt that way about me."

Lacy threw back her head, and laughter spilled from her lips. "I don't Ruth, but I made *you* believe, didn't I? And I didn't even have to wiggle my ass. That, big sister, is what being an actress is all about."

Ruth turned to Mark. "See how cruel she is? If I weren't so loyal, I'd have left long ago."

Mark watched Ruth stalk into the house before he spoke to his wife. "Are you happy now that you've proved a point?"

"Happy?" Lacy repeated. "Not exactly, but the point had to be made all the same. I meant what I said; I want her out of here."

Mark shrugged, pretending indifference. "She's your sister. If you want her out, that's fine with me. But think twice before you let her go. She does a lot for you."

"You don't know how it feels to have her in the house. Every day I dread coming home, knowing that she'll be here. It's even begun to affect my work."

Mark would never allow anything to interfere with Lacy's career. "What do you suggest?"

She sighed. "I don't know. Perhaps we should have a small

house built for her beyond the tennis courts. That way she wouldn't be constantly underfoot."

The memory of Ruth's unconventional lovemaking stirred Mark's blood. He had gone to her bed every night for the last two weeks. There was no pretense of love between them, only animal lust. He doubted that Ruth was capable of love any more than he was. But he liked having her at his beck and call, and a house of her own would give them more privacy. "That's a good idea. I'll talk to a contractor next week."

"Do it as soon as you can. You don't have to listen to her complain—I do."

"No," he said, lifting the morning paper to cover his smile. "I hear no complaints from her."

Chapter Fifteen

1940

Germany had conquered six European countries in three months. France, the last to fall, had been finished off in only nine days. England now stood alone against a ravenous Hitler, who seemed determined to gobble up the whole world. The Nazi dictator had bragged that he would soon march his victorious troops across England. But he hadn't reckoned on the courageous determination of the English people, or the valiant fighting power of the RAF, who courageously pounded back at the German Luftwaffe as they conducted their nightly air assaults on London and other targeted cities in England.

Andrew Mallory and volunteer pilots from every corner of the world had converged on a grateful England to join the ranks of the RAF. He'd spent three months in Toronto, Canada, learning to fly American Fairchilds. After that, he was transferred to Moose Jaw, Saskatchewan, for RAF training.

Now he was in England, welcomed with overwhelming appreciation by the English airmen. Their casualties were high, and the life of a fighter pilot was cheap, but the constant danger and living for the moment suited Drew's somber mood as he tried to put Lacy from his mind.

He hadn't heard from her since he'd left her looking heartbreakingly sad as Mark Damian had held her possessively—he really hadn't expected that she would contact him, but he had hoped. Lacy had made it clear that no matter what her feelings for him were, she would honor her marriage vows, and he knew she meant it. Sometimes he hated himself for being such a fool and loving a married woman; sometimes he felt that he hated her because he couldn't have her. But always the memory of her haunted him and tormented his every waking moment.

It was an overcast day with misty rain falling as Drew tightened the straps on his bright orange life jacket before climbing into the cockpit of his Hurricane. His gaze went to the picture of Lacy that was attached to his instrument panel. It was a publicity photo in which she was looking straight at the camera, and Drew felt as if she were looking at him. He touched her face and smiled. "Let's go, beautiful," he whispered.

Drawing in a deep breath, he fastened his leather helmet, adjusted his goggles, and gave the signal that he was ready for takeoff.

Cunningham, a British pilot who was always smiling and joking and never seemed to take life seriously, yelled to him, "You'll likely get your tail shot off, Yank. Where do you want the body shipped?"

Drew smiled wryly. "I'll just be buried alongside you, Cunningham. Because if I go down, who's going to protect your ass?"

The two men grinned, then saluted each other. There was a camaraderie among the pilots—deeper than friendship, deeper even than a brother's love, because they were all aware that their lives depended on each other.

"See you up there, Yank," Cunningham said. "Don't worry about the Jerries; I'll be flying your wing today."

The revving of the engines made further conversation impossible, so Drew turned to his instrument panel with a serious expression on his face. Today's mission was more dangerous than most, because they were on a daytime strike against a German munitions dump.

Miraculously they flew undetected until they reached their target, which was well camouflaged. They were flying low enough for Drew to witness the chaos their approach brought to the soldiers, who frantically scurried about, trying to man their antiaircraft guns. The first pass rendered the guns ineffective. They made a second and a third pass, leaving nothing but burning rubble behind.

"Well done," the squadron leader's voice crackled over the radio. "Take us home, men." Suddenly his voice rose in volume. "Enemy at two o'clock. Look lively, men—break out of formation—we're sitting ducks."

Drew glanced over at Cunningham, who was just to his right. He dipped his wing, and Cunningham dipped his in reply. In unison, the two drifted left and confronted two German Messerschmitts.

Drew rolled, then dove under the first plane, letting loose a volley of fire. The second enemy plane came up behind him, its guns spitting fire. Bullets penetrated the cockpit, and Drew felt a stinging in his side. He'd been hit, but strangely enough there was no pain, just a sudden numbness. He could feel death breathing down his neck, but it had little meaning to him at the moment.

He swerved, dove, and climbed, but the German stayed with him like a menacing shadow. Suddenly, in a flash of fire, he saw the German plane nose-dive, twisting and spinning downward. Good old Cunningham had scored a hit!

Suddenly Drew heard a loud volley of gunfire and saw Cunningham's plane burst into flame. He cried out as the plane exploded in air, leaving only fragments to fall earthward.

Drew had never known such anger. Until now, the air battles had merely been a case of taking an enemy plane out before it got him. Now it was personal. Where moments ago he had been the hunted, he was now the hunter.

Drew rolled over so he wouldn't lose sight of his prey, who was in the thin cloud just to his left. He looped his plane to head for the cloud bank to his right, trying to get his bearings. A quick assessment of his instrument panel alerted him that he barely had enough fuel to get back to England. But that wasn't important at the moment; Cunningham had to be avenged.

His senses warned him that the enemy was now behind him, so Drew did a split-S and touched the inside rudder, coming out of the clouds face-to-face with the German who had shot down his comrade.

Drew had the sun behind him and knew that his one advantage was that the enemy pilot was temporarily blinded. He opened fire, hitting his target. There was no elation, merely the satisfaction of knowing that the man who had killed Cunningham had just hit the ground in a burst of flame.

Drew had little time to contemplate his victory before another Messerschmitt was on his tail. He rolled and looped, trying to get behind the German plane, but it matched his maneuvers, letting loose a stream of bullets.

Drew and his opponent played tag in the clouds, but he couldn't shake the German pilot, who seemed to guess his next move before he made it. After five minutes of looping and rolling, he knew that he had only one chance, so he grabbed the throttle and took his plane careening downward. Flying full-out at three hundred miles an hour, he was only fifty feet from the ground when he leveled off, but he was still being followed by his determined pursuer.

He was light-headed and his mouth felt dry as he broke into a sweat. He had to remain conscious; he and his faceless assailant were in a struggle that wouldn't end until at least one of them was dead.

At such a low altitude, one wrong move would mean disaster. Just ahead, Drew spotted a spine of grassy hills. Dipping down so he was only thirty feet from the ground, he streaked toward those hills, maneuvering his plane back and forth to keep from being hit by sporadic gunfire from the plane behind him.

Drew's hand was steady and his eyes were keen as he gauged the distance to the hills. At the last moment, he slammed the throttle and his plane shot upward. He rolled to his side, leveled off, and glanced back just in time to see the Messerschmitt crash into the hill and burst into flame.

He checked his instrument panel and saw that the fuel was now dangerously low. He couldn't make it back to the base, and he didn't relish bailing out to become a prisoner of war.

He glanced at Lacy's picture, aching inside because he'd never see her again. "I'm going down with my plane, beautiful. Stay with me and give me courage. If I'm going to die, my death has to count for something."

With strong resolve, he turned his plane to meet another oncoming plane. Opening fire, he watched the German aircraft careen right, and a smoky trail followed it to the ground, where it exploded on impact.

At last there were no more enemy planes in sight and Drew owned the skies. His satisfaction was short-lived when he noticed that his engine was damaged and pouring smoke. Still, like a homing pigeon, he turned toward England.

He felt strangely calm as he removed his glove with his teeth and glanced at Lacy's ring circling his little finger. He would never hear her say that she loved him, and that was his one regret.

He dropped to a lower altitude, trying to conserve what little fuel remained. Time had no meaning as he cast a wary glance at the smoking engine, which could burst into flame at any moment. He was within sight of the English Channel when fire licked at the engine and the plane sputtered and started its final descent.

Out of fuel and on fire, Drew braced himself for a crash landing. The crippled aircraft sputtered, and the propellers fell silent. Gliding on the wind currents, he finally reached the channel. The sun had gone down, and he could see the twinkling lights of small fishing craft in the distance.

The impact with the water was jarring, and he felt pain shoot through his leg. With considerable effort, he managed to release his harness, knowing he'd have to get out of the plane or be carried to the bottom of the channel.

He climbed over the side, using his last bit of strength to inflate his vest. It was dark, oh, so dark, and the water bitterly cold. His leg hurt like hell, although he didn't know why. He knew he'd lost a lot of blood from the wound in his side, but he wasn't sure what other injuries he'd sustained.

As a feeling of peace descended on him, his thoughts turned once again to Lacy. How sad to die never knowing what it felt like to make love to her. Her face swam before him and his last conscious thought was of her just before he sank into a black void.

Lacy stood before the mirror, straightening the seams of her silk stockings. She reached for a simple black dress and pulled it over her head just as Ruth sauntered into the room.

Ruth watched her silently for a moment and then spoke in her usual acid tone. "You've got five secretaries working in the office today just to answer your fan mail. Do you know what one of the letters was about?"

"No, what?"

"It was from a network of hat manufacturers beseeching you to abandon your bareheaded look and take up wearing hats. They say you are killing their business. They even offered to supply you with free hats."

Lacy laughed. "It won't do them any good. Mark won't let me wear hats."

Ruth leaned against the doorjamb. "Do you enjoy the power, knowing you can dictate what women all over the world wear?"

"No, Ruth, I don't. If you must know, I'm tired of all the fuss."

Ruth watched her sister fasten a leather belt about her slender waist. "I, for one, am beginning to be bored by your wardrobe.

I'm sick of seeing you in black; it looks like you're in perpetual mourning."

Lacy slid her foot into her shoe. "I couldn't agree with you more. I'd wrestle you for that green frock you're wearing."

Ruth scowled. "My dress didn't cost half of what you paid for those black-market Italian leather shoes."

Lacy hoped to avoid quarreling with her sister this morning, so she changed the subject. "What are your plans for the day?"

"Oh," Ruth said bitingly, "I thought I'd play bridge with the ladies, then a round of tennis at the club—afterward, I thought I'd have tea with the mayor's wife."

"I'm in a hurry, Ruth," Lacy said impatiently. "I have an appointment with a newspaper reporter from New York."

"Speaking of newspapers, there's something in today's paper that might interest you. There's been a tragic accident."

Lacy fastened her hair away from her face with an onyx clip, knowing Ruth loved being melodramatic. "Oh?" she said without real interest.

Ruth watched her sister's face closely as she handed her the newspaper she had tucked beneath her arm. "Yeah. It's about that man who came here to see you—you know the one, that New York director."

Lacy's heart stopped. "Andrew Mallory? Something has happened to Drew?"

"That's the one."

Lacy had feared this day would come. Since Drew first joined the RAF, she'd listened daily to news broadcasts, afraid she would hear about his death, yet needing to know. With a trembling hand, she took the newspaper from Ruth, and the headline jumped off the paper at her: ANDREW MALLORY, BROADWAY DIRECTOR, ACE FLYER, AND WAR HERO, CRASHES INTO ENGLISH CHANNEL.

Scarcely breathing, Lacy quickly read the article. Drew had been on a mission somewhere inside Germany when his plane was hit. Before crashing in the English Channel, he had managed to shoot down three enemy aircraft.

Lacy's eyes were swimming with tears when she finally read that Drew had been rescued by a fishing boat and was now recuperating in Middlesex Hospital in London. Here the information was sketchy. The article said only that he had been wounded and his leg was broken.

She raised tearful eyes to her sister. "Oh, Ruth, he's alive!"

Ruth's eyes narrowed in speculation. "Yes, and that news obviously means a great deal to you."

Lacy hurried to the telephone and lifted the receiver to place a call to England. It didn't matter to her that Ruth was watching her every move—she had to know Drew's condition.

It took eight agonizing hours before the overseas operator could connect her with Middlesex Hospital. A crisp British voice came through on the other end of the line. "Matron Roston here. How may I help you?"

"Nurse, I'm calling from California to inquire—"

"California in the States?" the woman asked incredulously.

"Yes. I'm calling to inquire about a patient, an American lieutenant, Andrew Mallory."

"Patients aren't allowed to receive calls," the matron said primly.

"I don't need to talk to him," Lacy said in desperation. "I only want to know how he is."

"Are you a relative or a friend of the family?" the matron asked, beginning to relent.

"Yes . . . a friend. I'm Lacy Black, and I'm—"

"*The* Lacy Black from Hollywood, California?" Matron Roston asked excitedly. "I've seen all your pictures."

There was crackling on the line and the signal was growing weak. "Can you please tell me Lieutenant Mallory's condition?"

"Miss Black, of course I'll tell you anything you'd like." Apparently the name Lacy Black could work magic, even halfway across the world. "Lieutenant Mallory is recovering nicely from his wounds. For a while the doctors feared he would lose his leg, but it now seems to be mending. I'm sure he'll be glad to know you called to inquire about his health. Shall I give him a message?"

"No . . . yes, please. Just tell him I send . . . that we all send our hopes for his speedy return to America."

The crackling grew louder and the connection was broken. Lacy replaced the receiver and buried her face in her hands. Thank God Drew was out of danger.

Nurse Roston entered the sterile hospital ward where the wounded officers were recuperating. She walked directly to Lieutenant Mallory's bed and smiled at the handsome American. "I just had someone from the States call to inquire about you."

"So what's new?" one of his companions asked good-naturedly. "He's always getting calls from the States. Bet this one was female, too."

Matron Roston straightened Drew's sheets and plumped his pillow. "She was female, all right, but this one was different."

"Yeah," a British officer scoffed. "How could you tell over the telephone?"

The matron looked smug. "This one was Lacy Black, herself."

Drew grabbed the woman's hand. "Did she say anything else? Did she send me a message?"

"She said they were all waiting for you to return to the States, Yank."

One of the British officers looked at Drew with growing admiration. "You know Lacy Black—*the* Lacy Black?"

Drew smiled. "I know her, but don't ask me to introduce her to you. She's particular about the company she keeps."

One of the men laughed. "That can't be true if she talks to you. You Yanks are overpaid, oversexed, and, regrettably, over here."

Matron smiled at the teasing banter between the men.

Drew pretended seriousness. "I heard you needed someone to win the war for you. You certainly weren't doing too well on your own."

"A lot of help you are, lying flat on your back. The Jerries certainly picked you off easily enough."

Drew suddenly grew silent. He reached down and touched Lacy's ring, wishing he could reach out and touch its owner.

Chapter Sixteen

Lacy read that Drew had recovered from his wounds and was back in New York, working on a new play. The newspapers and magazines were filled with articles describing his bravery in battle, and she was secretly so proud of him. But mostly she was glad he was home safely.

She had hoped that with the passing of time she would forget about Drew, but she loved him more than ever. She remembered the way his eyes lit up when he smiled at her, and the devastated look on his face the day she had pressed her ring into his hand. She felt disloyal to Mark because of her feelings for Drew, so she tried to be more tolerant of her husband's shortcomings, although she could feel herself pulling away from him more and more all the time.

Gone were her girlhood illusions about Mark. He didn't love her, and he probably never had. They had not made love in a very long time, and she was glad he'd stopped coming to her room at night. Everyone thought she didn't know about the other women in his life, but she did. She'd known for years; it just didn't hurt or matter anymore.

* * *

The ringing of the telephone jarred Lacy out of a deep sleep. Since she was the only one at home, she lifted the receiver and said drowsily, "Hello?"

There was a long silence on the other end of the line, but she sat upright, her hand tightening on the phone. She knew without being told who it was. "Drew."

"How did you know?"

Oh, how she had hungered for the sound of his voice. "I just felt it."

"Yes, I know. We have that between us, don't we, Lacy?"

Her heart was pounding, and she closed her eyes, trying to picture him in her mind. "Are you well?"

She could imagine him smiling. "Good as new."

Her voice was breathless. "I was worried about you."

"Lacy," he said after a long pause, "I've reached for the phone many times to call you, but it took me until now to get up the courage."

"Why?"

"I need you. Just say the word, and I'll be on the first flight in the morning. I want to bring you back to New York with me. You belong to me—we both know that."

Oh, yes, she knew it. "I can't do that to Mark."

"But you'd do it to me," he said bitterly. "You love me," he insisted. "You know you do!"

She couldn't deny it. "Yes."

"Then why? Doesn't it matter to you that you are tearing my heart out? Don't you know that without you I have no life?"

She wanted him so desperately, it was like a physical pain. If there were only herself to consider, she would run to him and never look back. "Drew, there can never be anything between us. I'm Mark's wife, and I owe him so much. I could never betray his trust."

Her heart contracted at the pain she heard in Drew's voice.

"You are already cheating him by loving me," he said, even though he knew it was futile to think she'd change her mind.

"But he'll never know." She had to make him understand. "I owe Mark my loyalty, Drew. I can't leave him."

"Lacy, just let me see you . . . talk to you—hold you."

She knew if she didn't hang up, she might relent. "I can't talk any more, Drew," she said desperately.

"Wait, let me hear you say you love me," he urged. "Give me that much to hold on to, Lacy."

"I love you so much it hurts," she admitted with tears running down her cheeks. "My dearest love, I will miss you every day for the rest of my life." With a smothered sob, she replaced the receiver and broke the connection between them.

Mark sat at his desk, pondering the changes he had noticed in Lacy. She was distant, and no longer seemed interested in pleasing him. She was quieter, spending most of her time alone, and he wondered why.

Work had begun on a little house for Ruth behind the tennis courts. At night, when Lacy was asleep, he would sneak into Ruth's room and the two of them would unleash their passion until they were both exhausted. *If only Lacy were as accommodating as her sister,* he thought, *she'd be the perfect woman.*

"Mark," Lacy said, interrupting his thoughts as she came into his study and placed a bound script on his desk. "Barnard Christopher at Union Pictures sent this over by messenger with a note begging me to consider the starring role. I've read it, and I like it. I'm going to play Sister Mary."

"What in the hell are you talking about?"

"A Superior Woman."

"Lacy," he said impatiently, "every actress in Hollywood has her heart set on that part. I find it ludicrous that Barnard would offer it to you." He sneered. "You, playing the part of a young girl raised in an orphanage, who grows up to become mother superior of that same orphanage? Nobody would believe it."

She tried not to be hurt by his ridicule. "I can do it; I know I can. I've heard you say a thousand times that an actor always needs to grow."

Mark stared at her incredulously. "You're serious, aren't you?"

"Of course I'm serious. I want to play a part that will challenge my abilities. I'm tired of people dismissing me as merely a beautiful body. I have a mind, too."

Mark became angry. "Don't be ridiculous. If Barnard wants you, it's only because your name will command big box office turnout, not because of your acting ability."

"It's time I proved that I can act."

He threw his hands up in exasperation. "Do you know what your trouble is, Lacy?" he asked cruelly. "You've been reading too damn many of your own publicity sheets. They only say that you can act because that's what I told the publicists to print. Besides, you're not going to make a picture for another studio. I've told you repeatedly, Lacy Black works only for me."

She felt more and more as if she were a prisoner and Mark her jailer. If she allowed it, he would use her until there was nothing left of her. She might not be able to have the life with Drew that she wanted, but from now on, she would live her life with Mark on her own terms.

"I'm going to do this picture for Barnard," she said quietly. "I had hoped you would agree, but I'll do it without your approval if I have to."

"No, you won't!" he said, slamming his fist on the desk.

She leaned across the desk, glaring at him, something she had never done before. "Yes, I will."

Before he could recover from his shock, she turned and walked away, her head held at a defiant tilt. Lacy didn't see the hands that balled into fists, nor did she know that in defying Mark, she had made a dangerous mistake.

Mark's eyes narrowed and dark rage overpowered him. Maybe he should have reminded Lacy that she was expendable. Dolores had found that out the hard way, when she defied him. He picked up a pencil and broke it in half, wishing it were Lacy's neck.

A sudden thought struck him and he rummaged through the papers in the wall safe until he found what he wanted—the million-dollar insurance policy on Lacy's life. At the time he'd taken it out, it had been only a publicity ploy; he'd never dreamed he might collect on it. His eyes glazed over and he smiled. With a million dollars, he could pay off his gambling debts and the mortgage he'd recently taken out on Pinnacle Pictures, and still come out ahead.

He nervously thumbed through the policy as a plan began to take form. He sat forward, his eyes gleaming. What did it matter if Lacy died? He was losing her anyway. Women had always been trouble to him—but he had a way of dealing with them.

He scanned the double-indemnity clause with greedy eyes. If death was accidental, the policy would pay double—two million dollars!

Turning to his typewriter, he removed the paper, wadded it into a ball, and tossed it into the trash can. He had a new script to write. Usually his writing was uninspired and shallow, but he was so wrapped up in the plot of this story that it took on a life of its own.

It was about a famous Hollywood star who died in a tragic plane crash, and how her grieving husband rebuilt his life on the proceeds from her life insurance. Feverishly, his hands flew over the typewriter keys as his devious scheme unfurled.

When the finished pages lay before him, he trembled with excitement. He knew just how Lacy would die. And he would make it look like an accident so no one would ever suspect that she had been murdered.

Mark smiled at his own genius—he would make Lacy a participant in her own demise!

Chapter Seventeen

Lacy stepped out of the bathtub, feeling as if every bone in her body ached. She'd finished the final scene of another western in which she played a saloon girl who was reformed by the handsome hero and left her sordid past behind to become his wife. Now she could tell Barnard Christopher that she would accept the part of Sister Mary.

She slipped into her silk robe and belted it at the waist. Sitting at her dressing table, Lacy stared into the mirror. There was not a mark or a blemish on her complexion, no sign on her face that her heart was broken. She despised her platinum-colored hair; in fact, she had begun to despise many things about her life. More and more she wanted to leave Hollywood, with its artificial glamour. If only her fans knew how meaningless her life was, they wouldn't envy her.

She had no life outside her work and the endless parties she and Mark attended. Her everyday existence was as staged as any of her movies. Mark kept her isolated and she was never allowed to go anywhere without an escort; she was never alone, whether it was at the studio or at home. She had no real friend she could talk to, and she was lonely for meaningful companionship.

She climbed into bed and sank into the soft mattress, too weary to think anymore.

A moment later, the door opened and Mark entered, switching on the bedside lamp so soft light spread across the room.

"Are you asleep, baby?"

He hadn't called her that in a long time, and she stiffened, hoping he didn't want to make love to her. "No, I'm awake," she said, pulling the covers to her neck.

He sat down on the bed and took her resisting hand in his. "I haven't been much of a husband to you lately, have I?"

She searched his eyes, trying to judge his meaning, but this was a new mood that she hadn't seen before. "I don't blame you, Mark. I'm sure I have been a disappointment to you as a wife."

He smiled that boyish smile that she'd once adored.

"What man wouldn't want you for his wife, Lacy?"

"You are in unusually high spirits. Did you win at the races today?" she asked, trying to find a reason for his cheerfulness.

"I haven't been to the track in weeks." He raised her hand to his lips. "I've spent a lot of time thinking about you lately, and things are going to be different from now on. We're going to recapture what we've lost—you'll see."

She pulled her hand from his. "I'm not sure that's possible, Mark. You haven't even spoken to me since I told you that I was going to do *A Superior Woman*."

His eyes shifted away from hers. "Well, baby, I was wrong. I know that now."

She looked at him suspiciously. "Then you agree that I can do Barnard's film? If this is just a trick to get me to do another of your predictable pictures, it won't work, Mark."

"No, it's not that," he protested. "You were right about needing to grow in your acting. Will you just listen to this exciting new project I've written for you? If you decide against it, I won't object to your playing Sister Mary."

She closed her eyes, wishing he'd just go away. The roles he created for her were all the same, no matter what he said.

"This part will test your acting ability, and I think you'll be pleased. You realized before I did that you've outgrown the dumb-blonde roles." He saw a flicker of doubt in her expression. He stood and walked to the window, a self-satisfied smile curving his lips when he heard Lacy get out of bed and join him.

"Tell me more about this script, Mark."

"OK, baby." He kissed her cheek, and this time she didn't turn away. "And there's something else, too." His gaze stabbed into hers. "Maybe we should have a baby."

She looked at him questioningly, hardly daring to believe what she had heard. Could Mark have changed? He did seem different—but could she trust him?

"Would it make you happy to have a baby, Lacy?"

For a moment she was shocked into silence; then she replied as honestly as she could. "I don't know, Mark. At one time it would have been my fondest dream." She shrugged. "But now I'm not so sure."

He stared at her in anger, feeling that she'd somehow betrayed him—not that he wanted a baby, and not that he'd really let her have one, but he had expected her to be pleased with the idea. "What you mean is you don't want my baby," he said at last.

"As I told you, I just don't know."

"Baby, come to bed with me so we can talk more . . . intimately."

"No, Mark. I won't."

He wanted to strike her, to drag her to the bed and make her submit to him, but if his plan was going to work, he had to handle Lacy just right. "Very well. We'll let that go for now. Let's talk about my idea for your next movie." He sat down on the white damask sofa and held out his hand for her to join him there. "I think you'll like it."

Nervously, she sat beside him and didn't object when he drew her into his arms. But when he began to nuzzle her ear, she pulled away. "Tell me about your idea, Mark."

He settled against the high-back sofa and smiled. "For the sake of argument, let's call our heroine Jane Doe. Her husband is . . . the owner of a large corporation that's in financial trouble. She's the one with money, and he's afraid that she'll try to leave him. His dilemma is this: how does he get rid of her and keep her money at the same time?"

Lacy was intrigued—she could see the possibilities. "Oh, Mark, is it a murder mystery?"

"Yes, it is, baby."

She moved closer to him. "Tell me more."

"I got the idea when we took out that insurance policy on your life," he said daringly. "Our hero takes out a large insurance policy on *his* wife, knowing she has to die, but that he has to divert all suspicion away from himself. What do you think he does?"

Her eyes sparkled with anticipation. "What?"

"He arranges an airplane crash. Nobody's tried that angle before. Of course, since he doesn't have knowledge of airplane motors, he has to have an accomplice. So he pays some poor fool who works at the airport to put a defective hose on the gas line. Not a hose that's been tampered with, but one that shows natural wear."

"That's brilliant. Then what happens?"

"Our hero—"

"Villain," Lacy interjected.

"As you wish. Our . . . villain talks his wife into taking a trip by air on his company's private plane. Of course, the inevitable will happen. Imagine how the poor woman would feel at the moment when she discovers that she is going to die. Can you imagine the terror she would experience?"

Lacy shivered, more from the sinister tone of his voice than from the plot he was unfurling. "So far I like it."

Mark's voice became husky with passion. His own words were arousing him, filling him with desire for Lacy. "And when she realizes that her husband . . ." He moved closer to her and bent to kiss her lips, but she turned away and his mouth brushed against her cheek.

He straightened, pulling back.

Lacy clasped her hands and avoided his eyes. "Go on. What happens next?"

"You'll never guess how it ends," Mark said grimly, as he realized that she couldn't even stand for him to touch her.

She was glad he'd turned his attention away from her and back to his plot. "How does it end?"

"With our hero—or villain, if you will—pretending to be broken hearted and winning the world's sympathy."

She was puzzled for a moment. "Are you saying the man will get away with the crime and go unpunished?"

"Of course. He's a clever one, our hero—too clever to get caught. The movie will end with him attending the funeral and giving a eulogy that will move the mourners to tears."

Lacy looked at him doubtfully. "I think the public will insist he be punished."

Mark smiled indulgently. "You just be ready to give the performance of your life and leave the plotting to me." His hand moved up and down her arm in a caressing motion. "Our hero's speech will be the climax, and the audience can draw its own conclusions. He'll say, 'Ladies and gentlemen, I'm here today only because my wife would expect it of me. She would want me to go on because that's the kind of woman she was. I hope you will understand. I . . .' " Mark paused, his breath caught in his throat. It took him a moment to compose himself. Then his voice was deep and husky, with a tone of profound sadness, as he continued. " 'I hope you will forgive me if I can't say any more about my wife at this time. The pain is too new, the grief too sharp. I will end by adding a personal note. I once told her that she would break my heart, and she has.' "

Lacy shook her head. "I still think that he should pay for his crime."

"In a way he will. You see, he realizes deep down that she

was the only woman he ever truly loved and respected—as much as he was able to love. He created in her the ideal woman, and he will never find another like her."

"Mark, it is exciting," she admitted reluctantly.

"Does this mean you won't do Barnard's film?"

She hesitated, because she had so wanted to work with Barnard. "I'll tell him to find someone else."

Mark's eyes gleamed with triumph. "We'll begin casting as soon as I make sure there are no plot holes." He smiled. "This is the kind of part that draws the attention of the Academy. I wouldn't be surprised if you win an Oscar for your performance. Play it well, Lacy. Play it as if your life depended upon it."

"I shall, Mark. You'll be proud of what I do with this role."

He traced her lips with his finger. "I've always had great pride in you, Lacy. I want you to remember that."

"I know," she said softly, wishing things could be different between them.

"Lacy," he said, changing the subject, "something's come up, and I won't be able to go with you to the premiere of *Heart's Deception* in San Francisco on the twentieth."

"Are you sure? I thought there were some people you wanted to meet at the party afterward."

"I'll have to miss this one. But I'll be waiting for you to return." He gazed deeply into her eyes. "Perhaps then we can put our marriage right."

This was a Mark she didn't know, and she was puzzled, almost troubled by the change in him. "I hope so, Mark," she said at last. "We were happy for a time, weren't we?"

He touched her cheek softly. "You're so young, only twenty-one." For the first time, he felt a prickle of remorse. Lacy was truly a rare jewel, and he would miss her. But she had started to defy him, and it would only get worse. She had to be eliminated before he lost control of her completely. "No matter what happens, I want you to know this: I have come closer to loving you than I have any other woman."

"I know."

He pulled her to him, stroked her hair, and murmured in her ear, "I want to make everything up to you. After you return from San Francisco, we'll go away together and try to recapture the old magic. We'll make love all night, sleep late, and have our breakfast served in bed."

Lacy laid her head on his shoulder. She didn't love him, but they could make a life together. Drew's face flashed through her mind and she closed her eyes. She had chosen to remain with her husband; she had to forget about Drew.

Ruth paced her room like a caged animal. She'd seen Mark go into Lacy's room, and she jealously imagined that they were making love. Her body was on fire for him, and she wanted to scratch her sister's eyes out. She was sure he hadn't been with her sister since she had first seduced him; in fact, she doubted he'd been with anyone but her since that first time, because she'd satisfied him every night.

Mark would come to her tonight—he always did. Lacy couldn't fulfill his animal needs—only she could.

Ruth stripped off her clothing and lay naked, waiting for Mark—but he didn't come to her room that night, or the next, or the next.

Chapter Eighteen

Lacy dove into the water and swam the length of the pool, thinking how much Mark had changed. Almost overnight he seemed to have become the man she'd always wanted him to be. He was home with her every night and couldn't do enough to please her. He hadn't tried to make love to her yet, and she was grateful to him for being so sensitive to her moods. Perhaps they could make this marriage work after all.

She reached the end of the pool and had turned to swim back when she saw Mark approaching. She swam toward him and climbed up the steps to be wrapped in the oversize towel he held out for her.

With vigorous strokes, he dried her arms and back.

"I come looking for my wife and find a beautiful mermaid," he said, kissing the back of her neck.

"Have you finalized the plans for my trip to San Francisco?" she asked, taking the towel and wrapping it around her damp hair.

He moved away from her and sat down on the edge of a lounge chair. It didn't escape her notice that he avoided her eyes. "Yes, I have. Everything should go as smoothly as planned. Be warned that there will be a large turnout of fans at this premiere."

She remembered the time in New York when she had almost been crushed by a frenzied mob. She was suddenly afraid that it would happen again. "Mark, can't you come with me?"

He took her hand and pulled her down beside him. "Believe me, baby, if I could, I would. But you know I must put business first."

She nodded. "I know. It's just that I get so frightened of crowds."

His grip on her hand tightened until it was painful.

"Oh, God, if only you didn't have to go," he whispered.

She thought she saw tears in his eyes. "Is something wrong, Mark?"

He dropped her hand, and she watched as his eyes suddenly became cold and unfeeling. "No, nothing's wrong." He patted her arm. "Now, let's go up to the house and have Consuela pack for you."

Lacy slipped into her terry-cloth robe and followed him into the house. Something wasn't right, but she didn't know what it was. With Mark, she could never be sure of anything.

When they reached her bedroom, Consuela was already packing, and Mark interrupted her in his usual dictatorial manner. "No, Consuela, not the suit. She'll wear the gown with the black sequins," he said with a frown.

"But Mark," Lacy protested, "if I wear the sequins, I can't wear my emerald necklace." She picked up the jewelry case that held it.

"You're not taking the Raja Star," he said quickly.

"Why not?"

"It's too dangerous for you to wear unless I'm with you. It will remain here," he said, softening his words with a slight smile. "Besides, baby, you don't need any adornment."

She placed the necklace case in his extended hand. "I wish

you'd change your mind and come with me. You know how I dislike traveling alone."

He opened the black velvet box to assure himself that the Raja Star was safely inside and then closed it with a snap and laid it on her dressing table. "You won't be alone. You'll have your hairdresser, a publicity man, and George Levine with you. He'll be taking all the publicity shots. Your pilot will be Frank Hooper. I know you like him."

"But Mark," Lacy said in disappointment, "I have this premonition that . . ." She paused. "I know it's silly, but last night I dreamed that I would never see you again."

Mark lowered his eyes. "Don't be a child, Lacy. Now let's finish packing, and then we can go over the details of your trip."

Ruth entered the room and stood beside Mark. "I've never been to San Francisco," she commented. "I've always wanted to go."

Lacy gave her sister a quick glance. Even though they barely tolerated each other, she would welcome Ruth's company this time. "Why don't you come with me?" she offered.

Ruth gave Lacy a sly look. "I might consider it if you were taking the train, but I'm not flying; the very thought scares me." Secretly she was delighted that she would have Mark all to herself. Lacy would be gone five glorious days—surely in that time Mark would need a woman, and she intended to be available.

Lacy handed Consuela a black silk scarf and watched her tuck it into the trunk. "You would like San Francisco, Ruth. Please reconsider."

"No, I don't think so," Ruth said, looking up at Mark suggestively. "I have plans and don't intend to . . . change them." It gave Ruth great satisfaction to toss out hidden innuendoes that made Mark squirm. He needn't worry, Ruth thought contemptuously. Lacy wasn't even aware of what was going on right under her nose.

Dark clouds were gathering over the Pacific as the chauffeur-driven limousine hummed down the road. Even though it was not a cool evening, Lacy shivered and burrowed even deeper into her black mink coat. When they pulled up to the airport and Mark held the door for her, the first drops of rain began to fall.

Mark handed her the cosmetic case, then watched as the chauffeur unloaded the rest of her luggage.

Lacy glanced down the runway at the silver plane that Mark had purchased for the studio just a few weeks before. She turned to enter the small tin building that served as a waiting area, thinking he'd come in with her, but he pulled her into his arms.

"I'll say good-bye to you here, baby. I have an appointment later and I'll just make it if I hurry."

Lacy's heart grew heavy. "Good-bye, Mark. Take care of yourself."

His lips were warm against her cheek. "Lacy, Lacy, you can't know the pain I feel at this moment." His arms tightened about her and she felt his body quiver. "I never thought it would be this difficult. I could almost change my mind."

She glanced up at him, seeing torment in his eyes. "Then change it and come with me."

The look of pain quickly disappeared and he answered her cryptically. "No, where you are going, I can't go." He gently stroked his hand across her cheek. "Be a good girl, baby, and go on in. You're getting wet."

"Good-bye, Mark."

He seemed to come out of a trance and pulled her into his arms, kissing her passionately on the lips. At last he raised his head and released her reluctantly. "I love you, baby."

He turned away and, with a quick wave, got into the limousine, staring after Lacy as she entered the building.

"I had to do it, Lacy," he muttered to himself. "You left me no choice." With a deep sigh, he motioned for the chauffeur to drive on. Everything had been set in motion—there was no turning back now.

* * *

George Levine entered the waiting area and spotted Lacy. He rushed over to her and leaned down to brush her cheek with a kiss of greeting. He was the studio photographer and had known Lacy right from the start. The hairstylist and publicist had already arrived and were sitting in a corner of the airport, drinking coffee, deep in conversation.

"When Frank arrives, our entourage will be complete and we can leave," Lacy told George.

"The weather's getting nasty out there. That's why I'm late. Frank probably got caught in the same storm."

She smiled. "Don't worry; we aren't going anywhere without the pilot."

George sat down beside her. "Where's the boss? I thought he'd be here to see us off."

Lacy's lips tightened. "He was, but he had an important appointment. So he had to rush off."

George's eyebrows lifted quizzically. He could imagine what kind of appointment Mark had rushed off to, and he only hoped she was worth it. Sometimes Mark Damian was a real ass. He was married to the sweetest woman in the world and he treated her like shit. There wasn't a man at Pinnacle Pictures who wouldn't trade places with him, even for just one night, and the fool didn't even appreciate what he had.

Lacy could hear heavy raindrops hitting the tin roof, and she was about to comment on the storm when a rain-soaked Frank Hooper entered, removing his cap and slapping it against his thigh to remove some of the water. He shook his head as he approached her.

"I'm afraid we've been grounded because of the storm, Miss Black."

"For how long?"

"I shouldn't think it'll be safe to fly until tomorrow, but I'll remain here at the airport in case that changes. You should go on home, Miss Black. If the weather improves, would you like me to call you?"

"Yes, should the conditions change by midnight. After that,

go on home." She felt almost relieved as she turned to George. "Tell the others they can leave and we'll call them if the plans change. Would you drop me at my house on your way home?"

George nodded. "I'd be glad to."

Ruth had heard Mark come in moments ago, so she hurriedly fumbled through Lacy's closet until she found what she wanted. With her heart beating a loud tempo, she stripped off her clothes and pulled on the see-through black gown. She then moved to Lacy's dressing table and dabbed perfume behind her ears. Ruth's eyes widened when she saw the black velvet box that contained the Raja Star. Apparently Mark had forgotten to lock it in the wall safe.

With trembling fingers, she lifted the necklace and clasped it around her neck, staring at her reflection in the mirror admiringly. She might not be the beauty Lacy was, but men had always found her desirable, and Mark was no exception.

Ruth made her way to Mark's office, where she knew she'd find him. Not bothering to knock, she pushed open the door.

He was talking on the telephone, and he slammed down the receiver when he saw that she was wearing the Raja Star.

"What in the hell do you think you're doing? Take that off immediately."

She smiled secretly, choosing to misunderstand him. "All right, if that's what you want." She pushed the straps of the nightgown off her shoulders, and it fell about her feet, leaving her standing before him wearing only the necklace. "I'm always willing to oblige you, Mark." She ran her hand across her breasts, eyeing him all the while. "We are alone—I gave the servants the night off."

His eyes raked her curvaceous body, and his anger quickly turned to uncontrollable lust. In long strides, he was at her side, gripping her arms and burying his face against her ample breasts.

Ruth shivered with delight as his base instincts took control. He fondled her until she squirmed, her lips opening to receive his ravenous kiss. She flung her arms around him, pressing her body against his.

Mark picked her up and carried her up the stairs. She was vaguely aware that he took her to his bedroom, where he tossed her on the bed and unbuckled his belt.

"Bitch," he ground out.

"Yes, but you like it this way. We're both animals, Mark. Lacy could never satisfy you like I do, and you know it."

He was beside her, jerking her head back and staring into her face. "You'll never be Lacy. Get that thought out of your stupid head."

He trembled, trying not to lose control when she rubbed her now perspiring body against his. She felt his erection and smiled, nipping at his mouth with her sharp teeth. "No," she said hotly, "I'll never be Lacy. Aren't you glad?"

With a muttered oath, he pulled her beneath him. "I hate you," he muttered against her lips.

"Yes," she answered, her eyes glazed with passion. "I love the way you hate."

Lacy inserted her key in the front door and thanked George when he brought her luggage in. She wondered where the servants were, and went from room to room, looking for Ruth. When she reached Mark's office, she found the lights were on, but he wasn't there. Seeing her black nightgown on the floor, she picked it up and stared at it, puzzled.

Deciding that no one was home, she walked up the stairs. She would go to bed early, and if the pilot called her with word that the weather had cleared, she'd tell him they would leave in the morning.

At the top of the stairs, she noticed that Mark's bedroom door was open and light was spilling into the hallway. As she approached his room, a streak of lightning split the air.

The lights temporarily went off, and she stood in total darkness, waiting for them to come on again. That was when she became aware of the animal sounds coming from Mark's bedroom.

In one horrifying moment, Lacy realized that Mark had brought one of his women into their home. Suddenly the lights flickered and came on again, and she felt her stomach churn when she saw who was in the bed with him. She wanted to cry out, but no sound would come from her dry throat.

Her husband was making love to her own sister!

Mark and Ruth were so involved in satisfying their lust that they didn't even know she was there.

Lacy leaned against the door for support, feeling so hurt and betrayed that she wanted to die. She seemed frozen in place, watching Mark stroke Ruth's breasts while he moved against her.

"You tramp," he ground out hotly, as if saying the words aroused him further. "Whore."

"Yes, I am. But you must like it because you keep coming back to me," she said, panting. "Your little Lacy can't keep you happy, but I can."

Lacy wanted to leave, to run, but she couldn't.

"I don't want to think of Lacy," Mark said. "She'll never again make men lust after her."

With a strangled cry, Lacy moved to the bed, her eyes burning with anger.

Ruth was the first to see her sister. Her eyes rounded with surprise, and she shook her head, her eyes suddenly filled with shame.

When he saw her, Mark sat back, reaching for the sheet and pulling it over himself. Lacy should have been dead by now. "What the hell—"

At last Lacy found her voice as she looked pointedly at her sister. She had played this same scene herself in her films, but never as the outraged, betrayed wife. Always before, she had been the seductress lying in the arms of the unfaithful husband. The words she spoke were unoriginal; they might have come straight from the script of one of Mark's movies. "How long has this been going on, Ruth?"

For a moment Mark's face whitened. "Lacy . . . it can't be!"

"I wasn't speaking to you, Mark," Lacy interrupted him. "Nothing you can ever say will interest me again." She turned away from him and stared at Ruth. "I was talking to my sister and wondering how she, my own flesh and blood, could betray me."

Ruth got to her knees, holding out a beseeching hand to Lacy. "I—"

At that moment, Lacy saw her emerald necklace sparkling about Ruth's neck, and she almost strangled on her rage. With unleashed anger, she reached forward and tore it from her sister's neck. "You can have Mark, and welcome to him, but you can't have my Raja Star."

Without another word, Lacy marched to Mark's bathroom. Dangling the Raja Star over the commode, she cast a mocking glance in his direction. When he shook his head, she smiled and allowed the necklace to slide through her fingers and splash into the commode. With a feeling of satisfaction, she reached for the handle and flushed, knowing she'd never want to wear it again anyway after tonight.

Mark cried out, "Dammit, Lacy, what in the hell are you doing?" He leaped off the bed, wrapped the bedspread around him, and raced to the bathroom. Going down on his knees, he breathed a sigh of relief. The first flush hadn't taken the necklace all the way down. But just before he could reach it, Lacy flushed again and the emerald necklace disappeared in a spray of swirling water.

He looked from her to the phone, not knowing which problem to attack first. "I'll call a plumber," he said, rushing for the phone. Just as he picked up the receiver, he heard Lacy flush the commode again, and he knew that the necklace was gone forever.

Replacing the receiver, he walked slowly toward her, his eyes blazing with anger. "I could kill you for that, you stupid bitch.

That necklace was worth more than you'll ever be."

"Really?" she said in a calm voice that surprised even her. "Well, it isn't worth much now, is it?"

He raised his hand as if to strike her and she stared back at him, unafraid. "I wouldn't do that if I were you, Mark."

He dropped his hand, not knowing what to do. This was the worst night of his life.

Lacy shook her head. "Good-bye, Mark."

"What about me?" Ruth cried, for the first time realizing what all this meant for her.

"I never want to see you again, Ruth," Lacy told her. "You are the worse offender here, because you're my sister."

Ruth wondered why she felt such pain when she looked in Lacy's eyes. "I thought you would be in San Francisco."

Lacy looked at her in disbelief. "You think that excuses what you did?"

Mark knew that if Lacy walked out on him, he'd be ruined. "Baby," he said, almost tripping over the bedspread that was draped about his waist. "Let's talk about this."

"No! I'm going to return to the airport, Mark. The flight was canceled because of the storm, but I think Frank will fly me wherever I want to go, storm or not."

Mark stopped in his tracks. All his problems would be solved if she got on that airplane.

Lacy ran from the room and down the stairs, grabbing up her smallest suitcase and going into the kitchen, where the car keys hung. She took the keys to Mark's precious Cord and ran to the garage.

Inserting the key in the ignition, she slammed her foot on the accelerator and sped away. As she rounded the driveway, her headlights shone on Ruth.

"Wait!" Ruth cried. "I'm sorry. Please let me—"

Lacy gunned the accelerator and Ruth had to jump out of the way to avoid being hit.

Lacy was so numb, she wasn't thinking straight. The image of her sister and Mark making love was burned into her mind, and she knew she'd remember it for the rest of her life. She never wanted to see either of them again. In fact, she never again wanted to see Hollywood or anyone connected with it.

She needed to be alone for a time. Then, when she wasn't feeling so sorry for herself, she would go to New York. Yes, she would go to Drew!

Pulling off the road at an all-night diner, she found a phone and called Drew's number, suddenly needing to hear his voice. She was relieved when he answered.

"Hello."

"Drew, this is Lacy. I'm coming to you."

She heard his deep intake of breath. "How soon—when?"

"I don't know, but I'll be there if you still want me."

"Want you! You're all I think about. What happened to change your mind?"

"I can't talk about that now. I'll tell you everything when I see you."

"I don't care about the reason. Just hurry."

"Drew?"

He didn't try to hide the elation in his voice. "Yes, my love?"

"Thank you." She hung up, breaking her only connection with reality. Just knowing that he still loved her took the edge off her pain.

It was raining harder by the time she reached the airport. It was almost midnight, and she half feared the pilot would have already gone home.

With her suitcase clutched in her hand, she entered the building to find him having coffee with two other men she assumed were mechanics because of their greasy coveralls. When the pilot saw Lacy, he hurried to her.

"I was about to call you, Miss Black. It doesn't look like the weather is going to let up."

"I have to get to New York."

He looked baffled. "Not San Francisco?"

"No, I want you to take me to New York tonight."

"But Miss Black, all planes are grounded. It isn't safe to fly in this storm."

"I'll pay you well, but if you won't take me, I'll find a pilot who will," she said firmly. "I have to make a phone call, and afterward you can tell me your decision. Now, where can I find a phone?"

He led her into an office where the oily smell reminded her of her father's garage; he closed the door so she could have privacy. The telephone was on a desk piled high with papers. Lifting the receiver, she gave the operator the number. "Hello, George. This is Lacy. I want you to come to the airport at once and bring all the money you can get your hands on. And please hurry."

George didn't ask Lacy any questions as she stripped off her wedding ring and placed it in the palm of his hand.

"The ring is worth much more than the five thousand dollars I gave you, Lacy," he protested. "I can't take it."

She looked at him and he saw the misery in her eyes.

"I won't be needing the ring any longer, George. Hock it, give it to your wife, or throw it away. I just don't care."

His eyes were filled with compassion. "Is there anything more I can do for you?"

She extended her hand to him and he squeezed it. "No, you've been a prince. Thank you."

"I take it you are flying out as soon as this weather lets up."

"I'm leaving as soon as possible. And thank you for not asking questions, George."

"I know more than you think I do, Lacy."

She glanced out the window and watched a trail of raindrops make a path down the glass. "I know."

Chapter Nineteen

The rain had slowed by the time Lacy climbed into the seat beside the pilot. As he revved the motor, she closed her eyes, still too numb to think clearly.

"Miss Black," Frank observed, peering though his rain-spattered windshield, "there's a woman running toward us. Do you know her?"

Lacy recognized Ruth, who was waving her arms and trying to draw their attention. "Yes, I know her. Pay her no mind. Just take off."

"Yes, ma'am."

As the plane taxied forward slowly, Ruth caught up with them and began pounding on the door.

"Let me in. You can't leave without me. I haven't anywhere to go. Lacy, let me in!"

"Stop," Lacy instructed the pilot. She opened the door and stared at a very wet and frantic Ruth. "What do you want of me?"

"Mark's kicked me out. Please take me with you."

Ruth looked pathetic with her wet hair plastered to her head and rain running down her face.

"No. Just leave me alone, Ruth."

"I know what you're feeling"—Ruth was shouting to be heard above the engines—"and you have every right to hate me. But I'll make it up to you, Lacy—I swear I will."

Lacy could only stare at her. "What about your fear of flying?"

"The only thing I fear right now is being left behind."

"Get in," Lacy said in resignation.

Ruth scrambled into the back and settled in the seat. "Thank you; you won't regret this."

"I have many regrets, sister, dear, and most of them have to do with you."

Knowing she had to get away from Ruth, Lacy leaned over and whispered in Frank's ear, "I'm getting out. Here's another thousand dollars," she said, shoving money into his hand. "Chart your course for Snyder, Texas, and set my sister down there. No matter how much she protests, I want that to be your destination. Give her this money when you get there, and not before."

"But—"

"Please, just do it." Lacy was glad she had stowed her suitcase on the floor beside her, where it was within reach. Taking it in hand, she opened the door and jumped to the ground. After pushing the door shut, she waved for the pilot to take off.

She could only imagine Ruth's distress as the plane picked up speed and took to the air. She watched the lights of the tiny craft until it was out of sight and then moved in the direction of Mark's car.

With the windshield wipers swishing out a rhythmic beat, she turned the Cord eastward, wondering why she had remained so long in a marriage that was obviously wrong from the start.

Tears rolled down her cheeks, and deep, wrenching sobs tore from her lips. Now she could feel—now she would cry.

Lacy drove all night, putting as much distance between her and Mark as was possible. Early the next morning, she pulled into an obscure motor court. Before getting out of the car, she tied a scarf over her head and put on her dark glasses so she wouldn't be recognized. She slept most of the day, but by six she was on the road again, still heading east toward Drew and a new life.

The road stretched before her like a never-ending ribbon in the bright moonlight. She switched on the radio, hoping she could pick up a station. At first the radio crackled, and then she heard a man's voice and her hand froze to the steering wheel as she realized it was George.

"I'm Mr. Damian's assistant. As you can imagine, he's too broken up to talk. He's asked me to tell Miss Black's public that a bright star has disappeared from the horizon and we will never see her like again."

Lacy frowned. What was George talking about? Apparently the publicity wheels were already turning and Mark was trying to cover up for her absence.

George Levine's voice cut into her thoughts. "I was one of the last people to see Lacy Black alive. She asked me to come to the airport before she left, and I did."

"We will all miss her," the announcer said gravely. "Movies will never be the same now that the most beautiful woman in the world is dead."

Lacy was shaking so hard that she had to pull off to the side of the road. She turned up the volume on the radio.

"How can we be sure that there was a crash?" the announcer asked.

"The pilot radioed that he was having trouble and going down. He knew they were going to die because he asked the tower to tell his wife and children that he loved them. The control tower reported that they were in contact with them until the end. They heard a woman scream." George paused a moment as if he couldn't go on. He cleared his throat and said in

a choked voice, "Around two o'clock, Mr. Damian was informed that Lacy was dead."

"I'm sure there will be a search for the bodies," the announcer said.

"Yes, it's already begun. But it could take a long time to locate the wreckage, since it's believed they went down somewhere over the Sierra Nevada."

"Weren't they off course if their destination was San Francisco?"

"We can only assume the storm caused them to go off course," George said.

Lacy shook her head, unable to comprehend what they were talking about.

"Can you tell us anything else?" the announcer inquired.

"No, that's all we know at this time."

"Please convey our deepest sympathy to Mr. Damian. The world knows that they were deeply in love."

The theme song from *Mata Hari* came on, signaling an end to the interview, and Lacy sat there, too stunned to move. She tried to sort out what she had just heard. With heartbreaking clarity, she realized that there had been a crash and Ruth and Frank had died.

She was still angry with Mark, but she couldn't let him continue to believe that she was dead.

Lacy turned the car around and headed back in the direction of Los Angeles, until she remembered something that Mark had said to her. Her blood ran cold.

She could hear his voice as he told her about the plot of the new picture he wanted her to do—a plot in which the woman was killed in a plane crash that had been planned by her husband.

Once again she pulled off the side of the road and switched off the engine. How could she even think it? Mark was many things, but he was not a murderer.

She pressed her fingers against her throbbing temples. What

had he said about the script—the husband would make it look like an accident, a defective fuel line?

She closed her eyes. No, it wasn't possible. Still something nagged at her. Details came back to her, little things that all added up to something big. Mark hadn't wanted her to take the Raja Star with her on the plane; he had stayed home when he usually accompanied her on promotional tours; and like the husband of the tragic heroine in his script, Mark had insured her life for one million dollars!

The pieces fit together too well for it to be coincidence. But she couldn't believe that he had deliberately set out to kill her. She laid her head against the steering wheel, trying to find answers and thinking how close she'd come to death. "Oh, Ruth, poor Ruth, you weren't much of a sister, but you didn't deserve to die in my place."

Suddenly a coldness clamped her heart. Was it possible that the Mark she had once loved had wanted her dead? Could he have been having sex with her sister, all the while thinking she was on a plane that was destined to crash? Was he capable of such an atrocity?

She shivered—she couldn't think about that now. If she did, she'd lose her mind. Lacy started the car and turned around, heading east again. For the moment, she could prove nothing. The Cord sped on throughout the night. Lacy didn't know what she was going to do, but she couldn't go to Drew until she knew the truth.

Drew Mallory was at the theater going over the score for his new play. He didn't know when Lacy would arrive, but it was hard to concentrate on his work when all he could think about was her.

One of the dancers from the cast approached him with a forlorn look on her face. "Mr. Mallory, isn't it so tragic about Lacy Black?"

"What about her?" he demanded.

"Why, it's all everyone's talking about. I still can't believe it."

"Barbara, what about Lacy?"

"The airplane crash. Didn't you know? She's dead!"

Drew felt as though someone had just slammed a fist into his stomach. "You're mad. Why do you come to me with such lies? Don't you think I'd know it if she were dead?"

Barbara stared at him in bewilderment, wondering at his violent reaction to the news of Lacy Black's death. "It's true," she protested. "If you don't believe me, just ask anyone."

Drew closed his eyes, turning away. His voice was hardly audible as he spoke. "Everyone is dismissed for the day. Go home until further notice." Without another word, he moved up the aisle toward the exit, his every step an effort. His mind refused to accept that Lacy, his Lacy, was dead.

When he reached his apartment, he immediately grabbed a bottle of bourbon and took a deep swallow before switching on the radio. With unashamed tears in his eyes, he listened to the gruesome account of Lacy's death.

He didn't know it was possible to hurt so much and still go on living. She had been on her way to him when she had died. He took another deep swallow of the bourbon and dropped down onto the couch.

Beautiful Lacy, so alive; how could she be dead? She was supposed to be a woman of the world—a sex symbol—and yet, he had found her innocent and highly moral. He touched the ring that he never removed from his finger, knowing it was all he would ever have of her. Happiness had been within his grasp, only to be snatched away. He wanted to get roaring drunk so he wouldn't have to think.

How would he go on without her?

Mark had been receiving streams of callers for a week. It wasn't difficult for him to play the bereaved husband, because he really was grieving over Lacy's death. Everywhere he went, he received a barrage of sympathy, and he took it as his due.

One thing kept nagging at Mark. Ruth was missing, and the bitch had taken his Cord. He'd lost Lacy and the Raja Star; he'd be damned if he'd lose his Cord, too. Then he had second thoughts. If he alerted the authorities and they found Ruth, they might learn something from her that would make them suspicious about Lacy's death. She could have the damn Cord; it was little enough to pay to be rid of her. She would only be an encumbrance to him now anyway.

Mark went back to the house where he had lived with Lacy for four years. He was surprised at how empty it felt. His footsteps took him to her bedroom, where he sat on her bed as if he were waiting for her to come rushing through the door at any moment.

Deep pain ripped at him when he realized that he'd never see her again. He lay back on her pillow, and the air seemed to be filled with the sweet, exotic scent she always wore.

"I told you, Lacy," he murmured aloud, "that you'd break my heart one day, and you have."

In Albuquerque, Lacy stopped at a drugstore and bought a bottle of hair dye. In a motor court on the outskirts of town, she changed her hair back to its original color. Staring at the stranger who looked back at her in the mirror, she felt a sudden fear. She had gone from Lucinda Blackburn to Lacy Black, and now she had to become someone else again—just who, she hadn't yet decided.

Rummaging through her suitcase, she removed all the expensive black clothes and dumped them in the trash can, wondering what the maid would think in the morning when she cleaned the room. With satisfaction, she pulled a blue cotton dress over her head and arranged the shoulder pads. She had bought several inexpensive dresses, and it felt good to have a wardrobe that didn't include anything black.

She placed a floppy hat upon her head, deciding it would further her disguise, and wondered what the millinery industry would think if they could see Lacy Black finally wearing a hat.

With a quick assessment of her appearance in the cracked wall mirror, she decided that no one would guess her true identity. She looked nothing like a glamorous star, and besides, everyone thought Lacy Black was dead.

She tossed the hat aside and lay back on the bed. Hoping to fall asleep, she switched on the radio and listened to the soothing music of the Tommy Dorsey band. Suddenly the program was interrupted by a news bulletin that made her blood freeze. It was live-from-Hollywood coverage of Lacy Black's memorial service.

Feeling sick inside, she listened to Mark's voice as he delivered the eulogy. She'd heard the words before in what must have been his dress rehearsal: "Ladies and gentlemen, I'm here today only because my wife would expect it of me. She would want me to go on because that's the kind of woman she was—"

Lacy didn't need to hear any more. She knew what he would say by heart—she'd heard the script.

She turned off the radio and began pacing the floor like a caged animal. Mark had deliberately tried to kill her. But why?

Lacy didn't cry; she was angry, and she wanted revenge. She didn't know that it was possible to hate someone so much.

It hadn't mattered to Mark that the pilot had three children who were now without a father. And if they had flown out as Mark had planned, George Levine, the publicist, and her hairdresser would also have been on that plane when it went down.

She drew in a shuddering breath. Mark was evil—why had she not seen it before? She had been married to a monster!

Lacy stopped before the mirror and stared at herself long and hard. "One day I'll bring you down, Mark Damian," she vowed. "You'll fall so far, you'll have to climb up just to reach hell."

The large cathedral where Lacy Black's memorial service was held was filled to capacity with Hollywood's elite, while thousands of mourners stood behind the roped-off areas, hoping to get a glimpse of Lacy's grieving widower and the celebrities who were in attendance.

Mark, his eyes hidden behind dark glasses, accepted condolences in silence. The world was grieving because of the tragic end of a great star. She would not soon be forgotten; in fact, her legend only grew with each passing day.

Afterward, Mark went back to the house he'd shared with Lacy and remained in seclusion for weeks.

When he did emerge, he looked haggard, and it appeared that he'd lost weight. His first day back at the studio was spent making arrangements for the release of Lacy's last two films.

He sat at his desk, staring down on the lot, watching people scurry around like mice. He'd received a two-million-dollar check from the insurance company; no one suspected a thing.

He swiveled around and stared at the mound of papers on his desk. Somehow the joy had gone out of his life—he missed Lacy more than he'd thought he would, and he was haunted by memories of her.

He hit the intercom, and his secretary's voice crackled on the line. "Get me that new girl at once," he snapped. "Have the makeup and wardrobe departments stand by this afternoon."

A short time later, a pretty blonde entered, her enthusiasm clearly written on her face. "Oh, Mr. Damian, how can I thank you for this chance?"

He ground his teeth together. She would never replace Lacy—no one could. "We'll find a way, baby. You'll see."

The Aztec Theater was crowded, as it always was when a Lacy Black film was playing. If it hadn't been so dark, the small-town audience would have been shocked to see the sanctimonious Sam Blackburn amble in and take a seat at the back after the picture began.

He stared at a close-up of Lacy, knowing that only a father would recognize her as his little girl. She looked so like her mother, who had really been the love of his life. Suddenly, it was too painful to sit there any longer. With his shoulders hunched and his eyes moist with tears, he quietly left.

The old man's steps were slow, his back hunched as he

moved in the direction of his garage, up to his empty apartment, to spend another long evening alone.

If only he could tell Lacy that he now realized she had been his pearl and Ruth the swine.

Part Two
Ben

Chapter Twenty

With the radio as her only companion, Lacy drove until she was too exhausted to go any farther. Mostly she slept during the day and drove all night, always in an easterly direction, and always fearing that Mark would somehow discover she was alive and come after her.

She thought about returning to Snyder. But she couldn't go there. Her father wouldn't welcome her, and people from her hometown might recognize her.

It was after midnight and Lacy hadn't passed a car in hours. She needed to sleep, but where could she hide where she would feel safe? If Mark had connected the disappearance of his Cord with her, he might realize that it was Ruth who had died in the crash.

When she drove into Denver, she decided to get rid of the Cord. It was such an unusual car that it drew too much attention. Passing through the sleeping town, she headed the car up into the foothills, knowing what she must do. It was almost sunup when she stopped on a steep embankment. She pulled on the hand brake, got out of the car, and walked to the deep ravine, staring into the black void—an appropriate resting place for Mark's prized Cord.

In the distance, she could see the lights of Denver as the inhabitants stirred to life. Whatever she did, she must do it quickly.

Lacy was cold and frightened, and there was no one she could turn to for help—she would just have to help herself. Reaching into the backseat, she took her suitcase and set it beside the road.

She paused with her hand on the brake. There was always the possibility that the car would be discovered and traced back to Mark. She'd just have to take that chance.

She released the hand brake and jumped out of the way, waiting for gravity to do the rest. Slowly at first, the car moved forward. When it approached a sharp turn, it plunged into the air and, for what seemed like an eternity, was suspended there. Lacy watched in fascination as the car disappeared from sight. She could hear it grind against rocks, turn over, and at last come to rest at the bottom of the ravine.

The deed was done, and it gave her great satisfaction.

With a cold, bitter wind blowing in her face, Lacy gripped the handle of her suitcase and started walking back toward Denver. The sun was just coming up when a truck stopped to give her a lift, which she gratefully accepted.

She judged the driver to be somewhere in his forties, friendly and sympathetic. Lacy felt guilty for using her acting ability to convince the man of the tragic story she embroidered.

His hands tightened on the wheel in anger. "You say the man asked you to marry him and then took your money and abandoned you, little lady?"

"Yes, sir." She sniffed.

"A man like that ought to be horsewhipped."

"I just want to go home to my mama."

"And you will. Where's she live?"

"Kansas City."

"I'm heading up Salt Lake City way, or I'd take you myself.

But don't you worry; I'll see that you have the money for a bus ticket home."

"Thank you," Lacy said, feeling even guiltier because he was so nice, "but I have just enough money for a ticket."

He smiled, his rough face softening. "You'll be all right, little lady. You're pretty, and a good man will come along one day and make you a decent husband. Do you know," he said, glancing at her sideways, "you remind me of someone, but I can't think who at the moment."

Lacy pulled her floppy hat down at an angle and turned to look out the window. "I have that kind of face," she murmured.

The man sitting next to Lacy on the bus was reading a magazine that had her face on the front cover. She watched him thumb to the article that told about her death. For a long moment, her gaze focused on a picture of Mark in dark glasses, playing the bereaved husband. She was almost certain that behind those glasses his eyes reflected triumph instead of grief. She thought it was strange that there was no mention of her sister's death. Maybe no one had seen Ruth climb aboard the plane that night.

Lacy was anxious to get to New York, where she'd be just a face in the crowd, and she admitted to herself that she wanted to be near Drew, even though she could not let him know she was alive. Not yet.

More than anything, she wanted to run to the safety of his arms and have him hold her until the pain stopped. But she loved him too much to involve him in the ugliness and danger that shadowed her life. Her situation was complicated, and she was confused and didn't know what to do. The world thought she was dead, but in fact she was still legally Mark's wife and not free to approach Drew.

It was noon when the bus pulled into New York City, and Lacy couldn't help remembering the last time she was there. Then, she'd had a suite at the Plaza and the press had followed her everywhere she went. Now, there was no fanfare and no one cared who she was.

She found a modest walk-up apartment in Greenwich Village that consisted of a small bedroom, an even smaller kitchen, and a bath she had to share with three other tenants.

She spent the first few days cleaning and repainting the dingy gray walls and hand-sewing bright blue curtains for the bedroom and yellow ones for the kitchen. At last, exhausted, she stood back and looked at her small accomplishments. This was her new home and the first day of her new life.

Lacy was awakened by the sound of honking horns and rush-hour traffic. It took her a moment to remember where she was. Stretching her aching muscles, she washed her face and set the coffeepot on the burner. She had to look for a job. What was left of the money George had given her wouldn't last much longer.

Taking a steaming cup of coffee and yesterday's newspaper, she sat at the rickety table and scanned the want ads. What were her qualifications? The only job she'd ever had was acting, and she dared not pursue that career. She flipped through to the front of the paper, scanning it for any mention of Lacy Black. She was glad that the accounts of her death no longer made headlines. She hoped the world would soon forget she had ever existed.

With crushing sadness, she realized that she would have to establish a new identity before she could go job hunting. What name should she choose? She glanced through the newspaper, hoping to find something that appealed to her.

She was diverted by an article on the war in the Libyan desert. It told about the hardships experienced by the British soldiers, who were unaccustomed to desert warfare. Besides fighting the enemy, they had to endure the burning heat, thirst, and mirages that tortured and tantalized them into near madness.

"Mirage," she said aloud. "An illusion, something that isn't real . . . like me."

She would choose Mirage for the symbolism, and use her old name, Blackburn, because she needed to hold on to some part of her own identity. Mirage Blackburn—it sounded right.

Wouldn't she need papers to prove who she was—some kind of identification? She opened her handbag and flipped through her wallet. The only identification she had was a driver's license, but it was, of course, issued under the name of Lacy Black.

Feeling utterly defeated and heartsick, she laid her head on her arms. What was she to do? She had never been one to give up, not with her father, and not with Mark. She stiffened her spine and raised her head. She had to be strong now if she was going to survive.

She needed a diversion, something that would take her mind off her troubles, if only for a short time. She turned the newspaper pages to the entertainment section. Her eyes fell on an advertisement for Drew's new play, *Midnight Ghosts*. Checking her watch, she saw that if she hurried, she could make the matinee performance.

The play turned out to be a comedy. As Lacy sat in the darkened theater, she smiled at first, and then started laughing at the witty banter between the main characters. Life couldn't be so bad if one could still laugh. When the last curtain came down, she felt almost lighthearted. Just being in the theater, watching his play come to life on the stage, made her feel close to Drew, and she wanted to hold on to that feeling for as long as she could.

Reluctantly, she stood and merged with the departing crowd, dreading the thought of going back to her lonely apartment. She would feel more alone than ever now that she had touched Drew's world. It had been a mistake for her to come to his play.

People began to press in behind her, pushing until she stumbled against the man in front of her. A flash of horror, a distant memory, lingered at the edge of her mind as the crowd continued to shove her forward. Her breathing became shallow and quick and she froze in place. The last time she had left this theater, she had almost been trampled by adoring fans, until Drew rescued her. She clamped her hand over her mouth to smother a scream as people hemmed her in on all sides. When she heard a scream, it took her a moment to realize that the sound had come from her. Lacy lost her balance and flung her arms out to cushion her fall. She hit the floor hard, and a large man stumbled across her, pinning her beneath him. A crushing pain tore at her arm; and she was lost in total blackness.

At that moment, Benjamin Lord stepped into the crowded lobby and with one glance assessed the situation.

He knelt over the fallen woman, instructing the crowd to move back. She was beginning to come around, and he removed his jacket, placing it under her head.

"Can you move?" he asked with concern.

Lacy licked her dry lips as she tried to rise, but cried out and grabbed her arm. "I think my arm may be broken."

"Did you come to the theater alone, or should I fetch someone for you?"

"There is no one," she replied, biting her lip in pain.

Ben gently examined her arm, and frowned. When Lacy attempted to rise, he placed his hand on her shoulder. "I'm going to take you to the hospital."

She would have protested if the pain hadn't been so bad—all she could manage was a slight moan. The crowd parted as he carried her outside, but she saw nothing more than a blur of faces. Gently, he placed her in the backseat of a limousine that was parked at the curb. Tears of pain blinded her as he climbed in beside her.

"To the nearest hospital, Jenkins," he told his driver. "And hurry."

Benjamin Lord was an aristocratic-looking man in his late fifties. He was tall and distinguished, with gray at his temples and the kindest, softest blue eyes Lacy had ever seen. He wore a black pinstripe suit with a conservative gray tie. It was obvious to Lacy that he was someone of importance. She lay back, her eyes closed. For some reason, she trusted this man.

"However did you get caught up in that crush?" he asked gruffly. "When I reached you, they were practically trampling you. I hope a broken arm is all you have suffered."

She turned green eyes on him. "I don't know how it happened. I was going with the crowd, and I suddenly remembered . . ." She glanced up at him, wondering what he must think of her. "I was thinking about the play and not paying attention until I panicked."

A smile masked his look of concern. "It was good, wasn't it?"

"It was better than good—it was wonderful."

"I'm glad that you were impressed. The director, Andrew Mallory, is a friend of mine, and I'm proud of his every accomplishment." A smile formed on his lips. "But let me introduce myself to you. Benjamin Lord at your service, Miss . . . ?"

Before Lacy could answer, she felt darkness closing in around her, and she slumped into his arms.

"Hurry, Jenkins," Ben ordered. "I don't know how badly she's injured."

By now they had reached the hospital, and Jenkins pulled into the emergency entrance. Under his employer's instructions, he lifted the young woman into his arms and both men hurried into the hospital.

Ben brushed aside the receptionist, who wanted papers filled out. "Just get a doctor at once," he demanded. "There's time later to complete any paperwork you may require. Is Dr. Halstine on duty?"

"No, but his associate is on call," the receptionist replied stiffly.

"Contact Dr. Halstine and inform him that Benjamin Lord wants him to come to the hospital immediately."

The doctor who rushed forward recognized Ben and ordered that the injured woman be taken into the examining room at once.

Ben sat restlessly in the waiting room. Someone handed him a cup of coffee, and Jenkins appeared at his side with Lacy's handbag.

"I thought you might need this, Mr. Lord, to find out the woman's identity."

Ben had an aversion to inspecting the young woman's personal effects, but her relatives had to be notified of the accident. It was strange that her unstylish cotton dress didn't match the expensive alligator handbag. He opened it, finding the usual female belongings; lipstick, compact, comb. He removed her wallet and flipped it open, staring at the name on the driver's license.

"Lacy Black," he murmured in confusion. His eyes became speculative. No, this woman couldn't be Lacy Black; she was dead.

He flipped through the wallet, and was surprised to discover that the woman had several hundred-dollar bills in her possession. Feeling guilty for prying, he shoved the wallet back into the handbag, his mind in a quandary. Now that he thought about it, the woman did bear a resemblance to the deceased star. Perhaps they were related. There was a mystery here, and he intended to solve it.

Dr. Halstine came out of the swinging doors of the emergency room, smiling at Ben. "Well, your friend has a broken arm and a concussion. I'm glad to report that there are no internal injuries. I'll want her to remain in the hospital several days for observation, though."

Ben nodded grimly. "Can I see her now?"

"Only for a moment, Ben. I gave her something to make her rest. You know, it's not her injuries that concern me. It's her attitude. She doesn't seem to care if she recovers or not. If I ever saw a woman who had no will to live, it's our young patient." The doctor shook his head. "She told me how she was injured, but she wouldn't tell me her name. She insists that she has no close relatives or friends to notify. I find that strange."

"I don't know who she is or what her circumstances are," Ben said, "but I'll be responsible for all her medical expenses. I want her to receive the very best of care."

Dr. Halstine stared at the tall, stately man he had known for many years. It was said that if Benjamin Lord decided to run for president, he'd win by a landslide. He came from old money, and the Lord name was intertwined with American history. His great-grandfather had been one of George Washington's generals. His grandfather had established the family fortune in shipbuilding and banking. Ben, himself, was a friend of President Roosevelt's and was often invited to the White House.

"No doubt she will be grateful for your help, but we need to know her next of kin." He clapped Ben on the back. "Now, if you're through with me, I'd like to go back to my golf game."

Ben stood over the sleeping woman, more certain than ever that she was in some way related to the tragic star Lacy Black. Her eyes fluttered open and she stared at him in bewilderment. In this light, he was struck by her youth and vulnerability.

"Are you feeling a little better now?" he inquired gently.

"Yes, thank you for your concern," she said, her eyelids still heavy from the drugs she had been given. "I'm sorry to cause you so much trouble."

"My name is Benjamin Lord," he reminded her. "May I know your name?" he asked, putting a comforting hand on hers.

"I . . ." She licked her lips. It was time to assume her new identity. "I'm Mirage Blackburn."

He nodded. "Well, Mirage Blackburn, I don't want you to worry about a thing. I'll call on you again tomorrow." He searched her eyes. "In the meantime, is there anyone whom you want me to notify for you?"

She lowered her eyes, studying his strong hand. "No. There's no one."

"Then get some rest, and I'll see you tomorrow."

Mirage—as she now thought of herself—watched him leave. He was a very kind man, but she hoped he wouldn't return, because he would only ask her questions that she dared not answer.

She yawned as the medicine took effect. She was so sleepy. . . .

* * *

True to his word, Ben, as he insisted she call him, came to see Mirage the next day and every day thereafter.

Her room was filled with flowers and she found that she looked forward to his visits. She had never met a more interesting man. He brought her books to read and introduced her to the classics. She'd never had time to read before, and she was devouring them. In the evening he would sit beside her bed and they would discuss what she had read that day.

Mirage had been told by the nurses that Benjamin Lord was a very important man. But to her, he was both a godsend and a threat. He represented a safe haven in the confusion of her life, yet at the same time she feared his association with Drew.

The dining room at the Algonquin Hotel was crowded as Ben sat across the table from Drew, telling him about Mirage. "I've become attached to her, and I'm going to do everything I can to help her."

Drew looked at the man he loved like a father. In fact, his own father and Ben had been classmates together at Harvard, and when Drew's father died, Ben stepped in to fill the void he'd left. Not only did Ben advise Drew, he often put up the money for his plays.

"You are always championing the underdog, Ben," Drew said suspiciously. "How do you know you can trust this woman? She probably knows who you are and is just using you."

Ben shook his head. "No, she's not like that, as you'd see if you met her. She is a very troubled young woman, and I won't turn my back on her. She needs someone to care about her."

"Don't be too sure she didn't contrive the incident to get your attention. I've heard about such things happening."

Ben took a sip of wine and laughed. "You're beginning to see intrigue everywhere. I suppose it's because of your profession."

Drew leaned back in his chair and stared at his friend. "That may be true, but be careful all the same."

"If you want to meet her for yourself, you can come up to

Bar Harbor. I'm going to attempt to convince her to convalesce there when Dr. Halstine releases her."

"Do you think that's wise?"

"Don't worry about me," Ben said, changing the subject. "But I asked you here because I'm worried about you. You don't look well, Drew. You're much thinner than you were the last time I saw you, and I don't like those circles under your eyes. Have you seen a doctor?"

Drew glanced down at Lacy's ring. "What's wrong with me, no doctor can cure."

"Care to talk about it?"

Drew had always found Ben a most sympathetic listener, but he couldn't talk about Lacy with anyone; the hurt was too raw. "Not just now."

Ben was more perceptive than Drew realized. "Your problem has to do with the woman who gave you that ring, doesn't it?"

"How did you guess?"

"I've been watching the way you keep staring at it. I know it's a woman's ring, since it fits only on your little finger."

Drew's eyes were suddenly full of pain. "I can't talk about her yet, Ben. You see, she . . . died."

Ben paused with his wineglass halfway to his lips. "I'm so sorry, Drew. I had no idea. Is there anything I can do?"

"Only time can help, Ben. At least that's what the wise men say." Drew glanced at his watch and stood up quickly. "Gotta go now; I'm late for rehearsal. But take my advice and be wary of this woman. And don't think I won't come up to Bar Harbor to check on her for myself."

Ben set the new leather suitcase down and smiled at Mirage. "Dr. Halstine informed me that he is going to release you this afternoon."

Mirage looked crestfallen. She was going to miss Ben, and she realized that she might never see him again once she left the hospital.

"I called the manager of one of the department stores and

told him to have his people put together a wardrobe for you. He said they'd include cosmetics and whatever else a woman might need. If you find there's something missing, just let me know."

"Why did you do that, Ben? I'm already deeply indebted to you."

"Nonsense. I'm a selfish old man who has become very fond of a beautiful young woman and am loath to part with her company. I have a cottage in Bar Harbor, Maine, and I want to take you there until you are completely recovered. Since it's off-season, you can have privacy and no one will bother you."

"I couldn't possibly do that, Ben," she said, wishing with all her heart that she could. "I don't know what you think of me, but I'd never go off with a man."

He smiled. "Young lady, I'm old enough to be your father, and I'm flattered if you look on me as a threat to your virtue. But it's as I told you; I've grown fond of your company and look forward to you brightening up my life for a time. Is that too much to ask?"

She bit her lower lip. "I don't know."

"If it will make you feel any better, I've already hired a private nurse to look after you. So you see, we will be properly chaperoned. And there is a caretaker and his wife who live there year-round."

She looked at him, weakening. "I'd like to, Ben, but it doesn't seem proper."

He smiled. "We'll worry about what's proper when you are well. What do you say, Mirage? Will you make an old man happy?"

She glanced out the window to watch the first snowflakes of winter drift slowly downward; then she looked back at Ben, who seemed to be waiting for her answer. Maine seemed the perfect place to wait while the world forgot that Lacy Black had ever existed.

"Yes. I'll go with you, Ben. I owe you so much already, but I'll find a way to repay you somehow."

He moved closer to her and took her hand in his. "You have already repaid me by giving me your trust at last."

Chapter Twenty-one

As the chauffeur maneuvered the black Rolls-Royce up a steep cliff, Ben pointed out Windward House. It had been built in the Tudor style, and sat majestically on a hill overlooking the harbor. Surrounded by thick woods, it looked like a warm sanctuary from the heavy snowflakes that were covering the ground.

Mirage was huddled beneath a cashmere blanket with Ben beside her. There were still bruises under one eye, and her arm was in a sling, but her spirits were light. Ben had kept her amused all the way from New York. He was probably the most intelligent man she had ever met, but he never made her feel uncomfortable or ignorant, as Mark had.

"I thought you said you were taking me to a cottage—I don't call *that* a cottage," she said when she saw the sprawling mansion ahead of them.

"All the large houses you see here are referred to as cottages," Ben said with a slight smile. "It probably seems a bit pretentious, but I've called it that all my life. Many of the affluent families from New York and Boston once spent their summers in Bar Harbor. It's not as fashionable as it once was, though. Most of the families who used to summer here have found new play-grounds, but not me." He grinned. "I believe I like it better because of their absence. Some stubborn souls like me have retained their homes here, but only a few."

"I saw several hotels."

With a smile, Ben faked horror. "I believe that's why most of my contemporaries have moved on to what they call 'more suitable grounds.' Bar Harbor has become a favorite vacation spot for tourists, and I'm told it's favored by honeymoon couples."

"If this is only your summer residence, where do you live the rest of the year?" Mirage inquired.

"I occupy the top floor of the Lord Building on Park Avenue in New York. Although I must confess that I find myself spending more and more time here at Windward House and less and less time in New York."

Mirage was trying to understand Ben's life. "Mrs. Bittle, one of the nurses at the hospital, told me that President Roosevelt offered you an appointment as ambassador to the Court of Saint James, but you turned it down."

Ben smiled at her. "What else did Mrs. Bittle tell you?"

Mirage snuggled beneath the warm blanket. "She said you would be a good catch, but that many women had tried and failed to lead you into matrimony."

Ben's expression became grim. "I was married to the same woman for twenty-five years. When she died ten years ago, I had no wish to remarry."

"You've never been tempted?"

His eyes rested on her face. "Not for more than five minutes. Mary was kind and gentle, well-read and fascinating. I never knew a boring day with her. When she died, it was as if I lost my best friend. I'm not saying I haven't enjoyed the company of other women; I just never found one that would suit me as Mary did. I've never been one to settle for less than the best."

Mirage turned her face away from him. "You were most fortunate indeed, Ben. It must be wonderful to have that kind of marriage."

Have you been married, Mirage?"

She turned troubled eyes on him. "You may as well know now, Ben, that I don't want to discuss my past with you or anyone. I accepted your invitation to recuperate at your cottage mostly because I need time to think about my life and put the pieces back together."

"Perhaps you'll allow me to become your friend, and help you put those pieces back together."

She saw compassion in his eyes, and she believed in his sincerity, but her secrets were too dark to divulge, the danger still too real.

"Please don't ask me any questions, Ben, because I can't answer them truthfully, and I won't lie to you. There is much in my life that is uncertain, many problems that I haven't the strength to settle right now. When you find out about me, you may regret your kindness to me."

He patted her hand comfortingly. "I could never regret knowing you, Mirage, but I'll honor your wishes and not pry into your past. We'll just talk about cabbages and kings."

She smiled at his allusion to the Lewis Carroll poem he'd introduced her to.

"Do you play chess, Mirage?" Ben asked, changing the subject.

"No, I'm afraid not."

"Do you enjoy classical music?"

"I've . . . not been exposed to it," she answered, feeling out of her depth with this man. "Perhaps you could teach me," she suggested shyly.

Ben was pleased. This was going to be a most enlightening and exciting winter. For so long, his life had gone on in the same vein, never deviating from year to year. Then fate threw Mirage Blackburn into his path, and he felt young just being with her. She was running from something, and she was hurting. He wanted to help her, but first he'd have to win her confidence.

Jenkins opened the car door and Ben led Mirage up the steps.

On entering the house, she was awestruck. A black-and-white marble floor covered the huge entryway.

Ben ushered her into a large room where a cheery fire had been laid. She held her hands out to the warming flames.

"I like your cottage, Ben."

"I'm glad it pleases you. As I told you, the servants have the winter off except for Mrs. Brewster and her husband. They, along with Jenkins and your nurse, will look after our needs." He helped her into a chair and placed a soft woolen robe about her. "Are you feeling ill?" he asked solicitously.

"No. I'm fine."

Her eyes were troubled as she watched him sit in the wing-back chair across from her. "I want to tell you about myself, Ben, but I can't. All I can say is that you may be placing your life in danger by bringing me into your home."

"First you get completely well, and then we shall discuss what is troubling you."

At that moment, a woman dressed in a nurse's uniform appeared in the doorway, and Ben quickly introduced her as Kitty Merryweather, who would be looking after Mirage during her convalescence.

"I'm delighted to meet you, Miss Blackburn," the nurse said. "You must be weary after your journey."

Kitty Merryweather was in her early thirties and wore her hair severely pulled into a bun at the nape of her neck. Her hair was auburn and her face was covered with freckles. Her blue eyes were soft when she smiled, and Mirage warmed to her at once.

"I don't feel that I need a nurse, Miss Merryweather, but Ben insists that I do. I'll try not to be too much trouble to you."

The nurse took on a professional manner. "Your doctor advised me of your injuries and insisted that you will need rest. I've prepared a room for you, and I believe you should lie down after your strenuous trip."

Mirage watched the nurse walk up the stairs and offered Ben her hand. "It seems I have no choice but to follow her. Thank you for taking me into your home."

He held her hand gently in his grasp. "What man of my age wouldn't be happy to spend the winter with a beautiful young woman like you?"

Mirage was so grateful to Ben that she impulsively threw her uninjured arm around him and felt his arms tighten about her.

"Here now, none of that." Ben unclasped her arms and held her a little away from him. "You don't want to cause an old man to have a heart attack, do you?"

Mirage looked at his handsome face, which was surprisingly unlined. "You aren't old, Ben. I have never known anyone more vital than you."

He led her to the stairs and urged her upward. "You're going to be good for me, Mirage. Now go along with the nurse and rest. I'll see you at dinner."

When Mirage entered the bedroom, she was enchanted by its beauty. The white carpet and two wide windows gave the room an open, airy appearance. The huge poster bed had bright yellow chintz hangings and a matching bedspread. The furnishings consisted of a dressing table with a ruffled organdy skirt, and a couch and two chairs in yellow and white.

"I've already unpacked for you. You'll find a bath through those doors," Kitty said, while pulling down the bedspread. "Would you like to bathe before you rest?"

The bed looked so inviting, Mirage shook her head. "Perhaps I am a bit tired. I'll just lie down for a few moments."

The nurse helped Mirage undress and, when she was in bed, pulled the covers over her. "Sleep's what you need."

Mirage yawned. "I'll just close my eyes for a moment. . . ."

Before Kitty could tiptoe out of the room, Mirage was asleep.

Ben stood at the window, watching the snow pile up on the road. Before morning they would be snowed in, but that didn't matter. For so long he had felt a heavy loneliness, but now, since Mirage had entered his life, he found himself looking forward to each new day.

Mirage, however, was not at peace with herself. He could feel sadness and anger in her, and she had spoken of danger. What could have happened to her?

Kitty rapped on the open door, and Ben motioned her forward. "Is she resting?"

"Yes, sir. I wondered if you had any other duties you required of me?"

"No, Miss Merryweather, your only duty will be to tend Miss Blackburn. When she has no need of you, you are free to spend your time as you wish."

"Thank you, sir. I wanted to thank you for employing me. It's not easy to find a job in a private home these days."

He turned back to the window. "Just look after your charge, and we'll both be happy."

"Yes, sir." She moved to the door, knowing she'd been dismissed. She found this arrangement odd. What connection did her beautiful young patient have with the distinguished Benjamin Lord? Oh, well, it wasn't for her to question. She was hired to do a job, and she would do it to the best of her ability.

Mirage had been at Windward House for two weeks and was completely recovered, at least physically. Ben was always solicitous and kind in his treatment of her and had never-ending patience.

Although he spent most of his mornings in his study, he lunched and dined with Mirage. Today, for the first time, she had been invited into his sanctuary—his private study.

It was a large room with seven windows that faced the sea. The floors were of shining parquet, and the paneling was of waxed pine. The bookshelves were filled with leather-bound books and had beveled glass fronts. In addition to his heavy mahogany desk, there were three brown-and-blue-striped couches that faced a marble fireplace with carved lion heads.

"What an unusual fireplace," she commented as she entered.

"Yes, these carvings will probably outlast the house itself," he said, smiling. "It's good to see you looking so well, Mirage. I believe the doctor would pronounce you completely recovered."

"I owe it all to you, Ben."

He seated her on the couch beside him and picked up the book he'd been reading. "Nonsense. You owe me nothing."

She glanced at the book in his lap. "Did I disturb your reading?"

"Of course not. I sent for you, remember? I wonder if you'd be interested in this book. It's about famous jewelry."

Mirage glanced down at the picture of a huge blue diamond surrounded by sparkling white diamonds. "That's the Hope Diamond, isn't it?"

"Indeed it is. Quite lovely, but it carries a curse with it, you know. They say that those who own it meet with a tragic end." He turned the page. "And these gray pearls once belonged to Queen Elizabeth."

Mirage was beginning to feel uneasy, as if she knew Ben was leading up to something. When he turned to the next page, she gasped. There was a photograph of the emerald necklace that Mark had given her.

"This," Ben said, as her face paled, "is the Raja Star. It is said to have belonged to an Indian maharani, and it also carries a curse. It was last owned by the motion picture star Lacy Black. Isn't it amazing, Mirage, how buildings, cities, and even whole races can disappear, but something of beauty like this endures forever?"

She jerked her head up and stared into his eyes. *He knows,* she thought. *He knows who I am!*

"That necklace didn't survive, Ben," she said quietly. "No human eye will ever look upon its evil beauty again. You see, I flushed it down the toilet."

Chapter Twenty-two

A bitter gale raged outside the window, but Ben was aware only of the lovely girl who had just stunned him with her admission. Accustomed as he was to schooling his thoughts, he couldn't keep his eyes from revealing how shocked he was.

"You are Lacy Black," he said at last. "I knew you were hiding a secret, but I hadn't expected this. When the hospital needed your identity, I looked in your purse and saw Lacy Black's driver's license. When I noticed your resemblance to her, I thought you must be a close relative and perhaps kept her driver's license as a remembrance. I'm sorry to admit," he said apologetically, "that I don't frequent the movie houses, and I never saw one of your pictures. However, I've read many magazine and newspaper articles about you. Along with the rest of the world, I believed Lacy Black died in that plane crash."

Tears glistened in her green eyes. "I am dead, Ben. I'm one of the walking dead. I may not have been on that plane, but I might as well have been."

Pulling her into his arms so her head rested against his shoulder, he allowed her to sob out her misery. "Cry it all out, Mirage. Then you can begin to heal."

For a long time he held her, until she quieted. Then he handed her his handkerchief. "If you need to talk, I'm a good listener, and what you tell me won't go outside this room." He raised her chin. "But if you don't want to talk, we'll never broach the subject again."

"I want to tell you, Ben. I have to tell someone or I'll go mad. I just haven't known who I could trust."

"You can trust me."

"Yes," she said, laying her head back on his shoulder, "more than anyone I've ever known, I trust you, Ben."

"My time is yours, Mirage. Why don't you tell me everything?"

She dabbed at her eyes with Ben's handkerchief and sat up straight. "I wasn't much of a person, Ben. You wouldn't have liked me at all. I was weak and ignorant, and except for trying to do everything I could to please my husband, I succeeded only in my career."

"I have come to know you, Mirage, and I don't think that's true at all. Have you been so badly hurt that you have no feeling of worth?"

She tried not to cry. "Mark killed my soul, Ben, and he tried to kill me. He thinks he succeeded, but you see, the woman who died in the crash that night was my sister, Ruth. He's a murderer, and he deliberately caused the crash." Her eyes gleamed with a hatred so sharp that Ben clutched her hand to calm her. "Ben, Mark didn't even care that his deed would take the lives of other innocent people. If his original plan had worked, there would have been five people in the plane that night. As it was, the pilot left three fatherless children."

"Perhaps you should start from the beginning, Mirage. Tell me everything."

As she spoke in a surprisingly dispassionate voice, Ben could feel the pain of a young girl who had been deserted by a promiscuous mother, then rejected by a self-righteous father who never understood her worth. He felt her betrayal when her sister slept with her husband, and her despair and then anger when she'd discovered that same husband had planned her death.

When she finished speaking, Ben took her hand. "Let me tell you what I see, Mirage," he said gently. "I see an innocent young girl whose life is like an unwritten page. She was neglected and used by her family, who should have loved and protected her. Then she met a man, a charming but cunning devil, who saw her as his road to greatness. He took her away from the drudgery that was her life, but not for her benefit. He only used her for his own ends. I have seen your hunger for knowledge. But he used only your outer self and neglected the inner person. He was greedy and self-seeking, and you were his innocent victim."

Mirage looked at Ben in amazement. He seemed to know her better than she knew herself, and he had found good in her.

"And then," Ben continued, "fate stepped in and rescued you—gave you another chance. You can start with a clean slate, Mirage. You can make your life whatever you want."

"I can't, Ben. The driving force in my life now is hatred. Mark must pay for what he's done. I can't have a life until his villainous deeds have been uncovered for all the world to see."

"Hatred is a destructive force, Mirage. If you allow it to, it will turn against you and leave you bitter and tortured."

"I know that's true. My father was a bitter old man with no purpose in life but hatred and bigotry. I don't want to be like him, but I fear I have become so."

She reached out to Ben in desperation. "I can't seem to make a decision. Should I go to the authorities and tell them who I am and what happened? I'm not even sure that I could prove anything. Mark was very clever. It would only be my word against his."

"What do you want to do?"

"I want Lacy Black to stay dead."

Ben looked at her intently, feeling her torment. "Perhaps I can help you. Would you like that, Mirage?"

"Yes, Ben, I would like that very much."

He stood up and walked to his desk, lifting the telephone receiver. "This is my private line," he told Mirage. He spoke in a quiet voice and then waited for several moments.

The only sound in the room was the ticking of the clock.

"Hello, put me through to Mr. Hoover at once." He paused as if he were listening to someone on the other line. "I don't care if he is in a meeting. Tell him Benjamin Lord wants to speak to him."

Mirage's eyes widened. Could Ben be referring to the head of the FBI?

"Hello, Edgar, I have something I want you to do. I'll be in Washington at the end of the week." Another pause. "It'll be good to see you, too. What I have to discuss with you must remain confidential. Yes, I know you will, Edgar. Friday at one is fine. Yes, I can have lunch with you."

After Ben hung up the phone, he came back and sat beside Mirage. "Are you sure you want me to go through with this? We might find out things that you don't want to know."

"I have to know everything, Ben. Hold nothing back. Was that J. Edgar Hoover on the phone?"

"Yes, it was," Ben said matter-of-factly. "He's a friend of mine, and you can trust him completely."

"Will he have to know about me?"

"No. I'll protect your identity. I'll just tell him that I have an interest in Mark Damian's dealings."

Mirage shivered. "I feel somehow detached from my old life. It's something like the way I felt when I left Texas and ceased being Lucinda Blackburn and became Lacy Black. Now I've been forced to take on another new identity, and it's as though the other two never existed."

"Will you miss the adoration and glamour of the life you had as Lacy Black?"

"No. I never wanted that. I did like acting, but I didn't particularly like being a star."

Ben was quiet for a moment. "We could leave everything the way it is, Mirage. I must warn you, if I go forward with this investigation, there will be no turning back. Are you prepared to face whatever it reveals?"

"I can't leave it, Ben. I have to put my demons to rest." Her eyes were sad. "You see, I feel responsible for my sister's death, and guilty too, I suppose."

He patted her hand comfortingly. "Why should you feel guilty? You did nothing wrong."

"I should have died instead of her, and I have to know why I was spared. And I'll live in constant fear that Mark will discover it was Ruth who died and not me, and then he'll come after me."

"My dear, the investigation will not uncover the fact that Lacy Black is still alive. The only way anyone will ever know the truth is if you tell them."

"I don't think I'll ever do that."

Ben looked at the young woman with the soft brown hair and tried to see Lacy Black in her. She was beautiful, but it was a natural, classic beauty, not the dramatic, sculpted beauty of Lacy Black. Ben thought she was more lovely as Mirage Blackburn than she had been as the actress. "I have a feeling that you have a great deal of strength, Mirage. One day you'll take the misfortunes life has handed you and build a new life."

"Will you help me build that new life, Ben?"

His eyes softened. "Are you flirting with an old man, Mirage?"

She gently touched his dear face. "You know I don't think of you as old, Ben, and I'd never flirt with you. There can be only honesty between the two of us."

Mirage stood up, suddenly feeling self-conscious. She walked aimlessly around the room, examining a vase, a painting on the wall. She stopped at Ben's desk and picked up a picture of him and President Roosevelt on board a yacht. She dropped down in a chair and stared at Ben. "I have been told that the president is a personal friend of yours."

"Yes, Franklin and I go way back."

"Has he been to Windward House?"

"Yes. As a matter of fact, he sat in that very chair you're sitting in now."

"I'm very impressed."

Ben smiled. "He wasn't president then. And as for me, I'm much more impressed that Mirage Blackburn now sits in that chair."

"Why would you bother with me, Ben?"

"Because I like you," he said simply.

There was a long silence, interrupted by a rap on the door. It opened, and Kitty appeared with a tray. "I thought the two of you might like tea."

Gratefully Ben smiled at the nurse. Mirage was looking pale and he feared that today's ordeal had been too much for her. "Timed perfectly. We would indeed like tea, Kitty."

That evening after dinner, Ben and Mirage withdrew to his study. They sat together in companionable silence for a while, staring into the fire. Then Mirage knelt down on the Persian carpet beside Ben. "Teach me to talk the way you do," she urged.

"But Mirage, there's nothing wrong with the way you speak."

She lowered her head for a moment, and when she answered, it was so softly that he could hardly hear her. "I would like to make you proud of me."

He cupped Mirage's chin in his hand and raised her face until her eyes met his. "I don't want you to do it for me, Mirage. If you want to do it, do it for yourself, because it's important to you. Don't mistake me for Mark Damian. I accept and admire you the way you are. You don't have to change for me."

"Please, Ben, it is important to me." The face she turned up to him was vulnerable and pleading. "I want there to be nothing in the new me to remind anyone of Lacy Black."

He nodded. "Very well. I think the best way to proceed is by reading the classics aloud. I'll read a chapter to you, and then you will read one to me. I believe we'll start with Jane Austen."

* * *

Throughout the long winter, Mirage absorbed everything that Ben taught her. Sometimes at night he would hear her practicing her diction long after they had retired. He had never seen anyone so driven. She was a tortured soul, and there seemed to be nothing he could do to comfort her.

Each day she walked to the cliffs and stood staring down into the ocean, somehow finding peace as she watched the constant crashing of the waves against the granite wall. She was bundled up with only her face showing as she trudged along in the snow. Here in this peaceful haven, she regained her peace of mind. It was as if there were no world outside Windward House, and no man but Ben.

December 8, 1941

Lacy was awakened by Kitty shaking her. "Miss Blackburn, wake up. Something terrible has happened!"

Mirage sat up in bed, trying to focus her eyes. "What's wrong?"

"The Japanese bombed Pearl Harbor yesterday! Mr. Lord thought that you might want to come below and listen to the president's speech."

Mirage slipped into her warm robe, her heart beating with trepidation. Surely this would mean war for America.

Ben, Mirage, and Kitty sat together in stunned silence as President Roosevelt spoke: ". . . December 7, 1941—a date which will live in infamy . . ."

Ben, who knew the president so well, could hear the anger in his voice.

After the speech was over, Mirage turned stunned eyes to Ben. "We're going to war, aren't we?"

"I'm afraid so, my dear. I knew we couldn't remain on the sidelines for long."

"I'm frightened, Ben."

He stood up and offered her his arm. "Don't be. This was bound to happen, but we have a good man in the White House.

Put your trust in him and the valiant men who will stand between us and our enemy." He took her hand and led her toward the kitchen. "Come, let's have an early breakfast. Later, I'll try to get through to Franklin and see if there's anything I can do to help."

Weeks passed in unsettling frenzy as America prepared for war. The new year came and went with little celebration.

Americans turned their eyes to Europe and the Pacific. Mirage and Ben listened daily to reports on the radio, knowing that life in the United States would never be the same.

With the arrival of spring came a miraculous change to the land, and a change in Mirage. Ben, by showing her the first real kindness she had known in her life, had made her feel safe and secure.

He introduced her to a world of beauty, a world of culture, a world she had never known existed. She spent time poring over art books while Ben explained stylistic details and gave her information on the artists' lives. At night they dined formally, and Ben showed her which utensils were used for what course and taught her to enjoy elegant dining. Each day brought some new discovery.

Now Ben had summoned her, and she rapped lightly on the study door. He invited her to enter, and she found him sitting behind his massive desk. Silently, he indicated that she should be seated in the chair across from him, and Mirage became uneasy. It was almost as if he wanted to put a barrier between them.

"Is there something wrong, Ben?" she asked in concern.

"I wouldn't say that, Mirage, but I have a lot to tell you, and not all of it is pleasant."

She frowned. "The report's come in from Mr. Hoover, hasn't it?"

"Yes," he said, indicating a thick folder in front of him. "Would you like to read it?"

Mirage shook her head. "Not yet. Couldn't you tell me what it contains?"

Ben opened the folder and began to read from the first page, putting the information into his own words.

"This report gives detailed information on several people, including Samuel Blackburn and his second wife, Katherine, his daughters, Ruth and Lucinda, and a Hollywood producer, Mark Damian."

Mirage drew in a sharp breath and let it out slowly. "I'm ready, Ben. Please continue."

"On Samuel Blackburn, there's not much information. He is a widower with two daughters, both of whom he threw out of the house, and he now lives alone, a bitter and friendless old man."

Mirage leaned forward. "A widower . . . Ben, does that mean that my mother is dead?"

"I'm afraid so, Mirage. I'm sorry."

She shrugged, trying to pretend it didn't matter. "I never knew her, Ben. All I know is what my father told me about her. And none of that was good."

"Would you like to hear what the report says about her?"

She steeled herself for the inevitable. Somehow she was ashamed for him to know what kind of person her mother had been, but she nodded her head.

"Your mother, Katherine, was only sixteen when she married your father, and she ran away three years later."

"I know that already."

"What you may not know is that she took you with her when she ran away."

"I . . . no. I didn't know that," she said in amazement.

"It seems that your father was abusive, and she was hospitalized with a broken collarbone. After she was released from the hospital, her brother, Robert, came to take her and you with him to his home in Dallas." Ben's eyes were sad. "They were both killed that day, Mirage. They were thrown from the automobile your uncle was driving after they collided with a pickup. But somehow you survived. Your father came to get you, but refused to claim your mother's body. She was buried in her family's plot in Dallas."

"But why didn't he tell me she was dead? Why did my father lie to me all those years?"

"I don't know. Perhaps it was to hurt you—perhaps he couldn't admit the truth to himself."

"My poor mother. All these years I thought she deserted me, but she didn't. She really did love me."

"Take comfort in that, Mirage." His eyes dropped to the report and he turned the page. "Are you ready to hear about Mark Damian? I warn you, it isn't pretty. I can close the file now, and you'll never have to know about him."

"Surely it can't be any worse than what I already know. My God, Ben, the man tried to kill me!"

"That doesn't come out in the report, but the day your death was announced, he filed a claim on a million-dollar life insurance policy he had taken out on you."

Mirage nodded, and her eyes were sparkling with anger.

Ben's eyes met hers. "It seems that the policy paid double if your death was accidental. He collected two million dollars. And that wasn't the first time he came into money because of someone's timely death. The report says that his partner died in an automobile accident, leaving Damian as sole owner of Pinnacle Pictures." Ben cleared his throat. "It also appears that you were never legally married to Mark Damian."

"Of course we were married, Ben! You must have read about it in the newspapers."

He shook his head. "I said *legally* married, Mirage. Mark Damian may have gone through a ceremony with you, but he was already married, and his wife was still alive."

"Who was she?" Mirage asked through stiff lips, already knowing the answer.

Ben consulted the page in front of him. "The actress Dolores Divine. They were married in Dallas, Texas, just a few months before he supposedly married you. It appears she died mysteriously when her car went over a cliff. The authorities suspected foul play, but they had no suspect and no proof."

The suspicion growing in her mind was too horrible to think about. It seemed that people died when it was convenient for Mark. Mirage remembered the argument between him and Dolores a few days before her death. She now knew what the argument had been about, and she was convinced that Mark was responsible for Dolores's death.

Would this nightmare never end? Ben's disclosures seemed more like third-rate movie plots than real life—her life.

"I knew Dolores, Ben, and she wasn't a very nice person, but she didn't deserve to die like that."

Ben lowered his eyes to the report once more, reluctant to continue. He didn't want to judge Mirage, but he was disappointed in her because of what the investigation had revealed.

"There's more, Ben, isn't there?"

"I'm afraid so, Mirage. Edgar has informed me that he intends to alert the California authorities to the activities of the doctor who performed your abortion before you and Mark Damian were married. He has an abhorrence for abortionists that will not allow him to overlook the man's actions. But Lacy Black's name will be kept out of the criminal investigation; you can be sure of that."

"What are you saying?" Mirage's voice showed her shock. "Ben, I never had an abortion! Mark told me I had a mis . . . a miscarriage." Her voice had dropped until it was almost inaudible and she covered her face with her hands.

Ben saw her shoulders shake with the sobs she was unable to control. He came around the desk and held her in comforting arms.

She raised her tearstained face to him. "He killed my baby!" she cried, almost choking on her sobs. "He killed my baby, too."

All Ben could do was hold Mirage and rock her gently in his arms, waiting until her crying subsided. He was angry with himself for ever doubting her, and he pressed his face into her fragrant hair and whispered over and over, "I'm sorry, Mirage, I'm sorry. I thought you knew. How could you not?"

At last she had no more tears to cry. Ben continued to hold her.

"The happiest day of my life was when I found out I was carrying Mark's child. I wasn't even ashamed that we weren't married. Mark was angry, though, and wanted me to have an abortion, but I refused. Then one night—" Her voice broke. "One night he gave me some wine, and it made me sleepy. My dreams were horrible. There was a drunken man in my bedroom who kept telling me not to worry, that he was a doctor and he would take care of everything. Then I felt pain that was worse than any I had ever known. The next day, when I awoke, Mark was so sympathetic when he told me I had lost the baby during the night. I believed him, Ben; I had no reason not to."

She was quiet for a moment, remembering the night not long ago when Mark had told her that he wanted her to have his baby. He had been playing with her; she knew that now. He'd never had any intention of fathering a child. It must have given him some perverse pleasure to make plans for the future with her, while he was plotting her death. It wasn't something she could tell Ben, though; the betrayal was too personal to share with anyone.

"He's evil, Ben. He has to be stopped before he hurts someone else."

"We could turn him over to the police, but if they dig too deep into his past, they might find out things you don't want disclosed. You tell me what you want me to do."

Mirage managed to push all thoughts of Mark from her mind. One day she would have to deal with him, but not now. She would have to be stronger when she faced him, and she would have to be prepared to expose him to the world, and herself as well. "When the time is right, I'll settle with Mark Damian myself. He's my problem and no one else's."

Ben handed the folder to her. "This is yours, Mirage, to do with as you please. There are no other copies in existence; I have Edgar's word on that."

"You keep it for now, Ben. I haven't decided yet how I will use it."

Chapter Twenty-three

A brisk wind was blowing as Ben's sailboat cut through the waves, trailing a spray of water. Mirage laughed up at him as he tied off the rope. "I've never been sailing before. This is wonderful."

"Not been sailing?" he said in mock horror. "A landlubber on my boat. Men have walked the plank for less."

She tasted the salt air on her tongue. "We didn't have an ocean in Snyder, Texas, Ben. And if you know anything about Deep Creek, the only source of water, you'd know it was dry unless we had a rain, which wasn't often. You'd have trouble sailing a toy boat on it."

He smiled at the young beauty who seemed to be blooming before his eyes. She made him feel as if he could live forever.

"Ben," she said, voicing the thought she had been dreading, "it's time I returned to New York."

He tied off the wheel and sat down beside her, knowing it would be painful to let her go. "Where would you stay—who would take care of you?"

"I'll find another apartment, and I can take care of myself."

He took her hand and sat forward. "Mirage, I have something I want to say to you. Laugh at me if you want to, or just tell me what a foolish old man I am, but hear me out."

She was puzzled. "What is it, Ben?"

There was uncertainty in his soft blue eyes. "I would like you to be my wife."

She was taken completely by surprise. "Ben, I—"

He held up his hand to silence her. "Don't say anything yet. Just listen. I know there are many reasons for you to say no. I'm much older than you, for one thing."

She lowered her head. "I'm not right for you, Ben. You know what my life was like. I could never fit into your world."

He placed his hands on either side of her face and looked deeply into her eyes. "I know only that I love you, Mirage. It saddens me to think about you leaving."

"We can still be friends. I'll see you whenever you are in New York." She glanced up at the clouds gathering in the east. "You're an important man, and you know how people would talk if we were married. They would say that I only wanted your money."

"We'd know it wasn't true. Besides, I've never cared much about what people thought." He was silent for a moment. "Of course, if you don't care about me that way, I understand." His eyes met hers. "Do you care for me, Mirage?"

"Oh, yes, Ben. You are the finest man I've ever known. But I can't marry you."

He stood up, untied the wheel, and turned the boat back toward shore, not yet defeated. "We would be good for each other, Mirage. You need someone to take care of you, and I need someone to take care of. I've known marriages that have started out with far less going for them, haven't you?"

"Have you considered that someone may one day discover who I am? There would be a scandal, and I might even go to jail."

He laughed at her. "I think not. I'd never allow that." Then his expression became serious. "Consider what I've said. I won't rush you. Perhaps you will decide to make an old man happy, after all."

Bar Harbor was so beautiful, it seemed untouched by man's destructive hand. But Mirage didn't notice the beauty today. She had taken a walk along the bluffs overlooking the ocean so she could think clearly. She must decide if she was going to accept Ben's proposal. If she didn't marry him, she must leave this paradise forever.

She tried to think of life without him, but couldn't because he had become so much a part of her world. She had to weigh her desires against what would be best for Ben. No matter what he said, his circle of society friends would be shocked if he married a nobody, a woman with no past, or at least none that could be told.

A light mist hung over the blunted rocks that looked down on a restless sea. The cliffs seemed crafted by time and nature. In the distance, a small island rose like a mountain out of the waves. The sound of the rushing surf pounding against the rocks below reminded Mirage of man's harmony with nature, while the wind carried the song of the sea to her. Not far offshore, she could see playful seals propelling themselves out of the foamy spray.

She suddenly became aware of a yacht in the distance, its sails billowing in the wind. She watched as the craft grew closer and finally moored at the foot of the cliff where she was standing. For a moment she resented the fact that anyone would invade her privacy, for she had come to think of this cliff as hers alone. The land belonged to Ben, and he kept his own sailboats moored below at the boathouse.

Moments passed, and she could hear someone coming up the path. The man looked like a sailor, with his knapsack thrown carelessly across his shoulder. He walked with a slight limp, and she knew who it was even before he was close enough for her to see his face.

Andrew Mallory wore white pants and a blue-and-white pull-over sweater. His dark hair had been tossed by the wind, and with long strides he moved toward her.

For a long moment Mirage stared at him with an aching heart. His injuries must have been more severe than she'd thought to leave him limping. She turned her face aside, fearing he would recognize her, and yet almost wishing he would.

Drew hadn't noticed the woman who stood on the edge of the cliff until he was almost even with her. The sun was behind her, making it seem as if she were surrounded by a halo of light. For a moment he stopped to stare at her, thinking she was too beautiful to be real. She wore a green-and-white-print dress that was molded to her slender outline by a gentle breeze, and he felt strangely drawn to her.

Slowly he approached her, watching her all the while. She was young, probably in her early twenties, or even late teens. There was something vaguely familiar about her, and yet he could swear that they had never met.

But she was acting as if she knew him too. She was staring at him with the oddest expression, which caused him to stop and speak to her.

"Hello." Drew smiled. "Nice day, isn't it? I guess we've finally put winter behind us."

Her voice was deep and husky, as he'd known it would be, her eyes searching. "Yes."

"You aren't from around here."

Mirage lowered her eyes, trying to hide her hurt. Drew didn't recognize her, but why should he? He, like everyone else, thought she was dead. She had wanted so desperately to see him, and here he was near enough to reach out and touch, but she had to pretend to be an indifferent stranger. She almost gave herself away when her eyes dropped to his hand and she saw that he was wearing the ring she had given him when they parted. He still loved her, and she could be wrapped in his strong arms if only she would tell him the truth.

"No," she said at last, her voice choked. "I'm not from around here."

Drew touched his fingers to his forehead in a salute. "Good day to you."

Mirage didn't bother to answer as she watched him walk away.

Ben greeted Drew with genuine affection. "It's about time you came to see me. What beautiful woman has kept you from visiting an old friend? You could have picked up the telephone, you know."

Drew dropped his knapsack on the floor and shook Ben's hand. "I heard talk that it's you who's been distracted by an attractive female." He smiled. "I came to see if you needed to be rescued."

"I don't want to be rescued from this woman, Drew. She's special."

"I want to hear all about her."

"Come, I'll tell you about her over a martini."

"Lead on. No one mixes them like you, Ben."

Drew was seated on the bar stool, watching as Ben poured gin into a shaker of crushed ice and stirred it with a light hand. He then took two chilled cocktail glasses and dropped an olive in each before pouring in the chilled gin. For the finishing touch, he sprayed a mist of dry vermouth from an atomizer. With a smile, he handed one to Drew. "See if I've lost my touch."

Drew took a sip and nodded in satisfaction. "Very dry—just right." He watched his old friend. There was a spring in Ben's step, and a twinkle in his eyes. He looked better than he had in a long time. "Okay, tell me about this woman, Ben."

"She has a name, Drew. It's Mirage Blackburn. I believe that the two of you will like each other." Ben sat on the stool next to Drew, looking almost boyish. "She makes me believe that there's nothing I can't do, and makes me curse the fates that made me so much older than she."

Drew's brows came together across the bridge of his nose. "I may have already met her if she's walking on the bluff. Don't you think she's a little young?"

"There will be those who will say so. I'd hoped you wouldn't be one of them, Drew, because I've asked Mirage to marry me."

Drew took another sip of his martini to fortify himself. "I'd bet she couldn't say yes fast enough."

"Well, you would lose. My fear is that she may not say yes at all."

Drew could only imagine the woman's game. Get a wealthy old man interested in her, and then take him for his money. "Of course she'll have you. She didn't appear to be a fool to me."

"You have her all wrong, Drew. Wait until you get to know her."

Drew wasn't going to stand by while some little gold digger trapped Ben. "When do I get to formally meet Miss Blackburn?" he asked grimly.

"She'll be back soon." There was pleading in Ben's eyes. "Be kind to her, Drew—she needs kindness in her life. It's important to me that you two like each other."

At that moment Mirage appeared at the door. She had lingered on her walk, bracing herself for this meeting, but the coldness in Drew's dark eyes made her shrink inside. Her training as an actress came to her aid. She raised her head and stiffened her spine. With quick steps, she moved to stand beside Ben, feeling that he was her shield.

"Mirage, I'm glad you've returned," Ben said, taking her hand and raising it to his lips. "I know you've heard me speak of Drew Mallory."

Mirage managed a tight smile, while she quaked inside, afraid that Drew might recognize her. "Of course." She extended her hand to him. "I've seen two of your plays, Mr. Mallory, and I agree with the critics that you are a genius."

He touched her hand ever so slightly, and then drew his hand back. "Surely you flatter me, Miss Blackburn. Perhaps you should have read some of my earlier reviews, in which they branded me an upstart, and called me brash and strutting."

"I think I should say in Drew's defense," Ben interjected, "that when a man is brilliant and also young, critics are usually less than generous. For some reason, they like to see youth fail, and the aged actor, who can no longer remember his lines, succeed."

"Tell me, Miss Blackburn," Drew drawled, "where do you come from? I'm usually good at placing accents, but you have me at a loss. If I were guessing, I'd say your accent was upper-class American South, probably Virginia. Am I right?"

Ben chuckled at Mirage's stunned look. Her elocution lessons had borne fruit if she could fool Drew. He spoke up because he knew Mirage was reluctant to have anyone know too much about her background. "Would you like a cola, Mirage?" he asked, then moved behind the bar and opened the refrigerator.

"Yes, please," she said, easing herself onto a bar stool, but wishing she could go upstairs to her room.

"You aren't going to tell me that you don't drink, Miss Blackburn," Drew said acidly.

Mirage couldn't understand why he was being so critical of her. "I have no aversion to liquor, Mr. Mallory. But I'm honest enough to admit that I like colas better than mixed drinks."

"You sound too good to be true," he said in an insulting voice. "What other virtues have you used to impress Ben? Can I assume that you have a poor old mother at home who needs an operation, and you need money or she'll die?"

Ben let out an angry hiss, while Mirage stood abruptly. She knew how important Drew was to Ben, and she didn't want to be the cause of trouble between the two of them, but Drew wasn't making it easy. "If you gentlemen will excuse me, I'll just go to my room. I'd like to change before dinner."

Drew didn't see the hurt in Mirage's eyes, but Ben did. He turned on Drew angrily. "You have never given me cause to be ashamed of you until today. You just hurt the gentlest woman I've ever known. She's had a lot of sorrow in her life, and I won't have you adding to her pain."

"I don't understand you, Ben. Why can't you see the woman for what she is? She's after your money."

"You're a fool," Ben said sadly. "And if I could convince Mirage to marry me simply by laying all my earthly goods at her feet, I'd do it without hesitation, but she isn't interested in my money. After your actions today, I doubt that she'll have me under any circumstances."

"One of us has to be wrong, Ben," Drew said in a tone of voice that made it clear he didn't think it was he.

"I challenge you to decide which one of us it is, Drew. You may find that you don't know people as well as you think you do."

"You said you were ashamed of me today, Ben. Well, I have never had cause to doubt your good judgment before now. Why are you chasing after a girl young enough to be your granddaughter?"

"It's simple. She needs me. And more than that, I need her."

Drew slammed his drink on the bar. "I'll prove you wrong, Ben. I'll show her up for what she really is."

"If you hurt her again, I'll ask you to leave my house and not return," Ben warned. Though the words were painful to him, he continued: "I mean what I say, Drew. Don't make me choose between the two people I love most in the world."

Drew stalked out of the room, and Ben wondered why he'd had such an adverse reaction to Mirage. He had hoped they would like each other, but such an outcome didn't look promising now.

Dinner was stiff and uncomfortable. Ben tried to keep the conversation going, but halfway through the meal, it was apparent to him that Mirage and Drew never spoke directly to each other.

Mirage felt Drew's eyes on her, and she could hardly breathe under his probing gaze. Seeing him again made her realize that she had to tell Ben she couldn't marry him.

Against his will, Drew stared at Mirage. She wore an off-the-shoulder blue gown, and he couldn't help noticing how satiny her skin looked beneath the glow of the chandelier. Her face was lovely, there was no denying that, and her lips were full and enticing. Her soft brown hair was shoulder-length, and invited a man's touch.

Oh, yes, he could see why Ben was attracted to Mirage Blackburn. But Drew saw her as a conniving female who was only out for what she could get. He was more determined than ever to stop her from making a fool of his friend.

Mirage was glad when dinner was over and Drew excused himself to take a walk and smoke a cigarette. This left her alone with Ben so she could tell him she was leaving.

They moved into the living room, where Ben sat watching her pace before him. With a sinking heart, he knew that she had decided not to marry him. But he had not really expected she would—he had only hoped.

Mirage dropped down on her knees before him, her eyes bright with tears. "You know what I'm going to say, don't you, Ben?"

"Have you thought this through, Mirage? Are you certain you won't reconsider?"

"The best thing I can do for you is not marry you. We are from different worlds, and I wouldn't fit into yours any more than you would fit into mine. Don't you see that?"

His eyes were so sad that she almost relented.

"You haven't said so, but Drew's coming has convinced you that we aren't right for each other, hasn't it, Mirage?"

"Not entirely, but if this is how your friends react to me, think what everyone else would say."

He wanted to beg her to marry him, but he knew it would do no good. "I believe we would have had a good life together, my dear. There were so many things I wanted to share with you."

"I'm afraid that we can't even remain friends, Ben, because our friendship would only be misunderstood, and some people would make something ugly out of it."

"Will you at least allow me to help you?"

"No, I have taken enough from you. It's time I was on my own."

She pressed her lips against his brow and stood up, leaving the room quickly. She rushed out the front door and down the steps. A bright moon lit her path as she walked toward the high bluff. Already there was an emptiness in her heart that no one but Ben could fill.

Drew watched Mirage's pale outline as she stood on the cliff. He was glad to have this time alone with her so he could expose her for what she was. He couldn't go away and leave Ben in her clutches.

Mirage heard someone behind her and turned to face Drew. "You startled me. I thought I was alone."

"What's your game, Miss Blackburn?" he asked, cutting right to the heart of the matter.

She couldn't see him clearly because his face was half in shadow. It was painful to be near him and have him think ill of her. "I don't know what you mean, Mr. Mallory."

"You may be able to fool Ben, but I can assure you that I've met you before."

She took a step backward, with the intention of running away. Her worst fear had been realized: he knew who she was.

"Yes," he continued, "I've met you on the streets of New York and the streets of Paris, Miss Blackburn. You are one of those women who sell their bodies to men. The only difference between you and a common prostitute is that your price is higher."

Before he realized her intention, she slapped him. "How dare you say such a thing to me!"

He put his hand up to his cheek and smiled without humor. "I must have hit a nerve for you to slap so hard. If you want money, *I'll* give it to you. Just tell me the amount it would take to have you walk away from Ben and never bother him again."

Her eyes burned. "I'm not for sale, at any price."

He grabbed her and pulled her tightly against his body. When she tried to struggle, he captured her face between his hands. "I don't have to buy you. If I were of a mind to, I could have you for free."

She couldn't move as he lowered his head and his lips cruelly crushed her quivering mouth. The kiss had been meant to punish, to prove how easily he could seduce her and prove how unworthy she was of Ben.

But her soft lips ignited a fire in Drew, and he gathered her to him. She was reaching inside him, to a place in his heart that only one other woman had touched. Suddenly he resented her for intruding into the place that he had reserved for his dead love, Lacy, the perfect woman—perfect in life, worshiped in death. He had been with other women, but none had threatened his precious memories of Lacy as this one did.

Mirage felt her knees go weak, and she clung to Drew. How glorious it was to be held in his arms, to feel the heat of his body, to know he still desired her. For so long she had lived on the memory of every word he had spoken to her, and now he was touching her, kissing her, making her want him even more.

Suddenly Drew flung her away from him, his eyes tormented. "You're good—I'll give you that," he said in a tight voice. "You didn't kiss me like a woman about to be married to another man."

Mirage felt the hurt of his words like a wound in her heart. Of course Drew would believe the worst of her, because he didn't know they had met before—kissed before—and that she loved him.

"You don't know me at all," she managed to say in a raspy whisper. "You only think you do."

She was leaning against the trunk of a tree and he moved to her, trapping her between himself and the tree. "I know that you saw a chance to come into a fortune, since Ben has a bad heart and hasn't long to live. You have plans to become a wealthy widow, don't you?"

Mirage clutched at her throat. "Ben has a bad . . . heart?"

"Don't pretend you didn't know the doctors have given him less than a year to live."

Tears gathered in her eyes, and she quickly brushed them away. Her sweet Ben had never told her how ill he was. How like him to think of her and not of himself. "Thank you for telling me this, Mr. Mallory. You have helped me make up my mind. I have decided to marry Ben as soon as possible."

He grabbed her, his hands biting into her shoulders. "If you hurt him, I swear you'll pay, Miss Blackburn. There is nowhere you can hide to be safe from me."

Angrily, she pushed his hands away. "Don't threaten me. I don't care what you think, Mr. Mallory. You can approve or not. I care only about Ben."

Without another word, Mirage moved away from him, making her way to the house. She had to see Ben. She had to tell him that she would be his wife. She wanted to take care of him, to make sure his last days were happy. She did love him—not the innocent love she'd had for Mark or the all-consuming love she had for Drew, but with a gentle love that healed and nurtured, and that was what Ben needed.

She found him sitting where she'd left him, staring into the fire. She sat on the arm of his chair, and he smiled up at her.

"Ben, have you ever heard that it's a woman's prerogative to change her mind?"

Hope fanned to life in his eyes. "Have you taken that prerogative?"

"I have, Ben. I want to be your wife."

She almost cried out when she saw tears swimming in his soft blue eyes. He laid a shaking hand on her cheek. "My dearest Mirage. You have made me very happy." He clutched her to him as if by doing so he could absorb her youth and vitality. "How soon, Mirage?" There was desperation in his voice. "When will you marry me?"

"The sooner the better."

Chapter Twenty-four

Drew kept his anger under control while Ben happily told him the plans for his marriage to Mirage. "We've decided on a small private service that's to be held here at Windward House. I would be proud if you would stand up with me, Drew."

"I would have thought the future Mrs. Lord would want the world to know of her conquest."

Ben ignored the barb. "Just stand beside me on this, the happiest day of my life."

"You know I will," Drew said, deciding to relent. "Where's the honeymoon to be?"

"I've ordered my private railroad car to be made ready, and we're just going home to New York. It's what Mirage wanted."

"Ben, are you determined to do this?"

"I have thought of little else. I know you think I'm an old fool, Drew, but you don't know Mirage as I do. Give her a chance."

"I'll stand up with you, Ben, but don't ask me to sanction this marriage. I see only disaster ahead for you."

Ben shook his head in resignation, and then he grinned at

Drew as the irony of the situation became clear. "I've made decisions that have toppled empires and bolstered democracy. Don't you think I've acquired enough wisdom to choose a wife?"

When Drew didn't answer, Ben continued: "You have to trust that I know what I'm doing. Mirage is in the garden picking flowers for a bridal bouquet. Go to her and wish her well—do this for me."

Ben seldom asked him for anything, and Drew couldn't refuse this request. He feared the marriage would only cause Ben heartache, but he was helpless to prevent it.

Drew found Mirage sitting in the vine-covered arbor. She rose to her feet at his approach, and it didn't escape his notice that she avoided his eyes. He attributed that to a guilty conscience.

"I understand best wishes are in order," he ground out. "You got what you wanted, didn't you?"

Her eyes sparkled with anger. "If by that you mean I am happy to be marrying a man I love and respect, then yes, I got what I wanted."

"I'm not fooled by you as Ben is, Miss Blackburn. You don't have to pretend with me."

The green eyes she turned on him were reminiscent of other green eyes. *But she is nothing like Lacy,* he thought angrily.

"I know how much Ben cares for you, Mr. Mallory, and because of his affection for you, I am willing to overlook your rudeness. But don't continue this war between us, or you will lose."

"Is that a threat?"

"No. It's a warning that if you don't accept this marriage, you will hurt Ben. I don't care what your feelings are for me, Mr. Mallory, but I do care if he gets hurt."

"Just see that *you* don't hurt him."

She turned away, picked up an armload of pink roses, and walked toward the kitchen door, while Drew followed her with his eyes. Even the way she walked, the way she held her head, reminded him of his lost love. Would he never be rid of Lacy's ghost?

* * *

Mirage handed the flowers to Kitty and went directly to Ben's office, where she knocked on the door.

He admitted her with a smile.

"There is something I must talk to you about, Ben. I haven't told you before now because I know how close you are to Drew."

He watched her sit on the edge of a chair, nervously clutching her hands. "If it's about Drew's attitude toward you, I'm well aware of that. I won't have him treating you with disrespect."

"No, Ben, it isn't that. I have no complaints about how he treats me." She lowered her head, knowing this was going to be difficult. "I must tell you this because we've promised each other that our marriage will be based on honesty."

Ben stood near the fireplace, resting his laced hands on the mantel. "Then I'm glad you came to me with whatever's bothering you."

"Ben—" she raised troubled eyes to him—"I knew Drew before he came here. I knew him as Lacy Black, and we loved each other."

Many things were clear to Ben now. "Is that your ring Drew wears?"

"Yes, but he doesn't know me now, Ben. He thinks I'm dead."

"Are you telling me that you still love Drew and don't want to marry me?"

"I don't know how I feel about him, Ben. But I know that I love you and I want to be your wife."

He smiled and went to her, taking her hand and pulling her up to him. "Then I count myself fortunate, and I thank you for your honesty." His expression grew serious. "Mirage, I want you to think very carefully before you answer. If it's Drew you want, I'll understand. Although I didn't know the woman he loved was you, I've watched him grieve, thinking you were dead. He still loves you. Maybe you should tell him who you are."

She shook her head, feeling a lump forming in her throat. "No, it's best that he never knows. But I want you to know that nothing happened between us but a few kisses. I swear it, Ben."

He smiled. "I believe you."

"Then you don't mind that I once loved Drew?"

He searched her eyes. "I suppose what I need to know is how you feel about him now."

"I don't even like him at the moment, Ben. He's not the man I fell in love with. Perhaps he never was."

She looked into Ben's clear eyes, which seemed to peel back the layers of her mind and discern the tumult that was churning inside her. He knew how hard she was struggling with her feelings for Drew—he also knew that she had not completely won that struggle. "I will get over him, Ben. I promise."

"He still loves you. Tell him who you are."

She thought for a moment, then shook her head. "I'm not the same person he fell in love with. Let him go on believing that Lacy Black is dead. Promise me you will never tell him who I am."

He nodded. "If that's the way you want it, you have my word."

"I wish Drew would take my ring off his finger," she said wistfully. "It's just a reminder that can only cause pain to us both."

"And what about us, Mirage?"

Burying her lingering feelings for Drew deep inside, she answered him with sincerity and without doubt. "I want to be with you, to take care of you, to be your wife. I want to share your thoughts and tell you mine. I love you."

He pressed her to him. "I'm glad, Mirage. Because I don't think I could give you up to anyone—not even Drew." He was quiet for a long moment. When he spoke, it was with feeling. "I will tell Drew that I don't want him to come back if he can't treat you with respect."

She shook her head. "That's what you must not do, Ben. I couldn't live with the guilt if I was the cause of a rift between the two of you."

"So young and so wise," he said, softly touching her hair. "I don't deserve you, but I'm going to make you a good husband."

She took his hand and led him to the couch, where they both sat down. "Ben, tell me more about your first wife, Mary. What was she like?"

"Mary," he answered reflectively, "was delicate and often ill. But she was sweet and filled with kindness for others. Her one sorrow was that she couldn't give me children. I always wanted a child, but I pretended to her that it didn't matter. I believe she knew how I felt, however." He stared at the small hand in his. "My one regret is that I never was a father. Now I'm too old." He smiled apologetically. "I didn't mean to go into that. You wanted to know about Mary. When she died, I was devastated and thought I'd never love again. That was before I met you."

"Do you think your Mary would approve of me, Ben?"

He hugged her and laughed with joy. No one but Mirage would have asked that. "I believe Mary would very definitely have liked you. When she was dying, she begged me to find someone special and not to spend the rest of my life alone. She would have approved of my choice. I waited a long time for you, Mirage."

"Oh, Ben, I love you so much."

He drew in a deep breath. "And that's the wonder of it, my dearest heart—that you should love me."

The house had been filled with flowers, and Ben waited at the bottom of the stairs, with Drew at his side. There was no music and no fanfare as Mirage came down the stairs wearing a cream-colored gown, with a wreath of pink flowers woven into her dark hair.

Ben's eyes were shining as he watched her walk toward him. There was no mistaking the adoration in his look as he gazed at her.

Drew watched with a scowl on his face. He was still sure that Mirage Blackburn was a fraud, no matter how simple and unaffected she tried to appear.

The ceremony was short, and when it was over, Mirage went

into Ben's arms, laying her head against his shoulder and feeling loved and cherished. She would love and care for this man, and she would do everything she could to make him happy, she vowed to herself.

Kitty wished them the best, and Drew placed a reluctant kiss on Mirage's cheek for Ben's benefit. Then they all retired to the dining room, where a feast had been prepared. Ben toasted his wife with champagne, the happiness showing on his face.

The only blight on Mirage's happiness was Drew's brooding presence. She was relieved when he left, saying his yacht was ready to put to sea.

There was only a lamp glowing on the bedside table when Mirage came to Ben. He was propped on a pillow, his glasses resting on the bridge of his nose, reading a book. When he saw her, he removed his glasses and set the book aside.

His eyes moved over her as she stood just at the foot of the bed. The plain cotton gown she wore was one he had bought her in New York. His eyes moved over the curves of her lithe body, and up to the beautiful hair that framed her face and fell to her shoulders.

Mischief danced in her eyes. "Did I disturb your reading, Ben?"

He reached out to her and she gave him her hand. "To tell you the truth, I was reading because I was nervous."

She looked at him curiously. "You nervous, Ben? Why?"

He released her hand, his eyes dipping to study the floral pattern on the spread. "I am plagued with the thought that I might not be able to . . . that I can't . . ."

She smiled gently. "You underestimate yourself, Ben. You are a handsome man, and I find you desirable."

Panic still lingered at the edge of his mind. What if he disappointed her as a lover? He watched her hand go the buttons of her nightgown, fascinated, as if caught in a dream. Her gown fell to the floor, revealing the most beautiful body he'd ever seen—taut breasts, small waist, rounded hips, and long, shapely legs.

He was looking at Lacy Black, once named the most beautiful woman in the world. She was all that and more, and she belonged to him.

Mirage was filled with tenderness for this man who had given her a reason for living. She went to him and dropped down on the bed beside him. Boldly, she unbelted his green robe and pushed it off his shoulders.

Ben felt a burning desire in his loins that he hadn't felt in many years, and had thought he was incapable of feeling.

He closed his eyes as she slid her naked body against him and whispered in his ear, "I'm your wife. Whatever comes, we will share it together."

With desire raging through his body like wildfire, he ran trembling hands over her satiny skin. "I love you, Mirage."

"And I love you, Ben." She understood his feelings of inadequacy and wanted tonight to be special for him and for her. She had meant to give him the gift of herself with nothing held back, but suddenly she felt something she had never felt before.

His hands were expert, stroking, invoking passion in her that had never been tapped. Mark had been a selfish lover, wanting only to satisfy his own needs. Ben was gentle, loving, and not without the power to stir a woman's blood.

His lips gently settled on hers while his hands massaged her, causing her to arch her body to meet his caress. She had not known tenderness could evoke such desire.

She closed her eyes as Ben became more confident. He cupped and stroked her breasts until she ached with need.

When he made love to her, Mirage felt as if she were floating on a cloud of feelings and wild sensations. Never had she known so much pleasure.

At last exhausted, she lay beside him, her breath trapped in her throat.

Ben kissed her lips, and his mouth slid to her ear. "My wife, my wife, I've never felt this way before."

She looked into his eyes and touched his cheek. "Neither have I, Ben. I never knew it could be like that between a man and a woman."

He rolled over, his eyes clouded. "Don't say that if it isn't true, Mirage. Remember, we are going to be honest with each other."

She turned his face to hers. "Ben, I am being honest with you. I would never compare you with Mark, but he's the only man besides you that I've ever been intimate with. I never felt this way with him." She looked deeply into his eyes, hoping he would know she spoke the truth. "I never felt that kind of pleasure when Mark made love to me, Ben."

Tears sparkled in his eyes as he clasped her to him. "Mirage, Mirage, how can I say what's in my heart? How can I make you understand what you have given me?"

She kissed his face, laughing up into his eyes. "How strong is your heart, Ben?"

He grinned down at her. "Growing stronger all the time."

Her eyes gleamed like green fire, and her hand moved over his chest and downward. "Love me again, Ben."

And to his surprise and delight, he did.

Chapter Twenty-five

Mirage was astounded by the luxuriousness of Ben's private railroad car. The interior was covered with green brocade, and there was dark green carpet on the floor. At one end there was a wide bed with yellow sheets and a matching bedspread, and a Chinese silk screen divided the bedroom and bath from the rest of the car. Three couches covered in yellow silk and a dining table that could seat ten were at the opposite end.

On the trip to New York, she loved cuddling up in Ben's arms and having him read to her. His voice was deep and soothing, and many times he would read her to sleep.

Of course, Mirage looked forward to the times when Ben would take her in his arms and make love to her. She hadn't known that a man could love so unselfishly—but with Ben, his only thought seemed to be her happiness.

She was haunted by Drew's revelation that Ben had a bad heart and the doctors had given him only a year to live. She loved him, and she was determined to keep him well.

One night she had a terrible nightmare. She dreamed she was searching through the frightening shadows for Ben, but couldn't find him. She woke up crying and groping in the darkness and calling his name.

"Mirage, it's all right. I'm here. You're safe."

He turned on the light and held her close until she stopped trembling.

"Oh, Ben, I couldn't find you. I thought you had left me."

He brushed her hair out of her face and kissed her forehead. "I would never leave you willingly, Mirage. As long as I'm able, I'll be with you."

She clutched at his arm. "If only I could keep you with me always. Why couldn't I have been born thirty years sooner, so we could have a lifetime together?"

His eyes were sad. "It seems the gods sometimes have a strange sense of humor. They said to me, 'Ben Lord, you will meet the love of your life and she will love you in return. But we will make you an old man and her a young girl. Your time with her will be limited, so make every day count.' "

"Ben, I know about your heart; Drew told me. Why didn't you tell me how ill you are?"

"Because I didn't want you to marry me out of pity. Is that why you agreed to become my wife, Mirage?"

"I don't pity you, Ben. I pity me if I have to live without you."

His arms tightened about her. "I'll hold on to you for as long as I'm able, Mirage. But we both know that you will outlive me."

She took his hand and raised it to her lips. "I won't allow anything to happen to you. I'll take such good care of you, the doctors will wonder at your recovery. You will borrow from my strength, and I am strong, Ben."

"Sweet Mirage," he said sadly, "you will be my strength, but I'll be your weakness."

She kissed his mouth and drew his head down to rest against her breasts. "We will use each day as a gift to treasure and cherish. Then if one of us has to go on without the other, the one left behind will take out those cherished memories and relive them every day."

"No, Mirage, don't say that. If anything happens to me, I want you to go on living, not in the past, but for all your tomorrows."

Her eyes became misty. "Love me, Ben. I don't want to think about losing you."

He pushed her gown up and drew it over her head, tossing it on the floor. Their bodies came together in a gentle passion that chased all Mirage's nightmares away.

It was just before dawn when the train pulled into Penn Station. New York had not yet come to life, and it was strangely quiet. A porter carried their luggage up the steps to the street, where Jenkins, who had arrived ahead of them, waited to meet them. Mirage glanced at the tall skyscrapers as the limousine turned a corner and headed for Park Avenue.

"Ben, I know so little about your apartment. Tell me about it," she said with enthusiasm.

He laced his fingers through hers. "It covers the entire top floor of the Lord Building and has its own private elevator. It's quite comfortable, having four bedrooms, five bathrooms, and a living room with a magnificent view of the city. There's a formal dining room and an informal dining room, a kitchen that's a gourmet's delight, and a three-room servants' quarters. I thought you might like to redecorate it, since it hasn't been redone in more than ten years. But you can decide about that when you see it."

"I love to visit New York."

He chuckled. "Mirage," he reminded her, "New York is our permanent address. Bar Harbor is our summer home. We only remained there so long because you were ill at first, and then I wanted you all to myself."

She was quiet for a long time. "I'm nervous about meeting your friends, Ben. Suppose they don't like me?"

He'd had the same worry, but he tried to appear cheerful. "How could anyone not like you?"

Mirage moved quickly through the rooms of her new home, finding each one more magnificent than the last. She walked down a long hallway, where she saw several photographs of Ben with different people. Some she recognized as famous; others she didn't know at all. She paused at a picture of Drew. He was mounted on a horse and dressed in polo attire. She averted her eyes, not wanting to think about him today.

The master bedroom was huge and had the biggest bed she had ever seen. The carpet was light blue, and the bedspread and draperies were a darker blue. There were boxes stacked on the bed, and Ben smiled at her when she looked at him questioningly.

"I had one of the stores send over some things I thought you might need. You can look at them later and see if they suit you. Tomorrow you will want to go shopping for a new wardrobe."

She turned to him. "I don't need a new wardrobe, Ben. I have enough as it is."

She had such an unspoiled beauty, and cared so little for elaborate gowns, that Ben hesitated to point out the obvious to her. "I'm afraid that you will need the proper clothing for New York, Mirage."

She was pensive. "I hadn't thought of that." Her eyes gleamed with mischief. "As Mrs. Benjamin Lord, I suppose I have an image to project."

He laughed at her as she sashayed across the floor with her nose in the air, and he followed her out of the room to continue the tour of the apartment.

Mirage's feet sank into thick blue carpet as she entered the huge living room. She slid open the glass door to the balcony and stood with the cool breeze blowing on her face. Ben came up behind her and put his arms around her waist.

"Do you like it?"

"Like it? I love it! I don't want to change a thing."

"How about dinner, Mrs. Lord?"

She linked her arm through his. "I'm starved."

The waiter at the Stork Club beamed at Ben. "Mr. Lord, we haven't seen you in some time. I'll show you to your usual table."

Mirage was aware of the curious stares that followed them to a table near the window. Ben waved at several people, but didn't stop to talk. It became apparent to Mirage that she had become the topic of conversation, and soon people began coming by their table to speak to Ben, who proudly introduced her as his wife.

Mirage didn't miss the shocked reactions of the women, who smiled at Ben and offered him felicitations, but glared at her as though she had committed a cardinal sin. Most of the men, however, sounded sincere when they congratulated Ben. After a while they were left alone, but Mirage could tell that Ben was troubled.

She excused herself and went to the powder room to reapply her lipstick and regain her composure. Ben's acquaintances hadn't even given her a chance, but seemed to dislike her without knowing anything about her.

As she powdered her nose, she heard female voices coming from around the corner.

"Can you imagine Ben marrying such a young girl? And a nobody. I've never heard of her."

"We know what he sees in her," the woman's companion replied. "But what does she want with him?"

"Money, of course, dear. Gold digger, pure and simple."

Straightening her back, Mirage moved out the door, her head held high, her eyes on Ben, determined he wouldn't know how badly she'd been hurt.

The saleslady smiled at Mirage. "I believe you will be happy with your choices, Mrs. Lord. Shall I send them to your apartment, or will you take them with you?"

Mirage had dismissed the chauffeur in case Ben needed him. "Please have them delivered."

"I'll attend to it right away."

Mirage pulled on her gloves. "Can you recommend a good restaurant nearby?"

"There is a sidewalk café across the street. The food is very good, if you don't mind dining with the theater crowd. I have noticed that lately it has become popular with the women from the social register, so you won't feel out of place."

Mirage smiled to herself as she crossed the street. Snobbery was at its best in New York City shops. She found a table at the café and sat down, and a waiter magically appeared, handing her a menu.

"The fillet of sole is very good today, madame," he suggested.

"Thank you. I'll just have a salad and hot tea, please."

While Mirage waited for her order, she noticed that the two women who had been so vicious at the Stork Club the night before were seated at the next table. They had seen her, too, and now they purposely raised their voices so she could hear them.

"It's amazing who they'll allow to dine at the sidewalk cafés. Remind me never to come here again. It's so passé." The woman looked pointedly at Mirage.

Tears sparkled in her eyes, and she started to rise, when a hand fell on her shoulder. "Mrs. Lord, what a wonderful surprise to find you here. Ben is well, I trust."

She looked up to see Drew Mallory. "Yes, thank you."

"Do you mind if I join you for lunch?"

She bestowed a grateful look on him, wondering why he was being so pleasant. "Yes, please do."

He sat across from her, his dark eyes sweeping her face. The women at the next table looked taken aback, and then one of them smiled and waved at Drew.

"Mr. Mallory," the woman simpered, "won't you join us?"

"I think not, Mrs. Steadman," he said, not even bothering to get up when he answered her. "I have trouble digesting my food when the conversation bores me."

The woman gasped and turned back to her friend.

"Thank you," Mirage said in a soft voice. "I was about to leave."

Drew's eyes narrowed, and he lowered his voice. "There's no need to thank me. I'm doing this for Ben, not you."

She wanted to fling her glass of water in his face, but she held her temper and lowered her eyes. "Then on Ben's behalf, I thank you."

"Is the honeymoon over already? Where is your bridegroom?"

"I had to go shopping and decided not to put Ben through that ordeal."

"That must have set him back a pretty penny."

She gritted her teeth. "It's no concern of yours what transpires between my husband and myself."

Drew looked at her broodingly. "I assume you heard Walter Winchell's broadcast last night?"

"No. What did he say?"

"He asked the question, 'What elderly statesman and millionaire married a pretty young girl to have a companion in his golden years?' "

"Mr. Winchell is hateful, and should get his facts correct before he airs them."

"He merely stated what everyone else is thinking."

By now Mirage's food had arrived, but she couldn't eat for the lump that was in her throat. She pushed the lettuce around on her plate with her fork.

"If you will excuse me, I find that I'm not very hungry." She started to rise, but he clasped her wrist.

"Don't leave yet. Don't give those women the satisfaction of thinking they chased you away."

"It's not them, Mr. Mallory; it's you who makes me want to leave."

He released her hand and leaned back in his chair. "I have been hard on you, haven't I?"

"I don't like you very well."

He smiled at her candor. "Not many people like me, but I don't lose sleep over it."

"I'll bet that can't be said for the women," she said bitingly.

"You're a woman, and you just admitted you don't like me."

When she became silent, he pushed her teacup toward her. "Drink the tea. It's hard to come by these days, you know. If the war keeps on, you won't be able to get tea or coffee before long."

She took a sip, picked up her handbag, and placed money on the table. "Good day, Mr. Mallory. I hope you won't be a stranger. Ben would like to see you."

"You're still on your honeymoon," he reminded her.

Without a word, she turned and rushed away, hailing a cab.

Drew sat there long after she had gone. Why did he feel he had to punish Mirage every time they met? If she was good to Ben, what did it matter that she was younger than he?

He frowned. Because she was not as sweet and innocent as she appeared, and she was taking advantage of a sick old man. Then why had he felt the need to go to her rescue? Regardless of what he'd told her, he hadn't intervened for Ben's sake. He'd seen that she was being hurt, and he'd wanted to protect her.

Standing up, he hurried across the street. He'd return to the theater. The new stand-in for the star was pretty, and she had been issuing him an invitation that he meant to accept.

Chapter Twenty-six

When Mirage returned to the apartment, she tried to act cheerful. She told Ben only about her shopping expedition and running into Drew; she said nothing of the spiteful women she had encountered or how deeply they had hurt her with their cruel remarks.

Ben asked if she would like to go out for dinner, but she thought he looked tired, so she suggested they dine at home.

As they ate, she tried to draw Ben out about his illness, but he refused to discuss it with her. She did, however, make him promise she could go with him for his next doctor's appointment.

Over dessert of vanilla sherbet and raspberry cream, Ben handed Mirage a red velvet case, his eyes shining with eagerness. "A belated wedding gift," he told her.

She opened the box and gasped at the diamond necklace, bracelet, and earrings it contained. The stones were large and had a blue hue. She happily picked up the bracelet and held it to the light, watching it shoot out rainbows of color. "Ben, they are beautiful!" She jumped to her feet and ran to him, throwing her arms around him. "You're so good to me."

He pulled her onto his lap. "I want to lavish you with gifts so I can always see you as happy as you are now."

She ruffled his hair and planted a kiss on his nose. "Don't you know me well enough by now to realize that it isn't things that make me happy—it's you?"

"Will you forgive an old man's indulging himself then? I confess I did some shopping of my own today while you were out." He set her on her feet and took her hand, little boy–like, and led her to one of the guest bedrooms. There, draped across the bed, were several furs: a full-length ermine, a fox stole, and a floor-length mink with a hood.

She picked up the mink and buried her face in the soft fur. "You do spoil me, Ben."

He raised an eyebrow at her. "When your purchases came today, I noticed you didn't buy much."

"I wasn't comfortable spending—"

He held up his hand to silence her. "I opened you an account at the bank and you have charging privileges at several department stores. You are to use them, Mirage. You are my wife now."

"I don't know if you will understand this, Ben. Perhaps it's silly, but I feel guilty for having so much when there is a war on and so many people have so little."

He smiled at her, his eyes dancing. "Then pick out a charity you want to support, or several charities, and lavish time and money on them."

Mirage remembered the school she had formed for the migrant workers' children. "There is one organization that I'd like to continue to help. It involves children."

"Then you shall help them."

"You have a great deal of money, don't you, Ben?"

"Yes, my dear, a great deal."

"Then there is one thing I would like to do for myself," she said, draping the ermine over her shoulders and looking at her reflection in the full-length mirror.

"And what is that?"

"Promise you won't laugh."

His lips twitched. "I promise," he said solemnly.

"I want to take singing lessons. I believe I have a good voice; at least my high school music teacher told me I did. I'd like to develop that talent."

"Then you shall. But first, I have another surprise for you."

"Oh, Ben, surely not. You've given me enough already."

He reached inside his breast pocket and withdrew an envelope, extending it to her. "I think you'll like this."

She stared at the envelope return-addressed from the White House, and opened it with anticipation.

Dear Ben,

Eleanor and I would like to invite you and Mrs. Lord to a private luncheon at the White House on Tuesday, the 23rd. We both look forward to meeting your new bride.

Sincere wishes for your happiness,

Franklin

"Ben, I can't believe it—lunch with the president and Mrs. Roosevelt!"

"You'll like them, Mirage, and I know they'll like you."

Mirage was so nervous about the luncheon at the White House that she changed her outfit three times. At last she settled on a gray suit with a white silk blouse and white gloves. Ben decided he would show her the newly opened National Gallery of Art to take her mind off her nervousness.

As they walked through the rooms where famous paintings hung, many of which Ben had told her about, Mirage became so engrossed, she did indeed forget to be nervous. Her eyes shone when she saw two Van Goghs that Ben had donated to the museum.

Ben was enjoying her reaction, and he was amazed at how much she had absorbed from what he had taught her. "The

National Gallery opened only last year, Mirage, and from donations and auctions, you can see that we have acquired many wonderful paintings."

She came to a wall where Rembrandts were exhibited. Several self-portraits of the artist were displayed, and Mirage stared at one in confusion. "Ben, I thought they would have only originals in the National Gallery. Why would they hang a copy?"

He stood looking over her shoulder, his eyes sweeping the oil. "I can assure you this is indeed the original. What makes you think it's a copy, Mirage?"

Her first reaction was shock. Then slowly she smiled before laughing up at Ben. "Mark Damian thinks *he* has the original."

Ben observed the painting closer. "No. This was bought at an auction in Amsterdam and brought directly to this gallery. I'm afraid it is Mark Damian who has the copy."

Suddenly she felt sad. She wondered what Mark would think if he knew the painting he prized so highly was a fake—just as he was. She turned her attention to Ben. She didn't want to think about Mark, not yet anyway.

Franklin Roosevelt sat, his hand extended to Ben, a smile of genuine fondness on his careworn face. "Ben, it's been too long, my friend."

"Indeed it has, Mr. President."

Eleanor, looking crisp and cool in a light blue dress, stood stiffly beside her husband while he greeted Ben.

Ben moved forward and pressed his cheek against the first lady's. "It's always good to see you, my dear. You're looking well."

When the first lady smiled, her face became soft and her whole manner was transformed. "As glad as I am to see you, Ben, what I really want is to meet this lovely creature you married."

Mirage found herself the center of attention. The president wrung her hand, while Eleanor beamed at her. Over lunch, the Roosevelts put Mirage at ease. And she was fascinated when Ben and the president spoke of matters of state that she knew must be confidential, and they seemed genuinely interested when she expressed her views.

Mirage found herself drawn to the first lady, who was outgoing and had a way of making a person feel important.

"Is this your first trip to Washington, Mrs. Lord?" Eleanor inquired.

"Yes, it is, and I must say I'm most impressed. I can't make myself believe that I'm having dinner with you and the president. You are so kind to invite us."

"Not at all. Ben is one of our favorite people." Her eyes went to Ben. "Franklin and I have been worried about him, and we wanted to meet the woman who finally led him to the altar."

The president raised a glass to toast the newlyweds. "I'd say you got the best of the bargain, Ben—she's charming. May you always be as happy as you are at this moment."

After lunch, the four of them retired to the private living room, where Franklin lit a cigar. "Mrs. Lord—or may I call you Mirage?"

"Please do, Mr. President."

"Well, Mirage, how would you like my wife to show you through the White House? I'm told the Lincoln Bedroom is haunted, although I admit I've never seen President Lincoln." He clamped his shining white teeth on his cigar. "I wish I could summon him up; I'd like to ask his advice on the war."

Eleanor stood up, motioning for Mirage to follow her. "Come, my dear, I believe the men want to talk war. After a brief tour of the rooms, how would you like to accompany me to a hospital? I know the wounded there would love to meet a beautiful young woman such as yourself."

Mirage was aware that she was being honored, and she was glad, for Ben's sake. It was good to be accepted after the slights she had suffered in New York.

She looked at Ben, who smiled and nodded to her. "Go along, and make some soldier far from home happy."

* * *

That night at the hotel, Mirage told Ben about her day. "It was wonderful how Eleanor spoke encouragingly to the soldiers, and how they warmed to her."

"Eleanor?"

She smiled. "Yes. She insisted I call her by her first name. She is a gracious lady, and I feel honored that I got a chance to meet her."

Ben clasped her hand. "You charmed them both, Mirage. Franklin approves of my choice."

She removed her robe and climbed into bed beside him. "The war's getting worse, isn't it, Ben?"

"I'm afraid so."

"Seeing the wounded today made it all seem so real. Some of them were hardly more than boys." She raised herself up on her elbow and looked at him with troubled eyes. "Will we win this war, Ben?"

"We'll win," he assured her, as if he knew some deep secret. "But at what cost, and how will history judge us?"

"What do you mean?"

He looked at her apologetically. "It's nothing I can discuss with you, my dear."

She would not press him further, knowing the president must have confided in him.

At breakfast the next morning, Ben smiled and took a sip of coffee. "Eleanor has made you the rage, Mirage. I know human nature, and I'll wager that every hostess in New York will clamor for your attention now." He handed her the morning's edition of the *Washington Post*, and she stared at a picture of herself and Mrs. Roosevelt at Bethesda Hospital. She quickly read the headlines: "MRS. ROOSEVELT AND HER CHARMING COMPANION, MRS. BENJAMIN LORD, III, OF NEW YORK, VISIT WITH WOUNDED SOLDIERS.

"You can bet the article has been syndicated in newspapers across the country, Mirage."

She looked fearful. "What if Mark sees the picture?"

"He thinks you're dead. Even if he sees the headlines, he would never connect Mirage Lord with Lacy Black."

She nodded in agreement. Not one of the soldiers she had talked to yesterday had remarked that she reminded him of Lacy Black.

Mirage and Ben settled down to married life in the New York apartment. Ben had been right about her being the rage. Invitations arrived daily, most of which they turned down. They were content in each other's company. Mirage was reluctant to share Ben with anyone, fearing she would not have him for long. It was apparent that he tired easily, so she deliberately curtailed their activities.

Drew was their most frequent visitor, and of course, he was always welcome. Sometimes he would bring a beautiful woman with him; most of the time he came alone. For Ben's sake, he and Mirage had settled into an uneasy alliance.

1943

Mirage was happy with the progress she was making with her singing lessons. Her instructor, the temperamental Francisco Adolfo, praised her accomplishments lavishly. So far she had never sung for anyone but her instructor—not even Ben.

It was past nine when she rushed out of her bedroom, hoping to find a cab in the morning rush hour. She had only twenty minutes to get to her singing lessons. When she reached the living room, she stopped in her tracks. There was a new baby grand piano in the corner of the room by the window, and Francisco was sitting on the stool smiling at her, while Ben watched her face expectantly.

"Happy birthday, my dear," Ben greeted her with a smile and a kiss on the cheek. "Do you like the piano? Mr. Adolfo helped me pick it out for you."

She beamed at her husband. "I had forgotten it was my birthday." She moved to the piano and ran her hands over the smooth surface. "It's wonderful, Ben. But I don't play the piano, you know."

"You might say the piano is a gift for me, Mirage. I have never heard you sing. Will you sing for me now?"

The teacher nodded eagerly and said in a heavily accented Italian voice, "Sing, Mirage. I want you to show your talent to your husband." He looked at Ben. "She has perfect pitch, which not many can claim. She is a little shy until she starts to sing. But she has a voice like an angel, and the world should hear her."

Ben seated himself in his chair. "I have waited a long time to hear you."

She leaned on the piano, trying to decide what she would sing. She chose a song from *Madame Butterfly*. Her sweet soprano voice caught the high notes of "Some Day He'll Return."

From the first clear note to the last reverberating sound, Ben was stunned by the loveliness and strength of Mirage's voice. She indeed had a great talent.

"Sing another song," Ben urged. "Sing something just for me."

By now Mirage was feeling more confident, and she chose a contemporary song from *Oklahoma*, "People Will Say We're in Love."

When the last note died away, Ben stood up and applauded. "Bravo, Mirage, you were wonderful."

"Do you really think so, Ben?"

"I do."

"I told you she was good," Adolfo said with the arrogance of one accepting another's genius as his own creation. "She is ready to perform in public. It would be a shame if the world was denied her talent."

Mirage was embarrassed by Adolfo's flowery praise. "I sing only for my husband," she said.

"No, no," Ben said. "Adolfo is right; you should perform in public."

"At the Metropolitan," the Italian said, putting his hand on his heart and stabbing the air with his finger. "Yes, she will sing there."

Mirage laughed. "I wouldn't like that, Adolfo. I do have a desire to sing on Broadway, though." She looked at Ben, wondering if he would think she was being presumptuous.

He nodded. "I'll talk to Drew."

She shook her head as her breath became trapped in her throat. "Must it be Drew?"

Ben took her hand. "He's the best."

Chapter Twenty-seven

Drew looked at Ben as if he'd lost his mind. "You want me to do what?"

"I want you to audition Mirage for a part in your new play."

They had been sitting in the third row of the Mary Lord Theater, where Drew had been watching auditions for his new play.

"Surely you can't expect me to put an unknown, no-talent woman in my play just because you're my friend and she's your wife?"

Ben remained calm. "I wouldn't ask you to do this unless I felt she had talent. You should know that about me, Drew."

Drew's dark eyes spat fire. "She could wiggle her lovely ass and you'd think she was a prima ballerina. My God, Ben, have you lost all reason?"

Ben glared at his friend. "Don't go too far, Drew. The least you can do is listen to her. Then you can judge for yourself."

"I'm too busy to run around listening to every woman whose husband thinks she has talent. Besides, I need big names in this play. And if I don't get the backing, there may not be a play at all. These are hard times, Ben. I lost two years when I joined the RAF, and it hasn't been easy to break in again. Even though I've had successes, backers are reluctant to part with their money because of the war."

"How much do you need for this play?"

"I've put all my money in it, but I'm still short more than forty-seven thousand dollars." He looked at Ben with suspicion. "I don't like what you're implying."

Ben nodded. "I'll put up the forty-seven thousand, and take on any other expenses you incur. All you have to do is give Mirage a part, and you pick the part."

Drew leaned forward, resting his chin on his clasped hands. "If anyone but you made that offer to me, Ben, I'd tell them to go to hell."

"Is that what you're telling me?"

Drew sucked in a deep breath, knowing he couldn't turn Ben down. Ben had done so much for him over the years, paid for his education, backed his first show, never asking anything in return. He couldn't tell him no now. "Send her around tomorrow," he said in a resigned voice. "I'll try her. But if she isn't good, I won't put her in my play, even for you."

Ben stood and clapped him on the back. "You won't be sorry. She really is talented."

"Yeah, yeah, I know. And she's the most beautiful woman in the world." Drew sat there after Ben had gone, stunned by his own words, because he had once again unconsciously drawn a parallel between Lacy Black and Mirage Lord.

Mirage stood in the back of the darkened theater, where the only light came from the stage. Somewhere in that darkness Drew was watching. She felt her stomach tighten in fear, and she was sure she wouldn't be able to sing a note. She knew that Drew was auditioning her only to please Ben. What if she really wasn't good enough for Broadway?

She watched a woman come onstage with a confidence that she envied. She waited while the woman sang a few notes, and heard Drew's voice bark out, "No, no. That won't do. Next!"

The stage manager called out. "Mirage Lord, are you here?"

On stiff legs, she moved up the aisle. She knew when she passed Drew, but she didn't look in his direction. She climbed the steps and approached the stage manager. "I'm Mirage Lord."

The man looked at her with bored indifference while he handed her the sheet music. "What key?"

She swallowed hard. "I beg your pardon?"

Drew's voice came out of the darkness. "He asked what key you sing in, Mrs. Lord. You do know your key, don't you?"

"Yes. Key of G."

"One can only hope you can read music," Drew muttered.

She quickly scanned the sheet music and then turned to the man at the piano. "I'm ready."

Drew's eyes were fastened on Mirage. It was the first time he'd been able to observe her without being observed. She wore a modest blue dress with a wide white collar. Her hair was confined beneath a white bandanna, giving her the appearance of innocence and chastity. He leaned back, dreading the moment when she would sing her first note. He meant what he'd told Ben—if she couldn't sing, he wouldn't put her in his play.

Mirage was so frightened that she forgot to deliver the volume.

"We can't hear you, Mrs. Lord," Drew called. "That might be a blessing."

She refused to allow him to goad her into anger. Getting a grip on her emotions, she threw everything into the song. Her clear tones reached the far recesses of the theater. Drew sat forward, his eyes glued to her face. Ben was right: she was a damned good singer, and her voice could carry, too.

As Mirage gained more confidence, she began to relax. That part of her that was Lacy Black rose to the surface, and she mesmerized her jaded audience. Stagehands, prop men, and the stage manager stopped their work to listen to her.

Drew closed his eyes as her sweet voice went around and around in his head. When he looked at her again, he was reminded who she was. "All right, Mrs. Lord. That's enough," he said, breaking into her song.

Meekly, Mirage handed the music to the stage manager and moved to the steps to make her departure.

"Stop," Drew called. "If you're going to be in the theater, you'd better learn the rules. You will leave by the back door like everyone else, is that clear?"

"Yes, Mr. Mallory."

"Report to rehearsal tomorrow at seven sharp," he said grudgingly. "Have you ever been up that early, Mrs. Lord?"

Again, she knew that he was trying to goad her into anger, but she wouldn't give him the satisfaction. "I've always been an early riser, Mr. Mallory."

"Next!"

Mirage was too numb to be excited. When she entered the apartment, she found Ben anxiously waiting for her.

"Well?"

"I'm to report for rehearsal tomorrow. I can't believe it, Ben. I'm going to be on Broadway!"

"Did he say what part?"

"No. But I expect it to be a small one. I don't care if I sing in the chorus or just do a walk-on; I'll be on the stage."

He patted the couch, indicating that she should sit beside him. "You've missed acting, haven't you?"

"I love my life with you."

"But you have missed acting," he pressed.

"Yes, without realizing it, I suppose I have." She was thoughtful for a while, and when she spoke, she was troubled. "If I'm in the play, it will take time away from us, Ben. We won't be able to go to Bar Harbor this summer."

"It doesn't matter where we are, as long as we're together. I want this for you as much as you want it."

She curled up beside him, resting her head on his shoulder. "I'll make you proud of me, Ben."

"I already am."

* * *

The play was *Luck of the Irish,* a musical about an Irish immigrant who comes to New York looking for her brother and falls into the unscrupulous hands of a man who causes her downfall. In the end, she finds her brother, true love, and regains her self-respect. The lead was played by Sara Craven, who had been a star for years. Mirage was given the obscure part of a brothel keeper, Mrs. Dobbins, who was fifty, ugly, and unkempt.

If Drew expected her to complain about her part, he was mistaken. She was so happy to be in his play, she endured the hours it took to transform her face with makeup into that of an old hag. She was delighted that she had two songs.

Rehearsals were grueling, and they became even more so as the opening date neared. They were set for a trial run in New Haven in only three weeks. Ben had purposely stayed away so that Mirage wouldn't be nervous. He watched her come home each evening, tired but cheerful.

Drew was driving them all hard, including himself. But everyone from the star to the prop man was aware that he drove Mirage Lord harder than anyone.

Sara Craven even commented on it once to Drew. "Why do you push her so? She does everything right, and she has a better voice than I do. I expect she'll be a star one day."

He glared at her. "Just see that you know your part, and let me tend to Mrs. Lord."

Sara never mentioned it again, and neither did anyone else.

Mirage sat at the dressing table she shared with four other women, feeling sick with fear. Her hands were trembling so much, she couldn't hold them still.

"Got the jitters, honey?" one of the girls observed. "Just remember, this is New Haven, not New York."

"I don't remember my lines, and I don't think I can sing," Mirage said in a moan.

"We all feel that way at first, honey. But it passes. You'll see."

Mirage's entrance wasn't until the end of the second act, and she had to wait while the others came and went. The longer she waited, the sicker she felt. She longed for a wet cloth on her face, but she couldn't smudge her makeup.

At last the knock came on the door, and she jumped to her feet. "You're on, Mrs. Lord."

Her legs were shaking as she moved down the dim hallway. She reminded herself that Ben was in the audience, and that gave her courage. As she neared the stage, her fear began to diminish and her mind became clear. She swept into the spotlight, belted out her song, and moved through her part better than she ever had. She could hear her voice, but it was as if it came from someone else. She could hear the applause when she finished singing, but that, too, was happening to someone else. Were people laughing at her funny lines—yes, they were!

At last it was over. The people in the audience were on their feet, applauding. Mirage linked hands with the other performers for a curtain call, and the audience applauded loudly. Then the stars came out, and the audience went wild.

Everyone was running around backstage, congratulating everyone else.

When Mirage returned to her dressing room, a single pink rose lay on her dressing table with a note attached to the pink ribbon: *I love you, Ben.*

Hot tears fell on the rose. She hadn't disgraced herself or Ben tonight. Suddenly she looked up and smiled. Drew had done it; he had pushed them hard, but *Luck of the Irish* was a hit!

The New Haven critics raved about the play—they were even kind about Mirage's part. So with several minor adjustments, it went to Broadway. One of the changes was that Mirage now had three songs.

On opening night, Drew came backstage to make sure that everything was ready. There was an excitement in the air that hadn't been quite so evident in New Haven, and everyone could feel it.

He moved from one cast member to another, speaking a word

of encouragement. His job was over; he had guided them, and now when they stepped on that stage, he could only watch with the audience.

Mirage could hear him praise each performer in turn. When he came to her, his eyes locked with hers. "Try to remember to project more. Your voice tends to fade at the end of your second song."

She dropped her eyes, not wanting him to see her hurt. She had wanted more from him, but why should she expect it? He never missed an opportunity to humiliate her; why should tonight be any different?

As Mirage stepped onto the stage, she could feel the hot lights on her face, and she was aware of the people in the audience out there in that dark void, watching her intently. She played to them, she gave herself to them, and she sang for them alone. When her song died away, the audience applauded loudly, and that was her reward.

This time, Mirage was allowed to walk onstage by herself to receive her curtain call at the end of the performance. She was shocked and delighted when everyone in the audience stood, giving her a long tribute of applause. She bowed and backed up, but the crowd kept calling her name, and the stage manager urged her forward once more.

When she finally reached her dressing room, it was filled with flowers, mostly from Ben, but others from his friends in New York.

Cast members were running in the hallway, poking their heads into dressing rooms, congratulating each other. When she was dressed, she found Ben talking to Drew.

Ben pulled her to him and smiled down at her. "You were wonderful."

Drew nodded. "You did remember to project your second song." His voice sounded devoid of feeling. "The cast is all going to my place to wait for the reviews; you and Ben are welcome to join us."

Mirage smiled up at Ben. "Not me. I'm going home to put

my husband to bed. He's had enough excitement for one night."

"You go on, Mirage," Ben urged. "This is a very important night in your life. I wouldn't want you to miss it."

She linked her arm through his. "I want to be with you." She looked at Drew. "I'm sure you will excuse me from your party."

He shrugged. "Suit yourself."

Drew watched them walk away, feeling like a bastard. He had insulted her at every turn, was hard on her and humiliated her in front of the cast and crew, and she never broke and never complained. Was Mirage as good as she seemed, or was she only pretending?

Angrily, he turned away, wondering why he still had this driving need to humble her.

Ben smiled down at his sleeping wife. "Wake up, my dear. I've brought you coffee and several morning papers."

She sat up and pushed her tumbled hair from her face. "I can't read them, Ben. Just tell me what they say. Do they like Drew's play?"

He placed the tray across her lap and handed her a cup of coffee. "Fortify yourself."

Her face fell. "The reviews are bad, aren't they?"

He handed her the *New York Times,* already folded back to the reviews. "Go ahead, read it."

Reluctantly, her eyes fell on the article by the most respected reviewer, Brooks Atkins.

> At last, a play with substance and drama, expertly interwoven with comedy. *Luck of the Irish* kept me on the edge of my seat. Catherine O'Shea, played by Sara Craven, was brilliantly done. There were many memorable characters that will keep New York talking for months. But it is this reporter's belief that the tragedy of this play would have been too depressing had it not been for the fabulously funny Mrs. Dobbins, played by a newcomer, Mirage Lord.

> A natural at delivering comic lines, Mrs. Lord was not only believable in her role, but also sings like an angel.

The review went on, but Mirage could read no further. "Ben, he liked me. I can't believe it."

He handed her another newspaper, where she was pictured as the old hag, Mrs. Dobbins; right beside it was a picture of her without stage makeup. The caption read: *Beauty and the Beast. Can Beauty successfully play the Beast and make you laugh at the same time? If her name is Mirage Lord, she can. We predict a great future for this talented newcomer.*

"You can be proud, Mirage. You worked hard, and you are a success."

She pushed the tray aside and propelled herself into Ben's arms, and he caught her, laughing.

"I did it, Ben—I did it!"

He laughed delightedly. "Yes, you did, my dear. But I never doubted you would."

"Without you, it wouldn't have been possible. And if Drew hadn't pushed me, I would never have given my all. There were times when I wanted to scratch his eyes out, Ben. But as you said, he is the best."

Chapter Twenty-eight

1944

Times were hard as the war continued. Foodstuffs, leather goods, and gasoline were rationed. It was considered unpatriotic to wear stockings, since there was a shortage of silk and the new fabric, nylon. American women, always inventive, drew lines down the backs of their legs so it would look like they were wearing stockings with seams.

Luck of the Irish ran for a year before Mirage decided that she needed to spend more time with Ben. Lately he'd started looking tired, and she was concerned about him. She dreaded going to Drew with her decision, but she would not allow him to bully her into remaining with the show against her will. For all she knew, he might be glad to replace her.

Mirage found Drew in his office, seated amid the loose pages of a scattered script. She watched him for a moment before he noticed her, and she saw that he no longer wore Lacy's ring. At last, he must have gotten over loving her. It made her sad, but she was glad for his sake.

"May I speak to you, Mr. Mallory?"

He pushed a pencil behind his ear and swiveled in his chair to look at her. "Can't you see I'm busy?"

She raised her head and met his eyes. "I won't take up too much of your time."

"Sit down, Mirage." He looked at his watch. "You have exactly five minutes."

She dropped down on the edge of her chair. "I don't need that long. I want to quit the show."

He looked shocked. "Are you serious? What's the matter? Do you want a bigger part? More money?"

She ignored his derision. "No. I just want out."

He studied her face, wondering why in the hell she had to be so beautiful. "Of course you don't need money," he said cruelly. "Would you remain if I offered you the leading role? Is that what you're after?"

Mirage shook her head. "I have no ulterior motive. I've been worried about Ben, and I want to spend more time with him. I'm going to take him to Bar Harbor for the summer. Perhaps he can rest better there without the pressures of the city."

"You're too good to be true," Drew said, and the words were not a compliment. "Would you have me believe that you would give up a starring role in a hit play to look after an old man?"

"I don't care what you believe, Drew," she said quietly. "Your problem is that you think of Ben as an old man, and I think of him as the man I love."

"Ah, the devoted little wife."

Mirage stood up and leaned her hands on the desk so she was eye level with him. "I have taken your contempt for over a year and have said nothing because I wanted to show you I could be a professional. But I don't have to take it anymore, Drew. I'm giving you notice that I'm quitting the show so you will have time to replace me. If you don't like it, then go to hell."

Before she knew what was happening, he grabbed her and pulled her around the desk. She was trembling as he brought her resisting body against his. "Damn you, Mirage. I'm in hell every day. Don't tell me you aren't aware that you're torturing me—everyone else seems to know it."

"You . . . are hurting me," she said, feeling his warm breath against her cheek.

His grip only tightened. "Then hurt. Feel some of the pain that I feel."

"Drew." Her voice came out in a pleading whisper. "Why are you doing this?"

He captured her face and forced her to look at him. "I'm damned if I know, Mirage. At first I hated you because of what I thought you were doing to Ben. Now I'm haunted by you and I don't know why. Do you know that I still come to the play every night?" His hand tangled in her hair and he brought her face closer to his. "I come in time for the second act, just so I can hear you sing."

Mirage collapsed against him, trembling, and unable to move away. The attraction that had started as a seedling in Lacy Black had blossomed into full-blown love within Mirage Lord.

He pressed his rough cheek to hers. "I tried to tear you down, to prove that you were artificial and shallow. But you took everything I gave you and never broke. Every time I hurt you, it was like a pain in my own heart. I wanted to prove to myself that you were unworthy of Ben, but I found that the image you project to the world is what you really are."

Mirage tried to think of Ben, but Drew was holding her so close. At last she wedged her arm between them. "This is wrong, Drew—it must never happen again."

"I know," he said, burying his face in her hair. "Ben is the best friend I've ever had."

The mention of Ben's name was enough to bring her back to reality. "No, Drew, don't do this. We can't betray Ben's faith in us."

He released her, and she cried out at the misery etched on his face. "Don't you think I've agonized about that, Mirage?"

She picked up her handbag from where she had dropped it

on the floor. "We'll just pretend this never happened. We have to for Ben's sake."

Drew jammed his hands in his pockets as if he was afraid he would take her in his arms again. "Yet you don't mind tearing my heart out?"

"Oh, Drew, don't say it."

"Don't say what, that I love you? Don't say that you are so much a part of me that I can't take a breath without thinking of you?" He ran his hands through his dark hair. "Hell, I don't even know how you feel about me. For all I know, you may despise me—you have every reason to."

She moved to the door, gripping the knob tightly in her hand. "I won't betray Ben," she choked out. "I won't."

Drew was beside her, holding the door to prevent her escape. "Tell me you hate me; tell me you love me—just don't let me think that you are indifferent to me."

Slowly she looked up at him, feeling as tortured as he was. There was no joy in knowing he loved her, because the man they both loved stood between them. She couldn't bear to see Drew hurt again because of her. She softly touched his cheek. "You may not understand this, but I have always loved you. We both know that there can never be anything between us. We would hate each other if we hurt Ben. His heart—it would kill him."

He grabbed her hand. "A good-bye kiss, and nothing more. Give me something to hold on to during all the long, lonely nights." His lips were soft against hers, not kindling passion, but tender and loving, conveying knowledge of a love denied, and it was painful to them both. The driving hunger was there, but Drew kept it well under control—he had to, for both their sakes.

"I love you, Mirage, and I have only felt that way about one other woman. I need you, but I will let you go."

She quickly turned and rushed out of the room. She knew what Drew did not: that she was the woman he had loved both times.

* * *

Ben agreed to spend the summer in Bar Harbor. It was on the Friday before they left that the cast of *Luck of the Irish* gave Mirage a going-away party. The festivities were to be held at Drew's apartment. By the time Ben and Mirage arrived, everyone had already gathered, except the host himself.

It was sad to say good-bye to people she'd worked with for so long. There had been camaraderie between them, and she would miss them all.

Sara was playing the piano, and everyone broke out in songs from the show. Ben seemed to be having a lively conversation with the stage manager, and Mirage found herself looking around for Drew. She hadn't seen him yet.

They all urged her to sing one of her songs from the show. As she was lifted onto the piano, it occurred to her that she was performing for the last time.

Her eyes moved down the hallway and she saw Drew coming out of his bedroom, his arm draped around the shoulders of a woman she didn't recognize.

She concentrated on the words of her song, although her heart was breaking. Drew was talking and laughing loudly, and it was hard to be heard over him. Mirage had never seen him act this way, and it was obvious that he'd had too much to drink. It was as if he was being rude on purpose.

The woman he was with giggled and announced to the crowd, "You should see Drew's bedroom. He has pictures of Lacy Black everywhere. If I didn't know better, I'd think he loved a ghost."

"The perfect woman," Drew stated, smiling at Mirage mockingly. "She's incapable of disagreeing with me."

Mirage felt her face burn, and her heart was thundering within her breast. She slid off the piano at the conclusion of her song and found Ben. "I believe we should leave now. We have an early train in the morning," she told him.

Ben nodded in understanding.

"Wait," Drew said, slurring his words. "I want to drink a toast to Ben." He raised his glass, slopping liquor on the carpet. "To my friend." His eyes met Mirage's. "My friend who has everything."

Ben wasn't amused. He knew what Drew meant. He also realized that Drew would be disgusted with himself tomorrow when he was sober. Ever the diplomat, he raised his own glass. "To my friend Drew, who has had too much to drink and is going to have one hell of a hangover in the morning."

Everyone laughed because Ben had turned an awkward situation into lighthearted banter.

Nonetheless, he led Mirage to the door, knowing it was time to leave.

"Good-bye," she said. "I'll miss you all." Mirage took particular care not to look in Drew's direction.

Mirage and Ben spent lazy days fishing, boating, or just walking along the beach. He was tanned and didn't seem to tire quite so easily now.

One quiet day at home, Ben read to Mirage for a while; then she suggested that they have lemonade on the veranda.

She was wearing a crisp white skirt and blouse, and the wind ruffled her shoulder-length hair. Ben watched her staring out to sea, and he could feel a restlessness in her, though she tried to hide it. She was keeping something from him, and he guessed what it was. He hurt for the two young people he loved, because he knew they loved each other and were suffering because of divided loyalties.

He caught a wistfulness in Mirage's eyes. He wanted only her happiness, and it seemed that he was the cause of her pain.

"Would you like to return to the city?" he asked casually. "There's that Tennessee Williams play I'd like to see."

"I'm quite content here," she said. "Aren't you?"

"Yes, but then I'm not young like you. You should be where there is excitement, not nursing an old man."

She dropped to her knees and laid her head in his lap. "Don't say that, Ben. I love you."

He rested his hand on her silken head. "I know you do, Mirage. I never doubt that." He gazed at the dying sun as it seemed to be swallowed by the dark waters of the sea. "I'll always know that."

The lazy days of summer passed too quickly. Mirage noticed that the leaves were beginning to turn, and Ben predicted frost within the week. The mornings were crisp and cool and night fell early. It would soon be time to return to New York, but she wished they could remain in Bar Harbor. There was too much uncertainty for her in New York—Drew was there.

The day was sun-washed as Mirage walked along the beach. She had been thinking about Drew, wondering what he was doing, and agonizing over what beautiful woman might have captured his attention. A huge wave rolled in, leaping over rocks and dashing into the air. She raised her face, welcoming the cool spray.

Drew seemed to appear out of nowhere, as if her thinking about him had conjured him into being. He was standing against a huge boulder, watching her.

"Drew," she said, stopping in her tracks. "How long have you been here?"

"Long enough to observe your walk along the beach. I wondered if you were thinking of me."

She was near enough now that he could touch her, but he didn't. "Yes," she admitted truthfully. "I was wondering what beautiful woman had captured your heart."

Then he did touch her, tilting her chin up, his hungry eyes running over her face. "No woman can take your place in my heart, Mirage." He traced the outline of her lips with his thumb. "You know that without my having to tell you."

"The woman at the party—"

"She was less than nothing to me. Looking back, I think I brought her there hoping to hurt you. I can't even remember her name or her face. That wasn't worthy, was it?"

"Why would you want to hurt me?"

Slowly he lowered his head, his lips sliding across her damp face, which tasted like salt water. "I wanted you to feel some of the pain I was feeling."

"I did."

He swung her around, pressing her between the boulder and his body. "I need to feel you, to touch you. I was like a man without purpose when you left."

Mirage had thought she'd loved Mark when he had rescued her from her father, but she knew it had merely been gratitude. Her love for Ben was deep and peaceful; it calmed and nourished her spirit. But the love she had for Drew filled her with an aching, trembling need.

"Mirage," he murmured, pressing his hard, lean body against hers. "If I could have you just once to remember on cold nights when I ache to touch you."

A groan escaped her lips, and his mouth closed over hers, silencing her. His tongue plunged into her, sliding, circling, tantalizing her to the point of madness. No one had ever done this to her before, and her body quaked with a hunger so strong that she could hardly breathe.

The cry of a seagull circling above brought them both back to sanity. Drew raised his head, staring at her. There was such sadness in his dark eyes, such heartbreak, that it tore at Mirage's soul.

"I tried to stay away," he admitted. "I couldn't."

He turned his back on her and stared at the churning waves splashing against the shore. "I've told myself that I can never have you." He laughed bitterly and turned back to her. "Can you imagine me falling for two women in the world I could never have? There must be a lesson there somewhere, but if there is, I've missed it."

"Why did you come?" she asked almost accusingly.

He stared at her. "Because I've written the perfect play for you. The music was written for you. You must do this for me, because if you don't, I won't let anyone else do it."

"I can't. You know that."

His eyes dropped to hers. "I've already talked to Ben, and he says you will be perfect as my Helen of Troy."

"Ben can't know what torture it is for us to be together."

"Or what hell it is to be without you."

Chapter Twenty-nine

Auditions had started for *Helen of Troy*. Each day Mirage sat in the darkened theater behind Drew, watching him choose the remainder of the cast. Even though they spent so much time together, they never spoke of personal matters, but they were strongly aware of each other.

Work on the play was moving ahead rapidly. Workmen were busy making scenery and props, and cast members were being fitted for their costumes.

The makeup artist was applying eye shadow to Mirage's eyelids when Drew entered the dressing room. He watched for a moment before offering his opinion. "I believe she should have a beauty mark. No, higher up—yes, that's right. We want to accentuate her lips."

Mirage began to tense. As Lacy Black, she had worn a beauty mark in just that spot.

She could see Drew's image reflected in the mirror. He nodded in satisfaction and dismissed the woman, then spoke to Wanda, the wardrobe mistress, who was waiting her turn. "I want to watch you try the wigs on Miss Lord, so I can decide which one is right. Ignore the dark ones. My Helen of Troy is fair-haired," Drew said.

Mirage was paralyzed with a growing fear. "No," she said, putting her hands to her hair.

Drew gave her an impatient look. "Mirage, you should know that you have to wear a wig. You didn't object last time." He turned back to Wanda, who balanced a long golden wig on the tip of her fingers.

"No, that isn't quite right," he said, brushing past her and reaching for a platinum wig. "After all," he said in a bantering tone, "we're trying to remind the audience that men fought and died for Helen. Remember, she was the most beautiful woman in the world."

Drew pushed Wanda aside and pulled the wig over Mirage's hair. The smile froze on his face. His eyes met Mirage's in the mirror, and she saw bewilderment that slowly turned to anger. His mouth tightened and his dark eyes glittered.

"Get out, Wanda," he ordered harshly.

The woman hastily left the room, and Drew gripped Mirage's shoulders. Her eyes were pleading and frightened as he looked at every feature of the face of the woman he loved: the eyes, the mouth, the tilt of her chin that had haunted his dreams for years.

He suddenly loosened his grip on her and strode to a box of fabric, rummaging around until he found what he wanted, a length of black satin.

Mirage flinched as he came back to her, his eyes filled with fury.

"What are you doing?" she managed to choke out in a trembling voice.

He draped the fabric around her neck. "Shut up," he told her as he reexamined every delicate feature of her face. "My God, what a fool I've been, Lacy. Have you enjoyed yourself at my expense? Did you laugh at my stupidity?"

"No, Drew, I never did that."

He dragged her to her feet. "You are supposed to be dead.

What kind of cruel joke is this?" He shook her. "Tell me!"

Tears streamed down her face, and she tried to pull away from him. "Don't ask me any questions, Drew. I can't tell you."

He flung her away. "Does Ben know?"

"Of course he does."

He looked skeptical. "Ben would never marry another man's wife. And don't tell me that you divorced Mark Damian, because I'd know it if you had."

She started gathering up her belongings and stuffing them into a bag. "I have to go now, Drew." She ran toward the door, but he caught her and pulled her back.

"You'll go nowhere until you tell me what happened. Why did you allow me to believe you were dead?" His voice was raw with pain.

"I can't tell you—I can't."

He stared at her for a long time; then he released her. "You owe me an explanation."

She nodded. "I know, but not now. Let me talk to Ben first."

"When?"

"Today—right now."

"Go then. I'll be over tonight, and I want some answers when I get there."

She turned away and rushed into the hallway, too upset to answer when Wanda called to her. She bolted out the door and hailed a cab, needing to see Ben. He would know what she must do.

When Drew arrived at the apartment, Ben was waiting for him. He silently handed Drew a martini and motioned for him to be seated.

"Where's Lacy?" Drew demanded, glancing around the room. "Didn't she have the courage to face me?"

Ben sat down, looking as if he carried the weight of the world on his shoulders. "She was devastated when she arrived home today. I called the doctor for a sedative, and she finally went to sleep."

Drew's eyes became hard. "Why the deception, Ben? Why? I don't understand any of this."

"You have a right to be angry, and I'm sorry you've been hurt, but I think you'll understand when you know the reason why we allow everyone to believe that Lacy Black died in that plane crash."

Drew drained his martini and set the glass down on the table beside him with a snap. "You have my complete attention," he said.

Ben left his own drink untouched. "First, I must have your promise that what is said here will not leave this room. Second, and most important, I have to have your solemn oath that you will not go after Mark Damian."

Drew looked suspicious. "Why?"

"I won't tell you anything until I have your word."

Drew nodded. "You have it. Tell me."

Ben leaned in closer and lowered his voice, although no one else was in the room. "Mark Damian planned for Lacy to die in that plane crash, and he thinks he succeeded." His voice dropped even further as he revealed the tragic circumstances that had brought Lacy into his life.

As Ben had predicted, Drew's first reaction was to want to kill Mark Damian.

"That bastard! I'll get him for this!"

Ben shook his head. "Don't you think I would like to see him punished for what he did? But we can't do anything that might put Mirage at risk."

"Dammit it, Ben, you can't hold me to my promise."

Ben said simply, "I can, and I do."

Drew was battling with himself. At last he voiced the thought that had been haunting him since he'd discovered that Mirage and Lacy were one and the same. "Why didn't she come to me?"

Ben looked at him sympathetically. "I don't know. Perhaps she tried. When I first found her, she had just been to one of your plays. Who can say what would have happened if she had not ended up in the hospital that day?"

They exchanged a glance, both of them knowing how different their lives might have been if Lacy had not fainted at Ben's feet.

"I'm glad you know Mirage's secret," Ben said, "because you can do something for me."

"How can I help?" Drew asked.

"If anything happens to me, look after her. When I die, she'll be all alone and she'll need you."

Drew stared at him. "You aren't going to die, Ben. At one time the doctors gave you only a year to live. Obviously they were mistaken."

"I give all the credit to Mirage. She needed me, and I couldn't let her down." Ben's shoulders drooped. "But I'm weary, Drew, so weary. I can't last forever."

Drew covered Ben's blue-veined hand with his own. "I'll take care of her, Ben. And no one will ever hear from me her true identity." He stood up. "Tell her to report to wardrobe tomorrow and she can wear a dark wig. Impress on her that I'll never speak to her of what happened today, not unless she brings it up first."

"You're a good friend to us both."

"I love you both," Drew replied simply.

At first, when Mirage returned to work, she felt uneasy with Drew. But true to his word, he never spoke to her of the incident in her dressing room. In fact, he seemed to have little interest in her at all. Mirage would hear the others talking about him dating a different woman every night, and she tried not to think about him, except as the director of the play.

On opening night, Mirage stepped onto the stage as Helen of Troy and stepped right into the hearts of the audience. Wearing a flimsy white gown and golden sandals on her feet, and with her hair arranged in the Grecian style with a long, dark curl hanging over her shoulder, she was stunning. Her voice had never been better, and she opened to rave reviews. Tickets were sold out months in advance, except for the sections that were blocked off for military personnel, who were allowed to see the play for free.

Mirage was in her element when she was working. As when she had been making movies as Lacy Black, she studied the character so thoroughly that she became that person. The audiences adored her and kept coming back for more.

She was a great success, and became a respected actress, acclaimed throughout the world. Even the critics loved her. For the second time in her life, she had obtained stardom, and as two different women. Only Drew and Ben knew how great an accomplishment she had achieved.

Mirage's one heartbreak was that the doctor advised her she would probably never be able to have a baby. So she didn't suspect the truth when she began feeling sick to her stomach and was plagued by a weariness that wouldn't go away no matter how much she slept.

Not wanting to worry Ben, she made an appointment to see the doctor on a day he'd been called to Washington to meet with the president.

"I have your test results, Mrs. Lord," Doctor Halstine said, tapping his pencil on a green folder in front of him, "and it is just as I suspected."

"Is it something serious?" Mirage asked him anxiously.

"It's something you will have the rest of your life, but I wouldn't say it was too serious," he assured her with a smile. "You're going to have a baby."

Mirage stared at him for a moment, unable to believe what he was telling her.

"I would say you are about three months pregnant," he continued.

"But, Doctor, you told me I couldn't get pregnant because of . . ." Even now she couldn't bring herself to say the word *abortion*.

"No," he reminded her, "I said it would take a miracle for you to become pregnant. It doesn't happen often, but once in a while I do get to see a miracle. Congratulations to you and Ben."

Sudden joy washed over her. "A baby! Oh, thank you, Doctor—thank you."

His eyes danced with humor. "I can assure you, Mrs. Lord, that I had nothing to do with your situation."

She smiled. "I still can't believe it. I can't wait to tell Ben."

"I'd like to see Ben's face when you tell him. It's always been his fondest dream to become a father. Be sure you give him my best wishes." He cleared his throat. "I'll need to see you in another month; just tell my receptionist, and she'll make an appointment for you. Meantime, I want to get you started on vitamins."

Mirage left the doctor's office floating on a cloud. She still had trouble believing she was going to have a baby. At last she was able to give Ben something that no one else had.

As she sat in the cab on her way back to their apartment, Mirage tried to decide how best to tell Ben the news. Suddenly her thoughts were clouded, and she shuddered, remembering Mark's reaction when she had told him that she was pregnant.

Sometimes she'd allowed herself to think about the baby that Mark had torn from her body. The child would have been almost seven years old now if it had lived. In the secret recesses of her mind, she'd clung to the memory of that unborn child and mourned for it, believing she would never have another.

She touched her stomach, where Ben's child lay. With an aching heart, she spoke softly to the child she had lost. "I wanted you, and I would have loved you," she whispered. "And I'm sorry, but it's time I let you go and stop grieving for you." She pushed her troubled thoughts aside. Nothing must mar the joy of this day. Ben would be home tomorrow, and it would be their anniversary. She could think of no better gift to give him than a baby.

Mirage was napping when Ben returned from Washington the next afternoon. She woke to find him standing over her, his tie loosened and his jacket over his arm. She smiled and stretched lazily.

"You look very inviting, my dear," he told her, sitting down beside her and kissing her in greeting. "I know I sent you flowers," he said, looking around and noticing that the room was filled with a dozen flower arrangements. "I am just wondering which ones are from me."

Mirage laughed. "I have received congratulations on our wedding anniversary from the mayor, the governor, two senators, and a prince from some country I have never heard of. Your flowers are here," she said, indicating two long-stemmed pink roses tied with a green ribbon that lay beside her on the bed. "I didn't receive anything from the president, though," she said mischievously.

"As a matter of fact, you did. Franklin thought by letting me come home, he was giving you quite a present. He also sent his love," Ben informed her, "and so did Eleanor."

With a smile, Mirage swung her legs off the bed and slipped into her robe, belting it at her waist. She couldn't help noticing how tired Ben looked. These frequent trips to Washington were hard on him. "The servants have gone to bed. Why don't you take your bath while I make you something light to eat? If I know you, you ate nothing on the train."

"I'll only be a moment," he told her, glad to find a loving wife at the end of his journey.

Mirage made him a sandwich and a bowl of soup. He came out of the bathroom dressed in the blue silk robe she had given him for Christmas, his damp hair glistening in the candlelight from the table.

He didn't say anything when Mirage handed him a glass of champagne and took a champagne glass filled with orange juice for herself. She found that the thought of any alcoholic beverage made her queasy.

"We're staying in tonight, Ben. I wanted to spend our anniversary alone," Mirage said with a smile.

"This can't be much of an anniversary for you. Weren't the Cravens giving us a party tonight?"

"They still are," Mirage answered him solemnly. "But I made our excuses. I'm sure they'll understand when I tell them the reason tomorrow."

"Oh, and what reason will you give them, Mrs. Lord?"

"Well," she said matter-of-factly, "when a woman first learns that she's pregnant, she's nauseous most of the time, and the last thing she wants is a dinner party."

Ben pulled her down on his lap. "That's wonderful. So Sara is going to have a baby?"

"No, not Sara."

Ben's eyes searched hers. He was too afraid to hope, but Mirage was acting very mysterious. "What are you saying?"

Her laughter bubbled up. "Oh, Ben, I'm the one who is having a baby! This is my anniversary present to you." She was almost breathless with excitement.

"But how? I thought . . ."

Mirage took his hand and placed it on her flat abdomen. "The doctor said it was a miracle, Ben. We made a miracle."

He grabbed her in his arms and held her tightly as a tremor shook his whole body. "I can't believe it," he whispered in a choked voice. "I thought my life was perfect with you, and now it's even more so. Thank you, Mirage, thank you."

She snuggled against his chest. "I'm glad I could give you a baby, Ben, after all you've given me."

"Let's not start measuring who's given the most in this relationship," he said in a broken voice. "You might be surprised to find out it is you—even without counting the baby." He looked at her with a self-mocking smile that belied the tears shining in his eyes, and then his expression became serious. "What about your career? You'll have to leave the play. I wonder what Drew will say this time."

"He'll have no use for a pregnant Helen of Troy, Ben. I don't think even with my 'great acting ability' I would be able to fool the audience—especially in a few months, when I start showing."

"Poor Drew won't be happy about losing his star."

Drew was not happy when Ben invited him to dinner so they could tell him about the baby. He took the news in brooding silence, finally extending his hand to congratulate Ben, while bestowing a hard look on Mirage.

"You have a habit of leaving in the middle of a play, Mirage."

She beamed up at Ben. "I leave to prepare for the greatest role of my life—motherhood."

Chapter Thirty

1945

Mirage had never been happier, and Ben strutted around like a proud father. The pregnancy had been good for his health, because he refused to leave Mirage alone and had curtailed his travels. They both kept their social obligations to a minimum, preferring quiet evenings at home instead. As a result, Ben was rested and relaxed for the first time in months.

They were happy that they were able to engage Kitty Merryweather as the baby's nurse. She had taken such good care of Mirage when she had been ill, and they had complete trust in her. She'd already moved into one of the guest bedrooms and was helping Mirage put the finishing touches on the nursery.

Sadness did touch their lives toward the end of Mirage's pregnancy. President Roosevelt, the man who had been so dynamic in spirit and who had made his enemies tremble in fear, was dead of a cerebral hemorrhage. Ben was reluctant to leave Mirage so late in her pregnancy, but she urged him to attend the funeral at Hyde Park. Mirage mourned President Roosevelt's passing with the rest of the world, perhaps more than most, because she had met him and had been the recipient of his kindness.

Mirage was feeling restless. Since Ben wouldn't be returning until the next day, she decided that she and Kitty would use the tickets Drew had sent for the premiere of his new play, *Fly with Angels.*

During the first act, Mirage felt a pain so sharp it took her breath away. She gripped the arm of the chair until the pain went away. The doctor had assured her that the baby wouldn't be born for at least two weeks, or she wouldn't have attended the play, and Ben wouldn't have left her.

At intermission, she went to the ladies' room and splashed water on her face. There had been no more sharp pains, but there was a dull ache in her lower back that wouldn't go away. She wanted to see the end of Drew's play, so she didn't mention the pain to Kitty.

By the middle of the third act, Mirage realized that the pain was different now—more regular and becoming more intense. She was in labor!

Could she make it until the play ended? No, the pain was too severe.

Kitty was so engrossed in the performance that she hadn't noticed Mirage's discomfort.

"Kitty," Mirage whispered, "help me to the ladies' room, and then get Mr. Mallory. I believe the baby's coming."

The nurse's face whitened when she saw the pain etched on Mirage's face. She helped her up the aisle and seated her in a chair in the ladies' room, ordering the attendant to flag down a taxi. She then went in search of Andrew Mallory.

Drew burst into the ladies' room, unmindful of the startled looks he was getting from several women. He knelt down beside Mirage. "Can you walk, or shall I carry you?"

"Just allow me to lean on you," she said, gritting her teeth until the pain subsided.

In no time at all, she was installed in a cab that sped toward the hospital. Kitty had stayed behind to call the doctor and to try to locate Ben.

Mirage clutched at Drew's arm, her eyes wide and frightened.

"Hold on, Mirage," Drew said. "The hospital's just ahead."

The cab screeched to a halt and Drew jumped out, lifting her into his arms. Several nurses and an attendant were waiting for them, having been alerted by Dr. Halstine to expect their arrival.

"Let's put her on a stretcher," one of the nurses directed.

"No," Drew said, holding Mirage close to him. "She's in pain. I'll only hand her over to the doctor."

"Now, Mr. Lord," the nurse said in a condescending tone, "at this time, husbands just get in the way. Lay her on the stretcher, and I'll take care of her. The doctor is on his way. I can assure you that since this is your wife's first child, the doctor will get here long before your baby."

Not bothering to correct the nurse's mistaken assumption, he reluctantly placed Mirage on the stretcher, but she still clutched his hand.

"I'm frightened, Drew."

He bent and softly kissed her lips. "Don't be afraid. I'll be just outside the door."

It was four o'clock in the morning when a nurse informed a haggard Drew that Mirage had delivered a daughter and they were both fine.

"May I see her?" he asked. "I need to know for myself that she's all right."

"That won't be allowed, since you aren't the father," the head nurse replied stiffly. "We just got a call from Mr. Lord; he's on his way."

Drew's hands dropped to his sides as he moved to the window and stared out into the night. After a while, he straightened his tie and ran his hand through his hair. His footsteps were heavy as he left the hospital. Mirage didn't need him now; she'd have Ben.

* * *

Ben quietly entered Mirage's room. A single light glowed from a corner lamp, and she looked pale lying against the stark white pillowcase.

When she opened her eyes and saw tears on Ben's face, she felt her own eyes grow misty. "Have you seen your daughter yet?"

"No, I came directly to you. Dr. Halstine says you and the baby came through just fine." He squeezed her hand. "I'm sorry I wasn't here for you when you needed me."

"Don't reproach yourself," she said, smiling. "Drew was your stand-in." She looked beyond Ben. "Where is he?"

"I'm told he's gone already."

The nurse entered the room, carrying the baby, flanked by Dr. Halstine.

Ben released his hold on Mirage to reach eagerly for his daughter, and the nurse placed her in his arms. His eyes swept her from head to toe, and he was awed by how tiny she was. He was still wearing the cutaway and tails that he'd worn to Franklin's burial. Unmindful of his elegant clothes, he clutched the tiny infant to him.

"What do you think, Doctor?" Ben asked proudly. "Isn't she a beauty?"

"That she is. Six pounds and three ounces of perfect baby. She'll be as beautiful as her mother one day."

Ben looked from his daughter to his wife, and his shoulders seemed to droop. He knew he wouldn't be there when she grew up.

Katherine Delaney Lord was named for Mirage's mother. Never had a princess of the royal blood received more attention than Benjamin Lord's only offspring. Baby gifts came from all over the world. At the private christening, Sara Craven became Katherine's godmother, and Drew became her godfather.

At long last the war was over. There was celebrating in the streets of New York City. Ben and Mirage stood on the balcony of their apartment, waving small American flags and calling to the crowd below. Ben grieved that Franklin hadn't lived to see this day.

Sadly, the stronger their baby grew, the weaker Ben seemed to become. The doctor had ordered him to spend most of each day in bed, so a male nurse had been engaged to help Mirage look after him.

Warren Kendrick was a huge man with massive arms and a ready smile. Mirage secretly thought of him as 'the gentle giant.' He soon became as much a part of the family as Kitty, for both of them were indispensable.

Mirage decided to take Ben to Bar Harbor, where he always seemed the happiest. They packed up their belongings and were soon on their way. It seemed the closer Ben got to Maine, the lighter his mood became.

Two years had passed too quickly for Mirage. Next week they would celebrate Katherine's second birthday. Ben was sitting on the veranda, where he now spent most of his time, gazing out to sea.

Katherine waddled toward her father's outstretched arms, her chubby face showing her glee. She nestled in his lap, and he placed his hand on her curly head.

Mirage handed him his medicine and a glass of water. "You're her favorite person, Ben. She'd rather be with you than anyone."

He kissed his daughter's cheek. "I spoil her, but I want her to remember me, Mirage." He looked into his wife's eyes. "You won't let her forget me, will you?"

They both knew that he was slowly dying, but Mirage never let her mind dwell on that fact. She sensed that Ben needed her assurance today, and she nodded. "I'll tell her about you all the time, Ben. Katherine will always know that her father loved her. She will know that you were . . . are honorable, worthy, and the kindest man I have ever known."

He watched the wind ripple through her hair and reached for her hand. "You've had a good life with me, haven't you, Mirage?"

Her lips trembled as she turned to watch the sails of a yacht coming into port. "I never knew that life could be so good, Ben."

"Even if I took my happiness at Drew's expense?" he asked.

She turned to him quickly, searching his face. "Ben, don't say that."

"He loves you, and I'm glad. I know you won't be alone when I'm gone."

Kitty came out the back door and took a sleeping Katherine from Ben.

After she disappeared into the house, Ben continued: "I have sent for Drew. That will be his yacht docking now."

Painfully, Mirage realized that he wouldn't have sent for Drew unless he thought he was dying. She dropped to her knees and laid her head on his lap. "Oh, Ben, don't leave me. I need you; Katherine needs you."

Gnarled hands gently stroked her hair. "I hope my love has given you the strength to meet whatever comes with courage."

She could hear footsteps coming up the path, and she stood slowly, stiffening her back. "That'll be Drew. I'll leave the two of you alone."

"Go wash away the tears from your face and join us. I don't want to see any sadness today."

Mirage bent to kiss him, then went into the house, no longer fighting her tears.

There had been an article in the *New York Times* about Drew's engagement to a woman from an old New England family. Mirage had seen a picture of them together, and although the news stabbed at her heart, she hoped this woman would bring Drew happiness.

Later that evening, she watched Ben and Drew battle over a jade-and-ivory chessboard.

"You always were a worthy opponent, Drew, one of the few who make it a challenge to play the game."

"I learned from you, Ben."

There was a gleam of triumph in Ben's eyes. "Apparently, I didn't teach you everything." He moved his queen across the board. "Checkmate."

Drew studied the chessboard and shook his head. "You're too good for me, Ben."

"How about another game?"

"If you'll take it easy on me."

Mirage was seated across the room from them, reading a book. She felt Drew's eyes on her and looked up at him. He and Ben had talked a long time before dinner. She could tell by Drew's expression that he knew Ben was dying.

She got up and moved across the room. "Not another game, Ben. You need to rest." She picked up a handbell and rang it, summoning Warren. When the nurse appeared, he helped Ben to his feet.

"You stay with Drew, Mirage," Ben said. "Warren can tuck me in tonight."

She shook her head. "No, I'm weary. I'm sure Drew will understand if I go to bed early."

"Ben has asked me to take you sailing tomorrow, Mirage. Do you want to catch the morning tide?"

"I can't, Drew."

"Don't take no for an answer, Drew. All she ever does is sit at home with me. I want her to have fun for a change, and I insist you take her."

"I'll be waiting for you at six," Drew said.

Mirage nodded, wishing she wouldn't have to be alone with Drew. No matter how she tried to deny it, she loved him. Seeing him today had been very painful for her. She kissed Ben good night, checked on Katherine, and climbed into bed, hoping for a dreamless sleep.

It was a crisp morning, and the sun was just climbing into the eastern sky when Mirage made her way down the cliff to the boathouse, carrying a picnic basket over her arm.

Drew waved to her and called out, "Hurry aboard. I could use some help with the sails."

Agilely, she made the leap from the dock to the boat. It was good to feel the deck beneath her feet again. "I brought grub," she said, laughing up at Drew.

"Stow it in the galley, and tie this rope off for me."

Soon the yacht was under way, and Mirage stood at the helm, tasting the salty ocean spray on her lips. "I've missed this," she said, turning to find Drew staring at her.

"Have you?"

She ducked her head, disturbed by his nearness. "You must have sold the *Victory*. When did you get a new boat?" she asked, reaching for something to say.

"I've had the *Helen* for over a year."

Mirage steered the ship into the wind. "Is that the name of the woman you are going to marry?"

"So you read about that?"

"Yes. But I don't recall her name."

"I named the ship for the woman I love."

Why did it hurt so much to hear him speak of loving another woman? She had no right to be jealous. "Oh."

Mirage felt him behind her, and she glanced up into his face. "Helen of Troy, Mirage. *You* are my Helen."

Without knowing how it happened, she was in his arms, pressing her face against his sweater, glorying in the feel of his strong arms around her. He still loved her, and her heart was glad.

"I will never marry, Mirage. My heart's too full of you."

"But the article—"

"You know how those things get started. I dated the woman for over a month, and everyone had us married."

She moved out of his arms. "I wish you would marry someone and put me out of my misery."

"Don't talk to me about misery, Mirage."

She dropped down onto a seat, quickly changing the subject. "You know why Ben asked you to come?"

"Yes." He narrowed his eyes and glanced toward the east. "We had a long talk yesterday."

"Oh, Drew, he must be suffering so, but he never complains. I try to make his days happy, but I know he grieves because of Katherine."

"A man couldn't ask for a better wife, Mirage. You have made him happy. You kept him alive years longer than the doctors predicted."

Sadness was like a knife in her heart. "I want to keep him forever. He's my best friend."

"I know," Drew said, his eyes filled with misery. "Mine too." He glanced at the disappearing shore. "I don't know when I've seen the terrain so dry," he said, giving her time to compose herself.

She shaded her eyes and looked toward the distant horizon, searching for rain clouds, but there were none. The wind had suddenly intensified and the sea was becoming choppy. "I know. We haven't had any rain. The weather bureau says it's the driest summer we've had in years."

"Let's put ashore on that small island to eat our picnic lunch," Drew suggested.

"All right, but let's hurry. I don't like leaving Ben alone."

Their eyes met in mutual sadness, but no words were spoken. There was so much left unsaid between them. There always had been.

Chapter Thirty-one

The wind had grown stronger, and five-foot waves splashed on the rocks, sending a shower of spray cascading into the air.

Drew had been watching Mirage as she walked along the beach, picking up seashells to take home to Katherine.

"Mirage," he called, folding the blanket and lifting the picnic basket, "I think we should be heading back. The sea's getting pretty rough."

She looked toward the mainland, her body tensing. "Drew, that looks like smoke . . . or is it just clouds?"

He glanced toward Bar Harbor, noticing the black smoke that bellowed into the sky. "My God, there's a fire—a big one!"

They both ran along the beach, heading for the yacht. Drew leaped aboard and pulled Mirage on board after him. He started the engine and turned toward the west, his eyes on the smoke.

"I can see the fire, Drew," Mirage cried out. "Dear God, don't let anything happen to Ben and Katherine!"

A boat trip that should have taken no more than an hour turned into three because the wind had grown to nearly hurricane force. They watched helplessly as the fire spread rapidly out of control, all the while fighting to keep the *Helen* afloat. At times it appeared that all of Bar Harbor was burning.

Suddenly the southwest wind fell to a dead calm. There was an eerie silence followed by gale-force winds that pounded the coast of Bar Harbor, whipping the sparks into a raging inferno and sending the licking flames toward the town and ultimately up the hill toward Windward House.

The residents of Bar Harbor were like fugitives from a war zone, rushing through the choking darkness brought on by the surging smoke. They rushed to piers, their paths strewn with discarded treasures, as people chose life over worldly possessions. Floodlights illuminated the hopelessness of their situation. Escape seemed impossible—they were trapped. To the front was the danger of giant waves wrought by the storm, and behind was death by fire. It seemed that the whole world was aflame, as if God had wrought a harsh judgment against the community.

Mirage watched a curtain of smoke billow across the horizon, changing the summer paradise into charred ruins.

"Windward House is all right for the moment," Drew yelled. "The fire hasn't reached up the hill yet."

"Oh, please hurry!"

At last they approached the boathouse. Both Mirage and Drew leaped over the sides, wading through the water until they reached the shore. Mirage fell, but Drew lifted her up, and they both ran for the path that led to the house, Mirage praying all the way that her family was safe.

Even though it was afternoon, smoke made the sky dark as night. Someone had a loudspeaker and was advising everyone to evacuate by Shore Highway Three.

All Mirage could think about was her baby and Ben. Her feet flew up the steps that led to the house, and she stopped as she reached the top.

"Drew," she screamed hysterically, "the house is on fire!"

He took her arm and turned her to face him. "Listen to me,

Mirage. Ben and the baby will already have left. You wait here, and I'll make certain."

She clutched at his arm. "I'm coming with you."

He gripped her tightly. "You would only be in my way, and I'd be worried about you. Do as I say, Mirage."

At that moment, they both heard a child's cry coming from upstairs. Katherine was still in the house! Drew ran toward the inferno, entering the door just as burning beams fell about him.

Mirage tried to follow him, but spiraling flames kept pushing her back. "Ben, Katherine—God help them!" she cried.

She ran around to the side of the house, hoping to gain entrance through the kitchen. She saw someone staggering out the door. It was Warren, carrying Ben.

She ran to her husband, dropping down on her knees and taking him in her arms. "Oh, Ben, are you all right?"

"Katherine," he wheezed. "It's too late. . . ."

"Drew's inside. I'm going in, too," she said, jumping to her feet.

"Don't let her, Warren," Ben said in a weak voice. "Keep her away from the house."

The giant man looked at Mirage apologetically, but when she would have moved around him, he blocked her path. "I can't let you go in, Mrs. Lord."

"Move aside!" she cried, pounding on his chest. "I want my baby!"

At that moment, there was a thundering noise, and the ground trembled as the whole second floor of Windward House came crashing down into a burning mountain of fire.

Mirage twisted and turned, trying to get free of Warren's imprisoning arms. "Let me go—let me go!"

"Mirage." She heard Drew calling her. "It's all right. I have Katherine and her nurse. They're both unharmed."

Warren released his hold on Mirage, and she ran to Drew, ripping Katherine from his arms. "My baby, my sweet," she said between sobs, dropping to the ground and smothering the frightened child with kisses.

Drew dropped down beside Ben, searching his face in the light of the fire. "Are you hurt, Ben?" he asked with concern.

Ben grasped Drew's shirtfront, weakly pulling him closer. "Katherine, is she all right?"

"Yes, Ben," Drew assured him.

"Take care of them," Ben wheezed. "Promise me, Drew. Promise me."

Drew glanced up at Warren. "Was he injured in the fire?"

"No, sir. I got him out in time."

"Drew." Ben's voice became more insistent. "Promise me you'll take care of . . . Mirage and my daughter."

Ben's hand fell away from his shirt, and Drew realized that Ben needed a doctor. "You'll take care of them yourself."

"Drew, I can't make . . . it. I don't . . . have long. Promise me . . . you will. . . ."

Drew could hear the desperation in his friend's voice. "I promise, Ben. I'll take care of them."

With a soft sigh, almost a sound of contentment, Ben closed his eyes.

Warren moved opposite Drew and placed his hand on the pulse at Ben's neck. After a long moment, he looked up at Drew with sadness in his eyes.

"I'm sorry, sir, Mr. Lord is dead."

Mirage was unaware that Ben was gone. She was instructing Jenkins to bring a car around, since the fire hadn't yet reached the garage. "We need to get my husband to Ellsworth Hospital as soon as possible."

Drew went to Mirage, nodding for Kitty to take the child. Mirage's body was stiff and resisting as he took her by the arm. She knew the truth by looking at his face.

"No!" she screamed, fighting to get to Ben, but Drew held her firmly. "Let me go to him—he needs me."

Drew took her in a comforting embrace. "You can't help him now, Mirage. Ben is"—he choked on the word—"dead."

Deep, wrenching sobs tore from her throat, and she pushed Drew away, going down to her knees beside her husband. Taking his still-warm hand, she raised it to her face. "Ben, you can't leave me. Katherine needs her father—I need you."

She touched his dear face, which was plainly visible in the glow from the fire. He looked as though he had just fallen asleep. "Get up, Ben," she said to him. "We'll take you to the hospital. They'll know how to help you."

Drew pulled Mirage to her feet. "We have to leave now. The fire is spreading rapidly."

"But Ben?"

"Warren will take care of him. I have to get you and Katherine out of here."

"No." She stood up and faced him defiantly. "I won't leave Ben. You can't make me."

Drew realized he would have to push his grief aside if he was going to get them to safety. "You're hysterical, Mirage, and you aren't thinking clearly," he said, scooping her into his arms and carrying her to the car. "Ben asked me to look after you and Katherine, and by God, that's just what I'm going to do."

She fought him, trying to escape from his strong grasp, but he held her tightly. Kitty rushed behind them with Katherine in her arms.

Drew put Mirage in the car and took the baby from Kitty, placing her in Mirage's arms, hoping she would be reminded that the child needed her. "You have to think of Katherine, Mirage. Ben is beyond our help."

She clutched Katherine to her; the child was a small part of Ben that she could still hold. She buried her face against her, trying not to cry, for her daughter's sake. But Katherine didn't help.

"I want my daddy," she said, sobbing. "I want my daddy."

Drew helped Kitty into the backseat and called out to Warren, who was lifting Ben's lifeless body into another car. "Follow us down. The road looks clear, but the fire is advancing. Should we be separated, you know what to do."

"Yes, sir, Mr. Mallory. I'll take Mr. Lord's body to the morgue."

Mirage turned to look out the back window, satisfied that Warren was following them. As they came off the hill, bulldozers were clearing a path through the debris, allowing a long motorcade of frightened people escaping the fire to join a police escort.

Through a blinding haze of smoke, through flames and flying ash, buses and cars moved forward slowly, taking in stragglers as they went. The long motorcade twisted its way down the mountain, and it seemed as if the whole world were on fire.

When they reached the coast highway, Drew pulled over. "Can you drive, Kitty?"

"Yes, sir, I can."

"Then take the wheel; it'll be safe from here on. I'm going back to help."

Mirage grabbed his arm. "You aren't going back. I won't let you."

"I have to, Mirage. We all must do what we can. Make your way to New York. Have you got money?"

"I don't know. I don't think so."

He reached into his pocket and thrust some bills at her. "When you are safely away, stop at an inn and sleep for the night. I'll join you in New York as soon as I'm able, and I'll make all the arrangements that need to be made."

Mirage looked into his eyes. "Please be careful. I don't want to lose you, too."

As Kitty situated herself in the driver's seat and the car moved ahead, Mirage looked back at Drew, praying he would come safely through the fire.

Drew fought beside other courageous men against a fire that refused to die. The valiant firefighters hardly felt the blisters on their hands or heeded the smell of singed hair. Their blackened faces were smeared with soot, and their eyes were dull with fatigue. Their rubber boots covered blistered feet, and they ignored the burns on their faces and hands.

The peat bogs ignited and carried flames underground. Above ground, hungry flames fanned by the wind leaped from treetop to treetop, devastating everything in their path. The sounds of explosions from the intense heat filled the air.

Among the wildlife, old adversaries banded together to survive. The fox and the rabbit cohabited in water-filled ditches, while the wildcat and the deer swam to safety across shimmering ponds.

The legacy left by the fire was charred ruins and razed forests—a no-man's land.

Newspapers all over the world reported the tragic Bar Harbor fire, but more space was given to the honored statesman Benjamin Lord, who had lost his life that same night.

Mirage decided that Ben's funeral would be private, though heads of state from all over the world asked to attend. She sat like one turned to stone as Drew delivered the eulogy, crying only when she saw tears in Drew's eyes.

For weeks afterward she refused to see any visitors, including Drew. She moved like a zombie through the apartment, sitting in Ben's favorite chair, looking at photographs that had captured him when he was vital and alive. She could feel his presence so vividly that she was certain he was still looking after her and Katherine.

Her only joy was when she was with her daughter. During this time of grief, Kitty and Warren became her protectors, shielding her from curious reporters and the well-meaning people who wanted to express their sympathy to the Broadway star who had lost her husband.

At night Mirage would lie in bed, staring at the ceiling, listening in vain for the sound of Ben calling her name.

When she was stronger, she felt the need to return to Bar Harbor, and made the sad train trip alone. As the hired car made its way up the steep embankment where Windward House had once dominated the bluff, she saw only blackened ruins.

She dismissed the driver and walked around for hours. This had once been her haven, her sanctuary from the world; now it was nothing but rubble.

Only the marble fireplace with the carved lion heads seemed untouched by the fire. It was ironic that Ben had once told her the fireplace would outlast the house—he had been right.

She tried not to think about the night of the fire, for it had taken more from her than her home. It had devastated her life: it had taken her love—it had taken Ben.

Part Three
Drew

Chapter Thirty-two

The mood was solemn in the law offices of Lord, Bishop, and Bishop, where a group of people had been summoned to hear the reading of Ben's will.

Mirage, dressed in black, with circles under her eyes, greeted Palmer Bishop, Ben's former partner and lifelong friend. She also spoke to each one present, shaking hands and accepting condolences. There was Ben's business manager, the president of Lord Enterprises, and several servants who had worked for Ben for many years. Drew stood at the window with his hands crammed in his pockets, wanting to be anywhere but there today. He acknowledged Mirage with the merest nod.

"If you will all be seated," Palmer said, sitting at his desk and looking at each person in turn, "we will begin.

"As you know," he said, shuffling through the papers, "you have been asked here today because Benjamin Lord included you in his will. Molly and Thomas Brewster," he said, addressing the servants first, "Mr. Lord wanted me to thank you both for your years of devoted service at the Bar Harbor cottage. You have both indicated to me that you have no wish to move to

New York, so I'm instructed to advance you money to buy a house of your own and to pay you an annual income of ten thousand dollars for the duration of your lives."

He then turned his attention to the chauffeur, Jenkins, and his wife, Celesta, who was the housekeeper at the New York apartment. "It is Mr. Lord's wish that you both continue to serve Mrs. Lord in the manner in which you have in the past. He has instructed me to place money in an interest-bearing trust that will mature in ten years. I should make it clear that the money is yours whether you stay with Mrs. Lord or not."

"Of course we'll stay, sir," the chauffeur said gruffly.

There were several other smaller bequests before Palmer Bishop dismissed the servants and turned his attention to Mirage.

He handed her an official-looking document. "You will see listed there the various corporations owned by Ben, and others in which he had interests. All his assets, including companies, monies, artworks, and real estate, are left to you, with certain exceptions that we'll discuss later."

Mirage looked down the long list, unable to comprehend the magnitude of Ben's wealth.

"If you will turn to page ten, you will see that the assets come to a total of twenty-seven million dollars."

Mirage looked hopelessly at the attorney. "I know nothing about the operations of these companies, Mr. Bishop. Surely Ben didn't intend me to take over for him?"

Palmer Bishop glanced down at a document in his hand. "It was Ben's wish that you retain his business associates, Mr. Arnold and Mr. Curtis. He asked that you put your trust in their judgment, as he has always done."

"Yes, let it be as my husband wished," Mirage said, feeling numb and overwhelmed by the responsibility that had been placed on her shoulders. Ben had employed thousands of workers, and affected their everyday lives. How could she be expected to go on for him?

This time Mr. Bishop dismissed everyone but Mirage and

Drew. "The rest of the will concerns only the two of you."

Drew still stood at the window. He didn't like the proceedings, and he wished he hadn't been asked to come today.

"Mr. Mallory, won't you take a seat beside Mrs. Lord? I promise I'll not take up much more of your time."

Unwillingly, Drew complied.

"Mr. Mallory, my client wished me to express to you his feeling that you have always been like a son to him. Therefore, he has left to you the Lord theater complex, its grounds, and its buildings. He has also left you numerous other objects that are listed here." He handed a two-page document to Drew. "As you see, they are all personal items. Sadly, some were destroyed in the Bar Harbor fire."

Through a haze of pain, Drew looked at the list—Ben's ivory-and-jade chessboard. . . . He could read no further.

"Ben has asked that a sum of five million dollars be placed in trust for his daughter, Katherine Lord, to be given to her on her twenty-first birthday. Also, you will see listed on page twenty-three a number of family heirlooms he wishes to be handed down to her."

Mirage looked up at the attorney. "Thank you, Mr. Bishop. You handled a painful ordeal with grace and a professionalism that I appreciate."

"There is just a bit more," he told Mirage apologetically, turning to the last page of the will. "He asks that you, Mr. Mallory, look after Mrs. Lord and his daughter, Katherine. He beseeches you to be their friend, as you have been his. He hopes that you will always be there for them in their time of need."

Drew nodded. "I'll fulfill his wishes," he said with feeling. He turned his eyes on Mirage. "Mrs. Lord knows that I'll always be there for her."

Mirage pressed her lace handkerchief to her eyes. Ben was even reaching out from his tomb to care for her.

Mr. Bishop stood and extended his hand to Drew. "You may leave now. I have something of a personal nature to go over with Mrs. Lord."

Drew stood and shook the lawyer's hand. He then turned to Mirage. "Would you like me to wait for you?"

"No, thank you. I will want to be alone."

After Drew had departed, Palmer Bishop handed Mirage a large manila envelope. "Ben instructed me to turn this over to you."

She looked at him quizzically. "Do you know what it is?"

"No. It was put in my keeping before your marriage. It was sealed the day he gave it to me, and as you see, it's still sealed."

Suddenly Mirage knew what it was. It was the FBI's report on Mark Damian. She tucked the envelope beneath her arm and stood, extending her hand. "Thank you for your kindness, Mr. Bishop. I hope that you will advise me as you advised my husband."

"I'll do my best," he told her. He liked Mrs. Lord. When Ben had married her, Palmer, like many of Ben's friends, had had his doubts. But no longer. Mirage Lord had been a worthy wife for a great man like Benjamin Lord.

Mirage ached with loneliness as she moved through the rooms where she had spent so many happy times with Ben. She had given all the servants, including Kitty and Warren, the weekend off because she wanted to be alone.

Katherine was asleep, and lonely hours stretched before Mirage. She curled up in a window seat with the newspaper in her lap. She flipped through the pages, automatically turning to the entertainment section. As always, she looked at the advertisement for Drew's show.

Absently, she looked at the page with the Hollywood news, not really interested until she saw Mark Damian's name. She sat up straight, the breath tight in her throat as she read the article.

GRIEF STRIKES PRODUCER AGAIN

Mark Damian's second wife, Rosalinda Mitchell, met death when her car careened off the road on Mulholland Drive. Faulty brakes were blamed, and she was killed instantly. Mr. Damian was first devastated by the untimely and tragic death of his wife, Lacy Black, a star of great magnitude. Lacy died in a plane crash, and her body was never recovered. His second wife made only one picture, which was a flop at the box office. It is rumored that Mr. Damian never recovered from Lacy's death and keeps trying, without success, to mold women in her image. At this time, Mr. Damian is writing the life story of Lacy Black, in which newcomer Patricia Marlon will star on the big screen. It's this reporter's belief that no one could ever do justice to the mystical allure of the tragic star.

Mirage stared at the article, her mind racing back in time to when Dolores Divine's car had careened off a cliff on Mulholland Drive. She began trembling and couldn't stop. She was probably the only person in the world who suspected that Mark had killed Rosalinda Mitchell.

She stood up and moved to the window, staring down at the pedestrians moving around like tiny ants below. She was among thousands of people, and yet she still felt desperately alone.

She moved to the balcony and raised her face to the sky. "Oh, Ben, what shall I do? It's my fault that Rosalinda Mitchell is dead. If I hadn't been such a coward—if I had gone to the police after the plane crash—that poor woman would be alive today."

Suddenly her mind cleared, as if Ben had given her direction. Mark had to be stopped before he killed again. She remained on the balcony until long after dark, while a plan formed in her mind. If she went to the police now, there was no assurance that Mark would be convicted of his crimes. She wasn't sure she would believe such a far-fetched story if someone told it to her. No, the authorities would be no help—she was the only one who could stop Mark, and she knew just how to do it.

She was brought back to the present by the ringing of the doorbell, and she was tempted to ignore it. When the caller continued ringing, she pushed the intercom and said in an irritated voice, "Yes?"

"Mirage, let me in," Drew insisted. "I won't be ignored any longer. You don't take my calls, and you refuse to allow me into your sanctuary."

Drew was right. She had refused to see him because he was the one person who could intrude on her memories of Ben.

If she was going to deal with Mark, she might be in danger. She needed Drew to look after Katherine.

"Come on up," she said, pushing the button that would release the private elevator.

She met him at the elevator door. He hugged her and gave her a chaste kiss on the cheek. "It isn't good for you to bury yourself up here in your ivory tower and not see your old friends," he said. His eyes moved over her face, and he thought she was more beautiful than ever.

She linked her arm through his. "You will be my first guest since Ben's death."

They stepped into the living room, and he inspected her more closely. "How are you?"

"I'm numb. I still can't believe he's gone. I knew he was dying, Drew, and yet wasn't prepared to give him up."

"Why don't we go out for dinner? It's time you were with people. Everyone asks about you."

"I can't go out tonight, Drew. I gave all the servants the weekend off."

"Then I'll cook for us," he said, clasping her hand and pulling her toward the kitchen. "I'll make an omelet that has to be tasted to be believed."

He did seem to know his way around the kitchen. He opened a door and pulled out a skillet. "While I make the omelet, you choose the wine." He was thoughtful. "I think tonight calls for a light chablis."

Mirage felt as if a weight had lifted from her shoulders as she hurried to the bar and selected an Italian wine that she knew was Drew's favorite. Collecting two crystal wine goblets, she returned to the kitchen. Uncorking the top, she poured the pale liquid and handed Drew a glass.

He took a sip and nodded with satisfaction. She leaned against the cabinet, watching him dice peppers and add them to the pan.

He glanced up at her and smiled. "Aren't you going to set the table? Surely you don't expect me to cook and serve as well?"

She laughed. It had been so long since she'd felt lighthearted, and for the moment, she'd even forgotten about Mark.

They talked of trivial things over dinner. Then Drew told her about his new play. "It was made to order for you, Mirage. *Homecoming* is about a girl who returns to her small hometown after a long absence to find that she hasn't changed, but the people around her have changed their perceptions of her. She decides she must leave again, because she no longer belongs."

"I don't want to do a play, Drew. Not now. I have other obligations first."

He threw his napkin on the table. "What do you want to do? Sit around this apartment all day, living in the past?" He stood up and reached for her, pulling her to her feet. "Do you sleep with his ghost, Mirage?"

Drew muttered an oath and pulled her to him, his lips resting against her ear. "I waited, trying to give you time to grieve. I've never been accused of being patient, but I have been with you. We need each other. You knew I'd come for you sooner or later."

She turned her face so her cheek rested against his. "Yes, I knew," she agreed, not bothering to deny her need for him.

His arms tightened around her. "Have you any idea how a man can ache inside when he's denied the woman he loves? How many years I've wanted you." He closed his eyes, breathing in the scent of her perfume. "I can hold you now without guilt. You are mine, Mirage."

She could feel his urgency. Taking his hand, she led him down the hallway. She paused for a moment at Katherine's bedroom door and saw that her daughter was sound asleep.

She then turned to find herself lifted into Drew's arms. He lowered his dark head, his lips devouring hers. Always before, she had stopped him; this time she threw her arms around his neck, pressing herself closer to him.

Love, so long suppressed, burst into an inferno of passion.

"I won't stop this time, Mirage," he warned. "There is no one between us now."

For her answer, she pressed her lips to his, expressing all the tenderness she felt for him.

He carried her into her bedroom and placed her on her feet. For a long moment he allowed his eyes to feast on her. Because of her, he had been unable to fall in love with another woman. She had always been there inside him, making him compare all others to her.

He removed his tie and began unbuttoning his shirt as the flame of desire fanned to life. The glow in Mirage's green eyes was an invitation—she was his at last.

Mirage unfastened the hook at her shoulder, and her red silk dress fell in a heap at her feet.

Drew removed his shirt and tossed it aside. "I've wanted you for so long," he said in a choked voice, while he pushed the straps of her slip off her shoulders.

"I know," she said, unbuckling his belt.

Tenderly, he lifted her into his arms and placed her on the bed. She didn't turn away when his eyes ran over her naked body.

He had often imagined what she would look like at the moment of possession. He had not imagined that she would be so perfect. Her skin had the satiny glow of youth; her breasts were firm, her waist small. Her rounded hips tapered off to long, silken legs.

"Mirage," he said, allowing his hand to drift down her neck, across her breasts, and lower, to her stomach. "I want to savor every moment."

His body was hard and lean, a flawless specimen of maleness. She ached for him to hold her, to devour her with his lovemaking. She raised her arms, and he came to her without hesitation. They were locked in each other's embrace, their eyes closed.

She was absorbed by his strength—he was gentled by her softness.

He rained kisses on her face. "You're mine at last." He took possession of her lips in a soul-wrenching kiss.

Drew groaned with pleasure when she slid her silken body along his thighs. Gently he raised her above him and brought her down against him, sliding into her, going deep. He closed his eyes as tremors of pleasure rippled though him.

Mirage threw her head back, experiencing unleashed pleasure. She was aware that she was crying because their coming together was so beautiful. Their love-starved bodies arched in perfect unison.

When she cried out his name, he murmured hers over and over.

Afterward, they lay entwined in each other's arms. His hands ran over her, pressing her tightly against him, as if he were trying to absorb her into his body.

She softly wound a dark lock of hair around her finger. "I believe I fell in love with you that first night on the train, when you were so insulting to me."

He gave her a smile that twisted her heart. "I loved you even before we met. The first time you burst upon the movie screen, you landed right in my heart."

She looked at him in wonder. "How can that be?"

He shook his head and touched his mouth to hers before answering. "I'll be damned if I know. I can't explain it myself. That night on the train, I was afraid to approach you for fear my illusion of you would not fit the real person."

She arched her brow. "And did it?"

His hand moved up her arm and he captured her chin, gazing deeply into her eyes. "You were so much more than I could have imagined. When you left to go to your compartment that night, I sat there, unable to forget the green eyes that had stolen my heart."

"Is that true?"

"I can assure you it is. I had—and still have—your photographs plastered all over my bedroom wall. You can't imagine how it stifled my ability to take another woman into my sanctuary."

"I remember the night of the party at your apartment, you took a woman in there then."

"Only to make you jealous."

She didn't want to, but she couldn't keep from asking, "Did you make love to her that night?"

"No. I couldn't. That was the place I went to be with you, even if it was only the image of you."

A sob escaped her lips as he confessed his vulnerability to her. She touched his face and pressed her cheek against his. "I love you so much, Drew."

His grip tightened on her almost painfully. "When I thought you had died, I wanted to die too. Later, when I met you as Mirage, I felt drawn to you almost immediately and I couldn't understand why. I tried to fight my feelings, but I couldn't. The day I acknowledged to myself how much I loved you, I removed Lacy's ring."

She looked troubled. "I had noticed that you'd taken it off. Why did you do it?"

"It was difficult to let Lacy go—but you see, when I saw you onstage, you burst into my heart with the same intensity that she had the first time I saw her on the screen."

His lips touched hers in a kiss so tender her eyes misted. "Call yourself Lacy or Mirage, or change your name a hundred times; hide if you can, but I'll always find you and love you."

She picked up his hand and was about to kiss the palm when she frowned. "How did you get this scar?"

"It's nothing," he said, pressing her back against the mattress.

"You got burned the night you rescued Katherine, didn't you?"

"It's little more than a scratch."

"It was much more serious than a scratch, Drew. I can't bear to think that you were hurt and didn't tell me."

She pressed her lips against the scar, loving him for the man he was, and knowing he had suffered so much because of her.

"You have loved two other men besides me."

His voice had an accusing tone and she watched him turn away so she wouldn't see the hurt in his eyes. She knew he needed to hear how much she loved him. "Not Mark. I thought I loved him, but I now know I didn't. I was so young then, and he did rescue me from my father."

"Ben—you loved him."

She knew there must be no pretense between them. Their love was too deep and too untested, fragile at the moment, and would be even more so when Drew learned what she was about to do. "Yes. I did love Ben. He was my teacher and my beloved friend. He is the father of my daughter. I loved him deeply, but not the way I love you. You are the love of my heart, of my life. Perhaps I should tell you just how Mark found me and how I was transformed into Lacy Black."

He frowned, nodded, and listened quietly as she explained to him about her life, starting with her childhood in Texas and ending with the night Mark tried to kill her.

There was rage in the swirling depths of Drew's eyes. "Ben told me much of what happened to you, but made me promise to take no action. Now I must do something to stop Damian. He can't be allowed to get away with his crimes."

"Not *you*, Drew, *me*. *I* have to stop him."

There was an edge to his voice. "What do you mean?"

"I have been thinking for some time and I've decided to return to Hollywood."

"No, you're not!" Drew was visibly shaken. "That bastard is deranged. I don't want you anywhere near him."

"I have no choice."

"Think, Lacy—what would Ben advise you to do?"

Her voice was soft and her touch gentle as she reached out to caress his face. "Ben always left it up to me."

"Well, I won't." Drew pulled her against him. "I read an article about Damian's wife in the newspaper this morning."

"So did I. That's why I have to go. I know he's responsible for her death." She sat up, trying to gather her thoughts. "I'm the only one who can stop him."

"I won't let you go." His arms tightened around her like vises. "We'll figure out some other way to get him."

"I know the only way to get him." She moved out of his arms and off the bed. A chill struck her body, so she pulled on her silk wrap. "I read that he was making a movie about the life of Lacy Black."

Drew was immediately suspicious. "What are you thinking?"

"I'm thinking that no one can play Lacy Black as well as I can."

Drew pulled on his pants and went to her, gripping her arm. "I won't allow you to do anything foolish. We have a life together now, Mirage. I want you to be my wife."

"I can't make a life with you, Drew, until I've ended my life with Mark."

Fear for her tore at his mind, and he stared at her angrily. "And just how do you propose to do that? Do you think Ben would have wanted scandal to touch Katherine's life? Think of her, if you won't think of yourself."

Mirage covered her eyes with her hand. "I can't use the law to bring Mark down, Drew. But I have a plan that I believe will work."

"The hell you do. You're not going anywhere near that man."

She touched his arm. "Try to understand."

"I won't let you do it, Mirage."

There was defiance in her eyes. "You can't stop me."

Drew knew that he was going to lose her again. "If you go through with this, then we can have no life together. Ask yourself why you are doing this—is it because you want to stop him, or because you want revenge?"

"I don't know." Her eyes were clear and honest. "Perhaps it's a little of both. I only know that I must confront him."

"What do you expect me to do while you go after him?"

Her eyes were pleading. "In the event that something happens to me, I want you to take care of Katherine."

Drew's eyes were hard, and his words came out in a hiss. "You're insane if you think that you can take on a man like Mark Damian and win. He won't hesitate to hurt you if he even suspects who you are. No, I won't let you go."

"I love you, Drew, but you can't keep me from doing what I know is right."

"Then I'm coming with you."

"You can't do that either. Mark is my problem."

She kissed him on the lips and smiled sadly when he pulled away from her. "I love you."

"But do you love me as much as you hate Mark Damian?"

Chapter Thirty-three

Mark watched the camera zoom in on a close-up of Patricia Marlon. He pushed the cameraman out of the way and looked through the lens.

"She has too much makeup on," he snapped. "And anyone with sense knows that Lacy's hair was longer."

He shoved the camera aside. "Take her to makeup and use that life-size picture of Lacy I hung on the wall. Don't bring her back until she looks like a star."

Resentfully, Mark watched the makeup artist escort poor, frightened Patricia off the set. That woman would never be anything like his Lacy.

A deep, resonant voice spoke up from behind him, and he spun around to see the smirk on Sidney Greenway's face.

"You're playing a losing hand, Damian. That one will never make an audience believe she's Lacy."

"So you finally came?" Mark said grudgingly. "It's been three weeks since I left a message at your office that I wanted to see you. I thought you'd decided to ignore me, like everyone else does these days."

"I did at first," said Sydney, chomping on an unlit cigar. "And then curiosity got the better of me. I couldn't think of anything you and I had to discuss." Sydney had left the studio shortly after Lacy's death and hadn't spoken with Mark since.

"I sent for you because I thought you might want to direct my movie about Lacy's life, since you directed all of her pictures."

"I wouldn't direct that little nobody you call an actress if she was the only woman in Hollywood."

Mark held on to his temper, knowing that he couldn't afford to fight with Sidney—he needed him to make this picture a success. "You once said something similar about Lacy, remember?"

"Yes, but Lacy had a unique beauty that would have assured her success even if she hadn't had talent, which she also possessed in abundance. You never realized that about her, did you?"

Mark's eyes narrowed. "You were in love with her," he accused.

Sidney shrugged. "Wasn't everyone? How she ended up with a no-talent bastard like you, I'll never know. Don't ask me again to work with you, Mark. I happen to know that you don't have the money to pay my salary, and your studio practically belongs to the creditors. I also know that you've gambled everything away, and that you're in a drunken stupor for days at a time. See how your hands shake? Even now you want a drink, and it isn't ten o'clock in the morning."

Mark's eyes dimmed. "I don't have to take your insults, Sidney. Get out!"

"I'm leaving, but a word of advice before I go. Let Lacy rest in peace. There isn't a woman alive who can do her justice."

"I don't believe that's necessarily true." Both men spun around to see a woman move out of the shadows and into the spotlight.

Sidney Greenway knew the woman at once, because he'd seen her in three Broadway plays. He'd wanted to meet her, but no one had been allowed near her without an invitation. She looked elegant in her gray suit with the mink trim on the collar and a mink hat set atop her beautifully arranged dark hair. The diamonds that sparkled on her fingers and wrist were obviously genuine. What was a woman like Mirage Lord doing here?

Mark gaped at the beautiful stranger. She looked familiar, but he was unable to place her.

Mirage felt sick inside as she forced herself to meet Mark's eyes. She almost didn't recognize him, he'd changed so much. He'd put on weight, and his hair had thinned on top and was mostly gray. There were bags under his watery eyes, which suggested that he drank too much and too often.

Sidney smiled and moved toward her with his hand outstretched. "Mirage Lord, I'm delighted to meet you at last. I'm one of your biggest fans."

Mirage took Sidney's hand, trying not to show how pleased she was to see him again. She steeled herself to be cool and aloof. "You have the advantage over me, Mr. . . . ?"

"There's no reason you should know me. I'm Sidney Greenway."

She smiled at him. "Of course, the director. I have long admired your work."

Mark came forward slowly, his eyes drawn to the beautiful Mirage Lord. Of course he'd heard of her; she was the fabulously successful Broadway star who had been married to Benjamin Lord, the multimillionaire. In awe of her, he waited for her to acknowledge him.

When she turned her green gaze on him, Mark felt a chill go down his spine. He had once looked into eyes that were as green as hers.

"I assume you are Mr. Damian?" Her voice was clipped, her manner contemptuously cool.

"I am," he said, extending his hand, which she barely touched before she drew hers back.

"I've come to see you about an important business matter, Mr. Damian."

Mark couldn't help looking triumphantly at Sidney. "Shall we go to my office, where we can talk in private?"

"I'd like Mr. Greenway to come too. It's fortunate that you were here today, Mr. Greenway, because what I have to say includes you as well."

Both men were puzzled as they walked away from the soundstage and down a brightly lit corridor to Mark's office. Mark was playing the perfect gentleman, holding Mirage's chair, offering her a cigarette, which she refused, asking if she would like something to drink.

Sidney sat to her left, watching Mark with amused disdain. The poor fool didn't know how to act around a real lady.

When Mirage stood and walked behind Mark's desk to look at the painting hanging there, both men watched her silently.

She could hardly hide the loathing she felt for Mark. She finally brought her emotions under control and turned back to him. She knew his weakness, and she was about to exploit it.

"This isn't a very good copy of Rembrandt's self-portrait, is it?" she remarked airily. "I saw the original at the National Gallery in Washington, D.C., and this doesn't do it justice."

Mark looked from her to the painting. "You're mistaken, Mrs. Lord. This *is* the original."

She raised a cool eyebrow and moved back to the chair, where she sat down and crossed her long, silky legs. "I can assure you that I'm not mistaken, Mr. Damian. If someone sold this to you as the original, you were cheated. If you have any doubts, I suggest you call the curator at the National Gallery."

Sidney could hardly keep from laughing aloud at the stricken look on Mark's face. He was having the time of his life watching Mark squirm. Mirage Lord had struck Mark down, and he wondered if she was even aware of it. He stared into icy green eyes. Yes, she knew exactly what she was doing.

"I'm sure you are both wondering why I'm here."

"I sure am," Sidney said.

"I assumed that you would tell us when you were ready, Mrs. Lord," Mark said eagerly.

She tapped on the arm of the chair with long, manicured red fingernails. "It's very simple. I read in the paper that you are doing the life of Lacy Black, and I want the part."

Both men reacted with stunned silence. Sidney was sure she'd lost her mind, wanting the lead in a Mark Damian picture, when any producer in Hollywood would clamor to have her in his film.

Mark grew excited as he realized what it would mean for him to have Mirage Lord star in his picture—respectability, the acceptance of his peers instead of their contempt. He thought of the money the movie would gross all over the world.

"The part's yours, baby. I don't even have to think about it."

Her eyes flickered just the merest bit. "Don't be too hasty to accept, Mr. Damian, because I have stipulations that you must adhere to before we can come to an agreement."

"Anything you want, baby. You name it."

"First," she said, her eyes chilling him to the bone, "don't ever call me baby. I'm accustomed to giving respect and getting respect in return."

His face reddened. He reached into a drawer, pulled out a whiskey bottle, and poured a liberal amount into a glass. He took a quick gulp. "I'll try to remember that."

"Don't try—remember, Mr. Damian."

"All right. What else will you require, Mrs. Lord?"

"I understand that you're short of funds."

"I well, er . . . I don't—"

"Tell her the truth," Sidney prodded. He didn't know when he'd enjoyed himself more. "Tell her you're flat broke."

The look Mark sent him was poisonous.

"I thought so," Mirage said. "I'm willing to invest whatever money you need to make the picture."

Mark gasped. "Why would you do that?"

"It's not generosity, Mr. Damian. I'll expect half the revenues from the movie."

He thought for a moment. "I don't know. . . ."

She stood up. "Then we have nothing else to talk about."

"Now, now, wait a minute, Mrs. Lord. I might be willing to give you forty percent."

"Fifty," she demanded.

Sidney reared back in his chair. "Better go for it, Mark. You'll never get a better offer than that. Just her name on the marquee will bring in millions."

"All right, all right," Mark said grudgingly. "Fifty percent." His greedy eyes narrowed; already he was calculating his share of the profit.

"I have other stipulations, Mr. Damian," she continued.

He smiled. "I hope they are as easily met."

"They are quite simple. I will have complete control of the script, and complete say over any rewrites."

"Now, wait a minute. Lacy was my wife, and I knew her better than anyone did."

She stared at him coldly. "No one controls my performance on the screen but me."

"I agree," he said reluctantly. "Is there anything else?"

"Yes." She swung around to Sidney. "I want Mr. Greenway to direct the picture, at ten percent above his normal salary."

Sidney beamed. "I wouldn't miss this for the world. I'd have paid you to work on this picture, Mrs. Lord."

Mark took another drink to fortify himself and shook his head. "I don't want you on the picture, Sidney. Not after the insults you hurled at me today."

"I'll work with no one but Mr. Greenway, because I understand he always directed Lacy Black. That's my last stipulation."

Mark gritted his teeth. He had no choice but to agree. "I'll have the contract drawn up at once. We could go out to lunch, Mrs. Lord, and by the time we return, it will be ready for you to sign."

"That won't be necessary, Mr. Damian. I took the liberty of having my own attorney draw up the contract." She handed one to Mark and one to Sidney. "I believe you'll find everything is in order."

"I'm sure you won't mind if I have my lawyer look over the contract," Mark said, biting back his anger.

"Please have your attorney go over every word. I think you'll find it's just as we discussed."

Sidney pulled out his pen and signed his name in bold script. "It's good enough for me."

Mirage stood up. "I'll be in touch, Mr. Damian."

"But I don't have your address or telephone number."

"I'll call you," she said icily.

Both men watched as she left.

"This is the strangest day of my life," Sidney said, moving to the window and watching the elegant Mirage Lord climb into a black limousine. "God only knows why she'd want to work with you, Mark."

Mark was watching Mirage over Sidney's shoulder. "She's probably seen my pictures and admired them."

Sidney looked at him in disbelief. "Sure. And if you believe that, you'll believe that painting of yours is real."

Chapter Thirty-four

Mirage's California attorney had leased a large house for her on Bel Air Road. When she arrived, the servants and security guards had already been hired, and a monitered electrical gate had been installed at the base of the driveway.

She dashed up the steps and into the house, calling her daughter's name. "Katherine, Mommy's home."

Chubby little legs hurried toward her, and she scooped the child into her arms. "Oh, sweetness, I missed you." She glanced up at Kitty. "Has she been a good girl today?"

"She's been an angel," Kitty replied.

"Then I have a surprise for you." She reached in her handbag and pulled out a doll. "Look, she has curly hair, just like you, Katherine."

The child squealed with delight and planted kisses on her mother's face.

Mirage stood, handing her daughter back to Kitty. "Take her to the housekeeper and ask her to give her some cookies and milk. Then find Warren; I'd like both of you to come to the living room. I want to talk to you in private."

While Mirage waited for Kitty and Warren, she walked to the window, pulled the white curtains aside, and stared at the iron fence, where a uniformed guard paced back and forth. At first she had planned to leave Katherine in New York because she was playing a dangerous game with a dangerous man. But the day before she was to fly to California, she realized that she couldn't leave her daughter behind.

When she heard a knock, Mirage called for Warren and Kitty to enter. She invited them to sit down, and poured Kitty a cup of her favorite English tea, adding cream before handing it to her. Warren was partial to beer, and she offered him a bottle. These two had become almost like family to her, and she trusted them completely.

"I know that you both have many questions that I can't answer for you now. Perhaps I'll never be able to tell you why I'm here."

Kitty took a sip of her tea. "You don't have to tell us anything. If you came here, it's for a good reason. We'll do whatever you want us to do and ask no questions."

Warren nodded. "I'll not let anything hurt you or Miss Katherine," the giant man said with conviction.

"I appreciate that. I feel safe with you as our protector, Warren. But I want to caution you both not to allow strangers into this house under any circumstances. Warren, I'm putting you in charge of security. You will give the guards their orders every day. Kitty, I want you to oversee the servants."

Warren rubbed his giant hand on his trouser leg. "If you got troubles, Mrs. Lord, all you have to do is tell me, and I'll take care of whoever's bothering you."

She smiled at him, knowing he was sincere. "This trouble I have to take care of myself."

He stood up. "If there's nothing else, I'll just go on out and make sure the guards don't fall asleep on the job."

Mirage stood up and took his hand. "I want you both to know that you will have a position with me as long as you want it. I don't know what I'd do without either of you."

Warren looked at her with adoring eyes. "I'll never leave you. I promised Mr. Lord before he died that I'd keep you safe, and I mean to do it."

"Thank you, Warren."

When he ambled out, Kitty poured another cup of tea and handed it to Mirage, who sat down beside her.

"Mr. Mallory called three times today. He's worried about you."

Mirage was still hurt by Drew's behavior. After the night she'd told him that she must deal with Mark, he hadn't called or come to see her. Then the day she was to leave, he'd come by the apartment unexpectedly. But he was cold and distant. He'd asked if she had changed her mind about leaving. When she assured him that she hadn't, he'd turned and left abruptly without another word. Right now she wished she could feel his comforting arms about her. Facing Mark today had been an ordeal.

"What else did Drew say?"

"He asked that you call him."

Mirage stood up wearily. "Not tonight. I'm going to take a hot bath and go to bed."

Kitty stacked the china cups on a tray. "I'll bring Katherine to you before she goes to sleep."

Mirage was caught in the thrall of a dark and frightening nightmare. She could see Mark's face, not as it was today, swollen and blotched, but as she'd first known him when he was boyish and good-looking. She was running from him, running, running, but it was as if her feet wouldn't move. Up ahead she saw Ben, and she cried out to him to help her. Ben took her hand and looked at her with sadness as he disappeared. Then Drew appeared between her and Mark and he was armed with a sword. She cried out when Mark struck at Drew, and he fell down dead at her feet.

She was screaming, tossing, turning, trying to pull herself out of the nightmare, until at last she sat up in bed. Her body was trembling, and she was wet with perspiration. Feeling desperately alone, she reached for the phone. It seemed like hours before she heard Drew's sleepy voice.

"Mirage, what's wrong? Are you all right? You sound strange."

"I'm fine, Drew. I just needed to hear your voice."

He was silent for a moment. "I'm going to fly out there tomorrow. Something is wrong, and you just aren't telling me."

"No, don't come, Drew. And nothing's wrong."

"Mirage?"

"Yes?"

"I love you."

"Oh, Drew, I love you, too. I don't want to be away from you. I miss you desperately."

"Then I'll be out tomorrow."

"Please don't. Try to understand that I need to do this alone."

Again the silence. "I want to marry you, Mirage."

"When this is over, if you still want me, I'll marry you."

She could hear his sharp intake of breath. "Now that I've made love to you, I ache for more of you. Come home to me soon, Mirage."

"I will."

She heard the click on the other end. Once again she was alone with her fears.

Mirage walked down the familiar hallway to Mark's office. She braced herself for another face-to-face meeting with him. His attractive blond secretary, who had apparently replaced Helen, smiled brightly at her.

"Good morning, Mrs. Lord. I was told to show you right in when you arrived."

Mirage smiled tightly. "Is Mr. Greenway here?"

"Not yet. Mr. Damian wanted to speak to you alone first."

Steeling herself to see him again, she entered the office. Mark got quickly to his feet, crossed the carpet, and took her hand. She jerked it away and put some distance between them.

"You look beautiful, Mirage. I bet you wake up looking that way."

He was attempting to flirt with her, but what had been charming in a younger, more handsome Mark now seemed merely pathetic.

She sat down on the couch, but quickly stood when she recognized it as the couch where Mark had often made love to her. Filled with revulsion, she moved to the window.

It was apparent that most of the soundstages were closed, and there were very few people on the lot. Mark must be having serious financial troubles.

He came up behind her, so close that she could smell the whiskey on his breath. She forced herself not to move away.

"I suppose that many men have told you how beautiful you are."

She looked at him coldly. "More than you can count."

He stepped back a pace. This woman was too sure of herself, and he liked women he could control. But she excited him, for he believed that somewhere under that icy exterior was a hot-blooded female. She had married an old man—probably for his money—and he fantasized about showing her what a real man could do.

Mirage was watching him, and could almost guess what he was thinking.

"I'd like to see the script so I can read over it and make any changes I feel it needs," she said, getting down to business.

"Perhaps we could go to my house. We could take a swim and discuss the script in private."

She moved to a chair and sat down. "That's not the way I work, and I don't intend to change my habits now."

Mark settled on the edge of his desk, swinging his leg so that it was almost touching her. "You just aren't used to the way we do things in Hollywood. You'll find it different from the stage."

"How would you know?" she asked coolly.

"Well . . . onstage you do the same performance over and over, while we like to catch the scene with as few retakes as possible. It makes the story seem more . . . spontaneous."

"It's fortunate that I have the ability to read a script once and then recite it verbatim."

He looked at her oddly. "Lacy could do that, too."

"I'll take the script now, if you don't mind."

He walked around his desk, picked up a folder, and handed it to her. "I hope you like it. I wrote most of it myself."

"I'll let you know what I think of it after I read it."

She opened her handbag and held a check out to him. "I'd like a receipt, please. My accountant gets very upset when I don't keep receipts for him."

He stared at the fifty-thousand-dollar check. "I'll have my secretary make one out for you right now."

Mirage unfolded her long legs and rose, moving to the door. "Tomorrow will be soon enough."

"You aren't leaving, are you?"

She looked at him, her face frozen with icy contempt. "Do you have anything further to discuss?"

"No . . . nothing."

"When do you expect to start shooting?"

"Since everything's set up, I thought next week." He quickly thumbed through his calendar. "That would make it the twenty-eighth."

"I'll see you then."

He watched her leave, feeling slightly uneasy. There was something about Mirage Lord that troubled him.

Mirage's slippers were noiseless as she paced restlessly back and forth across the thick carpet, reading the pages of half-truths and lies that Mark had woven. He'd painted his life with her as a fairy tale, when in reality it had been a nightmare.

She drew a line through several pages and turned to the secretary she had hired. "I'll have some changes for you to type in a moment. We'll be working late tonight. Then I'll want them delivered to Mr. Greenway first thing in the morning."

Mirage picked up another page and felt as if she were going

to be sick. It was a scene in which Mark discovered her in Virginia, the daughter of a poor but proud country doctor. It was right out of the old publicity he'd invented for her, but with a twist. In Mark's new version, she'd fallen in love with him after he'd saved her from a runaway horse.

Her pencil danced across the pages, and her version began: *Step on a crack, break your mother's back!*

Mirage sat under the hot lights, directing the makeup man. A feeling of déjà vu took possession of her. The platinum wig was placed on her head, and she watched the makeup man's eyes widen in wonder.

"You look a lot like Lacy Black. I was here when she was, but I was just an assistant then and never got to apply her makeup."

She stood up, turning before the full-length mirror. The dress she wore was very like the one she had been wearing the first day she met Mark. It was the only realism that Mark had achieved.

She turned to her secretary. "Did you give the changes to Mr. Greenway?"

"Yes, I did as you instructed."

Mirage took in a deep breath to prepare herself for the inevitable. Surely she and Mark would have a showdown today.

When she walked onto the set, Sidney greeted her with a smile as he stared at her. "You startled me, Mrs. Lord. For a moment, I thought Lacy had returned to us. Your resemblance to her is remarkable."

"I've been told that on a number of occasions," she said, trying to act casual. She had known that people would begin to see the resemblance, and she was ready for it. If she had to, she would admit who she was, but she hoped it wouldn't be necessary.

"My secretary said that she gave you my changes."

He looked at her quizzically, but decided not to ask any questions. "I got them. It won't be too difficult to begin in Texas rather than Virginia. What I want you to do now," Sidney told her, "is practice a Texas accent so you'll be believable."

"I'll try my best," she said, easily slipping back into her old pronunciation. She turned to the first page of dialogue and began to read for him. " 'Step on a crack, break your mother's back.' "

"Excellent, excellent." Sidney nodded. "You must have seen her pictures, because you've captured her manner of speech exactly." He flipped through several pages. "I've had the number three soundstage set up for the apartment over the garage. We'll begin shooting that scene first."

Mirage's eyes ran over the people who had gathered. "Where is Mr. Damian?" she wanted to know.

Sidney moved close to her and said in a quiet voice so only she could hear, "I imagine he's on one of his drunks. We may not see him for a week or longer if we're lucky."

Mirage felt crushing disappointment. She had hoped that Mark would be there to watch the opening shots so he would see the changes she'd made; then she wouldn't have to go on with this farce. Perhaps Sidney was wrong and Mark would arrive later.

"Are you ready?" Sidney asked.

"Yes," she answered. "Let's get started."

Sidney looked through the camera, adjusting the lens. He zoomed in on Mirage and stared at her. She was talking to the man who was to play her father, and Sidney caught her side profile. He'd seen that profile before. He raised his head and looked at her, taking in every detail, and then went back to the camera. Cameras never lied; they saw what the human eye could not, and he had looked at that woman through the camera too many times not to recognize her now.

He was so shaken, it took him a moment before he could speak. "Would you mind doing the scene again?" he called.

Mirage nodded, taking her mark. As she moved through the scenes, Sidney knew without a doubt that Mirage Lord *was* Lacy Black. He was equally sure that Mark hadn't figured it out yet. What had happened to Lacy if she hadn't died in that plane crash? he wondered. What twist of fate had changed her from the meek, lovely little girl who did everything Mark told her, to the cold, beautiful Mirage Lord who was confident and very much her own woman?

He gathered his thoughts. There was a great mystery here. He would keep Lacy's secret and watch the drama unfold around him. She was after Mark—but why? She had to know that she was playing a dangerous game against a man whose mind was unstable.

"Let's begin again, Mrs. Lord. Everyone, take your places," Sidney said, signaling to his assistant, who called for quiet on the set.

"Ready, camera, action," he called, and the filming of *The Legend of Lacy Black* began.

Chapter Thirty-five

Mark woke with neon lights flashing in his face. His throat was dry, and he felt sick. The room was unfamiliar to him, and he tried to remember where he was. Sitting up, he buried his face in his hands. He remembered driving to Las Vegas, but he didn't remember anything that had happened since.

Feeling someone move beside him, he turned quickly to find a woman in bed with him. He stared at her, the heavy makeup, the bleached, strawlike hair, the flabby body. He must have been drunk to go to bed with her, he thought.

She opened her eyes, blinked, and smiled. "You look like hell, Mark." She slipped out of bed and plodded naked to the open whiskey bottle. "Here, honey. Take this—you'll feel better."

Mark downed the drink, and then looked at his surroundings. Rooms in cheap hotels all looked alike. "Who are you?" he asked at last.

"I'm Thelma, honey. Don't you remember?"

"No." He groaned, thinking that there was something important he had to do. "How did I get here?"

"You were in the casino, and let me tell you, honey, you

gamble big-time. I like a man who knows how to spend money." She sat beside him, reaching for his glass and taking a drink before handing it back to him.

He vaguely remembered playing blackjack. He also remembered losing. He pushed the woman aside and stumbled to his pants, which hung over the chair. Removing his wallet, he quickly counted the money. He had cashed the fifty-thousand-dollar check Mirage Lord had given him, and there was only five thousand was left.

He dropped down on the chair, his red-rimmed eyes staring blankly into space. He'd gambled it all away. He had to get it back—he just had to.

"What did you say your name was?" he asked.

"Thelma—Thelma Banks."

"Well, Thelma," he said, shoving a hundred-dollar bill at her. "Go out and get coffee. Lots of coffee."

She quickly dressed. "Are you really a Hollywood producer?"

"Yes."

"I never heard of you."

"Have you ever heard of Lacy Black?"

"Of course. Everyone knows about her."

"I was her husband."

Thelma nodded, not really believing him, but thinking she'd humor him anyway. "You said last night you'd put me in your next picture. Men have told me that before."

He looked at her with disgust. She might have been pretty when she was young. Now she looked like a hundred other overage and overweight whores. "Get me the coffee," he said in a growl.

"Are you going back to Los Angeles?" she asked.

"What day is this?"

"The third, I think."

He groaned. Shooting was to have started on the picture last week. He'd lost seven days out of his life. He felt himself drowning in desperation. "I've got to win the money back."

She shrugged. "You haven't been that lucky, honey. Maybe

you'd better take what money you have left and head home."

"Get out," he ordered. "Get out of my sight, and don't come back."

She opened the door. "Have it your way. But who's going to pick you up off the floor tonight when you fall down dead drunk?"

Mark threw his empty glass at her, but she ducked and hurried out the door, smiling to herself. She still had the hundred dollars he'd given her to buy coffee.

He dressed in his rumpled shirt and pants, then fumbled for the whiskey bottle. Lifting it to his lips, he drained it in one swallow. Staggering out the door, he headed for the casino. He had to win that money back before he could face Mirage Lord.

The movie was moving forward rapidly. Sidney hadn't felt this excited about a film in years. Mirage worked on the script at night, doing revisions that in no way resembled Mark's version, and turning them over to Sydney in the morning. Ordinarily, he wouldn't work under conditions in which the star had complete control of the script. But there were dark secrets being revealed with each new page, and he looked forward to reading the rewrites.

Mirage felt drained at the end of each day. Reliving her past was so painful that she would often go to her bedroom and cry before she could face Katherine. She waited for Mark to return, dreading the time when she must face him, but knowing that their final confrontation was close at hand. Each scene completed was evidence stacked against him, as the truth of their relationship was revealed on film.

The house was quiet, and Mirage heard only a barking dog in the distance. Glancing out the window, she saw the guard on duty at the gate. Tomorrow she would have to act out the bedroom scene in which Mark taunted her with the details of her own impending death. As she read over the words she had written, she clutched the pages of the script in her hand. Could she do that scene without breaking down? Yes, she had to, because it was the most important scene of all.

She walked to the bedside table and unlocked the drawer, lifting the revolver in her hand. Yes, it was loaded. She put it back in the drawer and relocked it.

When Mirage arrived on the set the next morning, there was a message that Sidney wanted to see her in the screening room. She went directly to him before going to makeup. She found him studying the rushes from the day before.

"You're talented," he said, motioning for her to sit beside him.

She had avoided looking at the rushes. Just acting out the scenes was painful enough; she didn't want to have to watch herself.

She sat beside him, not looking at the screen. "Acting is my profession."

"I know . . . Lacy."

She kept her eyes downcast. "Don't mistake me for the character I play."

"I know what I see through the camera lens, Lacy. I was your director and your friend for years, you know."

In the dimly lit room, she met his eyes, and he saw the first weakness in Mirage Lord—tears swimming in her green eyes.

"I was afraid that if anyone discovered me, it would be you, Sidney, but you were the only one I could trust to direct this picture."

"My God, Lacy. We all thought you were dead."

The projector had come to the end of the reel, and he switched on the lights. "What's going on here?"

"I *was* dead for a long time, Sidney. At least, I felt dead."

"Why did you come back? Don't you realize that Mark's a lunatic? When he sees this film, who knows what he'll do?"

"That's what I'm counting on, Sidney. I'm not the only one he's hurt. Don't you see, he has to be stopped!"

"I just read the last scene, Lacy. The bastard tried to kill you once; he'll try it again. We can't let him see this film."

"I know what I'm doing, Sidney."

"Do you? I hope you know I'll do everything I can to protect you."

"Thank you, Sidney. I'm sorry I had to use you in this way, but I couldn't tell you who I was."

"I know what really happened to you from reading the script. What I don't yet know is who died in the plane that night."

"The pilot, who had a wife and children, and my sister, Ruth."

"I see." He looked at her searchingly. "What do you plan to do with the film after it's completed?"

"I don't know. I didn't think it would get this far," she admitted.

"You said Mark had hurt others. Do you mean murder?"

Her green eyes were so sad. "Yes—murder. That's why I came back, and that's why he has to be stopped."

Sydney took her arm and guided her out the door. "Come on; we have a movie to shoot. I'll try to make it as painless as I can for you."

Mark was in a sour mood. It was the first time he'd been sober in over four weeks. His life was shot to hell. How was he going to explain to Mirage Lord where he'd been? More important, how would he tell her that he'd lost all the money she'd advanced him?

To make matters worse, when he got home last night, Patricia had cried and clung to him, demanding to know where he'd been and why he hadn't called. She wouldn't believe him when he told her that he hadn't even called his studio.

Women had always complicated his life. First Dolores, then Lacy and Rosalinda. But he'd taken care of them all. He might have to take care of Patricia, too. She was threatening to make trouble just because she had had a contract to star in Lacy's story and he'd replaced her with Mirage Lord.

He pulled through the gates of Pinnacle Pictures and waved at the guard. He knew what he would tell Mirage Lord and Sidney. He would tell them that he'd had to get away because writing Lacy's story had dragged up the past and it had been too painful for him to deal with. He'd had to go away to put himself back together. Yes, they would believe that. Well, Sidney wouldn't, but Mrs. Lord probably would.

He reached into the glove compartment and pulled out a bottle, taking a long swig. He was ready to face them now.

Mark looked at his secretary, his face twisted with rage. "What in the hell do you mean, they've almost finished shooting? And who told them they could have a closed set? I was going to launch a big publicity campaign and invite reporters."

"I tried to reach you, Mark," his secretary said placatingly, "but no one knew where you were. I had people calling me every day, demanding to know your whereabouts."

He wrenched open the door. "Mirage Lord has overstepped her authority. I'll kick that bitch off this lot!"

Mirage was doing the scene she had most dreaded. Dressed in a filmy nightgown, she was seated on a white sofa, next to the actor who played Mark. She hadn't had to memorize this scene; it was stamped in her mind forever.

Mark stood in the shadows, watching the actors portray his life with Lacy. He felt his knees buckle beneath him, and he grabbed hold of a prop to keep himself from falling. What were they saying? This wasn't his script. He stared at Mirage Lord and grabbed at his chest. She looked enough like Lacy to be her twin sister. He listened to the words the characters spoke, and fear splintered his mind.

The actor who was playing him was holding Mirage.

"Lacy, you'll be great in this movie. You always wanted a part with substance."

"That's wonderful, Mark. Tell me more."

"Our hero—"

"Villain."

"Our . . . villain takes out a large insurance policy on his wife and arranges for her to board a plane that will crash."

Mark was shaken. "Cut, cut! What in the hell's going on here?"

Everyone turned except Mirage, who was frozen. The time had come at last to confront Mark. Had he guessed who she was?

Sidney lit a cigar and looked at Mark though a screen of smoke. "We're making a movie here, Mark. Since you didn't see fit to be in on the beginning, don't come in at the end and disrupt us."

"Everyone leave," Mark yelled. "Go on, get the hell out."

Actors and crew alike scampered for the exit, and Sidney called out to them, "Be sure to report by seven in the morning. We want to do the scene at the airport."

Mirage stood up slowly, giving the performance of her life; she appeared calm, when she was actually quivering with fear.

"Where have you been, Mr. Damian?" she asked coldly. "Surely you knew my time in California is limited. We had to go ahead with the shooting."

"You had no right to begin my picture without me," he said in a snarl.

"Read the contract. It says the picture is to be finished by April first. That's less than a month away."

Before Mark could say anything, Sidney placed a protective hand on Mirage's arm. "Mrs. Lord and I will just be going along now." He grinned, watching Mark's shocked expression as he examined Mirage's face. The fool didn't suspect yet, but he would. Sidney wasn't about to leave Mirage alone with this maniac. "Hell of a good film, Mark. Glad you decided to tell the true life story of Lacy Black, no matter how bad it makes you look."

Mark watched them leave, wanting to call them back. There were things going on here that he didn't understand. He hadn't thought Mirage Lord favored Lacy, but in makeup and with the light-colored wig, she was a dead ringer for the star.

Mirage leaned against Sidney for support. She was still trembling. "Did I make a mistake?"

"My advice to you is to get on the first flight out of here and don't look back. I believe Mark's about to crack."

"I can't do that, Sidney."

He walked her to her car. "Isn't there some man in your life who can stop you from destroying yourself? Don't you know Mark's not worth it?"

He opened the car door for her, and she slid behind the wheel. "There is a man, but I'm afraid my insistence on coming here drove him away." She looked up at him. "Do you know Drew Mallory?"

"I know his work. Is he the one?"

She leaned her head against the steering wheel. "I'm afraid he's grown tired of waiting for me. I haven't heard from him in weeks."

"Go on home, Mirage. Lock your door and don't answer the phone. I'll try to keep an eye on Mark."

Drew picked up the phone and answered in an irritated voice, "Yes?"

"Andrew Mallory?"

"Yes."

"You don't know me. My name's Sidney Greenway."

"I know your work and your reputation. Not bad—in fact, damn good."

"I'd say the same about you, except this isn't a social call. If you care anything at all about Mirage Lord, you'd better get out here as soon as possible."

Drew clutched the phone and felt his heart quicken with fear. "Thank you, Mr. Greenway. I'll be there on the next flight."

Chapter Thirty-six

Mirage rushed through the nursery, gathering up Katherine's belongings and shoving them into a trunk. "Kitty, we must hurry if you're to catch the seven-thirty train."

"I don't like leaving you," Kitty said. Something dreadful must have happened to cause Mrs. Lord to react with such urgency. She'd come home from the studio a short time ago insisting that Kitty take Katherine back to New York on the next train.

Mirage pushed Katherine's favorite stuffed animal into a shoulder bag, knowing that her daughter would need the toy to sleep with. "When you get home, Kitty, go directly to the apartment and wait until you hear from me."

Kitty snapped the trunk shut and turned to Mirage with a troubled expression. "I'd feel a lot better if you were coming with us, Mrs. Lord."

Mirage glanced at her wristwatch. "I can't. But don't worry about me. Warren will take you to the station, help you get settled in the compartment, and wait with you until your train leaves. Then he'll come back here."

Mirage took Katherine in her arms and held her tightly. She

kissed her daughter on the cheek, loving her so much. She hated to send her away—but she had to because she wanted her out of danger. "Take good care of her, Kitty."

"You know I will. But I wish you'd—"

"No buts, Kitty. And don't worry; no one can get to me in this fortress."

Mirage carried Katherine to the car and handed her in to Kitty, who had reluctantly slid onto the backseat. She kissed her daughter one last time and stepped back to watch the car pull out of the gate before she went back into the house.

Mirage went into the nursery and picked up one of Katherine's blankets, which smelled like baby powder, reminding her of her daughter. Gently she folded it and placed it in a drawer. She had no time to think of anything but Mark; she had to have a clear mind so she could finish what she'd started.

Was that a noise she heard?

Moving into the hallway, she crept slowly toward the living room. Turning off the lamp, she moved to the window and looked toward the gate, where she could see the guard on duty there. No one could get in without his knowing it. A flash of lightning cut across the sky, like a sword of impending doom. How ironic that there had been a storm like this one the night the plane crashed.

An ominous silence settled over the house as she moved from room to room, making certain that the windows and doors were locked. When she entered her bedroom, she went to the night-stand and unlocked it, taking out the revolver. The gun was cold to the touch, and Mirage shivered as she spun the chamber to make certain that it was loaded. Before she changed her mind, she slipped the weapon into her purse so she could carry it around with her. Her stomach tightened into knots and she tried not to think about how frightened she was.

She had no doubt that Mark would come after her tonight, and she had to be ready for him. Tonight she might play the final scene of the life of Lacy Black. It was yet unwritten, and she didn't know how it would end.

* * *

Mark slid the reel into the projector and sat down in the darkened screening room with a half-empty bottle of whiskey beside him. He'd just see for himself what Sidney and that fancy New York actress had done to his movie. The scene he'd walked in on that afternoon had chilled his blood. No one could have known about that night he'd mocked Lacy with her imminent death—that is, no one still living.

His eyes were riveted on the screen, and when the first scene opened, he leaned back, watching a young version of Lacy walk down a dusty street. With makeup and lighting, Sidney had made Mirage Lord look seventeen, and it was uncanny how much she resembled Lacy at that age. Other than that, there was nothing unusual about the scene.

Suddenly Mark sat forward and his eyes narrowed. Snyder, Texas? Sidney must be responsible for that. Back when he'd been directing Lacy's pictures, she'd probably told him that she was from Texas. That was all right; no harm done.

He poured a glass of whiskey and tossed it down his throat, then poured another. It was unsettling how Mirage Lord had taken on Lacy's mannerisms. Of course, since he'd known Lacy so well, he could discern subtle differences that wouldn't have been apparent to anyone else. Mirage Lord had a sophistication that Lacy had lacked, but the camera was as kind to her as it had been to Lacy. This might just be the best film he'd done in years.

He sat there a long time, staring at the screen, mesmerized by what he saw. Memories of Lacy wound their way though his mind. His beautiful Lacy. He'd never been able to forget her. He'd loved her in his own way, and he'd spent years trying to re-create her without success.

Why had she left him? He buried his head in his hands and groaned. She hadn't left him; he'd sent her to hell! "Lacy," he cried out. "You are dead. Why don't you stay dead?"

The movie caught his interest again, although his vision was a bit blurred. The film hadn't been shot in sequence, but that wasn't unusual. The editor would put the scenes in order.

He watched a scene in which Lacy entered the house. What was happening here? She called his name; no one answered. He watched her enter a bedroom and then draw back, sobbing as the camera panned into the room.

He shot out of his chair when he saw the actor who played him in bed with another woman. Was that supposed to be Ruth? Suddenly the camera zoomed in on a replica of the Raja Star!

Lacy jerked it off her sister's neck and Mark's hand went out toward the screen as if he could stop her. He knew what would happen when Lacy walked into the bathroom dangling the priceless necklace in her hand.

Mark became so engrossed in the film that he lost touch with reality. It was as if he'd been jerked back to the past.

"No, not that. Don't do it! Don't flush the Raja Star, Lacy!" he shouted. He gripped the back of the seat, reminding himself that this was only a movie. He closed his red-rimmed eyes, trying to think clearly. There was only one other person who could know everything that had been revealed in these scenes.

Mark's vision cleared as he stared at the beautiful image that seemed to be mocking him, and he cried out in a strangled voice, "My God, Mirage Lord *is* Lacy!"

His eyes grew cold, his face twisted with rage. "You didn't die that night in the plane, did you, Lacy? You're still alive."

He threw his glass at the screen and watched whiskey run down Lacy's image, making it appear that she was crying.

Mirage moved restlessly around the dark room, turning on the radio and moving the dial, but there was nothing she wanted to listen to, so she turned it off. When the room was quiet, she heard a noise coming from the kitchen. Walking slowly in that direction, her heart in her throat, she pushed the kitchen door open a crack and screamed when a shadow moved across the floor. The door was jerked open, and she was flooded with relief. Warren was standing there with a bottle of milk in his hand.

"I'm sorry, Mrs. Lord. Didn't mean to scare you. I just came in to have some cold chicken and a glass of milk."

She took in a deep gulp of air. "Don't mind me. I'm just nervous tonight, Warren."

"I guess it's because of the storm, Mrs. Lord. You don't need to worry about anything with me here."

She smiled at him. "I know that. Did the train leave on time?"

"Yes, ma'am, it did. Would you like me to sleep in the living room tonight?" he offered. "I'd be comfortable enough on the couch."

Mirage considered his offer. It would be a comfort to have him nearby tonight, but surely the guard at the gate would offer enough protection. "That won't be necessary. Good night, Warren."

"Night, Mrs. Lord."

When she left, Warren sat down at the table, raised a chicken leg to his mouth, and then placed it back on the plate. Something was bothering Mrs. Lord that she hadn't told him about. He'd never seen her this scared before; not even in the Bar Harbor fire. He'd just take a turn around the house before he went to bed to make sure there was no one lurking about.

Mirage settled on the sofa to wait in the darkened living room, listening to the brass wall clock ticking away the seconds. It was after midnight, and her eyes drifted shut while her head fell back against the couch pillow. Suddenly she jerked her head up. Had she heard breaking glass, or had she only dreamed it?

She removed the gun from her purse and walked to the window to look out. It was raining so hard that she could barely see the gate. She didn't see the guard, but that didn't mean anything; she would expect him to take shelter from the rain. She placed the gun on the sofa and sat down.

The house was almost too quiet. Perhaps a glass of wine would help calm her nerves. She got up and flipped the hall light switch, sighing impatiently when it didn't come on. The storm must have knocked out the power. She felt along the wall to find her way.

When she entered the kitchen, she tripped across something on the floor, landing with a thud against the table leg. It look her a moment to catch her breath and shake off the pain.

Feeling along the floor, she tried to find out what had tripped her. When her hand touched warm flesh, she jerked it back. She'd felt a human body, and there was something warm and sticky on her hand.

Blood!

"Warren," she cried, shaking his limp arm. "Warren, what happened?"

A voice came out of the dark void, a voice that chilled her heart. "He can't hear you, Lacy. He put up a valiant fight, though."

"Mark!"

"That's right, Lacy. You knew I'd come for you, didn't you? Even your guard at the gate and your watchdog here in the kitchen couldn't keep me away."

She stood up, wondering if she could make it into the living room, where she'd foolishly left the gun.

"Don't move, Lacy," he said, as if reading her mind. "You can't escape me this time."

She backed against the wall, staring into the blackness and calling on all her courage. "I have to stop you, Mark. You've hurt too many people."

She cried out when she felt his hand close painfully around her arm. Even while she struggled to get away from him, she realized that he was too strong for her.

"Give it up, Lacy. It will go much easier on you if you just accept your death this time."

To her surprise, he led her out of the kitchen and down the long hallway, toward the living room, where he pushed her into a chair, his hand lying heavily on her shoulder.

"Haven't you killed enough people, Mark? Is there no remorse in you at all?"

His hand lifted from her shoulder and he paused before answering her. "I have only killed because others forced me to."

"That's not true," she told him. "We are all responsible for our own actions."

He laughed. "This will be another perfect crime. No one will suspect me of killing Mirage Lord. No." His voice was caressing, as it had been on that night so long ago when he'd told her of her impending death. "They'll think the man in the kitchen killed you before he took his own life—what did you call him, Warren? What a pity that you can't get trustworthy help these days."

"You're sick, Mark."

She felt something cold against her cheek—it was a knife blade.

"Sick? Maybe I am."

"You killed my sister," she said in an accusing voice.

"So that's why Ruth disappeared."

Mark's laughter chilled her.

"Then your sister finally got her dream. She always did want to be Lacy Black." His tone of voice turned harsh. "Then *you* are the one who took my Cord."

Mirage felt suddenly calm and somehow unafraid. "I took it and I sent it over a cliff with the greatest of pleasure."

His voice took on a little-boy plaintiveness. "You knew I loved that car." His hand moved down her hair and across her shoulder. "You're even more beautiful now, if that's possible, Lacy. I've had my fantasies about you ever since you came to my office as Mirage Lord, acting as if you were too good for me."

Sickened inside, she shoved his hand away in disgust. "I can't stand it when you touch me."

"That wasn't always true, and I don't think it is now. Nothing will ever change the fact that you belong to me, and I can do whatever I want to you."

"I was never your wife, Mark. You were still married to Dolores when you married me."

There was another long silence, as if he were pondering his words. "How did you find out?"

Mirage suddenly saw a way that she might be able to free herself. Mark was a coward, and he would hesitate to kill her if he thought someone would find out about it. "I have a file that the FBI compiled on you. There is strong evidence that you killed not only Dolores Devine and Rosalinda Mitchell, but your business partner as well."

Mark's hand bit into her shoulder and he placed the knife at her throat. "And what about you, Lacy? Do they suspect that I killed you?"

"They think I'm dead."

"Then you can't die twice, can you?" he asked meaningfully.

She decided that it would be to her advantage to keep him talking as long as possible. "When I first realized that you had tried to kill me, Mark, I was devastated. I thought you loved me."

"I did love you. I've never found anyone who could replace you."

"Then why?"

"It wasn't about the money, not really." His voice broke with a sound of regret. "I was losing you."

"You betrayed me with my own sister."

"Ruth was a tramp. She'd go to bed with anyone."

Lacy was surprised at the pain she still felt after all these years. "Yes, Ruth proved that when she went to bed with you."

Mark grabbed a handful of her hair and yanked her head back. "Cruelty from those sweet lips, Lacy. There was a time you would have done anything for me. Why did you have to change?"

"It wasn't that I changed, Mark. I merely became aware of the flaws in your character—and they were many."

"My worst flaw was carelessness—I should have made sure that you were dead. This time I'll watch the lifeblood drain from your beautiful body. Maybe then I won't be haunted by you anymore." He traced the outline of her face with the tip of his knife. "In my heart, I never loved anyone but you. Why did you stop loving me, Lacy?"

In that moment, the electricity came back on and the hall lamp flickered, spilling light into the living room and illuminating Mark's face. Mirage was surprised to see the tenderness in his eyes. She had to take advantage of his softer mood. "Do you really think you can kill me, Mark? You've never had to face one of your victims when you killed them. No, you always took the coward's way."

His features suddenly hardened and he jerked her to her feet. "I'll show you who's the coward. Die, Lacy, and stay dead this time!"

Mirage gasped when Mark plunged the knife into her chest. She was puzzled as she slumped to the floor. There was no pain, only a heavy weakness that washed over her like the waves breaking over the granite rocks at Bar Harbor.

She reached forward, knocking the lamp off the end table. "Why, Mark? Why did you do it?"

To her surprise, he dropped to his knees, pulled out the knife, and gathered her into his arms. "No! Lacy, don't die—don't leave me!" he murmured over and over as he rocked her back and forth. "Don't leave me. Don't leave me."

She struggled against him with all her waning strength, and he released her. Rising weakly to her feet, she stumbled to the sofa, fearing that Mark might come after her, but he just sat there on the floor, crying her name and staring at his blood-soaked hands.

"Lacy . . . Lacy, forgive me. I'm sorry."

Frantically, she searched among the cushions until her hand closed on the revolver. She lifted the gun and aimed it at him.

"I can't let you go on killing, Mark."

Tears were streaming down his face. "Go ahead and shoot. Put me out of my misery. Every day of my life has been a fight just to survive—I'm tired, Lacy. No one cares about me—I'm all alone."

His self-pity turned her stomach. There was no remorse in

him for the victims of his madness. "If you are alone, it's because you deserve it. You're evil; you have a malignant sickness in you that destroys everyone close to you."

He stood up, a stricken look on his face. "Is that the way you see me?"

She could feel blackness closing in around her. She couldn't die yet—not yet! She licked her dry lips and stood up on shaky legs. "Your mind is sick, Mark."

He looked puzzled and then nodded slowly. "You might be right. I wasn't always this way. I can remember the good times we had. Can't you remember them too, Lacy?"

She saw that the whole front of her dress was soaked with her own blood. No one could lose that much blood and live for long, she thought. If she was going to stop him, it would have to be soon. Already she felt dizzy and weak. "Mark," she said, knowing she had to make every word count, "you have only two choices. You can either give yourself up to the police"—she held the gun out to him—"or you can end it all here."

He walked slowly toward Mirage, his eyes locked on the revolver. "You do it for me, baby; pull the trigger—do it for me." There was pleading in his voice as he lifted his tormented gaze to hers.

"There was a time when I thought I could kill you, Mark, but I just can't do it." She felt a loud humming in her ears and knew she was about to lose consciousness. "I'm glad to know that about myself."

"You're dying, Lacy," he said, clasping her hand and shoving the gun barrel against his heart. "I want to die with you. You owe me that much."

The gun dropped from her hands and she fell to her knees. "I owe you . . . nothing."

Like a man in a daze, he moved away from her. "I'm not really evil. I didn't mean to hurt anyone."

Mirage's knees collapsed and she hit the floor hard. She had failed. She thought of Katherine, and she thought of Drew, with deep sadness.

Her eyes closed and she lay very still.

Chapter Thirty-seven

Mark's car sped into the night, sliding on the wet pavement when he rounded a sharp curve. Instead of slowing down, he increased his speed, racing along the rain-slick road as if he were trying to outrun his demons. But he couldn't escape them. For the first time, he had seen himself through someone else's eyes, and he didn't like what he saw. Lacy had said that he was evil, and she was right.

When he reached the twisting turn on Mulholland Drive, he jammed his foot on the accelerator. He was like a man possessed as the speedometer climbed higher and the car became harder to control. He was unconcerned when his car slid, almost going over the embankment. His hands gripped the steering wheel and he stared ahead of him into the darkness. He'd killed Lacy, and he had to be punished. Yes, he was evil, and evil deserved to be destroyed!

At a particularly hazardous turn, he steered the car closer to the edge. An agonizing scream built up in his throat, but no sound escaped his lips when the vehicle shot into the air and then took a nosedive. The car fell, slid, rolled, and crashed against a boulder.

Silence ensued. Soft raindrops fell on Mark's face, and his lifeless eyes stared into nothingness.

The rain had stopped and the clouds parted as the taxi turned onto Bel Air Road. Drew felt an urgency within him as he watched the rain run down the window. The thin beacon made by the headlights of the taxi revealed standing water in the streets. "How much farther?" he asked the driver. "Can't you go faster?"

"It's just ahead," the man informed him, then stopped before an iron gate. "This is the address you gave me, sir."

Drew shoved money into the man's hand and got out, watching the car pull away. Turning up the collar of his coat to protect himself against the rain, he glanced at the high fence. He made his way to the gate and turned the handle, only to find that it was locked. He frowned when he saw that the call box had been ripped out of the wall. Something was very wrong here.

Through the bars, he caught a glimpse of the dimly lit house. Sidney Greenway had thought that Mirage was in danger, and no iron bars were going to keep Drew from going to her. He had no trouble climbing over the fence and dropping to the other side.

The rain had stopped and the clouds parted, allowing a bright moon to light Drew's path as he hurried toward the house. When he reached the circular driveway, he came across the body of a man. He examined the body quickly and discovered the man was dead.

Frantically, Drew hurried up the brick pathway. He had to find Mirage before it was too late. The front of the house was locked, so he hurried to the back. He found the back door open and Warren lying on the kitchen floor, groaning.

"Mr. Mallory . . . help her . . . help her," the giant man said when he saw Drew.

"God, don't let me be too late," Drew prayed. "Mirage!" he called, feeling as if his heart had been ripped out. "Where are you? Answer me!"

When he went into the living room, he saw that a lamp had been knocked over and there were other signs of a struggle. Then he saw Mirage lying on the floor, still and lifeless.

"No, Mirage, no," he cried, gently lifting her into his arms. She was so pale, so lifeless, he was sure that she was dead. Hearing a noise behind him, he glanced up to see a man, but it wasn't Mark Damian.

"I'm Sidney Greenway. I arrived just ahead of you. The phone was ripped out of the wall in the kitchen, so I had to call an ambulance from one of the bedrooms. They should be here any moment."

Drew laid Mirage on the couch and tried to stanch the blood with a towel Sidney handed him. "She's alive, but she desperately needs medical attention," Drew said urgently. She was so lifeless, he had to place his hand on the pulse at her throat to assure himself that she was still breathing. "They need to get here soon," he said, glancing at Sidney grimly. "Real soon."

"I'll find the key to the gate and then I'll wait outside for the ambulance so I can show them right in when they arrive." He glanced down at Mirage. "She's one hell of a woman. I hope you know that."

Drew held her hand, wishing he could do more. "I've known it since the first night I met her. God wouldn't take her from me now. Not after I've waited so long for her."

Drew gathered her to him, unmindful that her blood soaked his shirt. "I won't let her die—I won't!"

The police and the ambulance arrived at the same time, and two men took Mirage out of Drew's arms and placed her on a stretcher. Both she and Warren were loaded into the ambulance. With the fierce expression Drew wore when he insisted on riding in the ambulance with Mirage, no one told him he couldn't.

The wailing of the siren sounded like the voice of doom to Drew. He had never been so afraid in his life. *Why had he let his wounded pride keep him in New York, when he should have insisted on accompanying her to California? If he'd been with her, this would never have happened. How could he go on if he lost her again?*

She was so pale, he feared she might die before they reached the hospital. He remained beside her, clasping her cold hand in his, trying to give her some of his strength, his warmth.

At the hospital, Drew paced the corridor while Sidney watched him. "Have some coffee," Sidney said, shoving a cup into his hand.

Drew took a sip of the hot brew and grimaced. "They've had her in the operating room for two hours. Wouldn't you think they could tell us something? And why don't they post guards at the doors? Mark Damian is still out there. As crazed as he is, he might come after her again."

"The police will find him," Sidney assured him. "It was good news that her man, Warren, is out of danger."

"Yes," Drew said dully, his eyes pain-filled. "There is that."

The doctor appeared at the door of the waiting room. "Which one of you is Andrew Mallory?"

Drew was afraid to breathe. "I am."

The doctor noticed the blood on Drew's shirt. "Has anyone seen to you?"

Drew glanced down at Mirage's blood, which had dried on his shirt. "I wasn't hurt. But tell me about Mirage. Is she . . . will she make it?"

"Mrs. Lord is in guarded but stable condition."

Drew let out an impatient breath. "Speak English, Doctor. What in the hell does that mean?"

"We had to do some repair work, but we were lucky there was no damage to her vital organs. She's lost a lot of blood, and we're giving her a transfusion."

Drew walked to the door. "I want to see her now."

"I can't let you do that. The next few hours are critical, and she needs her rest."

Drew stood eye-to-eye with the doctor. "She needs to know

I'm with her; that's what she needs. It'll take more than you to keep me away from her."

"You'd better let him see her, Doctor," Sidney said with a slight smile. "I wouldn't want to be the one to try to stop him."

The dark glance Drew cast at the doctor confirmed Sidney's warning, and the man stepped aside.

Drew moved quickly down the hallway, but when he reached Mirage's room, he stopped outside, mentally preparing himself for what he might find. In the room, there was but a single light over the bed, and Drew stood over her for a long moment. She looked so fragile, he was almost afraid to touch her. Her long lashes lay against pale cheeks. There were bruises and scratches on her face. He dropped into a chair beside her bed and took her hand in his.

"I'm here, Mirage. You have to get well for me and Katherine. We both need you."

She groaned, and her hand tightened on his.

"I won't leave you." He kissed her cheek. "You'll never be rid of me again."

Mirage awoke to find sunlight streaming through the open curtains. The room was unfamiliar to her. She ran her tongue over her dry lips, wondering for the moment where she was and why she was in such pain. She turned her head and saw Drew asleep in a chair beside her bed, and her confusion deepened.

Suddenly the whole horrible nightmare came back to her in a flash, and Mirage realized she was lucky to be alive, though she still didn't know how badly she was injured. How had Drew known she needed him? It took all her energy to raise her hand and lay it against his cheek. She watched him open his eyes and smile at her.

Drew saw the question in her eyes. "You're going to be all right." He leaned forward and brushed her forehead with his lips. "I'll call the doctor. He wanted to know as soon as you regained consciousness."

"No, not yet. I have questions. How did you get here?"

"Sidney called me."

"Warren? How is he?"

"He's recovering nicely and should leave the hospital next week." Evidently, she didn't know about the guard that Mark had killed, and he wouldn't tell her just now.

"Take me home, Drew."

"I will, Mirage. Just as soon as the doctor allows it."

"Mark's dead, isn't he?"

"Don't think about him. I have something important to ask you."

She nodded weakly, but her eyes were bright. "You don't have to ask. Yes, I'll marry you."

His smile erased the tired lines from his face. "You're pretty sure of yourself, aren't you?"

"Only about you." Then her eyes dulled. There was something that kept her happiness from being complete. "I must know about Mark. I have to know that he'll never hurt anyone else, or what I did has no meaning."

Drew took a deep breath. "Mark is dead. His car went over a cliff on Mulholland Drive. Ironically, he went off at the exact place where his wife, Rosalinda, lost her life."

Mirage shivered. "He meant to die. At the end, he realized what he'd become. Do you believe that?"

"I don't care how or why he died." He took her hand and raised it to his lips. "I only care that he's dead and he can't hurt you anymore."

He smiled down at her. "Now, I want you to think only pleasant thoughts. Think about becoming my wife."

The newspapers sensationalized Mark's death, speculating about all the mysterious deaths connected with him. One reporter was sure all the tragedy was caused by the curse of the Raja Star. After all, everyone who ever owned the necklace had died horribly.

Fortunately, Mirage's name was kept out of the newspapers. The day before she was released from the hospital, Sidney paid her a visit. He handed her a box tied with red ribbon. She was curious as she opened it, and even more curious when she saw that it contained a reel of film.

"It's the only copy of *The Legend of Lacy Black.* I thought you might want it."

Mirage handed it to Drew. "Please destroy it."

Sidney sighed. "It was my finest work, and no one will ever see it."

Mirage took his hand and pulled him down so she could kiss his cheek. "Thank you for being such a good friend."

Sidney smiled. "It's nothing, Mirage Lord. You see, I loved Lacy Black . . . when she was alive."

Epilogue

Los Angeles
2002

The public curiosity over the disappearance of Lacy Black had dissipated and the media now focused on a new Middle Eastern crisis. Delegated to the third page of the *Los Angeles Times* was a small article that almost went unnoticed:

> The remains of Lacy Black's pilot were claimed last week by his family. In an interview, his widow revealed that she had been receiving anonymous deposits to her bank account since his death, and that they have still continued even after his body was found.
>
> The burial of the unknown female passenger was paid for by an organization headed by the renowned broadway actress Mirage Lord Mallory, who is known for her charitable works. A spokesman for Mrs. Mallory and her husband, Broadway director Andrew Mallory, said that the family had no comment.

At one time Mirage had considered playing Lacy Black

in a film about the star's life, which may have been the reason she took pity on the unknown woman who died in Lacy's place.

There is still no word on what happened to Lacy Black. The mystery will probably never be solved. Is she out there somewhere laughing at us because of our obsession with her, even after all these years? Is she walking beside us on the streets, unnoticed and anonymous? As Garbo once did?

If you are out there somewhere, Lacy, we hope you have found happiness, because your art brought so much joy to so many, and left an indelible memory in our hearts.

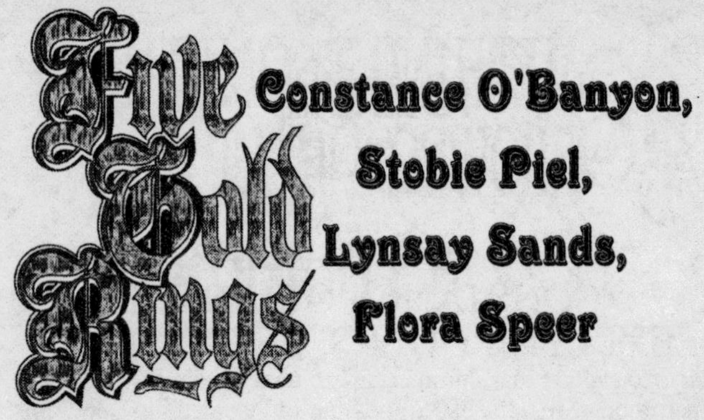

In the Year of Our Lord, 1135, Menton Castle is the same as any other: It has nobles and minstrels, knights and servants. Yet from the great hall to the scullery there are signs that the house is in an uproar. This Yuletide season is to be one of passion and merriment. The master of the keep has returned. With him come several travelers, some weary with laughter, some tired of tears. But in all of their stories—whether lords a'leapin' or maids a'milkin'—there is one gift that their true loves give to them. And in the winter moonlight, each of the castle's inhabitants will soon see the magic of the season and the joy that can come from five gold rings.

___4612-1 $5.50 US/$6.50 CAN

Dorchester Publishing Co., Inc.
P.O. Box 6640
Wayne, PA 19087-8640

Please add $1.75 for shipping and handling for the first book and $.50 for each book thereafter. NY, NYC, and PA residents, please add appropriate sales tax. No cash, stamps, or C.O.D.s. All orders shipped within 6 weeks via postal service book rate.
Canadian orders require $2.00 extra postage and must be paid in U.S. dollars through a U.S. banking facility.

Name____
Address____
City_________________________State_______Zip__________
I have enclosed $__________ in payment for the checked book(s).
Payment must accompany all orders. ❑ Please send a free catalog.
CHECK OUT OUR WEBSITE! www.dorchesterpub.com

Christine is shocked that she's agreed to marry. Her intended, Gavin Norfork, is a notorious lover, gambler, and duelist. It is rumored he can seduce a woman at twenty paces. The dissolute aristocrat is clearly an unsuitable match for a virtuous orphan who has devoted her life to charity work. But Christine's first attempt to scare him off ends only with mud on her face. And, suddenly finding herself wed to a man she hasn't even met, Christine finds herself questioning her goals. Perhaps it is time to make her entrée into London society, to meet Gavin on his own ground—and challenge him with his own tricks. The unrepentant rake thinks she's gotten dirty before, but he hasn't seen anything yet. Not only her husband can be scandalous—and not only Christine can fall in love.

___4805-1 $5.50 US/$6.50 CAN

RENEE HALVERSON

If André DuBois were a betting man, how would lay odds that the woman in red is robbing his dealers blind. He can tell beauty's smile disguises a quick mind and even quicker fingers . To catch her in the act he deals himself into the game, never guessing he might lose ghis heart process.

Faith O'Malley depends on her wits to succeed at cards, and experience tells her the ante has just been raised. The new gambler's good looks are distracting enough, but his intelligent eyes promise trouble. Still, Faith will risk everything—her reputation, her virtue—to save the innocent people depending on her. It won't be until later that she'll stop to learn what she's won.